TWIST
OF TIME

TWIST OF TIME

A THRILLER

GY WALDRON

FIRST FRUITS
PUBLISHING

Copyright © 2024 by Gy Waldron

First published in 2024 by First Fruits Publishing.

All rights reserved. No part of this book may be used or reproduced in any manner whatsoever without written permission of the copyright holder, except in the case of brief quotations in critical articles and reviews.

This is a work of fiction. Though grounded in historical documentation, it is entirely a creation of the author.

Paperback edition ISBN 979-8-8693-7816-3
E-book edition ISBN 979-8-8693-7817-0

www.Gy-Waldron.com

To Jadi, against whom all women are measured and found wanting

CHAPTER ONE

The nude woman's body had no head.
Homicide Detective Sgt. Kate Flynn first thought it was obscured by the thick undergrowth of sumac brush where the body lay. Moving closer, she was surprised to see only the stub of neck edged with a ring of dried, black blood. The rest of the neck was presumably attached to the missing head. For the average cop of thirty-five, the unexpected might startle; no head was very unexpected. But Kate was not average—she was a third-generation Irish cop with an IQ that hovered in the 140s. When she was a teenager and decided she wanted the same career as her father, a homicide detective, he began showing her crime scene photos from his cases. For Kate's eighteenth birthday, she watched her first forensic autopsy.

As a veteran cop, this missing head was no more than an underline in her crime scene notes.

She was keenly aware of the uniformed officer watching. His name was Lester Hicks, twice passed over for promotion. He was a dough-pudgy jerk and a gossip. Kate had been in the Santa Barbara Police Department little more than a year, having transferred from Los Angeles homicide as Detective Sgt. She was still fighting currents of male resentment and she knew that Lester was going to report back to the "boys" on her first homicide in Santa Barbara as lead detective. He was hoping like hell to say that she screwed up.

Lester cleared his throat to get her attention. "The hands are gone, too." He seemed pleased. "And the feet."

She moved in for a closer look. *The dumbass got that part right, the hands and feet were missing.* She looked for defense wounds and discovered a circular abrasion on the left wrist. From her pocket Kate produced a tape recorder and began dictating.

"Notes on Jane Doe homicide corpus: left wrist abrasion suggests possible handcuff attached to briefcase. No head—no dental. No hands and feet—no prints. Killer was very determined to prevent identification. This appears textbook, a pro."

Hicks grinned, showing broken teeth—a parting souvenir from his ex-wife, who finally took exception to his abuse. "I think she was killed someplace else and dumped here."

"Really? Damn, and I thought it was road rage." From his blank look, he obviously missed her sarcasm. The man was an imbecile.

"No, you're wrong," he argued. "Two hikers found her. Teenagers, a dude and a girl. They're waiting in my cruiser."

"You question them?"

"Yeah. They're spooked, probably the head thing. They came down off that upper trail." He indicated the dirt road about thirty yards above. "And here she was."

They were interrupted by the sound of a vehicle on the road. Kate expected to see the forensic van, but it was another Santa Barbara PD cruiser. The door on the passenger side opened and a man got out. The officer pointed toward Kate; he nodded thanks and began walking down the hill through the low underbrush toward her.

From habit, she sized him up as if writing a police description: height, five-eleven to six-one; weight, 185 to 195; age, thirty-eight to forty-three; even features, ruddy complexion; hair dark and close-clipped; wearing jeans, a leather jacket, and running sneakers.

Based upon the report from Homicide that morning, everything about him was wrong. He should be dressed in a monk's robe like the others at the Saint Joseph Monastery on the mountain above Santa Barbara. He should be pale and have a weird haircut. He was too young—shouldn't monks be older, like in the movies? And he definitely should not be attractive. Obviously, this was the wrong guy.

"Detective Sgt. Flynn? I'm Thomas Bardsey."

It was the right guy. "Thanks for coming," Kate said. "I thought you'd be wearing a monk's habit."

"I do at the monastery. Outside, we usually dress civilian. I came as . . ." He saw the body. "Oh, dear God."

"You reported a missing person two days ago, Denise Hollander. This woman was found this morning. Since there is no . . . uh, head, we hoped you could make an ID. You might recognize her from identifying marks on the body."

"I'm a monk."

"So?"

"I've never seen her naked."

"Oh. Right. Sorry."

"Besides, a head wouldn't help. I have no idea what she looks like."

"Didn't you report her missing?"

"Yes. But we've never met. She flew in from New York two days ago. We had an appointment to meet at the monastery. When she didn't show, I phoned her company in Baltimore and they said she arrived in Los Angeles. She had called her boss with her mobile phone while driving to Santa Barbara. I immediately notified the police." He frowned. "Isn't all that in my missing person report?"

"I haven't seen it yet. Homicide woke me at home and said you would meet me here." She looked him over. "I've never seen a monk out of uniform. I'm Catholic too—terminally lapsed."

"I'm not Catholic. I'm Anglican."

"I didn't know they had monks."

"Monks, nuns, the priests can marry. Also, some women priests. I like to say that we have all the problems."

Her laugh and the spark in her eyes surprised him; she was very attractive. His gaze shifted from her eyes to the dead body. "My only contact with her was by phone and email."

"What were you meeting about?"

"She was bringing me a manuscript. A diary, fourteenth century. Her company asked me to translate it." He added, "Celtic studies is my field."

Kate had no idea what that meant. "Is the diary valuable?"

He paused before answering. "Quite valuable."

"Enough to kill for?"

He paused again. "That would depend upon what's in the translation."

His pauses suggested he was being evasive. Great: a reluctant witness. Opening her writing pad, she scribbled a note. "Who wrote the diary?"

"A monk. A Templar Knight named Brychan."

"Spell it."

He did. "Rhymes with rye-kan. The 'ch' sounds like a 'k.' A Celtic term meaning royal bloodline."

"So, what is a Templar Knight?"

THE PEARL MOON was set in a black velvet sky in the coldest March the elders could remember. It was anno domini 1314. Sharp icy gusts stabbed spears at the two Templar riders and their packhorses. The younger, Sir Brychan, rode lead, his gray eyes reading the terrain. His huge companion, Sir Ursus, sat alert in the saddle as if awaiting an attack from the dark surrounding woods.

It was the third night since their escape through French King Philip's lines. They had pressed on for two hard days and nights of cold, dry camps. Despite a late freeze that coated puddles with a skein of ice, they did not risk wearing their white wool mantles that marked them as Templars. Since the brutal execution in Paris of Templar Grand Master Jacques de Molay, only days ago, King Philip's bounty on fugitive Templars had been paid in gold, not sous or denier.

That night, under the shelter of a towering spruce, they risked a low fire and roasted chunks of blood sausage on spits. Black rye bread and a comb of honey provided a meager meal. They also brewed a pot of precious kahveh. The roasted dark beans were finely crushed and boiled in water—a taste Templars acquired from Turks during the Crusades. Said to be a craving among them, its heavy aroma was often found in their camps. Because kahveh was Saracen, most bishops had prohibited its use. The ban was lifted when Pope Clement himself became partial to it.

Afterward the two men curled together, double-cloaked against the freezing wind, and slept in dreamless exhaustion. An iron chest sealed with lead lay between them. On its lid was carved the single word "VERITAS."

A few hours earlier, a lone scout from a band of outlaws heard the Templar horses moving in the woods and stealthily followed until they made camp. He waited until they bedded down, then went back for the others: eight predators who hunted these trails for anyone foolish enough to travel without escort. There had been no travelers for nearly a month, save for a caravan of merchant wagons under the protection of a troop of king's cavalry. The bandits in hiding could only watch hungrily as the caravan rode past. This time the scout reported there were only two men, six horses, and their packs—an easy prize.

IT WAS TEN days later when the High Sherif of Auvergne, Sir Gilbert de Bage, and his men rode upon the scene. They had been tracking the Templars for days. He was able to tell what occurred that night by the circle of bodies. Now weathered carrion, they lay in a broken ring as they had fallen, a feast for ravening wolves, woods rats, and carrion crows.

Sir Gilbert sniffed, believing he could still smell the feff of corpus rot. There was a prickle of hairs on his neck. He had heard many Templar stories as a young squire when he served his great-uncle Bors, who had been a Templar Knight in the last Crusade. The old warrior, when "drunk as a Templar," would tell tales hinting of the Order's mysteries. Sir Gilbert now read the signs: the two Templars surely must have been members of the Zealotes, which was a secret band within the Templar Order. Their fighting left a mark like no other.

The bandits' remains—gnawed bones, bits of leathery skin, and torn rags—were scattered in a rough circle around a space wide enough for two men fighting side by side. An odd assortment of weapons, a few swords, an axe, and a broken pruning hook marked the attackers as bandits, not soldiers. That the weapons lay rusting in the winter weeds meant no one had passed this way.

Gilbert immediately saw that this bandit attack was different. By day, they quickly overwhelmed travelers; at night, they killed their prey while they slept. Why had these been so foolish as to attack two Templars standing ready to fight?

The sherif was amused when he saw the answer. Inside the ring of bones where the Templars had stood were the charred ashes of their fire. Being fugitives, the Templars probably were not wearing their white mantles. Nor would the bandits know of the Zealotes' manner of always sleeping with one hand clasping a drawn sword. If awakened by any unusual sound, the two would be instantly on their feet, side by side, weapons ready.

His uncle had explained that Zealotes were paired in twos and drilled for countless hours in their peculiar stance, each sensing the other's move. When Zealotes battled in pairs, one warrior fought sinister, left-handed, so that any approach to them faced a lethal blade. The opposite hand held a dagger or mace. Zealotes had mastered fighting with a weapon in either or both hands.

Templar Knights were allowed to retreat only if the odds were more than three to one, Zealotes never: they won or died where they stood. Many of their brother Templars considered them fanatics. When a pair fought double-bladed, there was a Templar saying: "Two Zealotes, four blades, all dead."

Looking over the ground, the sherif counted seven skulls, two of them split from crown to jawbone by a powerful slash. One skull was missing. Eight against two, but it would not have mattered had there been a dozen. They were no match against two Zealotes of the Knights Templar.

TWO DAYS LATER, the younger Templar, Brother Brychan, edged closer to the fire and opened a scribe's case from the horse pack. It was a cherished present from his mother, Lady Gwynn, the year he entered the Templar Order. Placing it on the thick horse blanket, Brychan settled back comfortably against the high saddlebow.

The older Templar, Brother Ursus, placed the cracked kahveh urn where Brychan could reach it. He added a few dry sticks to the modest fire against the late afternoon chill. A light curl of white smoke rose from the blaze and filtered above through the spruce branches—not enough to give them away.

Brychan set out his writing tools, a crystal vial of fresh ground ink, four selected quills and a thin-bladed sharpener. From the scribe case he took out the diary given to him by Friar Luke, senior cleric in the Order. Its cover was of seasoned cypress finished in oiled leather with brass fittings, and so skillfully fashioned that if submerged in water, it would bob to the surface.

He blew on his fingers and selected a quill. Testing its point with his habitually ink-stained thumb, he dipped it, skimming the excess ink on the vial rim. "How many bandits did we fell two nights ago, Brother?"

Brother Ursus thought of it for the first time. "Six or eight. Too dark to be certain. Why are you writing about them?"

Brychan, surprised, looked up at him. "For a record. We neither buried nor prayed over them."

"No time."

"All the more that they be noted here." Brychan smiled a gentle reproach.

"They attacked us."

"But we did not wear our mantles. Had they known we were Templars they might have been afraid and therefore, spared."

"Or fought harder to get the bounty on us." Ursus scowled at the quill lines on the page. He had the natural mistrust of writing common among those who could not read. Less than half the Templar Knights could read or write; that was left to the brother clerics and priests of the Order. Even Grand Master de Molay was illiterate.

Writing was considered beneath warrior monks—the "Poor Soldiers of Christ." Ursus took justifiable pride in being illiterate, for it marked his warrior status. Brychan, who had been schooled from childhood by Cistercian monks, was an exception, but he was different in many ways.

Ursus warned, "Your diary will get us burned if we are caught."

"If we are captured, Brother, we will be truly blessed if burning is all they do."

Both men were Scots nobility. When talking with each other they spoke English or Scots Gaelic. They also spoke the Norman French dialect still used in some parts of the British Isles. Beyond their common languages, the two men differed greatly in age, size, and experience.

Brother Ursus was Sir Angus MacTeal, clan MacCallan, Templar Knight and monk. Due to his great bearish bulk, he was affectionately called Ursus Scotus—Scots Bear—and his bright red hair and beard added to that presence. A fearsome warrior of forty and four years, he was a master of all arms. He had fought in the final campaigns in the Holy Land, where he also learned a considerable amount of Arabic. After ten years of hard service he was initiated into the elite ranks of the Zealotes.

Sir Brychan of Houston, clan Howistean, was twenty-seven, a rangy six feet with a duelist's lithe body. When he turned twenty-one, he was knighted a Templar in Paris in the last group to be admitted. Seven days later King Philip the Fair of France ordered the arrest of Grand Master de Molay and all other Templars on Friday, October 13, forever known among Templars as Black Friday.

From that day, Sir Brychan was a fugitive, and there followed seven years in hiding. Then, in Paris, on March 19, on King Philip's orders, Jacques de Molay, a worn seventy, exhausted by repeated torture and seven years in prison, was taken from his cell and burned alive by slow roasting at the stake. Hours before his execution, a message was smuggled from prison through the mythic

Templar underground. It commissioned Brother Brychan a Zealote and charged him and Ursus with a secret mission to be followed to the death.

BROTHER URSUS SLOWLY drew his sword, clearing its sheath with a metallic hiss. "Can you keep watch for me while you write?"

Brychan glanced around. "Yes. Attend to your prayers, Brother."

Ursus stepped off three paces, one for each of the Holy Trinity. He laid his sword on the ground and knelt. Templars who strictly kept the Rule said twenty-four Pater Nosters and twenty-four Hail Marys daily, even when traveling. If they were Zealotes, one kept guard while the other prayed. The tradition came from scripture when Christ, on the night he was betrayed, asked his disciples to keep watch while he prayed. When outdoors, Zealotes always prayed with sword drawn and on the ground beside them.

As he kept watch, Brychan wrote in the meticulous script peculiar to the Cistercians. His diary did not record each day, but significant events were noted, like the recent outlaw attack. His writings also might include musings, jottings of verse, or an inspired moment of prayer written in Latin.

But his most private thoughts were written in Gaelic, for even in his precise Latin he did not have the words. Only Gaelic, language of the bards, could describe the visions of strange beings and glowing apparitions that came to him in their mysterious beauty.

To him they were not shadowy phantoms, but solid as earth under his feet yet light as a spring wind. They came in his sleep or at times when he thought he was asleep, only to discover that he had been in a trance and was hurled, as by war catapult, back to the present. Brother Brychan had "the sight," as did his mother and her mother before her, which was said to be marked by their gray eyes.

The diary was unusual in other ways. At the front were blank pages on which Brychan wrote. On the back pages were symbols and numbers, ciphers impossible to read without the key. The codes gave access to the Templar financial empire, by far the wealthiest order in the Church.

Brychan understood little of the "science of numbers" and less about cyphers. When charged with keeping the diary, it was explained to him that Templars had a system of banking using letters of transmittal called cheques, from the Arabic chess term *shah mat*: checkmate. With these documents, money was exchanged without coin or bullion being carried. Anyone could use them: clergy, nobles, kings, even the Pope himself. Merchants had become greatly dependent upon them. The system was so trusted that even after the fall of Jerusalem to the Saracens, now seventy years past, Templar cheques were honored everywhere, including the Muslim world.

Brother Ursus knew only that the Order had chosen Brychan to keep the codes and diary. Beyond whatever else it contained, the ciphers alone were worth the killing. But Brychan's writings in the diary, if they fell into the hands of Holy Office of the Inquisition, would mean indictment for heresy and witchcraft. That was certain burning.

AT THE SOUND of the cry, both men were startled. An animal? As they looked at each other it came again, a shriek of terror.

Ursus grabbed his weapon from the ground; Brychan stuffed the diary in his writing case and drew his sword. The wail came again from the woods on their left.

Brychan started to move, but Ursus stopped him with a gesture. Then Brychan heard it too, the sound of horses, not running but moving about.

TWIST OF TIME

Without a word, Brychan kicked out the fire. Ursus moved to his pack, took out a two-handed broadsword in its sheath and drew it. The two men exchanged a look indicating direction and still without speaking, moved into the forest.

About fifty paces into the thick brush, they came upon a rise in the ground. Beyond, they could hear the sound of men laughing. They moved up the slope quietly, their steps muffled by stiff, frozen weeds. Near the top they dropped down, crawling through thick ground wayz flecked with frost. They parted a growth of gray thistle and looked below.

In a clearing were four soldiers wearing the yellow livery of the King's cavalry, one on horse and three afoot. Two were holding a young woman on the ground. One of the men had pulled her skirt up to her waist; she was naked beneath. A burly third trooper had unbuckled his sword; his britches were down to his knees. As the girl cried out, he laughed, pulling at his huge erection.

At one side was a caravan wagon hitched with two horses. It was of a distinctive style—a bow-topped roof. Its red paint bore decades of weathering and was farded with leather and metalwork. On the ground lay the hacked body of an old man, his white hair wrapped in a red cloth.

Gypsies.

Brychan and Ursus looked at each other. With the King's price on their heads, to interfere would give them away to the soldiers. Besides, the girl was a Gypsy; this was none of their affair.

As they were about to turn away, the woman kicked the rapist hard in the ballocks. He yelped, sprawling to the ground. She twisted free and jumped to her feet, running. Two soldiers scrambled after her. One caught the back of her blouse as she frantically pulled away.

Cursing, the soldier yanked and ripped her blouse open, revealing her breasts and a crucifix on a chain.

"Jesus, help me!" she screamed.

Brychan and Ursus looked at each other astonished. Neither had seen a naked woman in years, nor ever heard of Christian Gypsies. But all Zealotes were bound by the first Templar rule: to protect all Christian travelers no matter who they were.

THE WOMAN WAS on the ground in a frantic struggle with three soldiers. One held her arms while a second choked her into submission; the rapist was on his knees between her legs, brutally forcing them apart.

The trooper on horseback, gleefully watching, sensed something. His hand was on his sword grip before he looked back. He turned into the powerful slash of a two-handed broad sword that almost cut him in half at the waist.

The soldier choking the girl looked up to see the mounted trooper tumble to the ground. Beside the horse was a Goliath of a man who charged with a huge broadsword. Two soldiers jumped up; swords drawn. The rapist's weapon lay on the ground midway between him and the giant.

A second warrior suddenly appeared out of the brush to their right. He carried a sword, but no shield. The giant halted his charge—a diversion until his comrade appeared. Now, in a well-practiced move, both men edged sideways in opposite directions, forcing the two cavalrymen to face out and become more separated.

The rapist was struggling, with his britches entangled on one of his spurs. His pants were wrapped around his knees; arse bare, erection withered.

The girl frantically crawled to the side, even more terrified. These two were not rescuers, only two more mad dogs to fight over the same piece of meat.

The giant roared, "Beauseant!" Swinging the broadsword in a great arc, he closed with the first soldier. The cavalryman defended with a two-handed parry. Each ringing clash took him another step, distancing him farther from the others.

Brychan attacked the second man with a flurry that forced his opponent to give ground. The trooper, a veteran sergeant, was bewildered; from its particular sound his opponent's blade was a Toledo. It could cost almost as much as a knight's armor, yet this magnificent weapon was wielded by one dressed rough, neither peasant nor noble.

Ursus continued his assault—a mix of quick slashes, spins, and turns. His broadsword, crafted especially for him, was almost five feet, longer than any the cavalrymen had ever seen. Brychan continued pressing his attack on the sergeant; the wily veteran began to give ground, tempting Brychan to overextend his blade.

Reading him, Brychan stopped in mid-swing, leaving the sergeant's arm extended. A swift inside slash caught his exposed elbow, severing the arm with a scream. Brychan, with both hands swinging the sword, slammed the sergeant's helmet with a sharp crack. As he was falling, a deep thrust took him dead center.

Ursus turned to face the rapist who had retrieved his sword. The soldier was big, but bulf and clumsy. He parried solidly against Ursus' battering, but with each backward step his britches crept down, exposing his arse. When his opponent's blade missed a desperate parry, Ursus slashed a scarlet gap across his lard-white belly.

The man groaned and dropped to his knees, grabbing at his spilling guts. With a merciful blow, Ursus severed his head.

Ursus looked at Brychan. "He was nae Scot. They love fighting bare-arsed."

All the cavalrymen lay dead. The fight had lasted less than a hundred-count.

The astonished girl watched them; one hand clutched her torn dress, covering her nakedness. She held a dagger from a fallen trooper.

Brychan raised his hand in blessing. "Peace, woman. We mean you no harm."

She snarled, raising the blade.

"We are Templars."

"Templars?" She suspiciously eyed their rough clothing. Both were clean-shaven, unlike Templars, who were known for their full beards.

"And fugitives," he added.

Dropping the dagger, she ran to the dead Gypsy. Falling on her knees she began wailing and throwing handfuls of dirt in the air and on herself in the Gypsy manner of grief. When she paused for breath, Brychan spoke.

"Your father?" he asked.

"Uncle." She looked at the dead soldiers, closed her eyes, and cursed a chatter of Romany sending their souls to hell.

Ursus scanned the surrounding trees, listening. "We must go. Their troop is close by."

Brychan turned to the girl. "Come with us." He ignored Ursus' angry look. "We'll take you to the nearest village."

Ursus shook his head. "Her wagon will slow us."

"Then she must leave it."

The girl indicated her uncle's body. "No. He is an elder, he must burn in the wagon."

Ursus, still looking at the trees, spoke in Gaelic. "Leave. Now."

Brychan knew well to trust Brother Ursus' instincts. His ability to sense trouble was a cause for wonder among their fellow Templars. Ursus explained that "he listened to the trees," which was the Celtic way of divining. Many believed that he simply had hearing like a fox, while others were convinced that God had given him a special gift.

Brychan motioned to the girl. "Come."

"He must burn in the wagon!" she insisted.

"Woman, get your belongings." Brychan's tone left no room for argument. He made the sign of the cross over the dead Gypsy.

While Ursus collected the cavalry mounts, Brychan unhitched the two draft horses from the Gypsy wagon. They were good stock, well-tended. He gave each a firm pat on their bruffed winter coats and offered a prayer that some lucky peasant might find them before the wolves did.

Ursus selected the largest stallion to carry his bulk and led the other horses to the Gypsy wagon.

When the girl appeared from inside the wagon, she was now wearing a long leather cloak lined with thick fleece. She carried a leather satchel and in the other hand a canvas bag of provisions: Gypsies never left food behind. Ursus took the parcels from her and hung them on the harness rig of one of the packhorses.

From the wagon seat, she nimbly climbed on a stallion, revealing a luscious flash of leg and thigh as she curled it around the pommel to ride sidesaddle. The glimpse took Brychan's breath away. As she confidently grasped the reins, he was reminded that Gypsies were notorious horse thieves.

With a grieving look back at her uncle's body, she followed the two knights.

By custom, when in the forest, Zealotes rode in silence to avoid their sound carrying. Brychan was relieved that the girl did not talk. He wondered if it was the nature of all Gypsies from their way of living apart.

As they were approaching their camp, both men sensed something was wrong. Ursus spurred his horse and broke from the tree cover with Brychan close behind.

They reined up, astonished. All their horses were gone. And the chest.

Ursus pointed to the skyline of a distant hill, which cut an arc into the setting sun. They could see the silhouette of three riders leading their stolen horses as they disappeared over the horizon.

Brychan spied his writing case on the ground half-covered by a blanket. Jumping off his horse, he ran and fell to his knees. With trembling hands, he opened it.

The diary was gone. ✝

Jake's was Santa Barbara's vintage diner, where savory, greasy fries in brown gravy were a cardiac hazard, and burly coffee in thick porcelain mugs could revive a coma. It was the police hangout for heavy carbs or a caffeine kick.

Kate and Thomas had come directly from the crime scene. Thomas was enjoying a second coffee as he watched her eat.

Kate was devouring the Lumberjack special: eggs, sausage, and a mound of hash browns high as the three flapjacks. At his look, she smiled.

"I never gain weight," she said. "I am going to donate my metabolism to medical science."

"As a monk, you'd starve in a week."

"Were you always a monk?"

"No. Were you always a cop?"

"Most women are curious about priests and monks. Wondering if—well, you know."

"I'm not gay, which is what you really wanted to ask. In another life, I had it all—a wife, a mortgage, even a bulldog named Merlin."

"You were married?"

"Yes."

"Divorced?"

"She died."

"Oh, I'm sorry. Why do we always think divorced first?"

"Maybe because you are divorced." At her surprise, he explained. "You don't wear a wedding ring; most married women do. You surely had offers. You must have taken one of them."

She was startled at how easily he read her. "Both of us were LAPD," she said. "I was homicide, he was vice. The perfect couple. Then one day he announced he didn't want to be married anymore." She paused. "Why do men always say that?"

"Do they?"

"Anyway, he left me for a girl barely in her twenties. A hooker he once arrested."

"That must have been—"

"It was. I resigned from LAPD homicide and came home to Santa Barbara over a year ago. They were short-handed in homicide and I had ten years' experience. Except for pissing off half the force who are trying to make detective, it's been boringly routine. Now thanks to you I get a murder, a mutilation, and your weird diary." She raised her coffee cup in a toast. "You've made my year."

"I keep thinking of Miss Hollander, poor woman. Killed and butchered simply because of the diary she was delivering."

"I wonder had it been a man whether he'd have been so horribly desecrated. Bastards. Brother Thomas, would you please take me, step by step, and explain how a monk safely cloistered in a monastery on a mountaintop in California gets involved in a homicide over a diary in this violent, evil world?"

She took out her notebook and waited.

"It all happened shortly after I came to the monastery. I've only been novitiate monk for a year."

"What does that mean?"

"A probation period; I am a few months away from my final vows. I was contacted at the monastery by Winslow Fallon, the head of Med-Tek. You've heard of him?"

She wrote his name. "Vaguely. One of those computer moguls?"

"And very eccentric. In addition to his multibillion-dollar empire, he has a passion for collecting rare books and manuscripts. Especially anything on the Templars. Like the diary."

"What makes the diary so special?"

"It is a legend in the rare book world. Some experts believe it is bogus, a fake or forgery. Others say it is cursed, bringing death to anyone connected with it."

"Sounds like voodoo."

"For seven hundred years it's disappeared then reappeared. Every time it appears, there's a murder—and usually more than just one. Recently it surfaced in the hands of Lazlo Reiner. He is the perfect image of the shady dealer. Despite Reiner's bad reputation, Fallon was convinced the diary was authentic and paid him two million dollars for it."

She looked as if she had not heard right. "Two *million?*"

"Then Reiner was murdered."

"With Hollander, that's two homicides. Looks like the voodoo is still working." She wrote Reiner's name. "Anything in the diary that could be a motive for murder?"

"Millions in hidden Templar wealth, according to the legend."

"Murder over a legend?"

"But based on fact. For seven hundred years, people have been killing for something in the diary. And just as I was about to get my hands on it, this happens. That's all I know." He shrugged.

"Okay." She nodded. "So, tell me more about the Templars."

"Forget all that stuff in popular novels. Good fiction, bad history. First, there is no proof that Templars were associated with Mary Magdalene. That's a myth. Second, there's no credible evidence they were connected with the Holy Grail. These Templar stories are legend and fiction written by three medieval writers, all novelists."

"Then who were they?"

"An order of warrior monks established in the twelfth century and lasting about two hundred years. They were highly disciplined and very secretive. Each Templar took a death vow of loyalty."

"Like the Mafia?"

"But tougher. Templars were considered by their enemies, the Saracens, to be the fiercest of the Crusaders, sort of an elite Special Forces. They answered only to the Pope, became his private army, and paid no taxes. In just a few years the Templar Order became the richest in the entire church—that's very, *very* wealthy. Eventually they became the main bankers of Europe."

"I'm a suspicious cop. What went wrong?"

"Jump to the year 1314. King Philip of France was nearly bankrupt and wanted to finance another war. He was already deeply in debt to the Templars. So, he came up with a simple solution—steal the Templar wealth. Working with the Inquisition, he created trumped-up charges of heresy. In a single day at the same hour, his troops raided every Templar site in every province, city, and town in France. It was the first mass arrest in history. But the treasure was gone."

"Gone where?"

"That's the mystery. Somehow, the Templars knew of the king's plans. Just days before the raid, they secretly moved approximately one hundred wagons full of their assets—gold, jewels, and various treasures. That's two hundred years of loot! Everything was loaded on eighteen ships. They sailed away and were never seen again. It was like robbing the Bank of England and coming up empty."

"I bet the king was pissed."

"He burned a hundred and fifty of their leaders at the stake. Several thousand more were tortured and imprisoned."

"Now *that's* making a statement. So, what happened to all the loot?"

"The king never found it. If the diary is authentic, it's the key to finding at least some of the Templar wealth. Conservatively, that's many multi-millions."

Motive: money, she wrote. "How did Fallon hear about you?"

"From my doctoral thesis on the wizard Merlin."

"King Arthur's Merlin?"

"That's him. King Arthur is probably a legend, but Merlin was real. He left writings that prove it. I discovered a document that gives a completely different picture and suggests that Merlin lived a secret double life. He wasn't just a wizard; he was also a bishop and became a saint in the Celtic church under another name. I dumbed-down my thesis and it was published as a pop-culture history. That's when Fallon contacted me."

"How did you get involved with this Celtic stuff?"

"By birth. My grandfather was a Scot and taught Celtic studies at University of Edinburgh. My father, an American, went there to study and ended up marrying the professor's daughter, my mother. Grandfather Andrew insisted that I be raised half-Scot. I spent every summer in Scotland with him. Gaelic became my second language."

Kate looked at her notes and frowned. "Thomas, the diary is evidence in a homicide. It's written in several languages and has a very complex history. Would you help us?"

"I need permission from my abbot."

She held out her cell phone. "Ask him."

TWIST OF TIME

• ○ •

Father Abbot Methodius listened impatiently on the phone as Thomas explained the situation. Methodius rolled his eyes. Thomas was totally unpredictable, from his controversial past to recently persuading Fallon to pay half a million dollars to the monastery for the diary translation. *Now he's involved in a murder investigation? He is a monk, heaven's sake!*

As Thomas continued talking, Methodius pictured the $500,000 in planned renovations fading before his eyes. He interrupted, "Brother Thomas, you must do everything possible to help the police recover the diary. Under no circumstances do we want to alienate Dr. Winslow Fallon."

After they left the diner, Kate decided not to go to the precinct. They were talking easily, which sometimes changed in official surroundings. She decided to drive to the bay. It was a perfect day and traffic was light, much like their mood: two people chatting instead of a witness interview.

As they talked, she became aware how different he was from the men she knew—mostly cops, detectives, a PI or two, and the occasional lawyer. Thomas was articulate, intelligent, and, though she would have denied noticing, attractive.

When she turned off the 101, in the mirror she noticed a dark sedan hanging three back. It was switching to whatever lane she took. She changed lanes again, and so did the car. But when it suddenly turned off at an exit, she decided not to mention it.

It was a decision she would soon regret.

CHAPTER TWO

The Santa Barbara wharf was less crowded than usual. Kate and Thomas sat on a bench savoring the ocean breeze with its heavy tang of salt. They watched a gaggle of brown pelicans disdainfully strut among a group of tourists.

"Thomas, I sometimes try and get another viewpoint in a homicide. You are unusually familiar with this case. Do you have any questions?"

"They may sound dumb."

"My dad, a second-generation cop, said the only dumb question is one you've asked before."

"Smart man. Okay. Since you don't have any witnesses, what happens next?"

"Find the diary; *it* is our case. Without the diary as critical evidence, there's no indictment. No DA would touch it. There are a large number of suspects. Since Fallon obviously didn't kill his own courier, he is eliminated. Given the diary's history of homicides, some of them must be connected. That means more leads."

"How do you keep track of all that?"

"Frankly, I try to think like a dog."

"A dog?"

"My dad's first partner as a cop was a German Shepherd named Shotzie. She taught him a lot. For example, when a dog enters a crime scene their nose also tells them information about the previous twenty-four hours. If I could do the same, I'd know how many people had been there, where in the crime scene they went and what they touched. Most of all, I'd instantly recognize them by their scent if we met, though I'd never seen them before. Homicide detectives spend a lot of effort trying to get the same results. First rule—think like the perpetrator."

"Then why would this perpetrator dismember Denise Hollander's head and hands to prevent identification, then leave the body on a trail in a public park where it could easily be discovered?"

"That was our first break. I think they goofed when they dumped the body at night. You saw the location; where you enter on that dirt road it appears you're in the woods. Actually, it's been a make-out spot since I was in high school. Lots of traffic. Whoever killed her doesn't know the area. That means they're from out of town and the murderer isn't some local soccer mom killing out of boredom."

"They followed the courier here?"

"And killed her. Now, I have a question. You said the diary might be fake?"

"Fake, or genuine, it is brilliant. Brychan was a linguistic genius. He wrote sections of the diary in four Medieval languages—English, French, Latin, and Gaelic. Fallon hired a team of translators to work on it. But he kept the Gaelic separate; that was to be my job."

"Why was the Gaelic different?"

"Medieval Gaelic is the hardest; it contains the most critical information." Thomas opened his wallet, took out a note, and unfolded it. "Brychan left a seven-hundred-year-old clue in English. Fallon sent me a copy." He handed it to her.

Kate read it aloud, stumbling over several words.

Beefor ye cross three werriors stand
Ant gurds ye last one of our band
Luves face schining shews ye wey
A werriors measure ends ye lai

She gave him a look. "This is English?"

"Middle English, around the time of Chaucer. Spelling was not yet uniform, but you can make sense of it phonetically. Three warriors stand before the cross guarding something hidden among a band or group."

"Boy, did I miss that."

"Then the last two lines are rhyming verse. 'Love's face shining shows the way; a warrior's measure ends the lay.' A lay is a narrative poem. This is like having the last piece of a puzzle but nothing that came before. Tricky?"

"Very. Obviously, the diary is a lot more than just evidence in a homicide."

The mountain road up to the monastery was a run of narrow tight turns with a steep drop-off on one side to a ravine below. The tires squealed in protest as Kate cornered the curves. Thomas nervously glanced at her.

"My dad had connections in Hollywood with the top stunt driver's school. For my high school graduation, I was given a course in high-performance driving."

"I can't decide whether to pray or jump."

Kate laughed; he was easy to talk with. Her reputation for

bluntness often caused critical evaluation reports from her superiors. She had a low tolerance for fools, whether smart-ass perps, difficult witnesses, or fellow cops. She had even tangled with a judge or two, which once cost her ten days in jail for contempt of court. At the LAPD, her fellow detectives referred to her as "BB" for brass balls. Though she pretended to be irritated, she liked it. Perhaps in order to overcompensate, she often wore skirts and heels on the job. She kept a change of clothes in her car trunk as the situation required.

Thomas was enjoying their rapport but found her attractiveness disturbing. Once in mid-sentence he found his eyes locked on her lovely legs. He forced himself to look away. It was a feeling he had not experienced in nearly two years. Why now?

At the crest of the mountain, Kate pulled in the parking lot of the monastery, passing a sign that said Saint Joseph's Anglican Celtic Order. With its all-white Spanish-style architecture it looked like a Catholic convent, which it once was. After Thomas got out of the car, there was an awkward pause.

"Thomas, I have to ask. Why would any man in this twenty-first century become a monk and live in a monastery?"

"Kate, that same question has been asked for over fifteen hundred years since the first Christian monks."

"In a convent, I wouldn't last a week."

She gunned the engine, waved, and drove away.

On the drive back, she was irritated by the paradox. There had been no interest in a man since her tortuous divorce. *Am I becoming attracted to a religious eunuch?* she wondered. The only man safer than a monk was either gay or dead. She made a mental note to call her therapist, Dr. Ruby Stein. Kate could already hear her laughing.

✠ THE TWO TEMPLARS and the Gypsy woman made camp under lofty towers of evergreen sighing in the cold north wind. Brychan was watching her as she moved about cooking their meal. She had told them her name was Sara, and that she was born in a caravan at Cádiz, Spain. She was preparing a stew of dried lentils with blood sausage and a winter hare that Ursus shot with his bow. From her spice bag she added wild onion, garlic, Spanish peppers, and black truffles. Brychan and Ursus shared an uneasy look: they believed truffles were poisonous, like most mushrooms. Sara searched for bread in the Templars' food pack. She unwrapped a damp linen bundle containing a rock-hard end of rye with a beard of black mold. Brychan stopped her before she threw it away.

"That's not food. It's for dressing wounds."

"Wounds? How?"

"Put the mold next to the wound and wrap it. Leave it two days, then do it again."

Sara wondered how anyone could believe such filth was medicine. She said a silent prayer that if she were injured, neither knight would attempt to treat her. She even heard that Gadjay kept dogs in their houses. All Roma dogs stayed outside unless they were sick. At night they ringed the camp—perfect lookouts. It was almost impossible to surprise a Roma campsite.

Brychan had seen few Gypsies; they had yet to reach the British Isles in great numbers. Arriving in France but a generation ago, she told him that they called themselves Roma or Romany. "Gypsy" was what outsiders, the Gadjay, called them.

From his interest in languages, Brychan had heard that Romany was unlike any other. A mysterious people, Gypsies told fortunes and possessed healing ways with animals, especially horses. They also crafted peerless silver and leatherwork. Known for their cunning, to be tricked by them was to be "gypped."

While she was cooking, Brychan talked with her. He was curious about how a Gypsy happened to be Christian. Didn't they believe in witchcraft? Sara explained that the Roma arrived in France as Christian pilgrims under protection of the Holy Roman Emperor. They practiced their faith in their own way, retaining old traditions. Their patron, Saint Sara, was said to have been a servant to Mary Magdalene. Sara was named after her.

Brychan watched, fascinated, as she worked. Her raven hair matched ebony dark eyes; she was wondrously bloss: well-proportioned, with large breasts. When doing woman's work, she moved gracefully; when riding a horse, she was gaynley as a man.

Ursus listened critically as they talked. Of all the orders in the Church the Templars were strictest about women. Her very presence violated their vows. A Templar must never be alone with a woman, private conversation with one was forbidden, and no woman could enter a Templar building or church without permission. To travel with one was unthinkable. Ursus feared that if they were discovered by another Templar they would be reported and made to serve the required year's hard penance.

The men were hungry and their first bites were a surprise, delicious and hearty. Ursus, assuming Gypsy cooking would taste foul, could remember nothing so good in months.

The Templar rule at meals was to eat in contemplative silence or hear scripture read by a brother. But this day had brought sufficient evil, as noted in scripture, and must be resolved. Sara listened as they tried to reason through their situation.

After the robbery they had searched the baggage, salvaging whatever they could. The thieves took the VERITAS chest, the diary, and their horses. But they left behind clothing, food, weapons, even their purse of money. What thief didn't steal money?

The robbers were traveling overland north, probably to Paris. But to follow with inferior horses would make catching them impossible.

To Brychan, the solution was to quit the trail, take a difficult overland route, and set an ambush.

Ursus was opposed. If they guessed wrong going overland, they could lose the robbers.

"Are you sure they are going to Paris?" Sara asked.

"It appears so," Brychan answered.

"The Roma go to Paris every year before Lent to sell to the crowds. We know trails to avoid the King's soldiers. You saved my life. I will lead you."

Brychan looked at Ursus who was shaking his head. "Brother Ursus, we are pursuing them with cavalry horses. The thieves ride our German breed, which are unmatched for endurance. Once they know we are following, they need only release the slow packhorses. Then we would never catch them."

Ursus understood horses better than anyone Brychan knew. In the Holy Land, the Bedouin who treated their horses like family, taught him. It was said that Ursus could follow a trail over trackless rock.

Ursus looked angrily at the woman: once again she was causing trouble, as was their way.

Brychan read his look. "Brother, the rule concerning women must be ignored when weighed against our mission. We must not fail."

To avoid further argument, Ursus rose and moved beyond the firelight. He stared at the trees silhouetted against the starry sky and while listening to the whispering night, from long practice, slipped into prayerful meditation.

TWIST OF TIME

* * *

SHERIF SIR GILBERT de Bage ordered his men to halt and make camp. It was too dark to continue tracking by torchlight. Even the relentless Templars would be forced to stop.

He had intensified the pursuit when he found eight dead bandits in the forest. It did not matter that the Templars slaughtered outlaws who would have been hanged immediately if caught. King Philip's bounty on Templars was paid in gold bezants. As High Sherif serving the Duke of Auvergne, Sir Gilbert could keep all bounty for himself. The bounty on two Templars was a small fortune.

When he began tracking the Templars, they had eight days lead. That changed when the sherif came across the bodies of four King's Cavalry and an old Gypsy.

At first, Gilbert doubted they were connected. Why would two Templars kill a total of twelve men in two skirmishes when they could simply avoid fighting? The sherif, who well knew weapons and modes of combat, had carefully examined the dead. His experience told him almost as much about the fight as if he had witnessed it; their different blades marked each warrior's action.

One Templar was extremely strong and a master of the two-handed broadsword. His first opponent was almost cut in half while mounted; another's ribs were crushed beneath his mail; a third was gutted and beheaded—all by this same warrior's powerful blade.

The second Templar, who slew the sergeant, had a sword that could pierce heavy mail; probably the new Toledo blade. They were expensive beyond any common soldier's means.

No Templar is a mere horse thief, yet two *on foot* attacked and killed four mounted King's cavalry and took their horses: proof they were either demons from hell or Zealotes. The sherif was surprised to discover that when he followed their trail, another set of tracks revealed the Templars also were tracking someone.

For three grueling days the sherif mercilessly pushed his men, closing the gap. The Templars were now but two days distant. They did not know they were being followed; surprise would give the sherif a critical advantage when they met. ☩

Thomas was out early the next morning after the homicide. He was in town having just made a delivery of Monk's Bread to the Community Food Bank. The job rotated among the monks and it was his turn.

The delivery truck was an ancient Econovan with a prima donna ignition that started on whim. After cranking easily that morning at the monastery, now when Thomas turned the key, it grunted, coughed, and died.

He got out and raised the hood without the vaguest idea what to do. Frustrated, he looked at the Saturday traffic passing by. He was offering a quick prayer when someone approached him from behind.

"Are you one of the Monk's Bread people?"

As Thomas turned, he was slammed in the head by a hard blow and dropped to the ground. When he looked up, there was a dark sedan backing toward him.

Two men jerked him to his feet and shoved him toward the car.

"Police! Hands in the air!"

All turned to see Kate, shielded by the open door of an unmarked car, showing a badge and pointing an automatic.

One man hit Thomas with his handgun and he dropped to his knees. Then both men jumped into the waiting car and cut across traffic so that Kate could not fire because of the other cars. In seconds they were gone.

She rushed to Thomas.

"Don't get up," she said. "I'm calling the paramedics."

Woozily, he managed to stand. "What are you doing here?"

She began dabbing his bleeding head with her handkerchief. "Yesterday, I thought we might be tailed, but who tails a cop? So, I followed you today to see if anyone was tailing you."

"Why didn't you tell me?"

"I would look silly if I were wrong."

"Next time, look silly."

"I am so sorry." His warm scent blended with the tang of lemon verbena from working the herb garden. She could almost taste him. "I'm taking you to the ER."

"No, I'm okay."

She saw he was going to be stubborn.

"Do you feel well enough to eat?" she said.

"Monks are always hungry."

"Good. Fallon is flying in on his private jet to meet us for brunch."

In a parked car half a block away, four men had watched the assault on Thomas. One of them, Sid Carver, swore. "Jeeeesus! How many people are after this monk?"

He touched instant dial on his cell. A voice said, "This is Victor."

"Carver. Big problem. Before we could grab the monk two guys out of nowhere jumped him. Then a cop appeared, and they took off. A cop! What should we do?"

He held up the phone for the others to hear. There were several seconds of silence.

"Where is the monk now?" the voice asked.

"With the cop."

"I'll report it to Leo. He will definitely want to meet with you. Be ready." The line went dead.

Carver, amazed, looked at the others. "That's frigging unbelievable! I've never heard of Leo personally meeting with anybody."

In a luxury suite at the Hilton off the 101 in Santa Barbara, Nora Pittman paced in irritation. Ravel Marinero, a man in his mid-forties, stood waiting impatiently. His dark olive face was born to have numbers under it on a police bulletin board. He wore a plastic windbreaker beaded with droplets still wet from a thundershower. His predator eyes followed her.

Nora, smoking a brown cigarette, moved through a maze of her Vuitton luggage strewn across the floor. She was in her mid-fifties and casually dressed in muted tans and browns. Some men would have found her attractive except for something in her eyes that cautioned trouble. It appeared when conversing with her: a lightning intelligence and direct questions.

"How do you know she was a cop?" she asked. "They usually work in pairs."

"She flashed a badge."

"Three of you, one of her, and you still didn't snatch the monk?"

"She was a cop! You didn't say the monk had police protection."

Nora didn't argue. In spite of his ordinary appearance, Ravel was an assassin with extraordinary skills. He worked alone, which was unique; most assassins work in teams. Of both Puerto Rican and Basque parentage, he was highly respected and on call with several extremist groups in Europe. She asked, "Would you recognize this cop again?"

TWIST OF TIME

"Anywhere."

"Next time, kill her and grab him."

She dismissed him with a nod. With a look of irritation, he left. After the door closed, she grabbed a porcelain table lamp and hurled it against the wall, sending pieces flying. She felt better.

Sid Carver and three of his team had been following the monk's van all morning waiting for the right opportunity to nab him. Suddenly, two men grabbed him and got away. Then a cop appeared—a total disaster. Now they were nervously waiting in a shabby motel room for Leo's arrival.

A few weeks earlier, Carver, known as the Broker, had been hired by "Mysterious Leo," as he was called, to put a team together to kidnap the monk. Carver had worked for Leo twice before: once, hiring a team to deal with a cartel selling stolen assault weapons, and then a political kidnapping. He'd never actually met Leo; connections were always through his middleman, Victor. Carver knew Leo by reputation: "*Super* nasty." During the illegal arms deal, when the other side discovered Leo was involved, they shaved their price. Carver was impressed. Now, because of their failure to kidnap the monk for Leo, he was also very nervous.

Only three of the team were with Carver that morning when the monk was snatched. It never occurred to him that he would have needed more. While he was waiting, he tried to estimate who was his weakest link so this didn't happen again.

Steiner, the "old man," was German, and his family had been part of the Baader-Meinhof terrorist group of the seventies. Wojowitz worked mainly for Israeli gangs operating in the States. His contacts seemed endless; he even kept close ties with rival Russian drug lords. Grigsby was Chicago mob muscle; his size came with a vicious reputation. Oddly, he was known to be henpecked by his very diminutive wife, a truth which nobody mentioned unless seized with a death wish. Alonzo was Colombian cartel; he seldom spoke but watched everything with a half-smile. Carter suspected the smile didn't change even when he pulled the trigger.

When Leo finally arrived, to Carver's surprise, he was alone. He had expected an entourage of flunkies. Leo was Black, another surprise, though it was known that he was not American. One look confirmed his bad-ass reputation. He was expensively dressed and had an attitude that reeked of power. It was said that some actually became sick in his presence when he was angry. Now, Carver believed it. Leo did not need thugs to intimidate.

Without a word, Leo carefully studied each face. Although they all were pros, this operation was too sensitive to rely on simply buying their services. Absolute secrecy was essential. Unknown to them, each was chosen with a vulnerable key that could be wound to his breaking point. Leo was the keeper of the keys.

Apparently satisfied, Leo stepped back. His slight smile did not reach his eyes.

Leo had spent a lot of time alone, and Carver could sense the unmistakable taint of solitary confinement. He was wearing black leather dress gloves in summer—no careless prints. This guy covered everything.

When Leo finally spoke, his voice was surprisingly soft. "The monk is your only priority. Understood?"

One or two nodded; nobody spoke.

"You never act without an order. Any order you get, you obey." He looked at Carver. "Is that absolutely clear?"

"Yes, sir," Carver answered.

Grigsby, the broody hulk, cleared his throat. "Look, when you say any order, does that . . ."

"It means exactly any order." Leo glanced at Carver for confirmation. Carver nodded.

Leo looked again at each face, fixing it in memory. "No failure. No excuses."

He walked out of the room. They all exchanged wary looks.

Before meeting Fallon for brunch, Kate Googled his name for background. His billions were not the result of some nerd working out of his garage. Driven by both a genius IQ and what was unexpectedly described as "multiple neurosis," he graduated high school at age twelve. After receiving a PhD specializing in brain research at Cal Tech, Fallon earned a master's at MIT in computer science. He immediately started his own company, Med-Tek, specializing in software for cutting-edge medical research. Though successful, the company was highly controversial.

Aside from legitimate research and development, Med-Tek's notoriety came from radical experiments with animals on behavior modification that utilized computer-chip brain implants; these were called BCI, which stood for Brain-Computer Interface. Many corporations had done similar experiments, but Fallon claimed his to be "the cutting edge in New Age therapy."

On Fallon's website Kate found a range of bizarre experiments. Rats were remote-controlled like toy cars. Most disturbing was a male chimpanzee named Butch implanted with a brain chip; he mounted a female named Sheba at the touch of a remote switch. Sexual intercourse was repeated again and again during the same session until Butch collapsed from exhaustion. Sheba, relieved, took a nap.

"Who needs Viagra?" Kate muttered.

Strangest of all, Fallon promoted his own controversy. Kate discovered a segment on his website devoted to negative comments from across the media. *Scientific American, Psychology Today, The Lancet*—all the press was unfavorable. Even *Rolling Stone* chimed in: "*Fallon is a triple threat: brilliant, creative, with the monstrous ego of an intellectual bully.*"

Kate wondered: who publishes negative commentary about themselves? Obviously, a supreme narcissist who is totally confidant in who they are. In a celebrity culture where media attention is vital, Fallon promoted his own controversy, which guaranteed continuous media coverage.

Kate was surprised to discover that he was also a famous gourmet, traveling all over the world to dine on exquisite meals prepared by superstar chiefs. Often these were filmed and featured on various network food shows which added to his celebrity.

Researching further, Kate ran Fallon's name through several police databases that cross-referenced criminal activity. It was a routine her father used on all names connected with a case, including victims, witnesses, and suspects. Occasionally, interesting data would turn up. He called it looking for the "edge."

Kate soon found an edge and a name: Gladys Pullman, a homicide victim who had worked closely with Fallon at Med-Tek. Kate wanted to find out more but would have to delay until after her brunch.

When Thomas and Kate arrived at the Four Seasons Hotel dining room she was surprised to find Dr. Fallon already there. It had been her experience that the more prominent the person, the longer the wait.

Kate mentally ran her assessment of Fallon: mid-fifties, brown eyes, hair professionally tinted to cover gray, height five-eight to ten, weight one-fifty to sixty. Build: pudgy masked by expert clothes styling. His face was framed in oversized black-rimmed glasses—a part of his signature look. He was said to be tailored by the most expensive shops on Savile Row and was never photographed without coat and tie. Despite his arrogance, there was an unexpected charm as he dominated the conversation. He was holding court.

Thomas listened to Fallon's small talk while they waited for drinks. It was odd trying to reconcile this congenial Fallon with the arrogant ass with whom he'd spent tedious hours discussing the Templar diary over the phone.

The drinks arrived—Chablis for Kate, beer for Thomas. Fallon raised his glass of mineral water in a toast.

"To happier circumstances," he said. Then the charm vanished. "I have suffered two devastating losses. The courier Denise Hollander, my assistant of sixteen years, was brutally murdered and is irreplaceable. The stolen Templar diary is priceless."

He turned to Kate and said, "Detective, you should know that I pride myself in a gift for retaliation."

"Hopefully, that won't be necessary." Kate was confident. "With our police coverage, the diary will soon be recovered, which will lead us to the killer."

"That's why I am offering five hundred thousand for information leading to the conviction of Denise's Hollander's killer."

"That is very generous."

"A term rarely applied to me, Detective Flynn." He appraised her knowingly and said, "Did Google mention that I married my stepmother the day after we took Daddy off life support?" He shrugged. "It didn't last. Passion is wrongly compared with fire; it is more like ice. When it's gone, everything begins to rot."

Kate was amused at the bizarre image. "No. Google didn't mention that."

Fallon glanced at Thomas. "I fear I have shocked our monk."

"I doubt if you fear shocking anyone," Thomas said.

"You see, Detective Flynn, when Brother Thomas and I began our association, I warned him that I am a militant atheist. As a fervent hedonist I embrace every indulgence—food, sex, everything except alcohol, which dulls both senses and intellect."

She savored a swallow of wine. "Mmm. You're right, I do feel dumber."

"May I tell you something about the miraculous brain?" Fallon reached in the breadbasket and held up a roll. "There's a theory that all ideas are *atomically* structured. The brain metabolizes solid food into abstract thought. How many thoughts in a slice of bread? Imagine— we may owe E equals MC squared to Einstein's bagel."

"An interesting idea," Kate said.

"Very." Thomas agreed. "Especially since you, an atheist, are paraphrasing the French Jesuit priest and scientist, Teilhard de Chardin."

Fallon frowned, irritated at being topped. "Let's talk business. Regarding the diary, my attorneys have managed to put limitations on its use."

"What limitations?" Kate asked.

"After you recover the diary, it may not be duplicated without a court order."

"I am not aware of any such law."

"It's being rushed through the California legislature this week. No national treasure in written form may be duplicated without notarized permission of its owner."

Thomas interrupted. "But the diary is not a national treasure."

"It is now. My attorneys have filed the paperwork. Only a few pages of the diary were duplicated for translation. The three I sent you. Are they safe?"

Kate frowned at Thomas; he hadn't told her. He avoided her look. "Yes, I have them."

Fallon, sensing the tension between them, played to it. "As you can see, Detective, your monk is also a man of mystery."

Kate agreed, "And so are you. How did you manage to limit our use of key evidence?"

"Power. And power is also knowing who to buy."

"In other words, a bribe."

"The perfect word. You should also know that I am bringing in my own investigative team to find the killer."

"And when you do, will you turn them over to the police?" she asked.

"It depends on how quickly they give me the diary. I will do every. . . ."

Thomas interrupted again. "You mean after you finish with them?"

"Precisely." He turned to Kate. "My attorneys assure me it would be very difficult to prosecute me should I find the killer in a foreign country and do whatever is necessary to recover the stolen diary."

"You think that's where he'll be?"

"It is certainly where he will end up." He smiled. The topic was finished; his Jekyll–Hyde charm reappeared. "Kate, do you like Mexican cuisine?"

"My favorite."

"Will you join me for dinner? I have a reservation in Cancún with a famed chef named Javier who is a genius with seafood, especially with a rare prawn he discovered. I'm told our meal will make it extinct. We'll jet back from Mexico tomorrow in time for you to go to work."

"Sorry, Dr. Fallon, I don't have time. Now I have to catch the killer before you do."

On the mountain road back up to the monastery, there was little conversation; both were still absorbed in the Fallon meeting. Rounding a turn revealed a dazzling panorama of shimmering ocean. Kate pulled over. Below, the cobalt Pacific was patiently carving the bay a wave at a time as it had for eons.

She asked, "Should I have gone with Fallon to Cancún?"

"It depends upon what you're willing to do for a Mexican dinner."

"Like trading my virtue for tacos?"

They laughed and watched the ocean, each absorbed in their thoughts.

Thomas was wrestling with the Fallon paradox: why was a scientist and atheist obsessed with the Templars, a religious order? He had hoped their meeting would clarify some questions but discovered only that Fallon had a complex agenda. Thomas was annoyed by something else—his irritation at the thought of Kate flying to Cancún with Fallon. Why did he care?

When Kate drove them into the monastery parking lot, she killed the engine but continued staring straight ahead. The anger she struggled to contain finally erupted.

"When were you going to tell me about the duplicate pages from the diary?" she said.

"Fallon swore me to secrecy. I had to respect that unless it became relevant to your case."

"The diary is missing. Those pages are evidence that it exists." She turned to him. "*That* makes it relevant."

"Kate, I'm sorry. I didn't mean to . . ."

"This is a homicide, Thomas. No more secrets. Agreed?"

"Then you should also know more about me. On the Internet, find my book and follow wherever that leads. Afterwards, I'll answer any questions. The title is *Merlin: Legend, Wizard, Saint*."

When she drove away, the questions were already forming.

At exactly eight the next morning, Kate arrived at the monastery. When she entered, she heard the echo of monks chanting somewhere deep within its walls. Brother Barnabas, the monk assigned to greet visitors, was wearing the distinctive habit of the order, a dark blue denim monk's robe with a red cord knotted at the waist. As a Catholic, Kate had seen many monks; they'd worn white, black, brown, or gray robes with a white cord tied at the waist.

Brother Barnabas seemed uneasy when she asked to see Brother Thomas.

"Please wait here." He disappeared down a chilly corridor, his steps sounding on the Spanish tile floor.

Given the sanctified atmosphere, Kate imagined taking off her blouse and running topless and laughing down the hall. Before she could enjoy the fantasy, Abbot Methodius appeared. He was in his late fifties, with an oyster pallor contrasting his blue robe.

"You wanted to see Brother Thomas?"

Kate showed her badge. "Detective Flynn."

"Oh, dear . . . Lord."

"What's the matter?"

"I don't know exactly how to—"

"What's wrong!"

"Brother Thomas was abducted last night."

Her gut wrenched. "Abducted?"

"Yes. He—"

"How in hell could he be abducted from a monastery?"

"Brother Barnabas was on night duty. Around one-thirty there was someone at the door. When he opened it, three men overpowered him and drugged him with a needle. When all the brothers were assembled, Brother Thomas was gone."

"Did you call the police?"

"No. There was a phone call. A man said that if we notified the police, they would kill Brother Thomas."

Kate flared. "God DAMMIT!"

The words echoed in the hallowed monastery for the very first time.

"Detective, you can't report this. Not until we have been contacted about his ransom."

"Ransom? For a monk? This is about that damn diary!"

Before Methodius could answer, an elderly monk entered. He was frail, nearly skeletal and wore thick glasses. Instead of aged wrinkles, his skin was a sallow parchment drawn over a skull that looked more like a museum artifact. There was a small bandage on the side of his head. Somehow, he looked vaguely familiar to her.

"Father Abbot, is there any more news about Brother Thomas?" he asked nervously.

"Please calm yourself, Brother Simon, or you'll be back in the hospital." He introduced them. "Detective, you may also recognize him as Dr. Simon Springer, the famed astrophysicist."

"Cosmologist," Brother Simon corrected.

Kate then remembered pictures in the media. The physicist-monk lecturing eminent scientists, his robe standing out in a sea of suits. She indicated his head bandage. "Were you hurt by the kidnappers?"

"No. Do you always jump to conclusions?"

The Abbot smoothly interrupted. "Brother Simon goes to the hospital regularly for dialysis. Last week he fell and injured his head."

Kate, annoyed by Simon's comment, pointedly handed her card to Methodius. "My phone numbers, in case you think of something." She looked from one to the other. "One question. Since they got the diary when they killed Denise Hollander, why abduct Thomas?"

Simon's look marked her as hopelessly dense. "Obviously, they need him to translate the diary. My God! You're a detective and didn't see that?"

CHAPTER THREE

Driving back to town, Kate was unconsciously speeding to match her racing thoughts. Brother Simon, the snotty little shit, was right. The kidnappers needed Thomas to translate, and she totally missed it. Incredible! From habit, she mentally focused to think like the opposition: as long as they needed Thomas, he would stay alive. Would he realize this and stall the translating?

When her homicide department found out about the abduction, it would become a kidnap-hostage situation and be out of her hands. She could already hear the SWAT order to "lock and load." She knew of a similar scenario from an LAPD counter-terrorist case; the hostage was killed in the rescue attempt. Zero sum: dead terrorists, dead hostage.

She decided to delay and not tell the department about the kidnapping. She would hold off for the next seventy two hours and work around the clock to find Thomas. But if she was wrong . . . Mother-of-God . . .

Right now, she needed help.

Det. Vicky Marroquin, a young forty, was the vivacious daughter of a Black mother and Latino father. She was the first non-Anglo woman on the Santa Barbara PD to make homicide detective. Vicky and Kate were Santa Barbara natives; both had gone to UCLA on scholarship. Vicky didn't finish but dropped out her junior year to marry. Though Kate's training and experience exceeded Vicky's, they perfectly balanced each other. When they worked good cop, bad cop, it was two worse cops. They were in tune like the cliché: they could finish each other's sentences.

During lunch at Jake's diner with Vicky, Kate explained the situation.

Vicky shook her head; she didn't like what she was hearing. "Let me be sure I understand. We search for the diary, we look for the monk, but we don't tell Captain Starger what we're doing?"

"Right."

"Kate, fooling him is trickier than a cheating spouse. If something goes wrong...."

"We could be fired."

"Right." Vicky shrugged. "Oh, hell. I'm in."

"In your place I would have said no."

"I almost did. What's next?"

"Witnesses. We've got abduction in the middle of the night and the monastery neighborhood has very little traffic. Let's hope for a roaming insomniac who saw something."

"Hernandez in Traffic owes me. He'll check the accident files. Kate, twelve hours gives them a big start. Your monk could be anywhere."

"Yep. I'll check private flights. Somebody on a gurney or with a team of bodyguards."

Vicky's instincts told her that Kate wasn't telling her everything, but she said nothing.

Back at her desk in Homicide, Kate made a call to Baltimore PD Homicide because Fallon's corporate headquarters were in

Baltimore. She was looking for information on Gladys Pullman, the murder victim who worked with Fallon. After annoying minutes of being transferred several times she found the lead detective, Lt. Dan Swartz. Their rapport was immediate, cop to cop.

"Dan, I couldn't find much information on Pullman's case."

"Not surprising. Fallon is a rotten piece of work. One of him in your life is enough."

"What happened?"

"We did a routine investigation on the Gladys Pullman homicide for the first forty-eight. But you could smell cold case coming. Fallon did a number on the media and it died."

"How did he pull that off?"

"Ever deal with a power player like Fallon? Money, contacts, politicians, and anything else he needs. He got the story buried. But I've got more in Gladys Pullman's file that didn't make the media. You want a copy?"

"I'll swap you my firstborn, if I ever have one."

After hanging up, Kate opened the courier Denise Hollander's homicide file. She was fifty-eight, unmarried, and had been Fallon's right arm. Her job was her life. There was data on her family—lots of nieces and nephews; she was the adored maiden aunt. For simply delivering the diary, Hollander was brutally murdered and mutilated. Kate felt a fresh rush of anger.

From the Hollander file she pulled her notes on Thomas' interview and locked them in her briefcase. There would be no documentation on Thomas until she was ready.

But fear still nagged. How was Thomas taking it? He was physically strong and mentally tough; monks required self-discipline well beyond the average person. How long could he delay?

Thomas' first sensation beyond pain was smell: fried frijoles. A headache hammered like his head was jammed sideways in a vice.

TWIST OF TIME

He realized he had been drugged; the effects were raggedly hanging on.

With eyes blindfolded, he lay on his back on a narrow metal cot with a bare mattress that reeked of old urine. One wrist was cuffed to the cot's iron frame; it barely gave when pulled.

He was aware of men's voices speaking Spanish from somewhere behind a door. Their radio played constantly—salsa music and Spanish talk radio. The rancid fried bean smell was stifling.

Mexico? Or hell?

Drifting in and out, he prayed fragments of Psalm 91. *The Lord is my refuge and my fortress . . . He shall deliver thee from the snare of the fowler . . . shalt not be afraid for the terror by night; nor for the arrow that flieth by day . . .*

Between prayers there was a collage of drug-sharpened images: Hollander's mutilated body, Fallon's droning obsessions, and especially the fascinating Kate Flynn. What was this attraction to her? Sexual repression fueled by monastic celibacy? For monks, that was a tiresome concept assumed by outsiders. But something about Kate beyond the sexual fascinated him, and that was much more dangerous.

Laughter from the next room jarred him back. *Focus. Think.* He was obviously abducted for one reason: to translate the diary. They blindfolded him so he could not identify them. Once it was removed for him to translate, he would see them. When he finished, they would have to kill him to avoid his identifying them in the courier's homicide. He must delay, delay. Just as he sensed that his mind was working, he drifted off in another blissful haze.

That night in her apartment, Kate sat at the computer with Watson, her twelve-pound tomcat dozing cozily in her lap. This had become so routine that whenever she used the computer at home, she needed the comfort of Watson's furry warmth. In the background, a Bach toccata by pianist Glenn Gould played in soft undertone. Kate usually had Bach playing whenever she was alone going over case material. It had been the background music of her life since college. To her, fugues with their intricate counterpoint were a musical metaphor of an ideal homicide investigation; CSI, DNA, ballistics, interrogation, autopsy, forensics—all fitting together with the precision of a Bach fugue.

Before she searched the Internet, she reviewed her notes about Thomas. Reading people was one of her strengths. She routinely made accurate assessments of witnesses, suspects, and perps. The FBI twice tried to recruit her as a profiler. She read Thomas as sophisticated and highly intelligent but with an unexpected naiveté. He had an appealing openness. What you saw was what you got.

On the Internet she found Thomas' book, *Merlin: Legend, Wizard, Saint*. Reading the reviews, she understood why he wanted her to find out about him from different sources. The book was highly controversial. History buffs loved it; academics attacked it. *The Atlantic* published an article on the ensuing scandal in which Thomas claimed to have discovered an unknown document proving Merlin's double life as pagan wizard and Christian bishop. It was dated from the late sixth century.

After questions were raised by some academics, lab tests proved the parchment was created no earlier than the eleventh century. It was traced to a notorious French master forger in the late 1700s.

When Thomas was being questioned for his PhD exam, the academic committee accused him of covering up the forgery to sell his book. Then, just days after the hearing, there was a personal tragedy. While Thomas was out of town at a conference, his wife, Lois, was killed in an automobile accident. Thomas's closest friend, Royce, was driving the car. They were returning from a weekend at a mountain cabin. It was perfect tabloid fodder: "*wife of controversial author dies during shack-up with his best friend.*"

Now Kate's interest was piqued and she continued searching. On another website she found a bizarre twist. An *Enquirer* stringer discovered that as an adolescent, Thomas was studied by the Rhine Institute, internationally known for research in the paranormal. Predictably, the tabloids branded Thomas "the psychic scholar," which further damaged his image among his conservative peers. At the next committee hearing, the psychic issue was raised. Thomas refused to comment. Shortly afterward, he withdrew from the program.

Kate was dumbfounded. Thomas a psychic? She hadn't the slightest belief in them. Psychics had been called in on two of her LAPD homicides. They couldn't find their ass with a bloodhound and an anal compass.

She intuitively felt that nothing about Thomas was bogus, but his naiveté might make him easily deluded. She turned off the computer, poured a Stoli on ice, and curled up with Watson on the sofa, drinking and thinking.

THE TEMPLARS AND the Gypsy woman had been traveling since daybreak. Though Ursus agreed to let the woman guide them, he kept an angry silence. Sara was amused but dared not show it. Ursus was well named—he was prickly as a bear sow.

Brychan glanced at him. "Your mood is foul, Brother Ursus. May we know the reason?"

"It is the Gypsy's fault that we were robbed." Ursus spoke as if she were not there. "When we helped her, the robbers stole the chest. True?"

"True, Brother. But how could we refuse to help her?"

"If you have the sight, why didn't you foresee that the robbers would steal the chest?"

Sara, astonished, looked at Brychan. He had the sight? Fortune-telling ran deep in Roma life. It was easy to fool the gullible Gadjay, but there were also readers who were truly gifted. Since the Church declared both the sight and witchcraft as heresy, why would God give the sight to a monk? Or was it the Devil's gift?

Brychan answered Ursus. "The sight has its own ways. Like the wind, it touches and moves on." He added, "It is said that only a fool reads for himself."

"Then, what good is it?" Ursus spurred his horse and rode ahead to reconnoiter a thick growth of greenery for possible ambush.

"Sir Brychan, if you read fortunes, maybe you are part Roma," Sara teased.

"No, I cannot read fortunes." He was amused.

Sara watched Ursus disappear into the thick woods. Although the two men hardly needed to speak to communicate, there was an unease between them. Unlike some Templars she had seen who kept only the appearance of monastic life, both Brychan and Ursus seemed sincerely devout. Their differences did not lie there.

"You two are an odd pairing. Are all Templars so matched?" she asked.

Brychan did not answer; it was impossible to explain in a few words. His thoughts were drawn to that day months before, when a secret document from the Grand Master was smuggled from prison.

Deep in the Forêt d'Orient, the fugitive Templars, about fifty-odd knights, sergeants, and troopers were gathered at the appointed place. After the Order was destroyed by King Philip, unlike many who fled to different countries, this small band stayed behind in France on orders from Master de Molay. They were instructed to hide in the forest and rejoin him when he was freed from prison by order of Pope Clement, which might happen at any time. They had no choice. They could but survive, endure, and wait.

For seven arduous years, Templar iron-clad discipline had held them together. Living off the land, they were also helped by poachers and peasants from their own meager stores.

While King Philip's soldiers scoured the country for the fugitives, the patrols did not venture far into the forest. The Templars, after years of combat in the Holy Land, had perfected Saracen ambush tactics. To be surprised by them meant death, for they could take no prisoners.

Now called together for a special meeting, the Templars arrived from their separate camps throughout the forest. A few defiantly wore their white mantles with the red Templar cross. In the breaking dawn light, they appeared as shadows in the heavy mist. The area was lit by a torch held by a raggedly uniformed sergeant. Friar Luke, still greatly revered, was wearing his Templar cleric's green robe, now much frayed and patched.

The friar explained that two separate messages had been smuggled from the Grand Master in prison. He opened the first parchment and translated its two sentences out loud from Latin: "We have appointed Brother Brychan a Zealote. He is to be paired with Brother Ursus. Signed de Molay, Grand Master, by Brother John, scribe."

No explanation was given.

There was astonished silence. Ursus looked in rage at Friar Luke as if he had written it.

All eyes watched Brychan who stared ahead at nothing. Though young, he was the best blade among them, save for Ursus. But, except for a few skirmishes with the King's patrols, he was unproven in combat.

Traditionally, Zealotes added to their ranks only proven veterans. Yet, Brychan was made a Zealote by special order of the Master. Known to all was the Templar maxim: "Zealotes answer only to Grand Master who answers only to Pope who answers only to God."

Resentment hung like stinging smoke. Many of them would have sacrificed all to be made a Zealote. Brother Ursus' eyes burned rage-hot. His last Zealote pairing was with Claude of Lorraine, whose combat legend nearly matched his own. When Brother Claude fell at Acre, in the Holy Land, he was pierced with five Saracen arrows before his final breath.

Ursus glared at Brychan. "A Zealote is a proven warrior. You don't know enough to stay alive." He spat and turned away in disgust.

In a quick move, Brychan's dagger touched Ursus' throat under the ear. Ursus slowly turned into the blade point. In warning, Brychan pressed, drawing a tiny drop of blood. He nodded to de Molay's letter. "I am now a Zealote by order of the Grand Master. You will obey it or be defrocked—the rule for disobedience."

The men watching were mute as mice. No one had ever pulled blade against Brother Ursus and lived. Brychan had drawn blood, a scratch the same as a slash.

All were witnessing the unthinkable: two Templar Knights about to kill each other in the presence of brothers. Since their founding in over two centuries, this had never happened.

Brychan and Ursus stood frozen like pointer and hare. Even with his throat cut, Ursus would quickly slay the young knight before dying. Brychan, for his part, faced a challenge that ended here or tainted all his days.

Slowly, Brychan raised his right-hand palm outward, waiting. If Ursus did the same and their hands interlocked, it would be the Zealote sign that they were paired.

TWIST OF TIME

Their eyes were unwavering as their palms touched; fingers then locked into a double fist. The *iunctus manibus*. It was the traditional silent vow. No matter their personal feelings, they now were sealed until death as paired Zealotes.

"Done," Friar Luke said, and on their locked hands made the sign of the cross. Then he handed the second document to Brychan. "Tell no one except Brother Ursus."

The Latin, as in the other letter, was written in the same scribe's hand. Brychan read silently then nodded that he understood.

Friar Luke whispered. "The chest is at Holy Cross Cistercian convent." He took the document back and held it to the sergeant's torch. It flared, instantly curling to ash; flashpaper.

"When?" Brychan asked.

"Tonight."

Brychan looked at Ursus whose eyes were blazing anger. Five years before, Ursus had been ordered by the Grand Master to kill Brychan if a certain prophecy he had dreamed was declared false—Holy Scripture's penalty for false prophecy. Fortunately, the prophecy proved to be true and Brychan was spared. Now, in a fatal irony, they were bound together on a mission that surely must end in death. ✢

Kate was early at her homicide desk after a sleepless night that a third Stoli didn't remedy. She was sifting through traffic reports looking for a possible witness. The phone rang.

"Detective Flynn? Fallon. I can't reach the monk."

She had forgotten to tell him. "Dr. Fallon, Brother Thomas is missing."

"What do you mean, missing?"

"He was abducted from the monastery."

"What! When?"

"Night before last."

"Why wasn't I told?"

"We've been rather busy here, Doctor." She couldn't tell him that the police also were not informed.

"That's not acceptable!" There was an angry pause. "Let me be very clear, Detective. I expect to be kept informed on every detail."

Kate bristled. "Dr. Fallon, why didn't you tell me about Gladys Pullman? She personally worked for you, yet you never mentioned that the Baltimore police have an open homicide case on her which centers around you and your corporation."

He was hesitant. "I . . . I didn't think it was pertinent to this case."

"Why does every dumbass think they can decide what is pertinent in a homicide? That is a police decision! *Me*. Understood?"

He ignored her insult; it would serve no purpose for them to quarrel. "I'm sorry, Detective. Frankly, it is very painful to talk about."

"I am afraid we have to."

"I'll discuss it just once. But if you mention it again, I will personally make this case a nightmare for you."

"No threats necessary. You're calling the shots. Let's talk."

"Very well. I am sure it is no surprise that . . . I have few friends."

She almost laughed. "Your honesty is refreshing."

"My work and the few associates that I trust are crucial to me. Both Denise Hollander and Gladys Pullman were the closest. Dr. Pullman was my top research programmer. One night after working late at the lab she disappeared."

"Disappeared, how?"

"She was abducted when walking to her car in our parking lot. She was never found."

"Any ransom demand?"

"No. But a week later some of her clothing was discovered in the woods. It was covered in blood. DNA confirmed it was Dr. Pullman's."

"What was the motive?"

"Corporate espionage. Immediately, some of our most sensitive data appeared in the news media and on the Internet. With this development the police upgraded Pullman's case to homicide."

"Anything else I should know?"

"Yes. I'm certain that a personal enemy is targeting me. Two of my closest associates murdered? Both work-related? Now you see why I put up the reward to get the killer. I want him; I will get him. I won't wait for the bumbling police."

"But Dr. Fallon. . . ."

"Keep me informed." He hung up.

Kate scribbled a note. She leaned back, looking at what she had just written: *What happened before the diary?* Denise Hollander was murdered for the diary but Fallon's associate, Pullman, was not. Something ugly was going on a full year before Fallon bought the diary and he was in the middle of it.

"Well, son-of-a-bitch," Kate said, and smiled. This routine homicide was becoming more interesting.

Fallon, wearing a white lab coat, moved quickly through his office suite and into his private elevator. He keyed a code and descended to the maximum-secure bottom level. The elevator opened into a glaring white corridor. There was a double door marked LAB 5 in raised letters; beside it was a state-of-the-art security terminal of his own design with interlocking ID systems. Fallon inserted an ID chip and placed his hand on a plate that read his palm and digital prints. This activated a retinal scan; he then said his name for a voiceprint. There was a soft bell as the computer confirmed his DNA chip.

The double doors automatically opened to an explosion of sound: a raucous celebration. A dozen or so men and women in white lab coats were drinking champagne. No one noticed Fallon.

His eyes searched a wall covered in large video screens rippling with everchanging data. Numbers and graphs danced an analysis of physiological readings. In the center of the room a massive mainframe computer was feeding the monitors. On it, foot-high letters spelled out the name GOLEM.

Facing GOLEM in an elevated medical examination chair, a pale man dressed in hospital blues sat with legs stretched out. His name was Herbert Longrieve. Late fifties and painfully gaunt, the bright blue of his luminous eyes contrasted with putty-toned skin. On his shaved head was a lacework of surgical stitching. The surrounding monitors were readings of his vital signs; an entire wall was laden with large video screens analyzing his real-time brain scans. No wiring connected him to the computer.

Nearby, two men were discussing sheets of printouts against the din of party noise. Both noticed Fallon at the same moment.

"Dr. Fallon, we tried to call you!" Dr. Meyer said. "At zero-nine twenty-three."

"Interface?"

"Total interface!" Dr. Lizerand beamed. He handed Fallon two printouts.

Fallon compared them. "Yes, by God!"

Lizerand pointed at the monitors. "Two-way communication! Impossible to tell the readouts apart. GOLEM can even make Herb piss on cue!"

Fallon added, "And Herb can give GOLEM his neurosis."

Both men laughed dutifully.

Fallon turned away and moved through the celebrants who parted like sea foam.

Longrieve saw him and brightened. Fallon took his hand, squeezing it. "Magnificent, Herb. No one else could have done it."

"Thank you, Dr. Fallon." His voice seemed weaker than Fallon remembered a few days ago. He looked up to see Dr. Meyer signaling. Fallon excused himself and followed the two doctors into an observation booth and closed the door. From here they had full view of the laboratory without the noise.

"Dr. Fallon," Meyer said, beaming, "when will you inform the government about our success on Project JANUS?"

"I'm not ready yet."

"But if it leaks to the media before we tell the government—my God!"

"Listen to me carefully." Fallon's tone dropped for emphasis. "Now the *real* work begins."

Meyer blinked, confused. "Interfacing a human brain with a computer *is* our real work. GOLEM and the human brain are now fused into one entity, JANUS. We are sitting on a major breakthrough! Why aren't you informing the DOI?"

"Because I expect JANUS to do more."

"More?" said Meyer. "The JANUS program can control human behavior. Alter personality. Manipulate sexual conduct. Create a military that will attack any target without question—an enemy army, a political rally, even an elementary school. What more do you want?"

"I want no further argument." There was a threatening pause. "Understood?"

Meyer blanched, Lizerand flushed, both nodded.

"There is something else," Lizerand cautiously added. "Longrieve's physical condition is deteriorating. Extreme fatigue. He is being literally drained by GOLEM."

"That was to be expected. Herb knew this from the beginning."

"But it's worse than we thought," Lizerand added.

Dr. Meyer nodded, agreeing. "As his physician I must warn you that if he does not get immediate rest, he could become comatose."

"No. Interface, twenty-four-seven. We can't risk breaking continuity."

"He is no good to you dead. Longrieve is unique."

"That is why you will keep him alive, Doctor. If he becomes comatose or dies, you will keep his brain alive. I suggest you start working on that."

Fallon turned and walked away.

Thomas, still blindfolded, was awakened by the sound of a car outside. He heard the room door open and the familiar footsteps of his jailers. Lighter, brisk steps followed: a woman.

He was uncuffed so that he could sit on the side of the cot. The blindfold was removed.

Thomas blinked at the brightness. It was his first look at his captors: two hard-eyed Latino men. There was a third man that he heard giving orders who always stayed in the other room. He looked down to see that they had dressed him in old work pants and a filthy denim shirt.

The woman was holding a black briefcase. She nodded for the two men to leave; they closed the door. She lit a brown cigarette, which had a distinctively sharp aroma. "I'm Nora."

When he did not respond, she set the briefcase on the table and opened it. She put on latex gloves and took out a package double sealed in clear plastic. She carefully removed an ancient book bound in scarred leather and studded with bronze brads worn smooth. She held it out to him. "The Templar diary," she said.

He looked at her for a moment, then took it. He was surprised at its weight; the leather cover was overlaying wood, probably cypress. With extreme care he opened it so as to prevent the full heaviness of the pages from resting on the spine, which could damage very old volumes. Unconsciously, he held his breath. He was holding seven centuries of history and legend—if it was authentic.

When he looked up at her, she smiled. "Translate the diary or they will kill you."

"You'll kill me anyway after I finish. Like you killed the courier Hollander."

"When that happened, I was a continent away and can prove it."

"Lady, has it occurred to you simply to hire a translator instead of kidnapping one? Scotland and Ireland are ass-deep in Celtic scholars."

"But none with your credentials: Celtic studies and the Templars." From her briefcase she held up his Merlin book. "You think I got your name out of the yellow pages?"

He didn't answer, just stared.

"Thomas, do you expect me to believe that you would let someone else do the translating? That diary is the last link to the Templars. You'd *kill me* to translate it."

CHAPTER FOUR

As Nora continued talking, Thomas sensed that her gift for annoyance bordered on genius.

Half-listening to her, he focused on the diary. Though he would have preferred to wear gloves to protect the page, to get the proper feel he needed to use bare fingers for this particular examination. Wiping fingers on his shirt, he lightly touched the page, following the sentences from right to left, opposite from the way they were written. Controlling his breathing to concentrate, he closed his eyes, trying to sense the vibrations of previous owners. There was an ancient Arab belief that this was possible with some documents; he personally had experienced it only once years ago. Now he felt his pulse rise, but that might have been from excitement.

"You need only translate the Gaelic," Nora explained. "I've read some of the French for an overview."

"Are you a linguist?"

"No. My French is fluent and I was able to muddle through some of the Latin."

"The Gaelic might be in an obscure Celt verse form. That redefines the word difficult."

"And an excuse to buy time. Thomas, let's understand each other. You will try to delay, hoping for a rescue that is not coming. If you are tortured, you may resist for a while. I can promise that it will be agonizing; they start with your testicles. And if you are accidently killed by some blundering thug with a blow torch, I won't get my translation. Accurate?"

"Extremely."

"Therefore, I'll make you a deal."

"Why would you offer me a deal?"

"Because I need the translation. Fast. The French language segment tells of thieves stealing an iron chest from the Templars. Afterward, whatever happened to the chest is written in what I assume is medieval Gaelic. Concentrate on that."

"A chest?" It was the first he heard of it. "Is this about the Templar treasure?"

She lit another cigarette. "I have no interest in a treasure."

"What's in the chest?"

"Whatever it is, I will destroy."

Her eyes had that strange look again; he wanted to keep her talking. "Why would you do that?"

"To stop Fallon." There was another enigmatic look. "Beyond that, the diary's monetary value doesn't concern me. After you give me the translation, the diary is yours."

"Oh, really?" He did not believe a word.

"You will own the Templar diary. You could write another book and this time, your source will be authentic. That might restore your ruined reputation. Then you needn't hide in a monastery."

"I wasn't hiding."

"However, once you own the diary you will face a new problem. You believe that because I have the diary, I killed the courier. So, when you have it, *you* become the prime suspect."

"Impossible. When the courier was killed, I was at the monastery with a dozen monks."

"Which puts you in the crime's arena. The final Mass is at midnight. Afterward, the monks retire to their cells. You could slip out, kill Hollander, steal the diary, and return before everyone is awakened at four."

"I don't have a car."

Nora took a breath then fired a quick barrage. "Hollander had a car. She picks you up. You butcher and dump her body. You have the diary. You hide her car. The distance where Hollander's body was found and the monastery is three-point-two miles. You walk back to the monastery before dawn Mass. Mission accomplished."

He was stunned. He had a motive and no alibi and had never once thought about it.

"Thomas, your choice is simple. Translate the diary and keep it, or spend eternity as fertilizer for some chicano's bean crop."

Captain Wade Starger was the living platitude of a cop's cop. Kate had known of his reputation even before her job interview two years ago. She learned to appreciate his quick intelligence and acid tongue. Though stuck behind a desk, he had a ruddy glow from living on his boat. His passion was the sea, with which no woman could compete. Starger would have made rank in any PD in the country. He settled in Santa Barbara because of the perfect climate, the magnificent bay, and his one true love, *May Belle*, his yacht. It drew young women like old money.

Starger held up her report. "What's going on, Kate?"

"What do you mean?"

"There is nothing here."

"That's all I have."

"A nude woman, headless, with no hands and feet was found in the boondocks and you're checking traffic reports? Did you think she was hit by a car in the middle of a forest?"

"Who said I was checking traffic reports?"

"Officer Lester Hicks. He has been reassigned to Traffic where he can do less harm. He saw you going through traffic files and reported it."

"Oh, *that* dumbass." She recalled his stupid comments at the crime scene.

"Be nice. It's the first idea he's ever had. He may have to take leave for burnout."

"I was looking for traffic incidents near the monastery in case anyone saw anything."

"What about the priest who reported the missing person?"

"Monk, not priest. He couldn't identify the body because he'd never seen her. We got positive ID from her company's DNA profile."

"They keep a DNA profile on their employees?"

"They're in medical technology. It's standard with them."

"Didn't you interview the monk? Where's that report?"

"He wasn't any help, so I haven't written it yet. Hollander was delivering a rare book to get the monk's translation. She never made it. I believe she was followed here, killed for the diary, and the perp and book are long gone."

"That's it?"

"It's all we've got. No witnesses, no physical evidence, no prints, no DNA. Rain washed any tire tracks on the dirt road. So yes, that's it."

"This case is high profile, Kate. I am under tremendous pressure from the Police Commissioner. Keep at it." He waved dismissal.

She stopped at the coffee machine feeling like shit. Starger was the main reason she had been hired; withholding critical information from him was blatantly disloyal. If her decision was wrong, it would be a career killer. No decent homicide department would touch her. It was a system where loyalty was valued above competence.

Kate moved through the room of droning detectives working their computers and phones. Vicky was waiting at her desk.

"Bad news, Vicky. Starger is bird-dogging us. You better bail while you can."

"Kate, Sgt. Hernandez found something." She held up a traffic report. "The night of the abduction there was an accident around 1:30 am. on Monastery Road."

"You're kidding!"

"A speeding car was coming down the hill from the direction of the monastery. It forced another car to run into a tree. Speeder kept going. The driver of the wrecked car didn't get a license number, but he is sure the other car was damaged."

"Paint and body shops?"

"I made a list while you were being grilled by Captain Salty."

Kate looked beyond Vicky to see Starger standing in his office doorway watching them. He closed the door.

Carver's team was once again crowded in the same shabby motel room, now cluttered with pizza cartons and empty beer cans. Cigarette smoke hung like a sour mood. They were waiting for Leo's phone call.

Carver was growing edgy. That made him stutter, which then triggered anger. Once when a woman laughed at his stammer, he pistol-whipped her. She was hospitalized for a month; he only served twenty days; she spent more time in the hospital than he spent in jail.

TWIST OF TIME

"Everybody, listen up," he ordered. "The monk was kidnapped while we watched. We better have some f-f-f- some answers." It slowed his stuttering when he forced himself not to swear. "Any ideas?"

Steiner was sitting on the bed cleaning his fingernails with the point of a sharpened ice pick. "Dis is not a normal operation." His thick German accent sounded like a bad B-movie. "A target you kidnap, you torture, vatever. But dis monk, vee watch but don't snatch. Then he disappears, dat's our fault?"

"What the f-f-f . . . do we tell Leo?"

Grigsby answered. "Don't admit nothing. Just tell Leo we are on top of it."

"D-d-damn Grigsby! Do you have any idea what will happen if we're caught l-l-lying to him?"

"N-n-no." Grigsby mocked.

The laughter stopped when the phone rang.

"Carver," he answered.

"Put me on speaker," Leo ordered.

Carver switched to speakerphone.

"What do you have for us?" Leo asked.

"Nothing new, sir. We're still w-w-watching the monk."

"How? Our sources report that he was abducted."

Carver blanched.

"If any one of you lies to me again, imagine the absolute worst in your life and it will happen. Find . . . that . . . *monk*!" said Leo. The line went dead.

Carver looked at them. There was not doubt on a single face.

Kate returned that afternoon from checking paint and body shops. She struck out. If Vicky didn't have better luck, they'd be in trouble. There were too many places to cover, and all they had was the color of the wrecked owner's car: Malibu Blue. There was a dark green paint graze left by the other car. But what if the owner took his time getting it repaired?

Waiting for Kate on her desk was a Fed Ex package from the Baltimore PD. Dr. Gladys Pullman's homicide file was twenty pages of reports and photos, plus forensic and CS data.

She read it, taking precise notes. (Her father had drilled in her that case notes must be kept current should another detective have to take over.) The attack had occurred late at night when Pullman was leaving the lab at Med-Tek. An attendant saw her being forced into a car by three men. The car drove away and she was never seen again. They had gained admission to the parking lot with fake credentials; the "extraction" was swift and clean. *Pros,* she wrote in the margin.

The package also contained first-rate crime scene photos. Six days after her kidnapping, pieces of a woman's torn and bloody clothing were found on a wooded path outside Baltimore by trail bikers. Forensics reported that the sheer volume of blood made fatality certain. The blood type, O positive, and the DNA on the clothes, definitely identified Pullman, Fallon's close associate.

Kate noted the similarities with Hollander's homicide. Her body was also mutilated and hidden in the woods. It was only found by accident because it had been dumped in the wrong place; otherwise, the MO was nearly identical with Pullman's, though a continent apart.

Kate drew a graph linking similar elements connected by threes. All three crimes showed the same planning. Pullman's abduction in Baltimore was the same MO as the street attempt on Thomas in Santa Barbara: three men and one car. At the monastery, Brother Barnabas reported that three men attacked him when he was drugged. Three men and a car in all three instances. Kate wrote: *Three homicides appear connected. How?*

TWIST OF TIME

* * *

After Nora left, Thomas slipped on the latex gloves and carefully opened the diary. Nora was right about one thing—nothing short of being abducted by aliens would prevent his translating it.

He scanned the medieval French and Latin; he had not looked at either since grad school. He estimated that nearly half the diary was Gaelic. As he predicted, a portion of it was written in bardic verse form. He would not have to fake delaying; this would be brutally hard.

With a magnifying glass Thomas examined Brychan's handwriting for a specific characteristic and, to his delight, found it: Anglo-Saxon script. It was particular to medieval England and gave Brychan's handwriting a unique style. This meant that he had learned to read and write in fourteenth-century England and nowhere else. It eliminated any childhood in France, where the Templars began. Brychan could not possibly have gone there until after adolescence. Revealing his youth and time of Templar recruitment, his handwriting held important clues to his past.

In skimming the Gaelic, Thomas discovered a passage where Brychan wrote about a Gypsy girl. *These overpowering feelings awakening again the terrible demon within.* He also mentioned *an overpowering lust.*

Thomas felt an instant connection. Brychan was struggling with celibacy, from which there was no relief without guilt, no compromise without sin. He and Brychan, both monks, shared the same problem separated by seven centuries.

Celibacy was a monk's gift to God, freely given. For Thomas it was often a struggle between Eros and God. He even made a covenant with his eyes, as scripture advised, to avoid temptation. Each time he saw Kate, the covenant was broken. With her, he seemed unable to control his thoughts.

He reread Brychan's words—*awakening again the terrible demon within.*

How painfully alike they were! He continued Brychan's narrative.

We had kept our hard pace overland and made camp early to give ourselves and the horses much needed rest.

BRYCHAN CAREFULLY LOOKED around the shallow defile where they made camp. It gave only slight protection from the witching March wind. He sat first watch while Ursus and Sara slept.

Staring at the fire, he saw the face that often haunted his thoughts and dreams: Vivyan, the wife of his brother, Duncan.

As a child, Brychan adored his older brother Duncan, following him like a playful shadow. They were different as noon sun and midnight moon. Duncan had little interest in knightly activities of dueling, jousting, and hunting. Brychan, though four years younger, soon surpassed his brother.

Lord Creighton despaired at this irony. Duncan who, as first son would inherit title, castle, and lands was woefully unfit to hold them. Warfare among Scots' lairds was a constant; estates and titles could be lost in a single battle or wrong alliance. Privately, Creighton feared that Duncan carried the curse that blighted his uncle Argus, who also avoided knightly pursuits. Instead, he spent all his time among the women as if he were one of them.

When Argus turned forty there was tragedy. Finn, his young Irish harpist, died of a fever. Argus seemed to lose his reason. One day he donated ten hides of land to the Church; the next day he was found dead, having fallen from the watchtower. All agreed it was an accident to cover the mortal sin of suicide. In the family it became a forbidden subject.

Brychan, as second son, was already destined for the Church. His mother, Lady Gwynn, was a scholar, unusual in women. Never would she give the knight's command to her son to return with his shield or on it. For Brychan, there would be no knighthood tainted by bloodshed. His quick mind had early marked him a scholar. She lovingly taught him to read even before he went to the Cistercians for schooling at Saint Andrew's Abbey. There, he studied the Quadrivium: arithmetic, geometry, astronomy, and music. Within a year he was composing Latin verses.

The Father Abbot delightedly told Lady Gwynn that Brychan reminded him of Jesus at age twelve confounding teachers in the Temple.

Each day after his school, Brychan entered another world. Rothgar, the Houston clan's master of arms, drilled Brychan, honing his skills as if he would one day become a knight, though both knew this was not to be. The veteran warrior marveled at how the young lad could sense an opponent's actions. Perhaps the rumor was true that Brychan had the sight from his mother. Could this explain his ability to anticipate an opponent's moves?

Lord Creighton's concern about Duncan eased when, in September of 1305, an arranged marriage was celebrated with Lady Vivyan, of clan Saint Clair. At twenty-four, Vivyan was already widowed, having been married four years to Colin MacVay, a wild rogue who spent his days hunting and nights wenching. Colin was accidentally killed in a tournament when a splintered lance pierced his throat. The Saint Clair family was delighted at Vivyan's marriage to Duncan Houston. Their joined estates and titles were a grand pairing.

Three months after the wedding, Brychan, soon to be twenty, returned home from his studies at the Cistercian monastery at Edinburgh to celebrate Christmas with his family. He was surprised to find that his brother Duncan had been sent on an errand to Ireland.

Vivyan, his new sister-in-law, greeted him joyously. With her luxuriant auburn hair and fierce blue eyes, she was even more beautiful than Brychan remembered at the wedding. He blushed at her attention as she begged to hear gossip from the city.

Brychan gravely explained that as a novice monk he had no knowledge of ladies' gossip. Vivyan teased that he was dreary enough to become an abbot before he was twenty-one. Brychan and his mother Lady Gwynn laughed at the image.

Late that night, Brychan was awakened. Someone was by his bed.

A glowing taper revealed Lord Creighton. "Come."

Pulling on his wool monk's robe, Brychan followed his father down the stone corridor sharp with December cold. Lord Creighton stopped at the library, unlocked the door, and motioned him to enter.

Though modest in size when compared to many in the region, Houston Castle was the only one for over two hundred leagues with a room devoted solely to books, numbering over fifty, counting scrolls. Brychan was struck again by mixed aromas of candle wax, parchment, and ground ink, reminders of the happy hours spent here with his mother. A robust fire blazed, unusual for the middle of the night. In its glow Brychan warmed his hands, obediently waiting.

The Lord's manner became formal. "I am your father," he said, "but also your lord and liege. Only King or Pope comes before me."

"Yes, fa—yes, my Lord." Brychan idolized his father, but must now address him formally. Whatever said here was blood-binding.

"Your brother, Duncan. . . ." Lord Creighton faltered. "Duncan has failed." He turned to a table cluttered with books and scrolls and grasped a bottle of wine. Thrice distilled the Dutch way, brandy, or burnt wine, was a new drink for which he had acquired a great liking. He pulled the cork and gulped, wiping his mouth on his sleeve. "Duty must be done for the house of Houston."

"My Lord?"

"Duncan has failed his duty."

"What duty?"

"He has not lain with his wife!"

In the following silence, Brychan heard the night wind as if moaning the Argus curse, his father's great fear. Duncan had once joked about it, but Brychan did not grasp the jest. Now he understood why his father's furious temper was directed at Duncan, even for some minor offense.

"Perhaps, my Lord, it is too early. Only three months."

Lord Creighton took another swallow, slopping more on his robe. "He has not lain with her. He never will." He slammed the table with his fist. "There must be a *blood* heir!"

Brychan knew the family chronicles from countless nights listening before the fire. Houston Castle, first a timbered fortress, was rebuilt in stone by great-grandfather Andrew with spoils from the Crusade where he served Richard Coeur de Lion. The greatly honored Houston title without a blood heir was a tempting prize and vulnerable to the strongest Scots taker.

His eyes fixed on Brychan. "You must do it."

Brychan barely whispered. "But that would be . . ."

"Would be following the command of your liege lord," a voice said.

He turned to see the dark silhouette of his mother framed by a window.

"Tell him," Lord Creighton ordered.

She came closer, the firelight revealing a deep sadness in her eyes edged with tears. "You will do as your liege lord commands.

Should there be sin in it," she looked at her husband, "it is on your father's head."

Brychan was confused. "But I am foresworn to the Church."

"And you will be," Lady Gwynn said. She moved to the table and picked up an ivory crucifix. "But first, this." She held the cross before his face. "You must never reveal your liege lord's command. Not even in confession. Only during your final unction. Then, God willing, the sin is passed on to your father," her voice faltered, "and to me . . . for my part in this."

"Swear!" his father croaked.

"And kiss the cross." Her face was now wet with tears.

Brychan's lips felt the chill ivory.

His father reached out and affectionately touched his shoulder; this hand that could cleave a man's skull with one blow was so light Brychan hardly felt it. Growling a curse, Lord Creighton clutched the brandy bottle and stumbling, left the room.

Lady Gwynn placed the cross back in its receptacle on the table and spoke. "Vivyan is waiting in her chamber. Tonight is the full moon." She looked at him. "You will lie with her. Every night, every day, until the next full moon."

It was the lunar cycle for breeding cattle and pigs. Brychan watched as she moved to a small altar where a single votive candle burned.

Lady Gwynn knelt on a prayer bench before an ancient Byzantine mosaic of the Blessed Virgin, more plunder from the Crusades.

The subject was closed.

BRYCHAN WAS STARING into the campfire, the remembrance so strong he had to bestir himself to be certain he had not slipped into a trance. He looked first at Ursus, still snoring, then to Sara who was deep asleep. From that first day, the sight of her lush breasts and flash of a perfect leg recalled Vivyan's memory. Now in the dancing firelight Sara's hair shined sable as a raven's wing. Her sleeping face was a child's, her small mouth curved like a cupid's bow, the same as Vivyan's.

He closed his eyes and whispered a desperate prayer against the haunting memory of Vivyan naked and the echoes of her erotic cries. He picked up the diary where he had been writing. Wetting his pen, he added:

It is a remembrance that has tormented day and night in all the years since. ✣

CHAPTER FIVE

Kate was at her desk at Homicide studying Gladys Pullman's Baltimore file when she was surprised by a phone call from Brother Simon. He was in the hospital for several hours of outpatient dialysis and asked if she would come by to see him so that they might talk. She did not want to spend time away from the case but agreed to go.

At the hospital she found Simon sitting in a chair and connected to a dialysis machine. He seemed no more concerned than if getting a haircut. She sat in a chair opposite, unsure why she was there.

"Thank you for coming," he said. "First, I must apologize for my harsh remarks to you when we first met."

"No problem."

"Oh, I sincerely meant what I said. But Father Abbot ordered that I confess my spiritual pride and humbly ask your forgiveness. Penance done?"

"Done."

"Good." He was uncertain how to begin. "I am very worried about Thomas and this kidnapping. He is not just a brother monk, but a friend and colleague. Our fields are similar: he, a historian; I a cosmologist. Both deal with time, past and present." There was a twinkle in his eye. "However, he also deals with future time."

"You mean all that psychic shi— stuff?"

"You are a skeptic?" He smiled. "My method is science, his method is . . . different. Neither is understood; certainly not mine. Look at string theory—multiple universes? We haven't even begun to understand this one." He shook his head in amazement. "Einstein wrote in a letter that 'People like us who believe in physics know that the distinction between past, present, and future is only an illusion.' Thomas once told me that for over two thousand years, the Druid wizards taught that past, present, and future are one. Incredible. They were two thousand years ahead of Einstein!"

"Brother Simon, your world is very different from what I expected. I thought that monks went to Mass, baked bread, and avoided women. But you are still working as a cosmologist and Thomas is an active Celtic scholar."

"All monks had careers before they became monks, Kate. In our order, they often continue their work. For example, Brother Mathew is also Dr. Edwin Twickham, a renowned geneticist. He is doing research involving monasteries."

"Studying monks?"

"No, rats. From the very beginning, monasteries all over the word had two things in common—manuscripts and rats that devoured manuscripts. The rats also ate monk's food, which is mostly vegetarian. Dr. Twickham believes that these rats, by eating this unvarying diet in monasteries for nearly two thousand years, have evolved to be a different species from those living outside monasteries. His research may reveal critical data about how diet affects physical changes in evolution."

"I see."

"I don't. I told Twickham his research is pointless! He should concentrate on something that will help monks be relevant in the world."

"I thought the whole idea of a monastery was to live apart from the world."

"Apart does not mean spiritually separated. We constantly pray for the world, even for those who don't believe in God. I promise you, a monastery is no place to hide from the world. The life is incredibly demanding." He changed the subject. "Have the police made any progress finding Thomas?"

She paused a nanosecond too long.

"Good Lord. You haven't reported it?"

"No."

"Why not?"

"His abductors killed the courier. They may have killed two more—a book dealer and a scientist in Baltimore. They are used to killing. In a hostage standoff with police, they would kill Thomas before giving him up. It's standard MO. My partner and I have about seventy-two hours to find him."

"May a scientist and meddling monk offer an observation?"

"Please do."

"Thomas told me what the diary might contain. I don't know how much he revealed to you."

"Not much."

"He believes there is much more involved than a Templar treasure. It has to do with manuscripts concerning a tremendous, disciplined power. Thomas' abductors are very sophisticated. You won't find them in your standard criminal database. To get them, you have to not just think outside the box; you must eliminate the box."

She smiled; he was tremendously likable. "Thanks, I'll remember that."

"The brothers right now are performing a rarely used ritual: a round-the-clock prayer vigil until Thomas is safely returned. Once, when we used it, the Berlin Wall came down. We like to think we did our part. As you work in your busy world, please remember, there are also a bunch of poor monks praying and wearing out their knees."

Thomas paced the small room thinking about Nora's offer of the diary in exchange for the translation. He heard someone at the door, then one of the Latino men entered with a pot of coffee and a plate of beans. The aroma told him that the coffee was burnt again. How difficult was it to make coffee? If his captors didn't kill him, their coffee would.

He ignored the beans, and poured a cup hoping it would give him a caffeine jolt. Returning to the diary, he found Brychan describing how the Templars interrupted their pursuit of the robbers to stop and engage in combat drills.

Three days since our last drill exercise. We are gaining on the robbers. When we overtake them, battle is certain, the odds uncertain. The two-man drill is our single advantage. It could determine victory or defeat.

From his research, Thomas knew that Templars greatly influenced battle tactics of that period. Though small in number, they were fierce and well-disciplined. They were often placed in small bands of a larger unit to lead the point of attack. Templars were special ops centuries before commandos and Special Forces.

He was fascinated by the paradox of non-violent Buddhist monks and their long involvement in martial arts. When the university offered free aikido classes, he and Father McCoy, the Catholic chaplain, took them together. Thomas lost four pounds and any illusions that he was a fighter. But he gained confidence that, in a threatening situation, he would not be helpless. In those long hours handcuffed to the bed, he decided that if he got the chance, despite being a peace-loving monk, he would fight like hell to escape.

But Nora played the diary like a chess master. Pride was his sin; his reputation as a scholar had been destroyed by false accusations. At that moment, he decided to take Nora's offer for the diary. But he would delay telling her so she would not think that he had been too easy.

That settled, Thomas returned to the diary.

We had been following the trail overland when we came upon a main road with many confusing tracks.

URSUS DISMOUNTED AND studied the ground. Tracking the robbers' horses overland had been easy. One packhorse had a peculiar side gait, making him unfit as a charger. But now the hoof-prints on the road were muddled among countless others. Ursus motioned to the right, toward Paris, the thieves' presumed destination.

"That way," he said.

"No. I think not," Brychan said.

Surprised, Ursus and Sara looked at him.

"That is the way north," Ursus insisted.

"But here, they turned south." Brychan urged his horse to the left with no explanation. Ursus remounted and they rode on in sullen silence. Eventually, they came upon horse manure dropped earlier that day.

Ursus dismounted and his fingers probed the sun-dried pile. Rubbing a sample between his palms, he smelled it with quick short sniffs, the Bedouin way. He looked at Brychan. "It's our roan."

"How far ahead?"

"Half a day." His look was grudging respect. Brychan had been right.

Sara was amazed. "Sir Brychan, was it the sight that told you which direction to take?"

"No." He looked at Ursus. "What thief does not steal money? One who fears breaking the eighth commandment—stealing. Possibly a priest?"

"What priest has the guts to steal from us?"

"A priest ordered to get the chest and the diary. Both the King and the Pope know of our charge from the Grand Master."

"How could they?"

"By torturing a brother Templar." Brychan added. "But if our robber is a priest, is he serving King or Pope?"

Ursus was instantly uneasy; to fight the King was bad enough. But the Pope? Wasn't that fighting God?

Brychan took a gulp of water from the pig's bladder canteen and handed it to Sara. "The King is north in Paris. Pope Clement is south at Avignon. Our robber priest is in a hurry to deliver his prize. Why would he go to Paris?"

Sara swallowed the sweet spring water, wiped her mouth, and corked the canteen. "Then," she said, "Avignon favors us. The south road leads to the Rhône. At Cécile landing, they can hire a barge to take them the long way to Avignon. If we hurry overland, we can still reach the Rhône today ahead of them." She looked at Brychan. "If you are right."

"*If* you are right," Ursus repeated.

Brychan said nothing, waiting.

Ursus looked fiercely at the Gypsy. He would sooner go to hell than follow a woman. "Lead us to the Rhône!" he ordered.

Thomas closed the diary—it was truly cursed. It had captivated him. He thumbed the legal pad full of translation notes. Oddly, his progress was much faster than anticipated. At times a difficult passage would suddenly become clear. This was happening more frequently. He returned to the diary, where the three reached the Rhône River near the village of Cécile.

Before dawn we pressed on, arriving ahead of our quarry. The day had dawned gray and chill but, as if a favorable omen, the sun suddenly appeared, warming the valley and the green ring of surrounding hills. A lone bird stopped in mid-song; there was an instant hush as if every creature awaited what was coming.

BRYCHAN AND URSUS were mounted at opposite sides of the trail that cut through a wooded glade. This was their chosen ambush site. Both studied the terrain—its grade and footing, where the thickest foliage and especially the direction of the wind that would carry their sound and spoor. Unseen beyond the trees they could hear the whispering rush of the Rhône.

To their front, the narrow pathway came down a shallow hill. They would be able to see anyone approaching for the full measure of a plainsong.

They had dressed for battle but without their white Templar mantles. Both wore hauberks—their long coats of mail—and a barrel helmet with flat top and face guard with its eye slits. Each was armed with sword and a long-bladed dagger—the misericord—which in skilled hands could pierce a mail coat.

Hanging from each saddle was a mace, the Turk weapon adopted by the Templars. The mace was so revered that, if lost, punishment was a year's hard penance. It was chosen specifically to fight Christians, for the Order had a rule against shedding Christian blood. The mace shattered more than cut, so bleeding was less than with a blade. Thereby the Rule of the Order was followed, and a favored weapon created.

Ursus made a final scan of the terrain. They had decided the best advantage would be to let them pass, then attack down-slope at their rear.

"Blessed Jesu!" Sara pointed to the distant hill.

Riders had just broken the far crest. Instead of the expected three, there were seven. Four cavalry had joined them.

"The Pope's cavalry, by their colors," Brychan said.

Ursus spat. "Two against seven; on foot, possible. Mounted, two against seven; bad odds."

"It's two against six," Brychan corrected. "One is a priest."

"You are both wrong," Sara said. "It's three against six."

FATHER PIERRE DU'BRAY rode point, in the front rank with the senior sergeant. He felt safer since the rendezvous with the Pope's men earlier that day. The troopers rode in column with packhorses at the rear. Father Pierre repeatedly looked back. He knew the Templars were somehow following, despite his taking their horses. Even just two Templars would attack the very gates of hell to recover the chest. Fear was alien to them.

The Dominican had carefully examined the diary. The ciphers were incomprehensible, but the writing in Latin and French was a clear indictment of Templar heresy. Only Satan knew what evil was written in the other language—maybe the Devil's own. Father Pierre, as an agent of the Holy Office of Inquisition, would turn the diary over to the papal prosecutors. The heretic Templar would be burned alive with his blasphemous diary feeding the flames.

On entering the glade, the sergeant signaled the troop to halt. "S'blood!"

The troop stared at a sight none of them had ever seen. A young woman riding bareback was galloping toward them, her dark hair flying. She was naked. A gift from heaven or hell: the soldiers began cheering. The rear ranks strained for a better look for the pathway was too narrow to go around either side.

Because of the yelling no one heard the clash at their rear. The last trooper in line only knew when a blade tore through his belly from the back. He was falling when Ursus jerked the sword free.

The next man turned, taking Ursus' mace full between the eyes, splitting his skull. He rolled backward over his horse.

Brychan, never having struck from behind, hesitated. Rules of chivalry dictated the first clash must be face to face; but this was different. As the cavalryman was turning, Brychan's swift blade cleanly severed head from neck. The knees locked and the headless body eerily held in the saddle a few seconds before falling.

In three quick blows the odds were changed.

As the next two troopers turned, both Templars yelled, "Beauseant!" and charged.

The one nearest Brychan cleared his sword as Brychan's blade caught his upper arm. A cross-slash severed his jaw and he twisted, falling to the ground.

Ursus' mace slammed the next man's helmet knocking him from his horse. Somehow, he landed on his feet; a second blow dropped him.

The last trooper wheeled horse and fled.

FATHER PIERRE STIFFENED in terror as the two Templars rode slowly toward him. He jumped from his horse and fell prostrate, his eyes clinched shut, hands trembling upward in supplication.

Brychan looked at Ursus. "A priest?"

"Smells like a Dominican."

At the sound, Father Pierre opened his eyes to see the Gypsy woman on a horse. She was now wearing a long leather cape, her naked legs lusciously dangling. Sara looked down at him with a taunting smile.

Pierre crossed himself and cursed: "Witch."

NOT A WITCH, Brychan wrote, *but an enchantress from whose spell it seemed not even heaven could protect.* ✝

In his private conference room, Fallon was meeting with the Bulldogs, Burns and Sawyer. They were licensed private investigators but kept separate from the Med-Tek corporation. Loyal to the last dollar, they were devoid of scruple.

Burns, a former bounty hunter, was front man and negotiator. Sawyer was the techie: electronics, photography, and ordnance. Fallon was amused by his contrasts—a nerdy thug.

They worked with a group of computer databases accessing personal information. Credit cards and banking, travel, telephone, medical, and pharmaceutical records. Personal text messages, too. The Bulldogs were a formidable corporate tool; they specialized in everything from blackmail to wet work. Also, both were dedicated sadists.

Fallon had first hired them during a tricky corporate merger. They acquired dirty background on two executives from the target firm. As a result, Fallon made more millions, and the Bulldogs had a contract for life.

Fallon held up a file. "I'm changing your assignment. Forget finding Denise Hollander's killer, for now." He handed it to Burns. "His name is Thomas Bardsey."

Burns opened the folder. "What's he done?"

"Disappeared. Find him. He's a monk." Fallon explained about the diary. "Which means somebody either kidnapped Bardsey or made him a better offer."

Sawyer spoke for the first time. "You want both the diary and the monk?"

"One is no good without the other."

Burns forced a smile. "Any restrictions on how we bring him back?"

"None. Have your fun. Just keep him alive."

Thomas' translating was interrupted by the sound of a car, then voices in the next room, speaking Spanish. Nora entered and the door closed behind her with the sound of the lock being bolted from the other side. She pointed to the diary.

"What do you think?" she said.

"Fascinating."

"How much longer will you be?"

"First problem, it's pointless to read just the Gaelic. Now I have to read the other languages for context. The Middle English I can hack. But the Latin is medieval church and mine is first-century classic and rusty. The next time you kidnap a translator, I suggest you also steal their reference books."

"Stalling? I told you—"

"I'm not finished," Thomas cut in. "Brychan was deliberately ambiguous in case the Inquisition got hold of the diary to use as evidence against him or the Templars. It would be impossible for them to translate. Hell, the CIA should add it to their codes. All of which makes getting into Brychan's head very tricky."

"And if you take too long, you're dead and I'm in deep shit. How do we lick this?"

Her use of "we" was a subtle manipulation and he played along. "It would help if you told me more."

"Like what?"

"What's in the chest? You said that you want to destroy it. Why?"

"To keep Fallon from getting it."

"Why is Fallon so important?"

"He and his team have created a supercomputer called GOLEM. He is also working on a top-secret government program, JANUS. Its mission is to completely interface a human brain with GOLEM. Do you realize what that means?"

"Mind control?"

"Much more. The interface subject is some poor bastard named Longrieve."

"Herbert Longrieve?"

She smiled at his surprise. "The Bobby Fischer of psychics. I also know that as an adolescent *you* were studied by the Rhine Institute. When Longrieve was there before you, he scored off the charts. He still holds the record in most categories."

"I thought ol' Herbie-the-nerdy disappeared."

"Fallon found him. He appealed to Longrieve's giant ego and buried him in money to become the GOLEM-JANUS interface."

"Why would Fallon need a psychic for GOLEM?"

Nora shrugged. "Maybe to analyze how a psychic's brain operates?"

"Already done. The Soviets in the sixties, with proven psychics. Psychokinesis works at the back of the brain. Precognition, the frontal lobes. There are also tons of studies by universities and classified projects by the CIA and Department of Intelligence going back decades, which of course, they deny. But what has that to do with a seven-hundred-year-old Templar chest?"

"Fallon is convinced that whatever it contains is critical to the GOLEM-JANUS project."

"That's crazy."

"That's Fallon. Maybe he thinks by interfacing with Longrieve, GOLEM will detect psychic energy."

"What energy?" Thomas argued. "It may simply be a brain abnormality. My own brain scans show an irregularity which has yet to be explained."

"Whatever breakthrough Fallon controls would be disastrous. I will stop him."

Thomas flared. "What in hell gives you the right to stop scientific research?"

"I'm a *zealous* fanatic," she gleamed proudly. "Had I been around during the Manhattan Project, believe me, there would have been no atomic bomb. What is the life of a few scientists compared with all who will die in nuclear wars and centuries of radioactive contamination?"

Thomas suddenly understood. Nora was like the Unabomber—kill real people to save imaginary thousands from a threat that may never happen. She was dangerously disturbed.

Nora continued. "I can't do anything about scientists toying with mass destruction, but I can do something about Fallon."

"How did you become so obsessed with Fallon?"

"Really? A monk, secluded in a monastery, who attends five masses daily and can never touch a woman, is calling *me* obsessed?" Her laugh was a rasping file. "I began by monitoring Fallon's experiments on animals."

"You didn't get data on GOLEM that way."

"No. That cost someone's life. But by God, I got it." She knocked at the door and pointedly looked at him. "Believe me Thomas, to get what I want, I'll do it again." The door opened. She slammed it behind her as she left.

Thomas was mystified. Nora had revealed Fallon in a new light. How did Herbert Longrieve, a psychic, fit in with Fallon's plan?

What was the medieval Templar connection to a modern-day intel operation? He knew they had discovered something important under Solomon's temple. They also brought the Shroud of Turin to Europe. In Spain they collected rare manuscripts from the Sufis who were famous for their studies in prophecy and precognition.

Now Fallon, Templar-obsessed, had recruited Herbert Longrieve, the highest-scoring psychic to work on his GOLEM-JANUS project. How did Fallon plan to use Longrieve? An earlier observation was reinforced; Fallon was far more dangerous than just his involvement in a homicide.

Otis Hardegree put down the paint sprayer and removed his mask. The boss wanted to see him at Bay 4. He swore, removed his gloves, and walked down the row of cars.

Jake, the foreman, looked up from his clipboard. "Otis, what in hell have you done now?"

"What do you mean?"

"Some cop is looking for you."

"Oh, that. Last night was our poker game. We was shooting the shit and talking pussy. This dude from a Camarillo shop said he was visited by a woman cop, a Latina with totally awesome tits. She was checking paint jobs, looking for a green four-door with a blue scrape. We got one, so I called the Santa Barbara police and left my name."

Jake gestured awkwardly. "Uh, this is a police detective."

Otis turned to see a woman standing behind him.

"The one *without* awesome tits." Kate smiled.

"Sorry, Officer. I was just kidding . . ." He flushed pink.

"No problem. You should hear how we girls talk about you guys." She pointedly stared at Otis' crotch. "What have you got . . . car-wise?"

Flustered by her comment, Otis led her to a dark green Ford two-door with banged bumper, deep fender ding, and a long blue scrape. The Ford looked brand-new. He showed her the work order. It was dated the day after Thomas' abduction.

"What's the delay?" Kate asked.

"Waiting on a paint color. When I told the guy it might take a few days, I thought he was gonna . . . he got upset."

Kate looked again at the order: a J. Ramirez with a Santa Barbara address. "Santa Barbara?"

"Yeah. You know how many body shops there are between here and there? Why come all the way to Ventura?"

On the drive back, traffic moved at a glacial crawl. Kate called Vicky on her cell. It was dark when, within minutes of each other, they pulled up at the address of J. Ramirez. No lights were showing but inside they could hear salsa music. It stopped when they knocked on the door. Then silence.

CHAPTER SIX

Kate and Vicky both unsnapped their holsters. Kate knocked again, no response. Vicky drew her Beretta and pressed it flat against the side of her leg, finger on trigger.

The door opened a crack, revealing a young Latino man. "Yes?"

"Mr. Ramirez?" Kate showed her badge. "Police."

"What do you want?"

"I'm Detective Flynn. This is Detective Marroquin. We'd like to ask you some questions."

"What about?" His eyes were cautious.

"Do you own a dark green Ford two-door sedan?"

"No. I mean, it's my wife's."

"Why is it being repaired in Ventura?"

"Is that a crime?"

"*Contesta la pregunta!*" Vickie snapped.

Her tone shriveled his testicles like frostbite. "My wife has gone to Texas to visit her folks. I was driving her car and scratched it. It's brand new. I wanted to get it fixed so she wouldn't know."

"Was this on Monastery Road?" Kate asked.

"Yeah."

"What happened?"

"I was speeding. I rounded a curve and scraped another car. Then they hit something, but I kept going. My insurance will make it good. I swear."

"Why didn't you stop?"

"I . . . I . . . was being chased."

Kate glanced at Vicky. "Chased?"

"It's personal. I can't go into it."

"Go there," Vicky said. "We're talking homicide."

"Homicide?" His voice cracked.

"If we go downtown," Kate added, "you won't be coming back. It's called obstruction."

"Look, I was with this . . . this woman. We were in bed. Okay?"

"Okay. So, what happened?"

"Her husband came home. And caught us."

"What's that got to do with your wife's car?" Vicky asked.

"He's a security guard. He carries a gun, man! I ran out in just my jockey shorts. Him and her got into an argument, so I managed to get to my car. I made it out of the driveway when he comes running out of the house with a gun. He was coming after *me*! I took off. He was in his car right behind me. That's why when I scraped that Ford I didn't stop."

"You took your car to the Ventura shop so the security guard would have trouble finding you?"

"Security guard, hell. My wife comes back tomorrow and her car is gone. Frankly, I hope the security guard finds me before she does!"

Kate and Vicky were sitting in the car still parked in front of Ramirez's house.

Vicky giggled. "Our suspect turns out to be a cheating husband running from his lover's husband with gun?"

"Hell, I was about to call SWAT for backup."

TWIST OF TIME

Giggles dissolved into laughter. When they recovered, Kate sighed, "Dear God, Thomas, where are you?"

Thomas closed the diary in its plastic covers, put it in the briefcase with his translation notes, and rubbed his tired eyes. The day's work had been exhausting. He estimated it was after eleven. He didn't wear a watch; at the monastery a bell tolled the canonical hours. Here, he tried to follow that same routine for a sense of control. Kneeling beside the cot, he began the prayer for compline. "Almighty God unto whom all . . ."

There was an explosion and the crash of glass. He switched off the table lamp. Immediately, he tasted the sharp tang of tear gas. Somewhere outside he heard shouts.

He rushed to the bathroom, wet a towel, and began breathing through it. As he came back into the room, the door burst from its frame. Two men appeared in black assault gear and wearing gas masks.

"*Policía! Vamanos!*"

One man motioned to him; the other went to the desk and grabbed the briefcase. Thomas, nearly blinded by stinging mist, was led by one of them. In the next room he saw two men on the floor, coughing. A policeman covered them while another was binding them with flexi-cuffs.

Outside, Thomas gulped air and wiped his burning eyes. Looking around he blearily saw for the first time that he was out in the country. The only light came from a single lamp on the small stucco farmhouse.

"You okay?" The man's voice was muffled by the gas mask.

The second man handed him the briefcase. "You better carry this."

Thomas took it and then realized that there were only three parked sedans. Where were the police vehicles?

A handcuff snapped on his wrist. "Get in the car!" the man ordered.

Before he could react, two shots fired inside the house.

"Shit!" One man wheeled around and ran back toward the house.

The other turned around to cover his partner. Thomas swung the briefcase hard, slamming him in the back of the head. He dropped like an anchor.

Thomas ran into the dark.

BRYCHAN WAS SPINNING in a chaos black as hell's abyss. Choking in a swirling void, his skin burned with countless stinging nettles.

Behind there were short bursts of strange thunder. Quick flashes of light revealed demons in black chasing him.

A voice shrieked in terror; it was his. He felt arms holding him, then recognized Sara.

"You cried out," she whispered. "Were you dreaming?"

It was not a dream but a trance, unbidden. "Someone is following us. Demons in black." He looked across the campfire to see Ursus staring. Then he realized that Sara's arms were still holding him.

In the Templar discipline, if caught in a woman's embrace, a knight would serve a year's penance in a cramped cell where he could not fully stand. Should there be any sexual contact, the penalty was expulsion from the Order. The woman would be branded to mark her before she went to prison for fornication.

Ursus' look was severe at this blatant violation of the rules of their order; it added to the already heavy burden they carried for disobedience, if discovered.

TWIST OF TIME

* * *

With no moon and only faint stars Thomas stumbled in the dark through a cultivated field. He was wearing his monk's sandals. A dim light was showing from the house behind him. He avoided looking at the light; it would delay his getting night vision. Suddenly he fell, sprawling in a tangle of bean vines stretching in the dark forever. Somewhere behind him he heard yelling.

He scrambled to his feet; there was more gunfire from the house. Whoever they were, they sure as hell weren't cops.

Thomas clutched the briefcase, a handcuff dangled from one wrist. Again, he fell in the tangled maze. His fingers felt the ground; there was about a foot width between the rows. If he could stay on this path, he would fall less.

Searching for something to fix on, he looked at the sky while concentrating on calming his breathing. A scattering of stars came into focus. He picked one in line with where he stood and began walking. He made almost fifty yards before falling again.

Half an hour later he was still moving through bean tillage. Occasionally, he fell, but not as often. When he broke on to a dirt road, he was able to walk briskly for another half hour. Finally, the road intersected with a paved two-lane. Ahead were signs on a post. In the dark he could make out a word: Oxnard.

Not Mexico! He was less than an hour from Santa Barbara.

After arriving home from the evening's fiasco, Kate did not go to bed. She was studying Gladys Pullman's homicide file when the phone rang.

"Hi. Remember me?"

"Thomas! Where are you?"

"Oxnard. A service station. Want to bail me out?"

When she drove up to the gas station, Thomas was waiting outside. His clothes were muddy; he had a week's growth of beard and a big smile.

Kate felt his arms around her for the first time. She was startled by her feelings. "Are you alright?"

He held up the dangling handcuffs. "Can you get this off?"

"Keep it on. Adds sexy macho to your monk's image."

At her apartment, she made coffee and they sat in the den. When he showed her the diary he babbled like a kid at Christmas. It was Babe Ruth's bat, Mark Twain's pen, Satchmo's trumpet, and a splinter of the True Cross all in one. He told her about Nora, her war with Fallon, and the GOLEM project, all interlinked by her warped logic.

Kate was incredulous. "You mean that woman who kept me awake nights is simply crazy?"

"Totally insane. First, she denies any connection to the courier Hollander's murder, then proudly admitted killing someone just to get information on GOLEM."

"That has to be the Baltimore homicide—Dr. Gladys Pullman."

"Who is Pullman?"

"Fallon's top researcher."

"That fits what Nora said. And you won't believe this—she offered me a deal. I give her the translation, she gives me the diary."

"Which makes you work for her. Crazy, but smart."

"She even explained how I could have sneaked out of the monastery and killed the courier. I almost believed her."

Kate laughed. "No way. You were the first one I eliminated."

TWIST OF TIME

"How?"

"You simply did not fit."

"That's not very scientific."

"Science gets convictions. Intuition and legwork get suspects. That's three generations of cop talking."

"Then who rescued me?"

Kate thought for a moment. "How about Fallon?"

"You said he was the only one you didn't suspect."

"But now I've had to rethink everything because this is becoming one hell of a case." She enumerated on her fingers. "Suppose Fallon killed Gladys Pullman for whatever reason. The diary being stolen leads suspicion away from him. When you are abducted, he even uses that. He finds out where you are because with his money his sources are better than ours. He sends a team to rescue you. But you blow everything by escaping!"

"Shoot at me and risk killing their translator?"

"Think. Did anybody actually shoot *at* you?"

"Now I'm not sure."

"Then, let's stick with what we know. Nora has admitted killing Pullman, Fallon's intel expert; that's capital murder one."

"What do we have on Fallon?"

"Nothing. Yet he's tied to everything. His courier, murdered. His close associate, murdered, the body never found. His book dealer, murdered. Fallon is like one of the Four Horsemen, Death, riding through everyone's lives." Kate shook her head. "Frankly, he's a first for me. I have never seen anyone like him."

Nora hung up her cell phone. Ravel had just reported that an assault team attacked and escaped with the monk and diary. He was on his way to meet with her when it happened. She was relieved. Had Ravel been there, he would have killed the monk. Terrorist MO: no rescue.

She dialed a number. Only when the person stopped swearing did she realize it was four in the morning.

Nora apologized, then asked, "Did Fallon know where the monk was held?" She listened. "No? Your check is in the mail."

She hung up, her thoughts racing. If Fallon didn't know, then who led the raid to free Thomas? Obviously, there was another player.

In the guestroom, Thomas lay awake despite aching fatigue. He and Kate agreed to look at everything fresh in the morning. An hour later he was still staring wide-eyed in the dark.

Kate, in her bedroom was sitting on the side of her bed; sleep was impossible. Thomas' return awakened feelings she had suppressed. The instant she saw him and felt his arms around her she realized how strong those emotions were. This was the last thing she needed—no personal involvement! She looked at the clock, three-twenty, too early to get up. She thumped her pillow into another shape and tried again.

Still wide awake, Thomas switched on his bedside lamp and opened the diary. He resumed reading Brychan's narrative just after the Templars' fight with the Pope's soldiers.

Our battle tactic worked. Surprise had been complete with the daring ruse by the Gypsy girl riding naked. Now we would discover whether our thief answers to King or Pope.

FATHER PIERRE SAT on the ground looking at the two Templars looming over him. He repeated, "I am Father Pierre Du'Bray, Dominican order, emissary for His Holiness and Supreme Pontiff, Clement."

TWIST OF TIME

From the way the younger knight had introduced himself, Pierre assumed that he was keeper of the diary. The one called Ursus was terrifying, striking down men like a demon. Prinkling with fear, the priest stared at Ursus. While cleaning bloody refuse from his mace, the warrior occasionally looked at him as if deciding how he should be cooked. It was rumored that Templars relished human flesh when prepared the Saracen way: the head with its brain spit-roasted in butter.

With a shudder, Pierre looked to see the Gypsy rummaging through the dead. The sun was blazing hot and the air rankled heavy with the stink of death—a mix of blood, mangled flesh, and the be-shitted corpses of man and horse. He had never smelled a battlefield—even a small one like this.

After the battle he had watched as the two Templars dismounted. They began chanting from their battle Psalms with their particular martial rhythm.

> *Blessed be the Lord my strength which teacheth my hands to war and my fingers to fight . . . For by Thee have I run through a troop, and by my God have I leaped over a barrier . . . Your right hand did sustain me, and Your battle cry made me many.*

PIERRE KNEW THAT Templars believed their war cry—"Beauseant!"—was revealed by God to make them appear greater in number to their enemy. It was true for he had just witnessed it.

Brychan jerked him to his feet. "Priest, tell us of your mission for Pope Clement. Refuse, and Brother Ursus will slowly skin the flesh from your body in the Saracen manner while you watch. It takes the better part of a day."

SARA WAS SCAVENGING from dead to dead, searching their saddle packs. She found canteens of sour wine, salt-dried beef, ground barley meal, chunks of rock-hard cheese, and stale loaves of black rye. Few spices, no peppers. Even the poorest Roma ate better than these Gadjay.

Looking at the battleground-strewn dead she shivered, recalling everything both terrifying and thrilling.

While waiting for the enemy she sat naked on her horse. She could feel the damp heat of the stallion between her legs. At the right moment, she urged the horse to a gallop. The instant the soldiers saw her, they began yelling. Even from a distance she knew that look on every face.

Her stallion surged full speed and from the horse's motion against her bare legs and pelvis, she felt a tingle growing with each stride. She was close enough to the enemy cavalry when, at the rear of the troop, she saw two of them tumble to either side, revealing Brother Ursus. Behind him was Brychan with a trooper riding in front. The trooper's head suddenly disappeared.

She watched Brychan, eyes blazing as he slashed another soldier who fell, spewing a stream of blood. At that same instant, her body exploded from groin to throat as she cried out.

It was like that first time under the covers in the dark, when her older cousin Carmen showed her how.

SARA PUT HER collection of salvaged food in a pile with their provisions as she watched the two Templars. On the ground beside Ursus was the VERITAS chest, its seals unbroken. The diary lay on top.

Ursus had collected two shields from the enemy dead. Now they'd be better armed in the next battle.

Brychan was questioning the priest, toying with him, a cat teasing its prey. The Dominican's color was sickly whey as he tried to answer.

"Priest, how long have you been the Pope's thief?"

"Sir Knight, I serve him at his pleasure. Whatever he . . ."

"What else have you done for him?"

"I was the emissary for His Holiness in Paris, two weeks past."

"What occasion, Dominican?" he spat the word in contempt. Dominicans were by far the greatest number in the Inquisition.

Pierre waned even paler. "On the occasion of . . ."

"The burning of Grand Master de Molay?"

Pierre managed to nod.

"You were there as the Pope's official witness?"

Pierre tried again but fear choked his words.

Brychan tossed him the canteen. "Shall Brother Ursus begin your skinning? He hates Dominicans even more than Saracens."

Pierre gulped the water and caught his breath.

Brychan tried again. "Where was the auto de fé, the place of execution? Notre Dame?"

"No. The Île aux Javiaux. An island on the river. They brought him there from Gisors Castle."

"Why there?"

"King Philip feared an uprising from the people. Some say de Molay was falsely accused."

"God's truth, he was. What else?"

"Another knight was to burn with him."

"Who?"

"Guy D'Orléans, the Templar novice master. But he died under torture because he refused to name those who were the last initiated."

Brychan whispered, "Oh, . . . no." Master Guy had been his mentor when he was among the last novitiates. Now Guy had died protecting him. Enraged, Brychan grabbed Pierre and shook him like a ruckle of bones. "Tell me *every* detail or by the Blessed Virgin I will burn you alive now!"

"De Molay was chained to the stake. The firewood was . . ."

"Every detail! What kind of wood?"

"I don't—green. Green wood."

"Soaked wet to burn slow?"

"Yes." He paused, remembering. "De Molay was strangely calm. When asked if he had any last request, he asked only that his hands not be tied so he could clasp them in prayer."

"Sweet Jesus." Ursus crossed himself.

"What then?"

"When the flames grew highest de Molay spoke loudly so that all might hear."

"What did he say?"

"De Molay called upon King Philip and Pope Clement to face God within a year."

"The *exact* words! What language?"

"French, of course."

"No! Think, priest!" Brychan jerked him closer, his voice barely above a whisper. "Did he speak *any* Latin?"

He squeezed his eyes shut, trying to remember. "Yes, some phrases. But I don't...."

"Did he repeat the word *confutatis*?" Brychan enunciated. "Con-fu-ta-tis?"

"Yes."

"How many times?"

"Thrice."

Brychan shoved him backward and Pierre landed hard on the ground. Certain he was to die; he crossed himself and covered his eyes.

Brychan looked at Ursus. "The Confutatis curse. There's going to be a new Pope. And King."

Sara stared in awe at the light in Brychan's eyes. ✣

CHAPTER SEVEN

When Kate awoke in her bedroom, she could hear Thomas in the kitchen. He had already showered and made coffee. His inner clock was still on monastery time.

They sat in the breakfast nook. "Kate, there is something I must tell you."

"Sounds serious."

"As a novice monk our order requires me to examine inappropriate feelings and confess them to that person. While I was a prisoner, I thought of you a lot."

She smiled. "I had the same problem."

"Then, it wasn't just me?"

"Thomas, face it. Our attraction was inevitable. We must keep it professional. If we don't, I could be fired because I'm a cop and you are a witness on my case. And I assume you, as a monk, could go to hell. Literally."

He nodded agreement. "So, what's next?"

"We should start informing people that you have escaped."

"I've already called Father Abbot. I knew they were doing our special prayer vigil. I wanted to report that it worked."

"It *worked*? You were rescued by people who tried to kill you."

"But I got away. We believe that all good comes from God."

"Is that theology off a bumper sticker?"

"Kate, I escaped. Q.E.D. *Quod erat dem—*"

"I know what Q.E.D. means. Thank you."

"Father Abbot said they were going to celebrate my escape."

"How do monks party?"

"Gorge on donuts."

"Sounds wild."

"We have our moments."

They laughed; the awkwardness passed.

"Also, I met your friend Brother Simon. I was very impressed."

"The *Christian Science Monitor* called him 'a human bridge between science and religion.' Simon advised Creationists that if their faith couldn't include science, their God was too small. He warned scientists that because their finite minds cannot prove the Infinite, that does not mean the Infinite does not exist. God should be subject to rigorous scientific investigation, heaven knows there's certainly enough data, which might yield even more science. Both sides call him the monk from hell."

"We met in the hospital where he was undergoing dialysis."

"Simon makes each dialysis an event. He even rides in an ambulance. After dialysis, they race with flashing lights to the beach where he lies in the sun and eats hot dogs. It infuriates Father Abbot, but what can he do?"

"Simon said you have a theory that the diary is not just about treasure, but also some extraordinary power. What did you mean?"

"You know of my early involvement with the Rhine Institute?"

"Thomas, since we are being honest, I do not believe in psychics. I used them on two LAPD homicides. A total waste."

"That happens. But there are also many psychics who have found victim's bodies that were hidden by their killers. Hundreds of times on record. Kate, there is no scientific explanation for psychic phenomena or prophecy. Yet, both have existed for thousands of years."

"What is the Templar connection?"

"Templars became famous for their prophecies. It began when King Philip used the Inquisition to destroy their order. A special court was convened to try them, and, despite very little documentary evidence, they were found guilty. Then the Templars predicted the deaths of four of their accusers, including King Philip. *All* died within the year."

"Another legend?"

"Historical fact. I believe the Templars discovered a system to develop psychic ability. If you can buy me enough time to work on the diary, I may prove it."

"No. You are going in hiding."

"What? Why?"

"That diary is physical evidence in a homicide. If my boss Captain Starger finds out that I haven't turned it in, I'll be back in a cruiser getting fat on French fries."

Thomas now realized that no matter how important the diary was to him, he must not jeopardize her. "Kate, what do you want me to do?"

"I know a place where you can work on the diary. I'll delay turning it in as long as I can. But I have to tell Captain Starger about Nora. Fallon had the diary declared a national artifact. That's FBI jurisdiction. They can throw a net over the entire country and get Nora."

"They won't find her. She's too smart."

"You give her too much credit."

"She has a solid alibi for Hollander's murder. You'd never connect Nora to her thugs who actually did it. You want Nora? Think like she does. She will do anything to get the diary. Let her come after me."

"That makes you a target."

"Kate, I'm not giving the diary up. Not to Fallon . . . nor to you."

"What!"

"Not until I am certain what Fallon plans to do with it."

"That's obstruction!"

"Nora convinced me that Fallon and GOLEM are incredibly dangerous. I have to know a lot more before I hand over the diary to him."

"And that's grand theft!"

"No, just a delay until I get some answers. And by using me as bait, you personally are doing something your whole department can't, which is setting a trap for Nora."

"How in hell did you become so devious?"

"Arguing with Jesuits."

Kate phoned Vicky to ask her to meet at Carlos' Cantina. It was frequented by an appreciative clientele who knew that chili Colorado was not a bowl of chili. They also had a tolerance for salsa that could peel tooth enamel.

When Kate left Thomas that morning, he was deep into the translation with a fresh pot of coffee and Watson curled beside him. The bastard cat had abandoned her for the novelty of hanging with another male.

Lupe, the waitress, brought Kate and Vicky two margaritas on the rocks. They had the kick of a pissed-off burro.

Kate savored an icy swallow, then said, "Thomas is free."

"What?" Vicky almost dropped her drink.

"Somebody abducted him from his kidnappers. But he escaped from them with the diary."

"Hoooooly crap!"

"It gets better. The bad guys work for a psycho named Nora. She had the courier killed for the diary. But there is not a clue who the second bunch of bad guys are."

"Where is the monk now?"

"Hiding where only God can find him."

"Captain Starger will find him before God does. You have got to tell Starger."

"And admit I covered up a kidnapping? Starger would fire us both."

"I knew that monk was bad karma."

"So, we'll use him to get Nora."

"As bait?"

"And I am the hook. When Nora makes her move, I may need help. Keep your phone on."

"Kate, this is getting way too personal."

"I *want* this killer! Every cop hopes for their big case. Mine just dropped in my lap—a homicide linked to a book legend. Which is tied to a billionaire mogul whose every move makes the media. Vicky, I'd follow this killer to hell to get him."

"Are you sure that's all?"

"What do you mean?"

"The monk, baby."

"He's just icing, he ain't the cake. We have both faced our attraction. Besides, he's a monk, for heaven's sake."

Vicky sensed that Kate's involvement made her blind to her own denial.

"Kate, we've got to get Nora before Starger discovers our deception or you can stick a fork in us and turn us over cause our asses are done!"

The small-frame beach house a few miles north of Santa Barbara had been in Kate's family for three generations. Her grandmother left it to her mother and the title was always kept in the succeeding grandmother's family name. On paper, it was untraceable to Kate. Nobody could track Thomas there, unless Kate had missed something.

She opened the patio door facing the ocean and was met by a wash of salt air. Thomas set his suitcase down. Brother Barnabas at the monastery had packed clothes, toiletries, and a few reference books, and then met them en route to the beach.

Kate spread her arms, showing off the room. "The family retreat."

Thomas could only stare. With the sun and sea behind her, the effect was stunning. Kate had that Irish coloring that fascinated men and women envied: creamy skin, dark auburn hair, and green eyes.

"My dad is a hard-nosed Catholic—Mass in Latin and fish on Friday. When I go to hell, Dad will be to blame. If he hadn't been such a fanatic I might not have lapsed." She indicated a table with pictures of the same woman at different ages. "That's my Mom. How he adored her! She died ten years ago so he made this place a shrine to the Virgin Mother." Kate nodded to a wall picture of Madonna and child. "But I still don't know who that woman with the kid is."

They both laughed.

After settling in, they sat on the patio overlooking the beach. Watson was tracking mice trails like a lion on the Serengeti. Kate opened a bottle of Cabernet and they watched the tide stretching each wave to reach the house pilings.

"Thomas, I'm honestly trying to understand this psychic stuff. Please help me."

Over the years he had stopped trying to explain the paranormal. But Kate deserved an answer, so he gave his best example. Lois's death.

"To give you some background, my wife Lois and I were having a rough patch. I sensed that she was unhappy but we didn't come out and discuss it. I was going to Cleveland for a week to lecture on Celtic lore at the Cleveland Museum of Art. I guess I was feeling sorry for myself because I took some of her letters to me when we were first in love. I would read them at night before going to sleep. I was actually reading one when the phone rang. It was Jean Abrams, my mentor at the university. Her voice was so strained I barely recognized her."

"Thomas, are you alone?"

"Of course. Why?"

"You may need to be with—I don't know how to . . ."

"Jean, what's wrong?"

"It's Lois. There was a car accident. She's dead."

Jean may have said something else but he didn't hear. He was seeing it again: the nightmare, the overturned car awash in hellish red and blue colors from road flares and emergency vehicles.

He heard himself ask, "How is Royce?"

"In critical condition." There was a cautious pause. "How did you know about Royce?"

Kate tried to make his explanation easier. "Yes, Thomas, I read about it in the tabloids."

"Then you may remember the headlines. 'Famous author's wife killed during weekend shack-up with his best friend.' "

"That must have been unbearable."

"A week before, I had overheard her talking to someone on the phone. She didn't know I was in the den. From her side of the conversation it sounded like they had just been together."

"Did you confront her?"

"No. I wanted to find out who the guy was. At this point in our marriage, I thought she had lost interest in sex. Instead, she lost interest in me."

Kate knew that humiliation. "Being hard on yourself is punishing the wrong person. Believe me."

"I assumed he was someone from her corporate world. Then I had a dream—Lois in a wreck riding with my friend Royce."

"Obviously, you were thinking of possible candidates; that triggered the dream."

"No. I *saw* it, Kate. Just like it happened. Every detail. Now Lois is dead and Royce is horribly maimed."

"And you feel guilty."

"What's the use of having psychic ability if you can't prevent something terrible from happening?"

"What could you have done?"

"Confront Lois. She was very fair. She would not have gone with Royce that weekend. She would have waited until I returned from my trip and we had it out. But because of my anger, I didn't tell her what I saw coming."

"Is this the first time you actually *saw* a dream event?"

"Yes. Never before."

They were interrupted by Kate's cell phone ringing.

"Detective Flynn? Fallon."

Kate looked at Thomas. "Dr. Fallon?"

"Any news on Brother Thomas?"

"Why don't you ask him?"

She handed Thomas the phone.

"Hello, Dr. Fallon."

"Brother Thomas? What happened?"

"I escaped. And I have the diary."

"Fantastic! Who kidnapped you? I must know!"

Kate, leaning close to hear, shook her head. "I can't really say, Dr. Fallon. They kept me blindfolded."

"Where are you now? The monastery?"

"No, someplace where it won't happen again."

"Good. Stay there. We don't need any more delays. How is the translation progressing?"

"I've barely started."

There was a silence. "That's all you can tell me?"

"So far, yes."

Another pause. "Brother Thomas, why do I get the feeling you are not being forthcoming?"

"Forthcoming? Why didn't you tell me about the chest? It would have helped to know what I am looking for."

"Who told you about it?"

"My abductors. They told me more than you did. Look, Fallon, translating the diary is tough enough, I don't need obstacles."

"Now that you know about the chest why can't you just concentrate on it?"

"Context. Brychan refers to the past when explaining the present and in different languages. What is in the chest?"

"That is not your concern. I insist you keep me informed on your progress!" He hung up.

Kate and Thomas shared a surprised look. Why was he so secretive?

Fallon, seething, tapped automatic dial. Sawyer answered at the first ring.

"The monk escaped and is hiding in Santa Barbara. Detective Flynn knows where he is. Find that monk!"

"Then what?"

"I'll tell you when you find him."

Kate poured the last of the Cabernet. They had moved to the den, where the tone changed from friendly discussion to straight interrogation. "What about all those psychic frauds?"

"There are lots of them. But there are also legitimate psychics. The best was Edgar Cayce."

"What made him different?"

"When Cayce was in a trance, he could mentally enter another person's body to discover ailments and suggest cures. A stenographer took down every word. Afterward, he had no memory of what he said. Kate, I've researched him. In over fourteen thousand cases I know of no instance of a Cayce fraud. He was devoutly religious."

"You are psychic and a monk; is there a religious connection with psychics?"

"Not really. One of the very best was an atheist. A Russian, Wolf Messing, was a favorite of Joseph Stalin. Messing's telekinesis was so powerful he was seen to knock a bird from a tree branch by just staring. Once, in a controlled test, he entered Stalin's dacha by walking past the guards as if he were invisible. That was witnessed and documented by Stalin's own secret police. Because of Messing and other psychics on their roster, Soviet parapsychology was 20 years ahead of everyone else."

"What kind of psychic are you?"

"A trance sensitive. The technical term is oneirology."

"Can you use psychic power to solve this homicide?"

"No more than you can. Out of a trance I don't get

premonitions, read palms, or see spooks. But last night I had a breakthrough on the diary. Brychan referred to a Muslim as Master Assam ibn al-Din."

"Why is that a breakthrough?"

"Brychan's calling him master means that he was Assam's apprentice. For a Christian monk, that was instant heresy. Back then, what you believed or didn't believe about God could get you killed."

"By following Templar orders Brychan was risking his life?"

"A death sentence. The Templars could not protect him from the Inquisition or King Philip. If I can find out why he took such a risk, I'll know why people kill for what is in the diary."

THE WEEK AFTER Christmas, 1306, Brychan, a twenty-year-old novice monk, after visiting his family at Houston Castle, returned to the Cistercian abbey at Edinburgh. The month with Vivyan seemed more dream than memory. He was told that Father Abbot wanted to see him immediately. Brychan's heart went cold with fear—had his sin been discovered?

When he entered the Abbot's chamber for the first time, he saw that the walls were laden with volumes, scrolls, and many wax candles. The aroma instantly reminded him of the library room where he'd spent many hours with his mother.

Reverend Father Jude was waiting behind a great oak table. Brother Gregory, his assistant, looked at Brychan with disapproval.

"You may go, Brother Gregory," the Abbot said. Gregory left and the Abbot motioned Brychan to come closer.

As he did, he saw folded manuscript pages on the Abbot's desk. Brychan froze. They were his private writings hidden under a plank beneath his bed.

"Please sit, Brother Brychan."

Brychan sat stiffly on the bench, desperately trying to rein his thoughts. He was obliged to look directly at Father Abbot whenever he spoke, but his eyes strayed to the manuscript in those thickly gnarled hands. They held his life.

From the beginning, his mother, Lady Gwynn, insisted that he record his dreams and visions. With God's gift came obligation. By studying his own written record, he would learn to separate true vision from false dreaming. In this he must be relentless to be worthy of his gift.

The Abbot unfolded the pages, which were evidence of witchcraft and heresy. He looked at a page, squinting one eye. Decades as a copyist had taken their toll.

"Do you recognize this, my son?" he said.

"Yes, Venerable Abbot." Brychan had left the writings securely hidden when he went home for Christmas. Entering a monk's cell without his permission was forbidden.

The Abbot gently admonished him. "The privacy rule of your cell does not apply to your Abbot. I have been reading your writings since you arrived. A monk must have no secrets from the Order. *Preserve me from secret faults, scripture says. God sees into every heart.*"

There was a brisk knock at the door. The Inquisition? Brychan locked his fingers to prevent his hands from shaking.

"Come in, Brother Justin," the Abbot called.

Justin entered. His demeanor was more battle-hardened knight than a monk. Each novice was assigned a mentor, and Brother Justin was his. Brychan heard that, years before, Justin had gained considerable fame in the joust. After he learned of Brychan's skill with the sword, during their daily recess, the two dueled with sharpened oak sticks dipped in red ochre while the monks watched and cheered.

The Abbot explained. "Brother Justin has told us of your unusual skill with arms. From his previous life that is expected, but you had no such past. How did this happen?"

"I was trained by my father's master of arms, Rothgar, a worthy gome."

"I see." Father Jude reached for a small bell and rang it. In the far corner of the room a narrow door opened and a man entered. He was tall and oak-solid with full beard and close-cropped hair. A scar scored his left cheek from ear to chin. His white mantle with a blood-red splayed cross at the left shoulder marked him a Templar Knight.

The Abbot introduced him. "This is Brother André of Tours, just arrived from the Templar preceptory in Paris."

Brychan stood and bowed slightly, as touching was forbidden for monks except when greeting with a holy kiss. From the look of Brother André, a kiss did not seem prudent.

Father Jude addressed the Templar. *"Frère André, Préférez-vous parler en Français? Notre Brychan parle le pauvre dialecte Normand que nous parlons toujours ici."*

"English is acceptable." His voice was a mastiff's growl and almost free of accent.

The few Templars that Brychan had seen were grim and forbidding. Brother André's countenance appeared hacked from craggy stone. It was not a face to meet in battle.

The Templar looked at Brychan for the first time. "Brother Novice," he said, "through your Abbot, we know of your promising skills. Our order does not seek candidates, they seek us. This is an exception. I am authorized by our Grand Master Jacques de Molay to offer you the opportunity to become a novice monk in the Knights Templar. If you successfully complete your novitiate, you will become a warrior monk, placing yourself, your soul, and your sword in the service of God."

André turned to Father Jude. "I must have an answer tomorrow, Venerable Abbot." He bowed and went out through the same door he entered.

Brychan could not speak. He had literally trembled to face Father Abbot, fearing the scarlet sin with his brother's wife had been discovered, and now, when it appeared certain that he would be burned for heresy, came this miraculous offer.

He remembered this moment as the most astonishing in all his twenty years.

CHAPTER EIGHT

BRYCHAN HAD NOT given his answer to Reverend Abbot and it was time. Outside in the bleak cold, he and Brother Justin sat where, in summer, a lush rose garden bloomed. Now the bushes, deep in winter's sleep, spread naked stems bristling with ice-covered thorns. Nearby, a statue of Our Lady watched with chill marble gaze.

"Tis a great honor, Brychan," Justin said. His breath blew a fine mist. "Would it had come to me at your age."

"I never considered any order but the Cistercians. Not Franciscans, nor Carmelites, and certainly not Dominicans. But Templars?"

"Hear me, Brother! They are warriors first. With no Crusade, they have become rich moneylenders. But by the rood, they are still Templars!" Justin jumped to his feet. "Mother of God! Is your blade quicker than your wits? As a Templar ye can pledge self, soul, and sword to God's service!"

"Yes, but I am not certain if . . ."

"Brother Brychan! Suppose, God willing, there is another Crusade! How will ye feel rotting in your books knowing ye could have been in the thick of it as a Templar, but refused?" Justin shook his head. "Zuggers! 'Twould drive me mad!"

IN A LIGHTLY blowing snow in February 1307, Brychan arrived in Paris and entered the city wall through the Temple Gate. He saw that the Templar preceptory had another wall surrounding it, a complete and separate fortress within the city. With its stone walls and high towers, it was the grandest in all the Templar Order, with the exception of Acre in the Holy Land.

Once inside, Brychan was ordered to change his white Cistercian robe for the gray of a Templar novice. It was to be worn over his regular clothing, for now he was neither noble nor monk. If he survived the rigorous training and was accepted by the Order, he would be given the coveted white mantle with the blood-red splayed cross. It would seal him as a Knight Templar and he would be buried in it.

In other religious orders a new name was taken with the monk's vows, but as a Templar, Brychan would keep his baptized name as a constant reminder of the world he had given up and the behavior expected from one of noble rank. Instead of the title novice, he would be addressed as Childe Brychan until he was knighted or dismissed as a failed candidate.

On the second day, he had an audience with Brother Guy d'Orléans, master of initiates. Sir Guy was revered for his considerable learning, having attended Oxford before becoming a Templar. He was also an intimate of Grand Master de Molay.

They met in the chancellery room where a fire burned, and a novice scribe waited to take down every word. Brother Guy questioned him, carefully considering each answer. When finally they discussed his gift, Brychan was assured that here it would be respected and encouraged to develop. In parting, the master cautioned, "I shall be watching you closely, Childe Brychan."

In the following days Brychan was surprised to discover that there were only seven novices. They had been training for months, except for Miguel the Spaniard who arrived only a week before him. Miguel was nineteen, small and pale with enormous dark eyes, and appeared an unlikely warrior. Brychan immediately sensed that Miguel would not survive the rigors of a Templar postulant. It was an instance where Brychan found his gift painful to the point of wishing he did not have it.

Four of the seven novices were from France and Normandy. Only one other was from the English Isles. He was called Childe James and was a year older than Brychan. In the days following, the two, one Scot and one Irish, forged a bond that would last all their lives.

James McGill was a boisterous Irish lad from a ranking noble family. Both being "Celts," they spoke Gaelic to each other, especially when they didn't want the Franks to understand. In the very first week, they were disciplined with three days on bread and water for rowdiness: they had laughed out loud.

James, like Brychan, was a second son, and would inherit neither lands nor title. "It was either the Templars or Franciscans," James explained. "Can ye see me-self a ragged Franciscan, where the most in life would be to receive a bleeding stigmata?"

"You'd have made a terrible Franciscan, Jamie. Better give your wily ways to the Templars. They'll use it to slay infidels."

"Now that's a true calling." James laughed.

In this new Templar world Brychan worked hard to adapt. He was accustomed to the Cistercian order where all monks had the same tasks: the five daily offices, manuscript copying, working fields, and tending flocks. They ate meat only on feast days.

Templars were different. All worshiped the five offices together and recited an additional twenty-five Pater Nosters daily. Being subject to combat, they ate three meals a day and meat thrice weekly. As a military order, their number was far less than their peak estimated at 150,000 worldwide a few decades ago. It had now dwindled to about 6,000 knights and men-at-arms.

Brychan's first task was to learn everyone's name and status. Ranking first were the white-mantled knights, which in Paris numbered twenty-eight. There were also approximately 260 brown-garbed sergeants and men-at-arms, which allowed seven to ten per knight for their particular battle tactics. They all drilled together—a system well established for almost 200 years. No other Crusader troops from any country were so consistently trained. In battle, Templars were unmatched among all Crusaders and the equal of any foe.

Next were the fifteen green-robed cleric monks: scribes who managed both banking and vast land holdings. They were headed by Friar Luke, a legend for his mastery of mathematics, geometry, and astrology. The clerics were also responsible for teaching the novices all 686 paragraphs in the Rule of the Order. These were memorized verbatim and recalled on command—a daunting task, especially for those unlettered.

Last in rank were the novices, like Brychan. They exercised daily in combat drill with the knights and sergeants. The most concentrated training was cavalry tactics. Templars were famed horsemen; it was critical to their success in battle. Each Templar was allowed three chargers, handled by a squire or sergeant. They were constantly rotated in battle so a Templar's mount was usually fresher than his opponent's. Horses were so regarded that one could miss a daily office if necessary, to care for them.

Finally, there was a separate group of five brothers requiring special care. Four were elderly knights, long retired. All were infirm and battle-scarred; one was blind and another had left his sword arm in the Holy Land.

The fifth, Brother Deagan, required special attention. Once destined to become a Templar knight, he became instead a permanent postulant. He lived in his cell, leaving only for meals and the canon offices. He was unable to remember names or faces, but knew all variations of the Mass and plainchants verbatim. He could recite hundreds of verses of scripture and all 150 Psalms in Latin without error—an incredible feat. Beyond this, he responded to no questions, shared no thoughts.

Brychan was surprised when Brother Deagan was appointed his exclusive responsibility. None of the other novitiates were so charged.

Every day Brychan led Brother Deagan to Mass. He watched as Deagan never faltered in scripture or chant, reciting entirely from memory. Even at meals, while a brother friar read aloud in Latin from scripture, Deagan silently mouthed the words.

Rarely did he acknowledge Brychan's presence. Brother Deagan, for the most part, did not seem to know he was there.

Both Brychan and the Spaniard Miguel were given a separate schedule from the others because of their gift. Brychan drilled with the others on the tilting field but afterward disappeared into the preceptory. No one dared to question why.

It began on a Monday following lauds. Brychan had returned to his cell and was washing himself with cold water, a daily penance. Brother André entered without knocking. Brychan had not seen him since his recruitment in Scotland.

"Follow me," André ordered.

Brychan trailed him through torch-lit corridors and down a winding stone passage never touched by daylight. When the torches ended, André took the last one and kept going deeper where the dark weighed heavy as Hades' cloak. Should the torch fail, Brychan knew he could never find his way back. André suddenly turned into a narrow passage. He stopped before a door and slid back its bolt.

They entered a great chamber that echoed their steps. In the center was a table with a single candle casting barely enough light to reveal the room's cavernous size.

Brychan turned to see André go back through the door. He heard the bolt slide and lock. He was alone.

Uneasily, he looked around. On the opposite wall was a huge tapestry of two knights riding the same horse: the Templar seal. Set in the wall were rows of iron fittings, some with rings. With a chill, he realized this was also a dungeon.

The door bolt clattered again. He turned to see André enter with another man who, from his dress was an Arab, by his dark skin, a Moor.

André presented him. "Childe Brychan, this is Assam ibn al-Din, your new master."

The Moor said something in Arabic to André, who answered and bowed. Brychan was surprised: a Templar bowing to a Muslim infidel? Without a word, André left. The Moor turned and looked at Brychan. Never had he seen such eyes—a gaze one surely could feel in the dark.

"You will address me as Master Din. Bolt the door. It will remain so whenever we are inside." His French had a Spanish accent rather than Arabic.

"Yes, Master Din."

Brychan went to the door. The sliding bar's edges were worn smooth by use and time. When he tried the slide, it jammed. He pushed with all his strength, sliding back and forth until it noisily fell in place.

He turned. Master Din was gone.

Brychan looked around. There was no other door. He rushed to the tapestry and pulled it back, certain there was a hidden door. There was only a stone wall lined with more bolts and rings.

"If I were an assassin, you'd be dead, novice."

The voice came from above. Brychan looked up into the darkness to see Master Din slowly lowering on a rope. He had swiftly ascended by a device pulled from the outside, while Brychan noisily worked the door slide: a simple trick.

The master's tone was accusing. "You just failed your first test. Where we will go, if you fail, you can never return. Failure there means madness."

Brychan now understood the cause of Brother Deagan's tragic affliction. He had been Master Din's novice before Brychan. ✝

"How's your monk?" Vicky asked. Kate was driving them in an unmarked cruiser to track down a lead on the Hollander homicide.

"Totally driven. Works round the clock on the diary. I've hidden him at our family beach house. I hope to heaven nobody tracks him there."

"You staying there too?"

"How else can I protect him?"

"Right," Vicky smiled. "And how is that going?"

"Great. Well . . . stressful." She sighed. "Hell."

"Yeah. A monk must be as bad as falling for a gay guy."

"Who says I'm falling?"

Vicky realized that Kate's attitude toward Thomas was changing and that could be disastrous. Unlike some police departments, the Santa Barbara PD operated strictly by the book. If Kate had an affair with a witness involved in a case, she would be fired. Yet she seemed in total denial.

The day after talking with Fallon, Burns and Sawyer arrived in Santa Barbara. They used a multiple-car system, renting two per day, never using the same make or color on succeeding days.

Sometimes both were in one car and, when they drove separate cars, they communicated by disposable burner cell phones.

They assumed that since Kate was working homicide during the day, she and the monk would only be together at night. The next day they began tailing her after work. When following her that afternoon, they lost her on a freeway when she made a quick switch at an off-ramp. Kate, routinely protecting herself, sensed she was being followed. That night they parked outside her apartment; she didn't show. Obviously, she and the monk were someplace else. But where?

At the Santa Barbara beach house Thomas was reading and taking notes on Brychan's narrative, which described a meeting with his Muslim master after a period of brutal training.

> *When I entered the chamber this time there was great change. Master Din was waiting but now the room glowed with light. Along the walls were seven blazing torches, and on the floor seven standing candelabra as tall as a man, each with seven burning candles thick as a warrior's forearm. All were repeated by sevens, following the Book of Revelation.*

MASTER DIN STOOD beside the table. On it was an iron chest bound with riveted straps. He motioned Brychan closer and pointed to a single word etched on the metal lid: VERITAS.

"Childe Brychan, do you know its meaning?"

"Truth, Master Din."

"Truth," he repeated. "I must prepare you. Your previous exercises were simple mimicry. Now, your path will be more severe."

Brychan wondered how it could be more difficult. During the

first month he performed a grueling series of chants daily; words repeated in specific order hour after hour in a peculiar changing rhythm until they made no sense and he was exhausted.

Master Din explained that their sound was as important as their meaning. "Each exercise creates a different vibration at your deepest center. Repetition increases sensitivity. Eventually, they will blend and become one sound. Then, a voice will speak to you through your gift."

After one particularly grueling session Brychan asked, "How do I know that I am doing this right?"

"You don't," Master Din snapped. "*It* chooses you."

THE DRILLS WERE like a bard's incessant chanting. One night, the sound awoke him from a deep sleep. His gift, his awen, usually worked through dreams and visions. It was from there the voice had spoken.

AT THEIR NEXT training exercise, Master Din was watching him as they stood before the VERITAS chest. "Can you recall the voice?"

Brychan closed his eyes and began the rhythmic chant in his head. "Yes, Master Din."

"Open your eyes."

Brychan saw that the chest lid had been raised.

"Hold the sound!" Master Din commanded.

But Brychan concentrated too hard and the inner voice stopped. He breathed deeply, enforcing relaxation from many hours practice. He broke a sweat; though he relaxed. After a moment it came back, a pulsing he could hear even when listening to the master.

From the iron chest Master Din removed a scroll of copper. It was of great age and covered with inscrutable writing. He took out two more, laying them side by side. Then another scroll, a parchment wrapped around two spindles of gold.

He unfurled the scroll to the first page, where Brychan saw three sentences in three different languages. "Can you read this?"

"No, Master Din."

From the folds of his robe the Moor produced a pointer, its silver tip in the form of a small hand. It was a treasured gift from Abram of Avila, a revered rabbi and renowned scholar. Master Din pointed to each line and spoke the words aloud; then, the translation. ✝

In Hebrew of the prophet Moses.
In Aramaic of the prophet Jesus.
In Arabic of the prophet Mohammed.
All read: "The Gift is not for gain."

Thomas made another note and underlined it. In Templar legends, among the treasures found under Solomon's temple were scrolls made of copper. He wiped his forehead, surprised to find a light film of stress sweat. He continued reading.

Master gave another warning. The scroll contained a discipline much more difficult than the previous exercises. Again, he reminded me of the terrible price of failure. I must risk reason, body, and soul without knowing why: my test of absolute Templar obedience.

Thomas closed the diary feeling uneasy, his fingers damp inside the latex gloves. He peeled them and wiped his hands while trying to grasp what he just read.

The Al-Din Discipline, which enhanced psychic ability, must be what Fallon was after. Finally, this was a direct link between the medieval diary and the present. But since Fallon could not translate the Gaelic portion of the diary, how did he even know the Din scroll existed?

Thomas got up from the table and stared out the window. He had spent his life thinking and acting independently, even when married to Lois. But this situation was different. From now on he would have to include Kate in every decision, for her safety.

When Kate arrived that evening after work, Thomas had dinner ready. The linguini with garlic, herbs, and white wine sauce was exceptional; he had learned a few monastery recipes. He waited until they finished eating.

"Kate, there is something we need to discuss about the diary."

"Okay, fire away."

"I've got to give you some background."

"It's been a tough day. Keep it simple."

"During the Crusades both Christians and Muslims committed the same blasphemy—they believed that killing each other was doing God's work. But the Templars were unique among Crusaders in that they played both sides. When they weren't actually fighting Saracens, they traded with them and engaged in scholarly debates, many of which were written down. As a result, they acquired great wealth, a wide range of knowledge written in books, scrolls, manuscripts, and many religious artifacts. By far the most important was the Holy Grail."

"You mean there actually was a grail? I thought that was just King Arthur fiction."

"The grail was real, but there is no definition of what it is. It is not mentioned anywhere in the Bible. The most popular belief says it was the cup from the Last Supper. And that centers on Joseph of Arimathea."

"The man who put Jesus' body in his tomb?"

"Very good, Kate."

"How did Joseph get the cup?"

"The evidence is circumstantial but convincing." He thought for a moment for the best example. "Kate, as a cop, imagine the Crucifixion as a heinous crime scene; the murder of a beloved rabbi. The night before, at the Last Supper, we know that John who almost certainly was a teenager, sat next to Jesus. He may have taken Jesus' cup because he sensed its significance since everyone drank from it. The next day John was the only one of the twelve at the Crucifixion. The other disciples fled, leaving Jesus to his fate. But Joseph of Arimathea, a *secret* follower, was there. With his servants, he took down Jesus' body from the cross for burial. If John had the cup from the night before, he probably gave it to Joseph for safekeeping because he was a prominent, wealthy man. Joseph may have used the cup to gather some of Christ's blood, making it a holy relic. After that, the cup ends up in England."

"How did it get there?"

"Joseph was an importer of tin from the British Isles, the source of his wealth. The Romans needed his tin to forge iron weapons. After Joseph became an evangelist, he went back to England. Many believe Joseph founded the Celtic church there. It is speculated that he brought the cup with him. Even the Roman Catholic church officially declared that England was where the Gospel was first preached."

"But after the Templars were destroyed why didn't they simply disappear?"

"The Templar mystique. They were associated with the Holy Grail, the Arc of the Covenant, the Shroud of Turin, the missing Templar treasure, and those mysterious manuscripts in the chest."

She was learning to read his pauses. "What's wrong?"

"Kate, I have to tell you something you are not going to like. I must find that chest and see what it contains before Fallon gets his hands on it. That means following the diary wherever it leads."

"Leave the country with two million dollars' worth of Fallon's property? What about all those crazies after the diary? Nora's killing crew? The goons who pulled the raid? And Fallon, the bad-assed billionaire? There's a whole frigging army after you."

"But I have the advantage."

"What advantage?!"

"I can track the diary; they can't."

"What if the diary is not authentic? You could be chasing some forger's scam. The last time you did that, it ruined your career."

"Kate, I have no choice. I must go to France."

Locked in an impasse, there was an uncomfortable silence.

"Then, I'll have to go with you."

"What?"

"The diary is evidence in my homicide case. I have to protect the diary and you. Thomas, you'd never make it to the airport, much less to France."

"Your department will never let you go."

"I won't tell them."

"That is extremely risky."

"But worth it if I catch the killer."

In the edgy silence, she poured a glass of wine that she didn't want and he finished his cold coffee. Neither mentioned another complication; they would be together day and night.

She moved toward the kitchen, then turned and looked at him. "This is going to be *very* difficult."

Leo's executive Learjet was circling Santa Barbara at 21,000 feet. It seated twelve: four forward cabin, eight rear. Carver sucked in the rich leather aroma.

A man sat by the cabin door facing him. From the moment Carver boarded, the man silently watched him. Thick-muscled and gorilla-hairy. He probably had to shave twice a day.

Carver tried a stare-down. Gorilla was unblinking as a shark.

The cabin door opened and Leo entered. Carver had to fight the impulse to stand.

Leo looked at the other man. *"Eu chamarei se eu o preciso."*

Gorilla gave Carver a final look, went in the rear cabin, and closed the door.

Carver nervously smiled. "Your f-f-friend is not very talkative."

"Try Portuguese." Leo sat in the diagonal seat.

The pilot's cabin door opened and a stunning blond woman appeared, a statuesque six feet. Carver's mouth gaped. He was rewarded with a look that told him he was dog shit on her shoes.

Leo frowned. "What is it, Andrea?"

"The pilot says that because of storms, we should re-route to Hong Kong or change itinerary. What do you want me to tell him?"

"I'll decide after we drop Carver off."

"I vote for shopping in Hong Kong."

"After your last trip, there's probably nothing left to buy."

She laughed, kissed his cheek, and went back into the pilot's cabin.

Carver was still focused on her figure as the door closed. Leo was human after all: he had incredible taste in women.

"Carver, what is this new development?"

"We spotted two men who arrived yesterday. They are following the woman cop."

"Refresh me."

"Detective Flynn. She's connected with the monk."

"Ah, yes, I remember."

"These guys are very good. She hasn't made them. Yet."

"Obviously, they're following her to find the monk just as you did. Stay close to them."

Carver hesitated, then said, "Wouldn't it be s-s-safer to snatch the monk before they do?"

"No. He must be free to go wherever he wants to lead us to the chest. After that, I assure you, we will take care of him. Permanently."

CHAPTER NINE

Thomas lay in the dark, exhausted, yet his mind would not shut down. The phrase from the diary—*The gift is not for gain*—was like a warning bell.

Brychan's problem 700 years ago was the same that Thomas wrestled with now. He was surprised to find the warning in three languages from three religious sources. It was as if the diary was taunting him. Was it divine retribution? Lois' death, Royce maimed, his own career ruined?

Back when he was researching his Merlin thesis, he had hit a wall. None of the leads were working out. He was dry; a dead end. Out of absolute desperation, he decided to use his psychic ability for research, using his "gift for gain." He practiced hours of intensive meditation. This should have relaxed him, but instead he suffered excruciating migraines. Finally, one night he had a dream with its distinctive trance imagery.

> *He was wandering through a library, an endless labyrinth of volumes, scrolls, and codices. Suddenly there was a great rushing sound like the breathing of a mammoth chorus. The books were*

alive, sucking up the air. He was suffocating. Then a voice said, "Do not read the past—go there."

He woke up to find himself standing in his bedroom staring into the dark.

He wondered: Was this instruction? A personal revelation through dreams? The Celtic term was *awen*, an energy force expressed through trance or dreams. Was this dream voice his awen? If so, it meant his Merlin discovery source was not academic, but a dream. Yet, it was absolutely central to his entire thesis. If he failed to disclose it, he was lying by omission. But neither could he reveal it to the academic committee. For that you don't get a PhD; you get a sanity hearing.

He checked the clock: 3:20. Kate was probably sound asleep in her bedroom. He turned on the reading lamp, slipped on the latex gloves, and opened the diary. Once again, he felt a sense of anticipation.

Kate was being awakened by Thomas.

"Kate . . ." he said.

She sat upright. Instinctively her hand slipped under the pillow for her Beretta. "What?"

"I'm sorry but I had to wake you. I found something in the diary that changes everything."

"Can't it wait 'til morning?"

"No." He held out a cup of coffee. "I just made this."

She took the cup and he turned on the bedside lamp. He sat beside her and opened the diary.

"I was translating Brychan's narrative and came across the phrase *'Gart na Beanacd.'* It's the old Celt name for a place called Bannock. Brychan's phrase translates as 'A dawn prayer before Bannock.'"

"Is Bannock a god?"

"A stream. The Scots word for stream is burn. And Bannockburn was a famous battle. It isn't in France, it's in Scotland. Brychan was praying before that battle; he was there."

"But he was in France. When did he go to Scotland?"

"I took another look at the timeline. In France, de Molay was executed in March 1314. That was when Brychan and Ursus received their secret orders. They must have been ordered to go to Scotland."

"Then where is the chest?"

"There is no mention of it."

"Maybe he hid it in France before he went to Scotland."

"No. Brychan was ordered to keep it with him, just as the Templar Grand Masters did. Once Bannock was mentioned, Scotland made sense. It was the main refuge for Templars after they were destroyed in France. Brychan says they were traveling northwest and mentions crossing two rivers, the Rhône and the Seine. One look at a map and I saw it. West of the Rhône is La Rochelle, the Templar port from which the eighteen treasure ships sailed. And Brychan needed a ship to get to Scotland."

"Where he prayed before the battle of Bannockburn. Damn, it fits."

"Everyone has been looking for the chest in France, where the Templars began. It's not there. We were about to make the same mistake. It's in Scotland."

"I'm having a minor crisis." Kate was sitting across from Captain Starger who impatiently tapped the desk with a yellow wooden pencil. She was late even though he had delayed an appointment to work her in.

"With you, Kate, it's never minor."

"Last year, my doctor, who has been seeing me since puberty, joined his brother's practice in Baltimore," she lied.

"Fascinating." Starger stirred a second packet of brown sugar in his hot tea.

"I have to fly there to see him. I'm taking sick leave for a week."

He snapped the yellow pencil in half. "Leave now?"

"Tomorrow. The Hollander homicide is stalled. Vicky can cover for me; she knows as much as I do. And there could be a bonus."

"What bonus?"

"The Baltimore police have a similar homicide connected to ours: a woman who worked directly with Fallon at Med-Tek. Kidnapped, murdered, and the body butchered, the same MO. I want to check it out while I'm there."

"You're going all the way to Maryland to see a doctor just because he used to treat you?"

"Chronic endometriosis. Don't worry, you can't catch it."

"Kate, there must be hundreds of gynecologists in Hollywood."

"Would you trust your balls to a stranger?"

He blushed. It was nice to know that some men still could.

Kate and Vicky were at Carlos' Cantina for an early brunch. Hidden under the table was a cat carrier with Watson napping inside. It was a restaurant violation, but Kate was almost family.

Vicky stared, unbelieving, and said, "You and the monk are going to follow the diary wherever it leads? Kate, that's crazy."

"Thanks. Just the vote of confidence I need." She opened her briefcase and produced two cellphones. She handed one to Vicky. "Burner phones. The last thing we want is somebody tracking us. Fallon is bound to call. What are you going to tell him?"

Vicky thought a moment. "If Fallon asks about you, I'll explain that you're in the hospital, female problems. Men hate talking about that stuff. If he asks about the monk, I'll say, 'What monk?' "

"Perfect. And thanks for taking care of Watson."

"I hate cats."

"Then Watson will drive you crazy trying to win you over. Don't fall for it. It's macho manipulation."

Lupe the waitress brought them two margaritas. Vicky teased the salty rim with her tongue. "Kate, if you get into trouble over there when you're supposed to be here, your career is dead."

"Yep. Either we find the chest, which leads to the prime suspect, or I'll end up writing parking tickets in a town not even on the map."

"Maybe you should reconsider."

"And lose my shot at the Big One? Never."

On her way to Santa Barbara, as she was turning off the freeway at State Avenue, Kate spotted them. A dark blue sedan pulled out, and three cars behind it, another sedan did the same, a double team. She slowed, they slowed. They were good but she was better.

She remembered what Thomas said: everybody was looking for the chest in France. Then she had an idea that caused her to laugh out loud.

Tremayne's Travel Boutique was a treasure trove of books, guides, maps, and pamphlets for any place this side of the moon. Kate spent about half an hour selecting material on France, everything from Paris street guides to cuisine tours. Whoever followed her into the store would know for certain where she was planning to go.

An hour later at the office of Windsor Tours, Kate sat waiting to see the agent. A grandmother with two shopping bags came in and took a seat. From her frazzled look, she really needed a vacation.

TWIST OF TIME

Kate booked for two on Air France with reservations at the Marcelle, a mid-priced Paris hotel. Thomas was financing everything with money from his book. Monks in the Anglican Celtic Order were allowed to retain some personal assets. Thomas had already given half his royalties to the order.

As Kate was leaving, she glanced again at the tired grandmother. She would have felt less sympathetic if she'd known that the woman, Mrs. Tolar, had also fooled the FBI, DEA, and the President's Secret Service.

Considered by many to be the best close tail in the business, Mrs. Tolar could follow a subject, change her appearance several times, and still not get burned. She was in her late fifties, plain with forgettable features. Spare as a rail, she watched her weight with austere discipline. Padding could be instantly added for plumpness or removed to appear thinner.

Though they had previously used her on several jobs, Burns and Sawyer did not even know her first name—she was simply Mrs. Tolar. It was rumored that her husband Marvin abandoned her and their daughter Marilyn, who had spent most of her thirty-two years in an expensive private sanitarium in New Jersey. Shortly after he abandoned them, Marvin disappeared. His insurance was substantial.

When Burns and Sawyer lost Kate in Santa Barbara, they put Mrs. Tolar on the next plane.

After frantically packing, Thomas and Kate barely made their flight to Paris. Kate didn't have to spot the surveillance; she could feel it.

Sitting together on the plane, Kate read the latest issue of *Forensic Sciences* and Thomas continued working on the diary. He resumed translating where the Templars had just ambushed the Pope's troops.

Laus Deo! After the battle we recovered both chest and diary.

BRYCHAN HAD FINISHED questioning the priest, but Father Pierre still shuddered the odd tremor. He watched as Brychan and Ursus carefully examined their re-captured horses.

Ursus tenderly ran his fingers over hips, hocks, and hooves, checking muscles and tendons. Named after the Great Barbarossa's warhorse, Dragon was a big German sorrel almost two hands higher than the average charger. He carried Ursus' bulk with ease; in battle the two fought as one. Splendidly trained, when charging in full combat gear Dragon could be guided by Ursus' shift in weight or guiding pressure from his legs without touching reins.

Brychan's stallion, Joshua, was named after the one whom God had given a "spirit of victory." Headstrong and vicious, he was a biter and kicker and always pushing to be first in the charge. Brychan delighted in him.

Ursus discovered an abrasion on Dragon's left hind leg. When he started to clean it, Sara opened her bag in which she carried herbs, potions, and various Gypsy medicines. Pushing his hand aside, she gently applied an ointment to the wound.

"With this he will heal faster," she said. After she finished, she gave Dragon a gentle rub around his mouth and kissed his velvet soft nose; he smelled of clover.

While the two knights were loading the packhorses, they discussed the best route to La Rochelle. It would take at least eight days or more, depending on weather. The hard March freeze had given way to April thaws and all roads were mud-thick bogs. At some point they would have to cross the Upper Seine where there were few reliable bridges.

Brychan offered Father Pierre a proposition. They would let him go if he swore on his priest's vows to sell the horses and give the money to the poor. He agreed, swearing by the Blessed Virgin and his mother's grave.

Father Pierre looked out on the field strewn with dead. "What of them?"

"As our Lord said, 'Let the dead bury the dead,'" Brychan answered.

"But four of them are Papal cavalry."

"Are they deader than the others?"

"We must give them proper burial!" the priest insisted.

Brychan threw his lance. The point jammed in the dirt between Pierre's feet. "Priest, digging five graves with that lance will take you all night. Better get started. Brother Ursus says the spoor of the dead is on the wind and there are wolves about."

Ursus and Sara were already mounted. Brychan pulled himself up into the saddle.

"Go with God, Dominican," he said. "If you can."

Pierre watched them ride away. *Let the dead lie*, thought the priest. Wolves had to eat too. He picked up the canvas sack of food, mounted up, and turned the horses south. Pope Clement, in selecting Father Pierre as emissary, had chosen well. Though deeply shaken by his experience with the Templars, the Dominican was consumed by ambition. He would not only die for the Faith; he would kill for it.

DESPITE THE QUICKENING dark, Brychan, Ursus, and Sara pressed on. She knew of a village nearby. Brychan preferred the safety of a forest camp, but Ursus said that Dragon was in need of a blacksmith.

For them to enter a town was dangerous. Two men in peasant's garb, traveling with a Gypsy girl, would draw attention. Above all, they must hide their Templar identity.

Saint Cyr lay in the folding lap of surrounding vineyards, which, despite a late frost, were touched with the first green of spring. The town was a stopover for the flood of pilgrims traveling to holy shrines to the south and east. At its center was a square around which the town buildings sprawled.

The three arrived to find a great bonfire and a crowd celebrating the end of Lent. That same day, a party of pilgrims had arrived, among them a large family of Bretons. The father, called Goulu the piper, was famed throughout the countryside. His daughters all sang and one played the Celtic harp. From the village came a drummer, a horn, a fife, and more singers. Mead flowed as from a sweet, honeyed river dammed up after forty lean days of "crabbed Lent."

The village innkeeper was called Roland and his great corpulence bespoke prosperity. He was also brew-master of a heavy-honeyed mead. Known throughout the province, Roland enjoyed good food, breeding fighting cocks, and the company of full-bodied women who differed from his spare wife, a pale creature who hovered like a shadow on the fringes of his fun.

Roland especially enjoyed talking with travelers. He collected their tales, gaining popularity in their retelling. Like a peasant reading weather signs, he read his visitors. Their accent, clothing, horses, and baggage revealed much more than they knew.

Sensing a good tale, Roland was drawn to the two strangers and the Gypsy wench. The giant was easiest to read: a warrior, by girth and gait, but there was something else. Roland chanced upon him at the stable feeding their horses. Ursus had removed his jerkin, revealing a weave of body scars. His right arm was nearly twice the size of his left from endless hours of wielding weapons. Perhaps he had been a Crusader; there seemed an aura of the East about him.

The one called Brychan was harder to read. Both men had the accent of the English Isles but this one spoke like a cleric. Roland suspected he was a churchman running away with the Gypsy—what man wouldn't? She was the type that drove a man to take leave of his senses. Even a Bishop would break his vows, ravaging her bloss body on the church altar and go to hell laughing.

While Ursus was out looking for the blacksmith, Brychan and Sara unloaded the packhorses. As Sara was untying the hitch, the heavy pack slipped. Brychan grabbed at the same time and their hands touched.

Before he could draw back, she took his hand. She kissed his fingers lightly, then caressed her face with his palm, which flushed at his touch.

Hearing Ursus' approach as he grumbled about the blacksmith's price, they moved apart just in time.

That night, a large crowd frolicked before the great bonfire as the two Templars watched. Over the years, Brother Ursus controlled his drinking through decades of monastic discipline. Few knew of his great thirst. Only rarely did he loosen the reins, and never within a religious house, or in the forest where ambush could be fatal. Saint Cyr offered a safe refuge. Tonight, he would drink.

Hoping to get the giant warrior talking, Roland kept Ursus' flagon full. He drank deep but said little as he watched the rowdy crowd. Brychan drank some wine; the Gypsy girl drank none. Roland eventually sensed that he would hear no tales worth telling. Finally, bleezed with mead, he fell into a drunken sleep.

Against the night cold, people huddled closer to the fire. A few were openly caressing, mostly young men and women. By twos, they began disappearing into the dark. A few men, looking around furtively, followed. It was an opportune time for drunken sex-play among all, peasant and tradesmen mixed. Fueled by lust, the great leveler, social status was ignored.

Old Goulu began another tune, his pipe joined by the girl's harp. The song was Celtic, for Bretons were the last surviving Celts in France. Breton songs were rooted in the ancient rhymes and tunes of Scotland, Ireland, and Wales.

Suddenly there came a ringing baritone in Gaelic—it was Ursus. The song was a bardic tale of war, love, and longing. When he finished there was a hush, so unexpected the moment.

The harpist nodded at Ursus and began another song. Again, he joined her. The Gaelic was meaningless to the villagers, but the sound of rhyming words and haunting melody brought thoughtful smiles and even a few tears as the song somehow touched heart and soul.

During the song, Brychan watched Sara, who sat with the women but continued to look at him.

The curfew bell rang, warning all homes to cover their fires for the night. The crowd thinned, the music ended, the old piper had fallen asleep.

Ursus was now solidly drunk. Brychan watched as the warrior wiped the mead dribbling from his beard.

"You are a man of hidden talents, Brother Ursus," he said. "I truly like you better drunk."

Ursus blinked bleary eyes. "And I you, when I'm drunk."

They tapped mugs and looked toward the fire. On the opposite side, Sara was listening to the women but watching Brychan.

He felt Ursus' hand touch his arm. "Brother, does not scripture warn to beware of the woman whose words drip as honey?"

TWIST OF TIME

Brychan quoted from Proverbs 5, the first verse that each Templar novice memorized. "For the lips of a strange woman drop as an honeycomb and her mouth is smoother than oil. But her end is bitter as wormwood, sharp as a two-edged sword." He nodded. "Yes, Brother Ursus, I pray it daily."

Ursus finished the verses: "Her feet go down to death; Her steps take hold on hell."

He nodded toward Sara. "Brother, you are playing with your very soul."

The tone was not accusing; instead there was a look Brychan had never seen: compassion. Ursus with his fierce struggle with drink, understood. The moment passed; Ursus rose and weaved his way to find more mead.

From across the fire, Sara's eyes held Brychan's. She was remembering the moment when their hands touched. Brychan's fingers knew both the mystery of writing and the killing power of a warrior. She sensed that they also knew the magic of making love.

She felt a quickening in her breast and wondered if it was even a greater sin with a monk. ✞

When Thomas and Kate landed at Orly airport in Paris, after twelve hours they were still deep in conversation. During the flight, Thomas read to her the Brychan and Gypsy story. Kate was fascinated—a passionate romance was the last thing she expected to find in a monk's diary. She also saw a parallel in their own lives, but was she just imagining?

As they passed through Gate 12, they did not notice a woman sitting in the waiting area who looked nothing like the grandmother in the Santa Barbara travel agency. Gaunt and severe with gray streaked hair and glasses, she sat reading the *Guardian*. She wore heavy tweeds and the sensible walking shoes of a British tourist.

From the airport to their final location was the critical part of the surveillance, for there was no way to be certain where they were going. Mrs. Tolar followed Thomas and Kate to Hotel Marcelle, where they checked in and reserved a car. After phoning her report to the Bulldogs, she was done. They would take over.

The next day she spent some of the bonus money shopping. She found three French dolls dressed in bright colors for Marilyn. There would be one for Christmas, Easter, and her birthday. All in all, it had been a good trip.

Carver was on the phone updating Leo. "We've found them," he reported proudly. "They flew Air France to Paris. They are staying at the Marcelle."

"Then why you are calling me from Santa Barbara instead of Paris?"

Leo swore in a language that Carver did not understand and hung up.

Nora and Ravel sat parked in her car on a dark side street off Union Avenue in Santa Barbara. It was their first face-to-face meeting since the monk's escape at Oxnard.

Looking at her, Ravel was frustrated by conflicting feelings. He often had sex with women with whom he worked; sex was a perk. Nora was his type. He preferred mature women, they knew what they liked and were often obliging to the odd desire. But Nora was all wires and circuits; there was no connection. Why not? Sex was a sport, not a head game.

Nora handed him an envelope. "Travel money and expenses."

He was suddenly all business. "Where am I going?"

"France. The monk and the cop have already left."

"A delay will make them harder to track."

"You aren't tracking them. You are tracking the people who are following them." She lit another cigarette and looked out the window. "I need your assessment of the situation."

"Assessment? A religious nut and a female cop. And you might as well know—after I finish, I don't want them dogging me. They'd never stop. I'll have to kill them both."

She barely nodded. "Then do it."

In Paris, immediately after arriving at the Hotel Marcelle, Kate made a phone call to Chief Inspector Niles Avery of Scotland Yard.

Several years earlier, Inspector Avery was closing in on a London confidence man, Chris Casswell. His usual targets were gay men, but this time Casswell made a fatal mistake: in a jealous fight he killed his mark. Despite the Yard's best efforts, he managed to escape. His trail led to San Francisco where he became a minor celebrity with the gay crowd. Then he disappeared again.

Scotland Yard liaison asked LAPD homicide for help on the chance that Casswell was drawn to the glamour of Hollywood. The case was dumped on the lowest desk in the pecking order, newly promoted Detective Kate Flynn. Her contacts in the gay community were tight through her team partner Detective Grove Tamblyn, a cop who was gay and out. He knew all the dirt and the bodies buried under it. After a few calls he discovered that Casswell was in Los Angeles; hard legwork did the rest. Casswell was arrested and deported into the waiting arms of Niles Avery and Scotland Yard.

Every Christmas Kate received by mail a two-pound tin of superb English toffee, compliments of the now-titled *Chief* Inspector Avery.

The night of their arrival in Paris, Thomas and Kate left the hotel by a back exit. They took a shuttle flight to London where Chief Inspector Avery met them. Instead of going through customs, they were registered with Scotland Yard, a professional courtesy that left no traceable record.

That same day, Fallon's Bulldogs discovered that Thomas and Kate neither checked out nor picked up their rental car. They simply disappeared.

CHAPTER TEN

Within twenty-four hours of Leo's call, Carver and his team were in Paris. Because of their varied backgrounds, they had numerous criminal contacts in Europe. They fanned out, each working his sources to find Thomas and Kate. One of them, Grigsby, stayed with Carver. Whenever the cop and monk were found, Grigsby would be the triggerman. Grigsby had also tapped his own contacts and was surprised when he was offered a two-day muscle gig paying five thousand euros. He could do it while the others continued their search. He asked Carver to call and get permission. To Grigsby's surprise, Victor refused his request.

It was their third day in Paris. Carver and Grigsby were seated outside Chevalier Rouge Café where the patio offered a view of the passing promenade. The lunch crowd had thinned and most tables were empty. Grigsby suddenly turned to Carver and said, "Okay, how much?"

"How much for what?"

"I'll give you a thousand euros to look other way for forty-eight hours. Nobody will know.

"Forget it."

"The team won't find the goddam monk for days. Meanwhile, you get cash for doing nothing."

"No."

Grigsby's huge paw locked Carver's arm like a bear trap. "I need that gig."

Carver's eyes shifted behind Grigsby. A Black man was approaching with two men walking on either side and two more were following. Leo.

"Oh, shit," Carver whispered and jerked his arm free.

Leo came up behind Grigsby and dropped a manila envelope over his shoulder. It landed on his coffee cup, spilling it.

"Goddammit!" Grigsby turned and saw Leo. He couldn't move.

Leo motioned for Carver to leave; he got up and blended into the passing crowd. Leo sat in Carver's chair and referred to the envelope. "Open it."

Grigsby instantly paled but didn't touch it. Leo held up a cell phone, his gloved finger ready to touch instant dial.

"If I make this call," he said, "a duplicate envelope will be delivered to the Chicago police and another to your wife. Do you know what happens in prison to excrement like you?"

Grigsby tried to speak but could only stare.

Leo stood. "Find the monk." He walked away, followed by the entourage.

On the envelope the café au lait was spreading like a brown curse.

When Thomas realized their destination was Scotland, he called Munro's Pub in Edinburgh. Caddy Munro was still proprietor. Their friendship went back to the boyhood days when Thomas visited his grandfather. Caddy was elated when Thomas told him that he was coming to Scotland and asked him to find a cottage to rent outside the city.

TWIST OF TIME

In London, they leased a sport BMW, a stick with four in the floor; Kate felt vulnerable without power wheels. Pushing the speed limit, she terrified Thomas and oncoming vehicles by driving on the wrong side for long stretches, miraculously avoiding a wreck. It was night when they arrived at the pub to Caddy's boisterous greeting. They had not seen each other for two years, when Thomas had returned for his grandfather's funeral. Back then, over shots of unfiltered single malt scotch that was clear as water, Thomas told Caddy of Lois' death and his intention of becoming a monk. Now Thomas and Kate were enjoying the atmosphere of the cozy pub as he remembered the convivial camaraderie of having a pint and playing darts with the locals. Caddy appeared with a huge platter of fresh smoked salmon, chopped green onion, and oven-hot soda bread. They washed it down with tar-black stout.

When Kate went to the rest room, Caddy said, "If she's what you get when you become a monk, I'm ready t' take me vows. You want to tell me what is going on?"

"She's a homicide detective."

Caddy stared, stunned. "Tommy, only you could become a monk and then find a woman like that. You're doubly blessed—a Scot with Irish luck."

"There's nothing between us."

"There will be, sure as sin." Caddy grinned.

When Kate returned, Caddy who usually flirted with every female from seventeen to seventy, controlled himself. They would spend the night at Caddy's apartment over the pub where he lived alone. Kate slept in the guest room and Thomas cramped up on the sofa. Early the next morning they left for the village of Newkirk, where Caddy had found a place for them to rent.

To Kate, the cottage had the fantasy of a movie set. Built in the early eighteenth century and once a working estate, the fields and pastures had disappeared piecemeal into the devouring suburbs. A pitched roof with two gables completed its Disneyesque silhouette.

Inside, a brick fireplace tall as a standing man dominated the main room. The ceiling was low, the doorways narrow, and stairs leading up to the two bedrooms were one-person wide. Kate, spreading her arms, touched both walls of the narrow stairs.

"Why does everything seem so scaled down?" she said.

"Many Scots don't waste money on frills like comfort."

He watched her go through the rooms, pausing to look and touch. The furniture was sturdy oak and walnut and hadn't known wax or polish in over half a century. Above the fireplace was an ancient flintlock, black-thick with rust. A brass umbrella stand housed a handsome collection of antique briar shillelaghs. Shelves lining the fireplace were jammed with books. In the air there still lingered a trace of the last cozy fire.

"Thomas, it's magical."

They shared a look. This was becoming harder than either imagined.

After they settled in, Kate went to the village for groceries while Thomas worked on the diary. Brychan's narrative contained an unexpected surprise.

On my twenty-first birthday I was initiated as a Templar Knight in a ritual sealed by sacred vow. I only reveal some of it now to deny lies by the combined forces of King Philip of France and the Holy Office of the Inquisition that was presented at the Templar trials.

There have been false accusations that the ritual included denying Christ, spitting on the cross, and the giving oneself to un-natural acts of lust with brothers. I swear before Almighty God, that during my ordination none of this occurred.

Brychan described how he presented himself naked following a ritual bath in cold water. Afterward, he put on a white linen jupon, the same as knights wore over their armor, but without the Templar cross.

There followed a day of fasting and meditation, and that night he spent alone in the chapel in prayer vigil where he humbly offered self, soul, and sword to the service of God.

At dawn, in the presence of eleven brothers, the number of apostles after Judas betrayed our Lord, the Master himself performed the ceremony while Friar Luke read the ritual. Several days before, to my immense joy, a parcel arrived by courier from my brother Duncan in Scotland. It contained great-grandfather Andrew's Crusader sword with which he served King Richard Coeur de Lion. With this honored blade I was dubbed a Templar Knight.

BRYCHAN DID NOT write about the other item in the parcel. At first it appeared to be a sealed manuscript scroll. On its cover, written in Gaelic, he read, "*God's Grace be with thee, dear Brychan. Vivyan.*"

Brychan, picturing Vivyan's haunting beauty, said a prayer blessing her. He broke the seal and carefully unrolled a magnificent ink drawing of Vivyan's two-year-old son, Andrew. Drawn from life, it was the work of her brother Erin, a Benedictine monk, gifted artist, and manuscript illuminator.

Brychan kissed the drawing, for he realized that he would never embrace his son.

It was Thomas and Kate's first night in the cottage and they were determined to keep busy. Each set up a workspace: Kate on the dining table and Thomas across the room ensconced at an ancient pigeonhole desk.

"Thomas, how soon do you think we can actually start looking for the chest?"

He flipped through the remaining diary pages. "Three days. Maybe less."

"See this?" She held up a folder thick with documents. "The courier Denise Hollander's case file. Just so you know, getting Nora is my priority, chest or no chest."

"What's your plan?"

"In my scenario the diary leads us to the chest. You notify Fallon that you are ready to meet and give him the diary. That will draw Nora like flies to honey."

"How will she find out?"

"Nora somehow knows Fallon's every move. She was able to get sensitive information about his research. I believe that she is tapped into a leak. We will use the same leak. When you meet with Fallon, Nora will be as close as his shadow. So will I."

"Pretty smart, Kate."

"No. Desperate. How else can I explain being in Scotland using a seven-hundred-year-old diary to catch a killer in sunny Santa Barbara?"

Three hours later Kate closed her file. "I'm going to bed."

"I'll stick with it. I don't want to lose Brychan's train of thought."

She touched the diary, fingers tracing the scarred leather. "Thomas, by our following the diary, isn't Brychan actually directing what we do?"

TWIST OF TIME

"I had the very same thought." His hand touched hers. "Sleep well." He watched her go up the stairs and shut the door to her bedroom. It was several minutes before he was able to concentrate on the diary.

The scene Brychan described next must have happened immediately after he became a knight.

Though I have previously written of Brother Ursus, I feel compelled to explain how our first meeting led to our fateful mission from the Grand Master.

IN THE FIRST week of October 1307, after compline, the monks were returning to their cells. Brychan was called aside by Friar Luke.

"Follow me," he told Brychan. "Speak to no one."

In a torch's dancing shadows, the friar led the way down a narrow stone chasm. Like during his experience with Brother André, this winding stairwell plunged to even a greater descent into the womb of Mother Earth. It gave the term "Templar underground" a veritable meaning.

Finally the passage angled and beyond was an iron door lit by two torches. Two Templar Knights stood guard, swords drawn. When they recognized Friar Luke, one motioned for them to enter.

Inside, Brychan was astonished to find a chapter hall capable of holding several hundred knights. On the far wall hung a huge tapestry of two knights on the same charger: the Templar seal. Beneath it stood five men and, dominating the group, Novice Master Guy d'Orléans. Next to him was Master Din and, on a table between them, the VERITAS chest.

At one side, two sergeants attended a flaming brazier in which glowed hot irons. Even from the distance Brychan felt the heat.

Opposite Master Guy was an enormous man in full battle gear, the most formidable warrior Brychan had ever seen. The eyes piercing though the slits of the face guard were fixed on him.

Brychan saw from Brother Guy's position he was the ranking Templar. His usual learned tone was now more commanding.

"Brother Brychan, I order you to recall the vision you reported to Master Din a few days before you became a knight."

Brychan had been reluctant to speak of it, but the dream was so disturbing that he told Master Din, who reported it to Grand Master de Molay. An order came back from him: Watch; pray; be ready.

Brother Guy said, "Brother Brychan, I must personally hear your dream."

The sergeants at the brazier stopped working. All eyes were on him, including the giant who seemed never to blink. That look must have turned many a warrior's bowels to water.

"It was a dream," Brychan began, "not of sleep but of vision. They have a different feeling. There was a thick fog and the sound of a great warhorse. Then a charger appeared on which were two Templar Knights mounted double. The horse stopped and refused to move but they urged him on. He became entangled in a great mass of undergrowth, and the more he struggled, the deeper he sank. Both knights spurred him and he attempted to jump free. He fell and the vines writhing like ten thousand vipers smothered them all. The vines were fleurs de lis."

Brother Guy crossed himself. "Yours is the third vision we have heard. The first was Brother Alexi, the Slav. He saw two Templar Knights on the same horse beset by hounds black as Dominicans' robes. They were torn apart and their bodies devoured by fleurs de lis. Also, Miguel the Spaniard reported a vision: two Templars on one horse were all burning fire. They rolled on the ground to stop the flames, which became fleurs de lis, which then smothered them."

Brychan was surprised to hear of Miguel, who had disappeared several weeks ago. He feared to ask about him because of his premonition that the delicate Spaniard would not survive his apprenticeship.

His look did not escape Brother Guy. "Something else, Brother?"

"Miguel. I am worried about him."

"Brother Miguel is very ill. He has fallen into a coma. If he recovers, he will be taken back to Madrid. I am told that is unlikely."

"I will add him to my prayers."

"Best you include our entire Order. Two of our brothers have the gift of interpretation. According to them, the two knights on one horse are the Templar Order; the fleur de lis is obviously the sign of King Philip. He will attack us, God forgive him."

The men looked at each other in surprise—all but the big warrior, whose gaze was still fixed on Brychan.

Brother Guy continued. "As a result of these three visions, Grand Master de Molay has ordered that all our treasury in France immediately be transported to the Templar fleet at La Rochelle. The sacred manuscripts from Jerusalem are to be placed in nine coffers and sealed. They will be taken to secret locations." Master Guy indicated the VERITAS chest. "That is number nine. Because of its contents, it alone is marked VERITAS."

From beneath folds of his robe, Master Din produced a scroll on gold rods: the meditation discipline upon which Brychan had spent endless hours. With a solemn look at Brychan, he carefully placed it in the chest.

Brother Guy indicated the huge knight. "This is Brother Ursus. He is our ablest warrior and a Zealote."

Brychan did not know what Zealote meant. He only knew the similar term from scripture—Simon the Zealot, the most radical of the twelve disciples.

The two sergeants began sealing the VERITAS chest with the sizzle and smoke of molten lead. Brother Ursus looked from Brychan to the coffer. He seemed unaware that Master Guy was speaking about him.

"Brother Ursus has been guardian of the VERITAS coffer since the fall of fortress Acre. You, Brychan, will join Ursus as guardian. Take it to Holy Cross Cistercian abbey outside the city. Hide there until King Philip attacks or these visions are declared false." He gave a warning look. "Brother Brychan, if the King does not attack, your prophecy is false. According to Holy scripture, false prophets must be slain."

Brychan looked at Ursus; now he understood his stare. The slaying would be his to do.

Friar Luke moved to Brychan and presented a volume covered in leather and brass studs. "This diary has my poor jottings in the front portion. Guardians of the diary must write whatever happens to them. Now you must record your mission and all that transpires. In the back you will find ciphers and codes."

"Ciphers? I know little of numbers, Brother."

"Listen to him, knight!" The voice was Brother Ursus. Then he said in Gaelic, "Listen and remember his words."

Ursus was a Scot!

Friar Luke handed Brychan a folded parchment. "This is the key for unlocking the codes. Memorize and destroy it."

In the past Brychan had struggled vainly with numbers. Moreover, when Friar Luke tried to explain to him the movement of earth around the sun, it was blasphemous! Didn't the Church teach that the sun moved around the earth? Friar Luke was quoting from heathen Arab writings. But for his devout reputation and great learning, he would have been burned for heresy.

Friar Luke continued. "The ciphers are for our banking in France,

TWIST OF TIME

England, Spain, and Italy where vast sums are kept. The codes access these accounts."

"Now you must go," Sir Guy ordered.

Ursus kneeled before the chest. Brychan, uncertain, awkwardly did the same. Friar Luke said a brief prayer in Latin.

Brychan saw Ursus' hand resting on the coffer, then watched his finger tracing a deep scar cut into it like an iron wound. Previously, when Brychan asked Master Din about the mark, he was told only that it happened at Acre.

FIFTEEN YEARS EARLIER in March of 1297, Acre, the last Crusader stronghold in the Holy Land, was under siege. A walled city of some 80,000 souls, it was the very last fortress. With its back to the Mediterranean, the massively engineered walls had endured many sieges and changed sides many times. Once again it was in Crusader hands.

Now after only forty days, Acre was falling to a great Marmaluke army equipped with two hundred siege engines. Two of them were the largest ever built. Named Furious and Victorious, each required a hundred pairs of oxen to move into place. They dwarfed even the great Roman war machines that had not been surpassed for nearly a thousand years.

Templar Grand Master William Beaujeu was in charge of Acre's defense. Though there were Crusaders serving under various dukes and a contingent of Knight Hospitallers, the main force defending it were Templars.

The day and night bombardment of shattering boulders and the undermanned defensive positions allowed for small Saracen raiding parties to slip inside. Soon the walls would be breached and over 200,000 Saracens would overwhelm the defending 800 Templar Knights and 16,000 foot soldiers. Their defeat was certain.

Sultan al-Ashraf Khalil, the Marmaluke leading the Saracens, had vowed to destroy Acre and rid the land of the Franks, which is what the Muslims called all Crusaders. That it was now a Templar fortress was especially fitting, for they were the most hated and equally respected. While other captured nobles were ransomed, Templars were usually beheaded. Saracens did not want to fight them again.

Ursus was thirty-three years old when he arrived at Acre and had served in the Holy Land for ten years. In that time, he earned a fierce reputation, and due to his great size and Scot's red hair, Saracens called him Aldubu al'Ahmar—the Red Bear.

When the Templar rallying call came, Ursus responded though he knew Acre was doomed. Since the beginning of the siege, nearly 20,000 citizens had managed to flee by boat from the seaward side, leaving 60,000 still trapped in the city. They were but days from capture.

Ursus and three knights were riding with Grand Master William Beaujeu down a winding street leading to the back of the Templar Church. It had temporarily served to house the treasury, books, and scrolls. Just a week before, everything was shipped to Crete. Only a single chest remained: the VERITAS chest that every Templar Grand Master kept with him.

As the four knights came on the square, they encountered six mounted Saracens. Both groups were surprised; a confused fight began. Four Saracen cavalry attacked while their two mounted archers released a flurry of arrows.

Master Beaujeu was pierced under the left arm. With a defiant roar, he pulled the arrow out, then fell from his horse.

Two Saracens broke off fighting to finish him.

Ursus charged, overtaking the two from the rear. He plunged his sword into the back of the first Saracen, who tumbled taking the sword with him. Ursus leaped from his charger, sending the second Saracen and horse rolling to the ground. A single blow of his mace finished the Saracen.

When Ursus reached Master William, he was alive but deathly pale. Two knights joined them; the third had fallen with the Saracens.

Ursus could see that William was dying. "Take him to the church," he said.

The Master raised his hand with two fingers extended, indicating a direct order. "You must take the VERITAS chest to Cyprus."

When Ursus tried to protest, William gasped, "Obey!"

They carried Master William into the church, where he died on his shield.

URSUS WAS LUGGING the VERITAS chest through a twisting warren of rubble-littered alleys. The coffer was designed as a two-man carry but Ursus' size and great strength made it appear to have been fashioned particularly for him. Working his way through deserted houses and back streets, he continued toward the Templar preceptory where a hidden underground tunnel led to the docks. A sergeant had been sent ahead to hold the last boat for him.

He turned onto a street to see a lone Saracen eating a melon at the stall of an Italian fruit vender he had just slain. The Saracen swung his blade. Ursus blocked it with the iron chest, but the blade cut a gash in it. Before the soldier could strike again, Ursus slammed the coffer in his gut, dropped the chest, and seized him by the neck. A shriek locked in the Saracen's throat as his windpipe snapped and he was thrown rolling to the ground. Ursus picked up the coffer and continued on to the wharf.

The bay water was a swirl of bodies and debris as oarsmen pulled the boat away. Ursus watched a great column of red and black smoke billowing from behind the city walls. Most of its

60,000 helpless survivors would be slaughtered, the rest sold into slavery.

Ursus later heard what chroniclers from both sides reported: on the last day Saracen and Crusaders were mingled in a fierce fight at the center of the city. In a final irony, the great central tower, weakened by catapult and fire, collapsed, crushing warriors from both armies.

Acre had fallen, ending two hundred years of the Crusades. ✝

Thomas put down the diary when he sensed Kate's presence. He looked up the stairs; she was standing in her bedroom doorway watching him, her sheer nightgown forming teasing shadows.

All good intentions faded in a single moment. He came up the stairs and when they kissed, both were trembling. She took his hand, led him into the bedroom, and closed the door.

Afterward, they lay in the dark, still holding each other. Neither spoke; words were meaningless.

Finally, she sighed, and said, "Well, you certainly haven't forgotten how."

CHAPTER ELEVEN

When Fallon received the Bulldogs' report that they lost Thomas in Paris, instead of being angry, he was elated. Thomas' disappearing with the diary meant that he discovered something tremendously important. That Kate was involved confirmed it. From Fallon's Templar research there were only three countries where Brychan would have taken the chest. Since Fallon already had his Bulldogs in France, he added two teams, one in Spain and another in Germany, where he had his strongest contacts. Within sixteen hours all his two-man teams were working round the clock with a hundred-thousand-dollar prize to the team that found them.

At Homicide, Vicky Marroquin was sitting at Kate's desk reviewing the CSI photos where Hollander's body was found. She did this re-checking from habit. Three years earlier on a complex case, she spotted a detail previously missed, which became key evidence in rendering a guilty verdict.

Kate's phone rang. "Yes," said Vicky.

"This is Dr. Fallon. Who are you?"

"Detective Sgt. Marroquin."

"Where is Detective Flynn?"

"On sick leave."

"Sorry to hear that. Nothing serious, I trust."

"Female plumbing."

"I would have bet she didn't have any." There was a nasty chuckle.

Vicky gritted her teeth. "Is there something I can help you with, Doctor?"

"Yes. Any news on the Denise Hollander homicide? I assume you are covering for Detective Flynn since you are answering her phone."

"There's nothing new to report."

"A difficult case, I imagine." His tone was slimy as mucus. "Please give Ms. Flynn my sincere wishes for a speedy recovery."

"Certainly, asshole," she said, and hung up, relishing the insult. The bastard didn't believe her; he was not even surprised. She dialed Kate's burner phone and left a message that Fallon called and did not buy their story. Now what would he do?

Thomas was sitting at the kitchen table watching early dawn light filter through the windows. Kate was deep asleep when he slipped from the bed.

His first thought on wakening was surprise; he did not feel guilty about having made love to Kate. Guilt should come naturally. You didn't have to go looking for it. Sweet Jesus! Couldn't he do anything right? Because he did not feel guilty did not mean that he wasn't. He was so mesmerized by what happened that he was unable to think beyond the present moment.

He made coffee and, though reluctant, began his morning novice discipline. During their first year all novices began each day with the Inquisition exercise. He must review why he chose to become a monk; question every thought; confront every doubt. Abbot Methodius had cautioned against making a decision about a vocation during any stressful period, yet Thomas became a novice shortly after a career scandal, the bitter shock of infidelity and the tragedy of Lois' death. He seemed incapable of following rules, a dangerous trait for a monk.

He thought back to when he first heard of the Anglican Celtic Order. The media had given unwelcome coverage to the psychic controversy about his Merlin book. He was surprised when he received a letter from the order supporting his use of the psychic for research. Included was historical material on two famed nineteenth-century archeologists, the English Frederick Bligh Bond and the Italian Umberto di Grazia. Each man had claimed a paranormal connection leading to their own extraordinary discoveries. Thomas found the order's letter comforting at an extremely difficult time. Later when he decided to become a monk, the ACO was the first he examined. It followed some practices of the early Celtic church and did not consider the psychic either heresy or Satanic, but a gift from God. Many of the first converts to the Celtic church were Druids where the paranormal was a commonly accepted part of life.

After he became a novice monk, he found himself hoping for a sign that he had made the right choice. Ironically, it came in the unlikely person of Fallon. His offer to pay the order for Thomas' translation of the diary seemed a unique opportunity to use his gift to serve God. But before he could even begin, the courier Hollander was murdered and he met Kate.

When he finished the Inquisition exercise, he wrote the required summary: *I confess that I am a novice monk who used another man's two-million-dollar property without his permission. I am involved in a murderous intrigue. I have had sex and have possibly fallen in love with a woman."* It was the worst summary ever submitted in the long history of the order.

Thomas looked up to see Kate standing in the kitchen doorway watching him.

"I was afraid it might be gone," she said.

"What would?"

"That hungry look. After the way I slept, I may never let you out of my sight." She indicated the diary. "Absolutely nothing stops you, does it?"

"Actually, I was thinking about us. Kate, this is . . ."

Her fingers touched his lips. "Please, *please* don't spoil it by analyzing."

He didn't. He pulled her on to his lap. It was another hour before he returned to the diary.

In the conference room at his laboratory, Fallon was checking the GOLEM readouts as doctors Lizerand and Meyer watched. Since achieving interface with GOLEM, Longrieve's precognition tests showed an increased efficiency of seven percent.

"It's working," Fallon said as he puffed a cigar in satisfaction.

"But fatal if it continues." Dr. Lizerand held up a handful of printouts. "These are latest on Herb's body functions."

"Summarize, Doctor."

"The seven-percent efficiency increase has cost Herb an overall drop in his vital readings. His blood, kidney, and liver enzymes are highly abnormal."

"Deteriorating even faster than we predicted," Meyer said.

Fallon nodded; he saw it coming. "The Cayce syndrome. When Edgar Cayce increased his psychic readings to help more people, his health suffered severely."

"Cayce!" Meyer bristled. "I'm a scientist, Dr. Fallon. I know nothing of the psychic because it does not exist. Longrieve's so-called psychic ability is simply his hyper-normal ability to concentrate. He could stand on burning coals and it would not waver."

"I agree with Meyer," Dr. Lizerand cautiously added.

Fallon was surprised. "You think I selected Longrieve only for his ability to concentrate?"

"Are you saying there is some psychic agenda?"

"Yes, but not as you dimly understand it. Accurate prophecies are in every culture. There should not be any, yet they exist! And there is supporting medical data. Proven psychics have abnormal levels of melatonin. Longrieve's is triple the norm. There is nothing mystical! All the mumbo-jumbo, voodoo, and rituals are simply exercises that focus the psychic's concentration. With GOLEM we will greatly improve that."

"GOLEM is a goddamn computer!" Lizerand shouted. "How can there be some psychic integration?"

Fallon turned to Meyer. "Doctor, you have been tinkering with Longrieve's brain. What would happen if he were conditioned with a psychic discipline? Could GOLEM access it through him?"

"I don't see why not."

Fallon smiled. "Which would then add a psychic element to a supercomputer."

"How do you know that this psychic discipline even exists?" Meyer challenged.

"GOLEM discovered it three years ago."

After showering, Kate slipped into an exquisite silk kimono, a gift years ago to her mother from the Tokyo police department in honor of Kate's father. She curled on the sofa and opened her laptop. Thomas was working at his desk. She was looking for connections between the Pullman and Hollander homicides. The material was growing stale—a perfect setup to miss something important. "Thomas, I need a break. Is there anything I could help you with?"

"Lord, yes. Would you search the Internet for clan histories, find the Houston family, and check their archives? We're looking for a letter Brychan wrote to his mother. Though it was not translated, Fallon scanned a copy to have forensic graphologists compare it with the handwriting in the diary. Brychan wrote both. Fallon was going to have me translate the letter after I finished the diary. But now I need to read that letter, wherever it is."

While Kate began searching Scotch heritage websites, Thomas returned to Brychan's narrative.

After winter's heavy snows, spring brought great floods that destroyed many bridges. The old piper's family had crossed the upper Seine and would know the best place to cross. Though the father spoke only the Breton dialect, his daughter Alva the harpist also spoke French.

✠ BRYCHAN FOUND THE harpist to be a tiny waif with huge bright eyes. After he asked where they had crossed the Seine, instead of answering, Alva baited him.

"I will tell you only if you first tell me something," she said.

"What is that?"

"Everyone is talking. Some say you are a priest running away with the Gypsy. The huge one, from his singing, must be a bard. But others say you all are merely thieves."

"Which tale do you believe, little one?"

"You and the Gypsy, of course."

"And if I deny it, would you still believe me?"

She shook her head.

"Then, believe what you will, but do not say that I admitted anything. Now tell me where you crossed the Seine."

"First, a bargain."

"Bargain?"

"Take me with you," she pleaded. "I can play harp for your bard. I know many songs, and I can learn his and teach him mine. I can even be his woman."

Brychan laughed, picturing Ursus' reaction. "How old are you, girl?"

"Fifteen. My sister already had two childer by then."

"You want to run away with two thieves and a Gypsy?"

"Oh, yes! Yes! Last autumn a troubadour asked me to go away with him. He said we would play before many lords and ladies."

"Why didn't you?"

"My father set the dogs on him."

"You want me chased by dogs?"

"No. But am I not pleasing to you?"

"Alva! You must not offer yourself to . . . ." But who was he to lecture anyone? "You would be in constant danger. Now tell me where you crossed the Seine."

He was the one she wanted but she dare not show it. "The bridge at Liége is washed away. We went south to the old miller's bridge at Calvière crossing."

Brychan held out his hand, revealing a gold besant. "For your dowry."

Her eyes widened. She had seen but never touched one. When she took it, he folded his hand over hers.

"Promise you will stay with your family." He squeezed her hand. "Promise?"

She nodded quickly. But she knew that unless God showed her otherwise, it was a promise she would not keep.

FATHER PIERRE WAS traveling south on the road to Avignon after leaving the Templars the night before. Failing to find a peasant's hut, he had spent a miserable wet night in the rough. Worse, he must prepare himself to report his failure to the Holy Father. Pope Clement, though French, demanded much from his Inquisition agents. Pierre could expect no leniency.

He reined his palfrey to stop. Approaching around a turn were five riders; the leader was obviously a knight. His cloak bore a red chevron: a sherif. God was favoring him!

Sherif Gilbert saw a man in Dominican black with an assortment of horses, three carrying combat harness and tack. That he traveled without protective escort was most unusual.

After exchanging greetings, Father Pierre presented credentials with Papal seals. He told what had occurred with the two Templars and that they stole a chest he was personally delivering to Pope Clement.

The sherif feared that the Inquisition might be involved. The priest showed documents with a Papal seal: authority equal to the King's. That Gilbert could not read did not matter; the beribboned Papal seals were enough.

Pierre explained that the Pope's letter gave him full authority to enlist help to recover the chest. He added that in addition to gold payment there was also papal preferment; special indulgences would be granted.

With a lifetime heavy with sins and the prospect of many more to come, Sir Gilbert found this as tempting as the money—almost.

Pierre raged. "The Templars are possessed by Satan himself! They have taken up with a Gypsy witch! In our company were two veteran cavalry and four Papal knights! Two Templars killed five of the six!"

"Only two Templars? How?"

"They were bewitched by the Gypsy! Naked as Babylon's whore, she cast a spell on them. They were cut down like wheat. The two Templars escaped scart-free with 'naer a wound."

Sir Gilbert had done his share of campaigning. He saw that there was more strategy than witchcraft in the Templars' attack. After questioning further, he understood: a diversion in front by the woman, a surprise assault in their rear. Besides, these were Zealotes. On horse, the two could have beaten all six without the help of a naked woman. In his own troop were four veteran cavalrymen. Against two Zealotes, they would be quickly defeated.

"Father Pierre, where are the Templars going?"

"La Rochelle. I heard them discuss the route."

"Which way?"

"North by west."

"First, I must see the Baron de Ville."

"No! We must continue the pursuit!"

"Priest, you have five dead! I found eight rotting bandits and a day later, four of the King's cavalry cut to pieces—all the work of these two Templars. You will use your papal authority to order the Baron de Ville to help us!"

"Ask for more soldiers?"

"No. Archers."

Pierre saw that the sherif could not be persuaded. "Where is the Baron de Ville?"

"Saint Cyr."

IN THE VILLAGE, word spread quickly of the arrival of the sherif's soldiers and a priest. Pilgrims immediately flocked to Father Pierre for confession. With Lent only three days past, there was already much to confess. Everyone wanted to arrive at the holy shrines with sins shriven. Father Pierre set up an outside confessional where he sat on a bench as each confessor kneeled beside him.

At the inn, Gilbert drank deep, wiped his mouth on his sleeve, and belched loudly. Roland nodded appreciatively at the compliment on his mead. They were at table; the room was empty of people save for two servants.

Three times a year, the sherif passed through Saint Cyr, where custom demanded that he call on the Baron de Ville. He always stayed at the inn. Roland did not suspect that his neglected wife, starved for attention, found comfort with the rugged sherif, who took his pleasure where he found it.

"This is not your usual time to visit, Sir Gilbert," Roland observed. "Why so early?"

"Templars. Two fugitives and a Gypsy whore."

Roland's flagon stopped midway to his mouth. "Then they *were* Templars!" He laughed. "The big one stank of the Crusades. God save me, I was right!"

"Bide they here?"

"Left this morning. Even before they could drink a stirrup dram for journey's luck."

"Where did they go?"

"Truth, I cannot say. But they spent time with the Breton family. I saw the young Templar talking with the peasant girl who plays the harp."

FATHER PIERRE WAS hearing the confession of the village smith, who was mumbling a pathetic tale of lust for his boy apprentice, when Sir Gilbert interrupted.

"The Templars were here; they left this morning."

"Where are they?"

"A Breton family knows."

"I just gave an old Breton confession. I could hardly understand him."

"Find him and question a girl harpist."

"Yes. After I finish th—"

Gilbert jerked him to his feet. "Now, fool!"

Father Pierre turned to the blacksmith and made a hurried sign of the cross, absolving him of all sins. Before the blacksmith got halfway to the stable, despite his confession and a waning will, he was anticipating seeing the apprentice.

"YOU WANT TWO of my archers?" Baron de Ville asked.

"Yes, your Lordship," Gilbert answered with a slight bow of his head. "The best and quickest. But not crossbows. Awblasters take too long to reload."

The Baron sat behind the great table in his manor hall—their usual meeting place. "And they are fugitive Templars?"

"Aye. One wields a mighty blade. A warrior of most passing prowess."

"Then why do you ask for only two archers?"

"My Lord, we will be pursuing at night. Our company is four cavalry and a priest. Two expert archers will allow us to keep a goodly pace. More men at night will slow us."

The Baron considered; most men would have asked for a dozen archers. The sherif for all his swazz and swagger knew his craft. "How much will you pay?"

Gilbert presented Father Pierre's beribboned letter. "The Dominican is emissary for His Holiness Pope Clement. This authorizes recruitment of men and supplies." Casually he added, "I suspect the Inquisition is involved."

The Baron choked on his wine in mid-gulp. The Holy Office—he wanted no problems there. "What else do you need?"

"Fresh horses—your best. No expense must be spared on the Holy Father's business."

FATHER PIERRE FOUND Goulu the Breton and his daughter Alva among their camp of relatives. He took them aside and began questioning. He fixed the girl with a stern gaze, copying the ruthless interrogators he had observed during Inquisition trials.

Alva met his brusqueness with dumb silence.

The old piper nervously glanced at the cavalryman accompanying the priest. The trooper had one empty eye socket and the shattered remains of a hideous face cleaved by a battle-axe that he had miraculously survived.

Pierre turned from the girl to the old man. "The Templars travel with a Gypsy witch—a venial sin. They have stolen a diary that belongs to Mother Church—a mortal sin. They have killed to keep what they stole—a deadly sin." Pierre pointed accusingly at Goulu and shouted, "And it is even a greater sin to protect enemies of the Holy Father!"

Alva was remembering Brychan's gift of the gold besant for a dowry she did not have. So, he was not a priest—no priest would be so generous. She would not reveal the gift lest it confirm him a thief. "He only asked me where we crossed the Seine."

"Where was that?" Pierre asked the old man.

The piper's accent was thick as Breton cheese. "The bridge at Calvière."

BRYCHAN, URSUS, AND Sara, having ridden hard all day through rain and mud-mired roads, made early camp. With a dawn start they would reach Calvière crossing before midday.

While the three slept, Sherif Gilbert, with cavalrymen, two archers, and a lagging priest rode by torchlight throughout the cold moonless night. ✝

Kate, in searching for Brychan's letter to his mother, located the small Caithness Archive Museum in Edinburgh on a narrow backstreet. The museum's purpose was to collect histories and documents of clans devastated in the battle of Culloden Moor in 1746. Some families were so decimated they never gathered again as clans. Among them were the Howisteans, Brychan's clan. What remained of their family records, tartans, and trophies were housed in the Caithness museum.

Thomas phoned the curator, Cornelius Higgins. He mentioned that his grandfather was the Celtic scholar and author Dr. Andrew MacLaird. Higgins instantly warmed and they made an appointment for that afternoon.

The building was a nineteenth-century brick manor house in a grim neighborhood whose better days were a century past. Inside, Thomas and Kate found heavy dark paneling and mismatched odds of shabby furniture. The walls were covered with an array of framed tartans, some marked with black stains of ancient blood. On the walls were etchings of clan chiefs and engravings of battles all but forgotten outside Scotland.

Cornelius Higgins, in his seventies, was wizened and bald, with stray wisps of white fringe. In his cluttered office they were served an excellent gourmet tea. Higgins was instantly smitten with Kate. When he left the room to get a book, Thomas muttered, "Just what we need, a horny curator."

"I think he's sweet," Kate purred.

Higgins returned with a volume titled *Roots of The Celtic Church in The Early Christian Era,* personally autographed, which he proudly read aloud. "To Cornelius Higgins, with scholarly respect, Andrew MacLaird." The curator added, "It is your grandfather's first edition."

Thomas asked, "Considering the dazzling title, are you surprised there was never a second?"

After tea, Higgins led them down a musty corridor lined with book-cluttered shelves and the aura of the ghosts of ancient clansmen. The hall ended at a small conference room where Higgins had prepared a display of the Houston clan, Brychan's ancestors. On the library table was the yellowed page of a genealogy tree and a large piece of tartan blackened with stains of blood. Framed beside it was the Houston crest: two greyhounds, each rampant at either side of a gold shield. Beneath an hourglass was the family motto: "In Time." Next to it was a safe deposit box and a long bundle wrapped in a woolen cover.

"The Houston family," Higgins said. "Their lands were within a few hours travel to Edinburgh. Before you examine the letter, may I show you our museum's finest treasure?"

Thomas brightened. "Please. I'd very much like to see it."

Higgins removed the wool cover revealing an ancient sword miraculously unmarred by rust, dent, or stain. "It belonged to Lord Andrew Howistean, the clan patriarch. He served with King Richard the Lionhearted."

Thomas' heart skipped. Brychan's sword: physical evidence that he had returned to Scotland. It was no longer speculation from a single line in the diary.

Higgins handed the sword to Thomas, who hefted it with boyish delight.

"Now the letter." Higgins opened the safe deposit box and removed a clear plastic folder. Inside was a single page of a worn parchment; the bottom was missing.

Thomas examined it through the plastic. "What is its provenance?"

"There is no date. Dating of personal letters came later. The bottom of the page where the signature would be is missing. It is addressed in Middle English to 'The most Gracious Lady Gwynn of Houston, clan Howistean.' The rest is in Medieval Gaelic and believed to be written by her son, Brychan."

Thomas instantly recognized the handwriting but asked, "How can you be certain that Brychan wrote it?"

Higgins referred to the genealogy tree. "Lady Gwynn had two sons," he said. "Duncan the eldest and Brychan. Duncan inherited both lands and title. He married and had a child, Andrew. Brychan, a second son without title, presumably entered the Church. Which explains no offspring."

"Why does that mean he wrote the letter?" Kate asked.

"Duncan, like many of the nobility, was illiterate. Brychan, as a cleric, was the logical person to have written it. After that, Brychan disappears from the family history."

Thomas quickly scanned the letter. "Could you make me a copy of this? I'll trade you a copy of my translation."

"Done!" Higgins agreed. "Do you have any idea what the letter concerns?"

Thomas glanced at Kate, trying to suppress his excitement. "It appears to be a farewell letter to his mother. Written before a battle."

"What battle?"

"He does not say. But this part," said Thomas as he pointed to a line, "is quite clear—'a battle in which I know I will not survive.'" His eyes met Kate's. "Brychan predicted his own death."

It was growing dark as they drove back to the cottage.

"It's incredible, Thomas—Brychan predicted his death?"

"It's called the seer's curse. Both Nostradamus and Merlin did, too." Thomas was still trying to fit everything together. "Brychan is known only as a second son. There is no record that he was a Templar. How was all that lost?"

"Brychan was a fugitive on the run and carrying something very valuable. He covers his tracks and Templar identity so well he disappears from the family history."

Thomas was amazed. "And for centuries fooled everyone. But *how* did he do it?"

Burns and Sawyer's black BMW was safely following a half-mile behind. When Kate and Thomas arrived at the cottage, Burns and Sawyer parked a block away and watched them go inside.

Burns dialed his cell phone. "They just left the museum. Staying at a cottage about an hour from Edinburgh."

"Excellent," Fallon answered.

"How did you know they would be at a museum?"

"In Paris they disappeared. My people found no trace of them in Spain or Germany. Eventually Thomas would have to go to Edinburgh, to translate a document at the museum as part of our agreement. Fortunately, you got there ahead of them."

"Then why wait? Let us go in, kick ass, and take the diary."

"Who would translate it? You? You can't do the Times crossword." He didn't want to discuss particulars over the phone. "Thomas Bardsey knows more than anyone where the chest might be. When he finds it, then you move. Understand?"

"Yes, sir."

"Lose him and you lose your fat contract." He hung up.

For several minutes Fallon sat motionless, concentrating as if reading an opponent's chess moves. There had to be a reason other than the museum letter for Thomas to change direction and suddenly go to Scotland. Obviously, that was where the diary led him. Against all logic, the chest was in Scotland.

CHAPTER TWELVE

Brother Simon awoke late again. Always an early riser, his sleep patterns were changing for no apparent reason. He had missed prime, the first daily office, but because of his age and poor health he had not been disturbed.

That morning he found a spot of blood on the pillow from either his nose or ears. Another organ about to fail—what was another symptom, more or less? He did not call the doctor.

Normally he slept well for a man his age; now his sleep was blighted with confused dreams laden with conflict. A constant ringing in his ears, tinnitus, had returned—probably an allergy reaction to his numerous medications. Most disturbing was another sound, a number repeated over and over like an irritating jingle. It would come and go, totally beyond his control.

The ultimate terror—losing his mental faculties. His wasted body, maintained by a dozen medications, was almost past concern. His mind was where he still lived.

He desperately needed to talk with Brother Thomas, who had been in hiding since his escape. Anxiety aggravated Simon's condition and Thomas' abduction seemed to intensify his symptoms.

Like a mutating virus: if it lost one source, it fed on another part of the same host.

Inexplicably, at that instant, there came the string of seven numbers, like a partial equation. Soon he feared that he would be an idiot savant, able to recite pi to a thousand digits but not remember the same oatmeal breakfast he ate every morning.

He desperately needed to talk with Thomas before his faculties deteriorated further.

"All I know about your Merlin book is from the tabloids. I want to hear it from you," Kate said.

"You'll think you're in bed with a lunatic."

"Great! I've never screwed a lunatic." Kate snuggled against the solid press of his weight. She was learning something of sexual obsession and eagerly indulged it. "Tell me about your Merlin."

"My Merlin . . ." He hunched back against the pillows. "Historically, there really was a sixth-century genius called Merlin. There are authentic writings by him. Written in verse, he made predictions and prophecies, many of which came true."

"Like Nostradamus?"

"Except hundreds of years earlier. Many experts believe the legendary King Arthur's Merlin was based on this fifth century seer. Others link his writings to Bishop Dubricius, a Celtic church saint of the same period. My thesis attempted to prove that Merlin led a double life as Saint Dubricius."

"A saint with a double life? There may be hope for me yet. How did your book get you in trouble?"

"Stupidity. In my psychic experiments, I had used a Celtic wizard's meditation device called the awen. I decided to try it on the Merlin research. After a week of intense meditation, I had the same dream three nights in a row."

"About Merlin?"

"No. About a seventh-century document written by a Celtic monk named Penda of Iona. I dreamed that I found it. Penda wrote that one of the monks of his order was present at the death of Bishop Dubricius, who confessed that he had lived a double life."

"How did that happen?"

"The Celtic church and the Roman church had just combined, and Rome was deciding which Celtic saints would be included with theirs. Penda knew the Dubricius-Merlin connection and wrote a letter to the Pope protesting that Dubricius not be included as a saint because as Merlin, he was guilty of heresy, sorcery, and witchcraft."

"Before receiving last rites, did Dubricius admit he was Merlin?"

"No. But he did not deny it, leaving it open to question. There were striking similarities. Each was born to a woman who was raped, had a child, and became a nun. Both men were gifted healers. Both were linked to King Arthur. Bishop Dubricius crowned him; Merlin fought beside him and was his chief advisor. And finally, Merlin and Dubricius died on the same day during an eclipse of the sun. Two men, same legends. But it all makes sense if both were the same man."

"But why would Bishop Dubricius need a double life?"

"His gift, precognition. Back then the Roman church considered it sorcery. But Dubricius was from the Celtic church. He believed it was one of God's gifts, like healing. As Merlin, he was obligated to use it to help others. And he did. He lived long enough to become counselor to five kings."

"What was Penda's connection to all this?"

"His letter to the pope requesting that Dubricius not be considered a saint because as Merlin, he was guilty of heresy. The document I found was part of that letter proving both were the same man."

"How did you find the letter?"

"Penda was a known Celtic writer, so I concentrated on libraries and colleges with the largest Celtic church material. I discovered it at Saint Dennis Divinity in north Scotland. It was a single page of vellum written in Latin. I made photocopies and wrote my Merlin book."

"What went wrong?"

"Academics are notoriously jealous. Some questioned its authenticity. But I had done the usual lab tests, x-rays, infrared, spectra, and chem analysis. Unfortunately, the letter I found was the work of a notorious eighteenth-century forger named Chignon who used it in a scam of his own. I was fooled like everybody else. But I was accused of covering this up to protect my book sales. I couldn't reveal my psychic connection of discovering Penda without casting further doubt among my academic peers. I could only plead an honest mistake, which it was. The academic committee didn't buy it."

"And then your wife was killed?"

"That finished me. I withdrew from the academic dogfight and was discredited." He looked at her and shyly smiled. "Now you know my dark secret."

"Baby." She sweetly kissed his mouth. "Dull, you're not."

After Kate was asleep, he lay awake, their conversation still churning. He went to the desk and opened the diary. For some time, he had felt an uneasiness about the translating. Once more he compared the diary pages with Brychan's letter to his mother.

Then, he saw it—the capital "B." It was the same as in the diary and in the letter he wrote to her. He looked at his own written notes. All three letter Bs were the same. And 700 years later, there's his handwritten B, the same as Brychan's as if no time had passed.

Could he have unconsciously copied the B while translating? He had written his name, Bardsey, thousands of times and though signatures did modify over time, there was hardly the slightest change in the B. All three were nearly identical.

Reincarnation? He had dismissed the idea before. A bit shaken, he returned to the diary determined not to think about it for the present.

Brychan's narration had switched to verse; he often was inspired to write a short rhyme about God or courtly love. Thomas usually scanned it and moved on, but this was different. Brychan had forced an iambic meter: ten beats per line on the first four, eight beats on the last two. Why the difference this time? Thomas worked out a rough rhyme in English to get the verse feeling.

As Joseph came to England's misty shore
To preach and hide the cup and crown he bore
So we two come and in his steps abide
A sacred treasure in this place to hide
As Joseph's legends so begot
I cast myself with Joseph's lot.

The next morning, he read it to Kate.

"What does it mean?" she asked.

"Joseph coming to England to preach has to be the same Joseph who placed Jesus' body in his tomb."

"And the cup is the Holy Grail?"

"It must be."

"What is the crown?"

"Jesus' crown of thorns. Legend says he brought that too."

She read the next line. "'So we two come and in his steps abide.' Who? Brychan and Ursus?"

"They fit. And 'in his steps abide' must refer to Joseph's steps because, like him, they have come on a mission. As Joseph hid the grail cup, they are hiding the chest."

"But what does 'Joseph's legends so begot' mean?"

"Not clear. And, 'cast myself with Joseph's lot' could be either 'lot' as in his fate, or a grave plot. Brychan loves double meanings. Joseph traditionally is connected with his own tomb where he placed Jesus' body. Since Brychan predicted his death, 'cast myself with Joseph's lot'. . ."

"Could refer to Brychan's own grave?"

"Yes, like when he wrote in Middle English. 'Before the cross three warriors stand, guarding the last of our band.' Obviously the three warriors would have to be statues instead of actual people. You might find statues before a cross in a church or a burial crypt. There are literally thousands of Celtic crosses all over Great Britain."

"Where do we start?"

"The tourist bureau; historic sites."

"What happens if we locate the tomb?" she asked.

"We have to take a look inside."

"Which is probably a felony. Let's hope he's not buried in Westminster Abbey."

From Nora's description, Ravel was able to spot Sawyer. He was coming out of MacNaughton's chemist's shop in downtown Edinburgh. Sawyer got in his car, where another man waited, obviously Burns.

Ravel followed as they tailed the monk and cop for the rest of the day. Watching them, he assessed their skills. Better at surveillance, they might use muscle if necessary but were more comfortable with photography, wiretaps, and computers. From long experience he could see if they attempted wet work, it was not their style. He would not need additional manpower to deal with them.

Kate sat at a dining table cluttered with tour brochures they had picked up that day. "I hope I soon get a feel for this stuff. I don't connect with anything here."

"Keep at it, Kate. Life isn't long enough to search all the wilds of Scotland."

He returned to Brychan's description where they had reached the upper Seine to make their crossing.

Though we could not see beyond the hill, we heard the rush of the flood-swollen Seine. Brother Ursus, riding ahead on point, stopped. I have written before of his astonishing ability to sense danger. He had that look now. I listened but heard nothing unusual.

"WHAT IS IT, Brother?" Brychan asked.

Ursus, still listening, turned Dragon into the gusting wind sending their spoor in the opposite direction. "Horses."

Brychan and Sara watched as he rode back up the rise from which they had come. When Ursus motioned, Brychan rode up the hill to join him. In the distance, breaking the far hillcrest, were seven mounted soldiers. An eighth rider was struggling to keep up.

Ursus pointed. "The lagging one rides like a woman. Does he seem familiar?"

"Who is it?"

"The Dominican I didn't skin." He looked back at the bridge. "We'll make a stand on the other side."

Brychan silently cursed for letting the priest go. He turned Joshua and galloped back toward Sara, motioning for her to ride on to the bridge.

Ursus delayed a moment to study the approaching horsemen. They must have seen him for they suddenly increased their speed.

When Brychan first saw Calvière Bridge, he was surprised that it had withstood the swift flood. Built from rough timber, it was narrow with uncertain footing due to frequent repairs. Just wide enough for a single team of oxen or horses, the crossing could only be made by man or beast at a walk.

The three slowly crossed in single file. Below, the churning flood pounded the pilings, causing the whole structure to shudder.

When halfway across, Ursus stopped and dismounted.

"Brother Ursus, even you cannot hold here against seven. We must cross over and take a stand there."

"Archers." Ursus's teeth clinched the hated word.

"Then it will take both of us."

"Two cannot beat them on open ground. But here, one can delay." He pressed Brychan's arm. "You must carry out the Master's charge."

"No!"

"You are sworn," Ursus reminded him. There was no more to say. From the weapons packhorse he removed his rolled mail coat.

Brychan looked up the hill where the troops would soon appear. Their mission now hung on a single dreadful decision. "Brother Ursus, we must stay together!"

Ignoring him, Ursus continued dressing for combat. He slipped on the hauberk mail coat, over which he pulled the white mantel; his last fight would be in full Templar dress. In a finishing touch, he looped the blood-red rope around his waist, the same red as the Templar cross, Christ's blood. He looked at Brychan. "Brother, you are guardian of the chest. Go with God."

Watching, Sara could hardly breathe. In spite of Ursus never accepting her, he inspired deep feelings of respect. She struggled against her tears.

Brychan was locked in helpless frustration. He could only watch as the greatest warrior he knew prepared himself for a battle he must lose.

Ursus selected the triangle battle shield taken from the earlier attack and lay it aside. He hung his heavy mace at his right side, the sheathed battle sword on his left. He picked up the two-handed broadsword and swung it with both hands, getting its feel.

Ursus smiled grimly at Brychan. "I can't hold them long, Zealote." It was the first time Ursus had ever called him that.

WHEN SHERIF GILBERT and his men came in sight of the bridge they halted. All stared, scarcely believing what they saw.

In the center of the bridge was a dead horse forming a barricade behind which a huge Templar stood. The Saracen stand, it was called. Neither Gilbert nor his men had ever seen one. No honorable knight would slay his horse then stand behind it to fight. Saracens facing defeat commonly used this tactic. It meant no surrender, no quarter.

The sherif uncorked the wine flask and took a deep swallow while evaluating the situation. On the narrow bridge, only two men side by side could make a frontal assault. Positioned behind the dead horse the huge warrior would have the advantage against any attack by foot.

A mounted attack was even more difficult. The horses could not charge on the narrow bridge with its uncertain footing. A horse would not step over a dead horse; they would balk. Charging, they would jump over, but here it was not possible. Should the attacker's horse get too close, the Templar would kill it with one piercing thrust of his sword, adding a second horse to the barrier.

Gilbert looked beyond the bridge to the hill behind. The other Templar and Gypsy girl were riding up a winding slope. They led two packhorses. One of them surely would be carrying the Templar coffer.

The sherif watched the two riders reach the hillcrest and then stop, looking down at the bridge. Apparently, the knight would not leave without seeing his comrade's fate. Gilbert knew that once in the forest beyond, the lone Templar had the advantage; he would surprise each pursuer one at a time. They must quickly defeat the Templar on the bridge before the other one escaped into the woods with the chest.

He ordered his men to dismount and the two archers to target the warrior on the bridge. They would shoot continuous volleys at close range, wounding the Templar sufficiently for the others to attack him on foot.

The four cavalrymen drew their swords and, by twos, closed ranks behind the bowmen who were moving into closer range.

The archers were armed with the French cavalry bow, smaller than that carried by foot archers. Copied after the Saracen bow, its range, though limited, was highly accurate. Matched against a knight and beyond reach of his lance or blade, it was a duel the archer always won.

From the hill, Brychan and Sara watched the bridge below. He was mounted on Dragon, Ursus' charger; Sara rode Brychan's Joshua.

As the archers and soldiers moved into position, Ursus waited behind the dead horse, sword and shield ready. He stood tall challenging the foot soldiers to close combat.

The bowmen let fly. The first missed; Ursus deflected the second with his shield. Once having the range, the archers began shooting rapid volleys.

Ursus moved, weaving and turning, showing his experience against Saracen archers. As the barrage continued, several grazing wounds were stopped by his mail coat. Then, an arrow struck deep in his left thigh. As he bent to grasp it, a second slammed his shield arm at the shoulder. His armor blunted it, but this would limit his shield movement.

Brychan watched in frustration. The archers, having scored, now increased the speed of their barrage. Even from this distance, he could hear the deadly sing of arrows.

Another arrow ripped into Ursus' left leg. As he bent to break the shaft, one pierced his right side. He doubled in pain. If he pulled it out, he would hemorrhage; he must break it to swing his sword arm freely. Grabbing the arrow, he clipped the shaft with a chop of his blade.

Sherif Gilbert looked up the hill, fearing that the knight and Gypsy would leave. They were still there. The Templar on the bridge was wounded in the thigh, leg, and side. The sherif now ordered the first two foot soldiers to attack.

They moved around the archers and edged forward, shields front, swords ready. Both tried to engage Ursus at the same time, but the dead horse was an obstacle. The first trooper's blow was deflected by Ursus' shield; with a swift under-thrust, Ursus' blade pierced the soldier deep center. Gutted, he sprawled over the dead horse.

As the second trooper charged, Ursus dropped low, his blade slicing both knees. The man howled and dropped, rolling in agony.

Ursus stepped over the dead horse and, with one hand, grasped the mail at the back of the soldier's neck. With a great heave he dropped him over the railing into the raging water. Screaming, he was instantly sucked under.

Ursus leaned against the rail fighting for breath as the next two men cautiously moved in for the kill. He seemed to wait a moment too long, then stepped over the dead horse and bent down.

As they rushed, he raised up, surprising them with the two-handed broadsword. Neither soldier could check his momentum. Ursus half-severed the first man's head and he dropped. The second blocked Ursus' slash but was off balance. With a powerful overhand cut, Ursus' blade sent his helmet flying.

Gilbert stared in disbelief: he was watching a master combatant. Four troopers lay dead in as many breaths. He shouted his admiration—"A luflych warrior!"—and gave a solemn salute. Ursus acknowledged with a nod and a wave of his hand.

Ursus picked up a shield from one of the dead. He took a new position, crouching behind the dead horse barrier. With two shields as cover, now he could wait them out. Ursus looked up at the top of the hill to see Brychan still watching. Ursus waved him on in a desperate plea. Brychan's leaving would force the sherif to attack on foot.

Brychan waved agreement. He gave the sign of the cross in final blessing and rode away.

Gilbert cursed; he could delay no longer. When he told the archers to stop shooting, they looked at him in surprise.

The Sherif dismounted and drew his blade. "Attack!" he shouted.

The bowmen shared an uneasy look as they drew swords. This was not their specialty.

Seeing their intention, Ursus now painfully stood. Though gloved, from habit he spat on his hands and grasped the two-handed sword. They could sense the doomed warrior smile beneath his faceguard, taunting them.

Beyond the hill, Brychan and Sara had reached the edge of the woods. It would be perfect refuge; the hard ground left no tracks. They need only avoid breaking foliage and they would be swallowed in the forest's thick cover.

When he suddenly reined Dragon in, Sara knew his intentions even before he spoke: "Take the horses and ride on."

"Sir Brychan . . ." she pleaded, but he turned Dragon and rode back up the hill.

On reaching the top, he stopped. On the bridge below, he saw Ursus and the sherif facing each other across the horse barrier. Both archers lay dead: quick work of the broadsword. Ursus was bleeding from a slash in his left arm. With only one usable arm, he drew his battle sword.

Brychan spurred Dragon down the twisting, ragged slope.

The sherif attacked with sword and dagger. He feinted quick moves, drawing the weakened Ursus out. Their blades rang in a brisk flurry, Ursus' sword went flying from his hand.

Gilbert, leaping on the dead horse, swung a blow to Ursus' helmet, then stabbed his dagger deep, penetrating the mail.

Ursus growled in pain and rage. Gilbert fiercely hugged him, forcing the blade deeper. Ursus clutched the mace at his belt and with a last desperate swing, slammed Gilbert's face. The sherif dropped to his knees. Jerking with convulsions, he collapsed.

Brychan jumped from his horse and ran across the bridge to Ursus. He was sitting, back against the rail, the knife hilt-deep in his chest. Brychan touched the handle to remove it, but Ursus shook his head. Gasping for breath, he could not speak. He raised his hand and Brychan took it, locking in the *iunctus manibus*. Brychan felt him slip away.

Looking to heaven, he roared a cry of grief.

When he finally looked at the hill beyond, Brychan saw the

mounted figure of Father Pierre watching. Then the Dominican turned his horse around and disappeared over the ridge. ✣

Kate awoke suddenly. She had been asleep nearly two hours and Thomas had not come to bed. She went into the living room and found the lights out and Thomas staring.

"Why are you sitting in the dark?"

He jumped at her voice. "I was working."

"In the dark?"

"I was reading the diary, but at some point, I was seeing what was happening, not reading it."

"You are pushing yourself too hard."

"Ursus is dead."

"Ursus has been dead. For centuries."

"Yes, but it happened just now. I *saw* it." He looked at her. "Kate, what in God's name is happening?"

After they went back to bed Thomas immediately fell asleep. Kate lay wide awake. From long habit of working several cases at a time, she would gather bits of data which she would later recall when needed. Tonight, Thomas had given her something to consider. She first noticed a connection when Thomas said that instead of dreaming, he actually saw the event. As a cop, when evidence on a case changed, she looked for what caused it. Now she saw it: Thomas had always been reading from the diary when this occurred. Although she didn't believe in the psychic, she observed that Thomas' so-called psychic ability was changing. As a cop she didn't need to understand the psychic; she followed evidence. She would watch him closely to see if there was a pattern. Then, she would confront him.

CHAPTER THIRTEEN

The next morning, Thomas awoke, depressed, with images of Ursus' death lingering like fragments of a nightmare. It was some minutes before he was able to work on the diary.

> *The day after the Feast of Saint Augustine we commended Brother Ursus' soul to God and committed his body to the earth as a Templar fallen in battle. We chose the nearby Saint Gilles Abbey.*

✠ BY JUNE OF 1314, Saint Gilles, an Augustine abbey, was in sad disrepair. Decimated by a plague three years running, there were no more than a dozen surviving monks from over two hundred. Because of its ill fortune there were seldom visitors.

Abbot Etienne was surprised when a knight appeared at the gate seeking permission to bury a warrior slain two days before—a Templar Knight. After a generous donation of three gold besants, the Templar was welcome to rest until the Resurrection with the Augustine brothers.

To the Abbot the party was very unusual: a knight, his dead comrade, two magnificent chargers, and a Gypsy girl leading the packhorses. Because of the relentless heat and the ravaged body, burial would be the same day.

The Templar was laid out before the altar and a requiem Mass celebrated. Afterward, the monks chanted plainsong as they escorted the body in solemn cortege to the cemetery.

Ursus was placed in the raw earth wrapped in his mail hauberk and Templar mantle and with his helmet strapped on. Whether buried in a grave, crypt, or church, a Templar's armor was his coffin.

Brychan carefully bent Ursus' left leg at the knee over his right, marking that he died in combat. The long sword, which had been fashioned especially for him, aligned on his body. Brychan felt that no one else was worthy to wield it and therefore buried it with Ursus. A winding cloth made from a monk's cowl covered his face; the earth was shoveled over him.

Brychan and Sara spent the night at the monastery. The Abbot was ultimately disappointed, for though they karped well into the night, he discovered nothing about the knight, the Gypsy, or how the Templar died. The gold besants also purchased eternal silence.

At Calvière Bridge, the death of a sherif and five or six men remained a mystery. It was said that the bridge was cursed. When it washed away in the next flood, mystery became myth, and in a few generations, that too faded.

MASTER ROUX, A Templar shipmaster once famed as the Navigator, was a bandy-legged mariner who seemed shaped by the hard winds and rolling seas where he spent his life. When Brychan searched for him on the docks of La Rochelle, his questions were met with silence or a shake of the head.

Brychan heard that the Navigator was at sea when King Philip raided the Templars. All Templar ships in port were confiscated and their masters imprisoned. Within a year they were all released. Shipmasters who might be convinced to change sides were too precious to squander by burning at the stake.

Afterward, it was rumored that the Navigator had charted himself a different course. Under the protection of powerful lords, he became a smuggler, some said pirate. The choicest booty often found its way to the hands of his lord protectors.

For four days Brychan searched the La Rochelle waterfront but there was no sign of a Templar Master Roux. Each night he rode back to the Gypsy camp at the edge of the forest where Sara had found refuge for them. There were a dozen or so wagons parked in caravan where the Gypsies spent the winter crafting silver and leather to sell the rest of the year.

Sara had been warmly welcomed, for she had relatives there. She and Brychan were not married and therefore were accepted—he was her "protector." If she married other than a Roma, she would be an outcast. Like Jews, Gypsies were strictly forbidden to marry outsiders. Gadjay were the same as gentiles and so called in the Romany tongue.

Brychan stayed in her cousin Raynold's wagon and Sara with a wizened matriarch Doloria, called the sad one for the curse of outliving husband and all her children.

On the fifth day, just before sunset, Brychan was surprised when the Navigator appeared at the camp. Master Roux still wore the Templar beard, but his hair had grown bushy as a haystack. With him were two men, sailors by their look. They boldly rode into the camp, despite being met by fierce barking dogs and a ring of sullen Gypsy men. The Navigator demanded to see the Templar Knight, Sir Brychan. In La Rochelle, Brychan had not identified himself by name, as knight or Templar, nor mentioned the Gypsy camp, yet, there stood the Navigator. Word had quickly moved through a world still strongly influenced by the vanquished Templars.

"Well, Sir Knight, I am here," Roux announced. "After you spread my name before every ship and whore's bed in La Rochelle, what now?"

"I was ordered by—" Brychan stopped. How much could he trust a Templar, now a pirate? After the trials and burnings, some Templars had enlisted in King Philip's service. These were not trusting times.

"By Master Guy to find me. Yes, I know." Navigator sharply eyed him. "I was expecting two Zealotes. How, by all the Holy Sacraments, did they pick you?"

"There were two of us." Brychan hesitated. "One died."

The Navigator's tone was still suspicious. "I never saw a Zealote with less than thirty years."

"I was the last chosen."

He looked at his companions and said, "The final pickings." Neither of his men smiled. "And when we met, Templar, you were supposed to say . . .?"

"Deo soli gloria." The meeting was so unexpected that Brychan forgot to use the password phrase.

"Confutatis," Roux responded, and raised his hand for the *iunctus manibus*.

Brychan paused, reminded of Ursus' death. "Confutatis." Their hands clasped. He added, "May he who falsely swears—"

"Die condemned." Roux finished the password phrase. "You have the VERITAS coffer?"

"I do."

"Are you taking it to Scotland alone?"

"Yes, God willing."

"Tell me, Sir Brychan, what is to be your cunning disguise, a Templar running from the king?"

"A horse trader. With four fine chargers, two German-bred, for delivery in Scotland."

Roux grunted. "Not bad."

"In Scotland I must find . . ."

"Stop! If I am tortured, I cannot tell what I do not know. Have you ever been examined by the Inquisition, Sir Knight?"

"No."

"You will be. Apparently, you are too stupid to avoid it." He peered deep into Brychan's eyes. "Merciful God—the angel protecting you must be the busiest in all the heavenly host."

"When do we leave for Scotland, Navigator?"

"Soon. Then I can return to the safety of piracy." He looked around. "How is it you're in a Gypsy camp?"

"A Christian Gypsy led me here."

"Christian Gypsy?" Roux snorted. "We must talk, Zealote. I've a long ride back to La Rochelle."

"Then stay the night."

"And wake up with my throat cut?"

"Hospitality is a *law* among Gypsies, not a courtesy. Any stranger, even an enemy, who is harmed, brings a curse on the entire camp for one generation." Brychan added: "I have learned a little of their wisdom."

THEY SAT BEFORE a campfire eating mortreux, a thick stew of rabbit and chicken laced with savory herbs that Sara prepared. As she served them Roux's eyes followed her; he smiled but made no comment.

"Zealote, we sail in two days. We take the route south of Jura. I will land you off coast at Argyll. Then, you're on your own."

"Argyll will be perfect," Brychan said.

"We must be careful. Inquisition rats are thick as flies on carrion since the death of the Pope."

"The Pope is dead?"

"S'blood! You don't know? Pope Clement died a fortnight ago.

At Avignon. Never has good news traveled so fast. Now there is but one pope, not two."

Brychan looked at Sara. "De Molay's prophecy . . ."

She remembered that Brychan predicted they would be getting a new pope. His gift spoke true.

"Then, the king is next," Brychan said, crossing himself.

"God grant it!" Roux laughed. "They say the Holy Father died bleeding from the bowels. A new pope is not yet selected. The Inquisition uses this time to increase their power." He noisily sucked a bone then tossed it to a waiting hound. "Templar, a Dominican weasel with several soldiers was asking about you. He did not appear concerned for your spiritual welfare. They have posted a reward." ✣

After half an hour Thomas finally finished reading the last pages of the diary. He then re-read a few pages and closed the book, staring in disbelief. He had translated every word from "I, Brychan Andrew Houston," to the last very last words: *"Deo soli Gloria."* To God alone the glory.

Kate came from the kitchen; one look told her. "You've finished."

"Yes. And you're not going to believe me."

"Try me."

"Brychan suddenly changes his narrative—there's not another word about the chest. Not a clue where he hid it. Just a repeat of the verse he wrote in English: 'Before the cross three warriors stand / Guarding the last of our band / Love's face shining shows the way / A warrior's measure ends the lay'—which means we don't know any more about where the chest is than if I'd never translated the diary!"

"You mean that's all he wrote?"

"No. It gets worse. After the poem, he wrote about his failed mission."

"Brychan failed?"

"For some reason, he didn't deliver the chest where he was supposed to. He does not explain why. Instead, his last writing is about the New Jerusalem prophecy."

"What is that?"

"The big one. Remember the other Templar prophecies, the predicted deaths that occurred right on schedule?"

"Yes. But how does—"

"The New Jerusalem prophecy says that the Templar Order will be secretly restored and there will be another great conflict between Christians and Muslims."

"When?"

"The Third Millennium."

"You mean now?"

"Yes, now."

"Thomas, do you believe that?"

"If you follow the news media, how can you not believe it? Especially when you realize that many Templar prophecies were accurate."

"*That* is unnerving."

"And look at us. We are following the Templar diary and doing everything it says."

"But we can always stop."

"I can't."

"No," she said. "Neither can I."

"Also, there's another question. Since Ursus was dead, who is Brychan referring to about two of them coming to England?"

Kate smiled. "I know who gets my vote."

✠ THE GYPSY WAGON moved down the twisting forest road through a darkening gloom. The distant clouds were swollocky as before a storm. Darkness would quickly fall as a covering cloak.

The woman drove so the man beside her could work at his leathercraft. But the man's hands lay idle. His gray eyes were the wrong color for a Gypsy. Brychan kept his gaze down whenever they passed anyone.

They appeared to be horse traders on the road to La Rochelle. But the dried mud on the ill-groomed horses could not hide that they were prime stock. A keen cavalryman's eye could spot the two German-bred chargers. Obviously, they were stolen: these were Gypsies.

BRYCHAN AND SARA had been arguing since the previous day. Once they got to La Rochelle, he would sail the Navigator's ship for Scotland, and she would return to the Gypsy camp. But Sara insisted that she must go to Scotland with him.

After another long silence Brychan repeated, "It is too dangerous."

"Was it too dangerous when I shamed myself naked before those pig-raping soldiers? Too dangerous when I am hiding a Templar wanted by the king? I am a *Gypsy*! If they find me with you, they will first brand me, then either imprison or burn me."

Brychan had been told that his mission in Scotland would be fatal. Even if not, he could never return to France. He did not tell Sara. If she went to Scotland and he died, what would happen to her? There were few Gypsies in all the British Isles. Where would she find refuge?

They continued looking for a place to camp and shelter the horses. The heavy smell of approaching rain and rumble of thunder warned of the threatening storm. Another flare of lightening illuminated a field with a grain storage lean-to. It would have to do.

Pulling off the road, they were hit by swirling wind and rock-hard hail. The horses were yawing against the tether lines when a sheet of icy rain hit like a wave from raging Neptune. Brychan jumped off the wagon and ran to the team, leading them toward the lean-to.

As Sara unhitched the team, Brychan managed to tie the four chargers to a railing. The wagon would have to block the opening, or the horses might panic and run. Just as the last horse was tethered, a tide of water rushed down the hill. Sara fell, then Brychan, rolling in a flash flood of water and mud. He yelled for her to get inside. She managed to climb up in the wagon and closed the door.

Brychan worked his way down the wagon tongue. He heaved hard, but the front wheels were axel deep in mud. He fell again. Pulling with all his weight, the tongue freed just enough and swung across, blocking the opening, and protecting the horses. Gasping from the rain's freezing cold, he climbed on the wagon and opened the door.

Inside, it was dark; Sara had not lit a lantern. He sensed, rather than saw her, as she held out a sheepskin for him to dry off with.

"A rain with hail fevers the lungs. Take those wet clothes off," she said.

"More Gypsy superstition?" He was shivering. He stripped and rubbed himself vigorously with the thick wool sheepskin.

She rubbed his back with another. "Turn around."

When he turned, there was a flash of lightning through the window. She was naked. She had removed her wet clothes, but there was not enough time to dress before he entered the carriage.

After a frozen moment, he lifted her in his arms, their mouths devouring. Carrying her to a bunk, he laid her down. When he thought better and tried to pull back, she fiercely pulled him on top of her.

She remembered Cousin Carmen's warning about the first time: expect little, give all. Then, no Gadjay woman can take him from you.

Deep into the night her rapturous cries blended with the howling storm.

At first light, Brychan awoke with Sara asleep in his arms and a terrible realization. He would readily die for his mission but did not have the will to go on without her.

A knight's first test is to honor his vows; a monk's is to serve only God. As both knight and monk he had failed. ✟

Thomas was listening to Kate in the shower and thinking how totally she engaged all his senses, her taste, her unique feel when they made love. Each time was magic, followed by the fear that it would suddenly end—the price for forbidden love.

Saint Augustine, when obsessed with his mistress, prayed, "God give me abstinence, but not yet."

Please, God. Not yet.

He forced himself to return to the diary. *What have I missed? A play on words? Some trick cypher or encryption? Surely, there has to be more.*

Kate came from the bedroom with her notebook. "Thomas, I want to try something. Let's look for the chest the same way we would look for a body."

"I've never looked for a body. Where do we start?"

"With basic police work. A seven-hundred-year old crime, like any other, still has motive, means, and opportunity. We don't know where he hid the chest, but we may be able to discover when he hid it, which gives us a start. What's the last date that Brychan is in France?"

"Back then, only churches kept calendars. The common people weren't concerned with exact dates. Something important was on or near a church feast day." He translated the Gaelic aloud: "Three days before the Feast of Saint Augustine, Brother Ursus sacrificed himself in combat for the Master's mission. *Requiescat in pace.*" He closed the diary. "That would be the last week of May."

"And by June twenty-fifth, Brychan was at the battle of Bannockburn."

"Which gave him four weeks before the battle. He sails to Scotland, that's a day or two, then goes overland to his destination. But for some reason he fails his mission. Now he must decide where to hide the chest and find another Templar to bury him with it, as his secret order from the Templar Master demanded."

Thomas shuffled through tour pamphlets and found the map from the tourist agency. "That means Brychan had only a few days from landing on the coast to get to Bannockburn."

"How far could he travel in a day?"

"In good weather about twenty miles."

"Two days, that's forty miles. Mark that on the map."

Thomas put a ruler along the map scale, which was ten miles to the inch. With the center at the Bannockburn battlefield, he drew a four-inch circle.

Kate pointed, "Somewhere in that circle there has to be three statues before a cross."

"Kate." He shook his head. "Don't *ever* stop thinking like a cop."

The next morning, they began where Brychan ended—at Bannockburn. Thomas had been there often with his grandfather; now he wanted to see it with fresh eyes. But the entire battlefield had been developed as a tourist site complete with a theater, 3D presentations, school tours, and merchandizing everywhere he looked. Tempted at first to check everything new, instead Thomas decided to walk the battlefield remembering how his grandfather brought the battle to life with his scholar's insight.

Bannockburn was a wide meadow edged by the river Forth. Once, when he visited the Gettysburg battlefield, Thomas experienced severe depression when he sensed a lingering aura from the slaughtered thousands. But at Bannock, a wide stream meandered pleasantly with no hint of its bloody past.

After they had been walking a few minutes, he pointed and said, "This was the ground the Scots were defending. They were led by King Robert Bruce, whose army was formed in infantry defensive units called schiltroms, its men armed with twelve-foot-long spears. Bruce used them differently—he trained them to be offensive attack units. His strategy at Bannockburn became legend.

"First," said Thomas, "he chose this terrain carefully. The meadow was between the river Forth on one side and Bannock stream on the other. This left the English attacking army very narrow ground to maneuver. The resulting Scots victory was miraculous."

Kate teased him. "What's miraculous is that you knew about this place but never connected it with Brychan."

"Maybe if I were a smart homicide detective, we'd be opening a bottle of champagne over the Templar chest."

"Cheap shot." She laughed at his retort. "But our search area isn't just the battlefield. In the twenty-mile radius, we're actually probing a circle of a thousand two hundred and fifty-seven square miles give or take."

At his surprised look she smiled, "Darling, I give great math."

After an hour of looking over the battle site, they drove to Stirling Castle, which stood on the dominant hill just minutes away.

"Stirling Castle was the main reason for the English invasion," explained Thomas. "There was a saying—'He who holds Stirling, holds Scotland.' It was the last castle in Scotland still in English hands and had come under siege by the Scots with a small force. English King Edward was marching on Stirling to attack the Scots and relieve the siege. To make matters worse, Robert Bruce's wife and daughter were hostages inside the castle. If King Edward's army defeated Bruce at Bannockburn, then reached Stirling and broke the siege, Bruce would never see his wife and daughter again."

"Imagine trying to fight a battle with that on your mind," Kate said.

As they were talking, they spotted a docent tour guide and introduced themselves. She was delighted to learn that they were from California.

"We are on a research project," Kate explained. "Do you know anything about three medieval statues of knights standing before a cross in this area?"

"Doesn't sound familiar. And I was with the tourist bureau before I came here."

"We asked them. No luck."

"Did you talk with Eleanor Harbin? She knows all the sites. Ellie has her own agency. She specializes in tours of the ley lines."

Kate looked at Thomas. "Ley lines?"

"Many sites like Stonehenge are laid out on ancient lines called leys that are perfectly surveyed and run for hundreds of miles." He turned to the docent. "Where can we find Eleanor Harbin?"

"Two blocks north of Edinburgh University on Chelsea Street. It's called Lady Ley Tours."

Kate smiled at Thomas. "Sexy title."

Burns and Sawyer waited for Kate and Thomas in separate cars at opposite ends of the Stirling tourist parking lot. They were talking by cell phone.

"Why would they think the dingus is hidden in a public place?" Sawyer grumbled.

"Why you bitchin'? They're doing our work for us."

Ravel, patient as a lurking spider, also waited for Thomas and Kate in his car parked among the tourists. This was the first time Kate and Thomas had gone someplace other than tour offices. He considered reporting it to Nora but decided to wait. This might be just another dead end.

Kate and Thomas walked to their car unaware that they were being watched. Before getting in the car Thomas to a final look at the battlefield.

"I don't get it, Kate," he said. "Brychan came here fully committed to die for his mission. Why did he fail?"

✠ BY THE YEAR 1314, Brychan was resolute in carrying out his mission, which took him to the Franciscan monastery at Whitburn. He was looking for a former ranking Templar who was now at this monastery.

One morning just after Prime, Brother Mathias was disturbed to hear that he had a visitor. Having abdicated his Templar oath on papal orders, he had taken new vows as a Franciscan. This was his first visitor in three years. He instantly tasted the coppery fear so different from battle where the most lost was your life. This visitor could jeopardize his very soul.

Mathias had been a Templar of note, serving in the Holy Land under Grand Master de Molay as his aide-de-camp. As such, he was privy to some of the Order's most guarded secrets.

Known then as William of Cameliard, he became Templar Master at the preceptory in Aberdeen. Following the Papal decree that all Templars must enter other monastic orders, William was accepted by the Franciscan order as Brother Mathias.

He paused at the refectory door, whispered a brief prayer, and crossed himself before entering to meet his visitor. One look and he recognized the type: a warrior with aging eyes in a young face. Assuming a formal manner, he introduced himself.

"I was Master William of Cameliard. Now, I am called Brother Mathias."

The visitor bowed respectfully. "Brychan Houston, Knight Templar."

"There are no Knights Templar," Mathias said bluntly. This knight might be a spy sent by the new pope to test his obedience. Since the death of Pope Clement, it was not clear which way the wind blew. A wrong move could mean the stake. He had witnessed three Inquisition burnings and remembered the scalding aroma of flesh-tainted smoke. Those screams were very different from the battlefield and never forgotten.

"Why have you come, Sir Brychan?"

"I was ordered to bring you the VERITAS coffer."

"I am no longer a Templar. I am bound by a papal bull; I can have nothing to do with any Templar matter. Even discussion is forbidden."

"But I was told you would know what to do."

"You must take the chest someplace else. There are no Templars to give it to. It would mean excommunication and eternal damnation for all of us."

"Where can I go? Scotland is our last refuge."

"And soon there will be no Scotland. The English army numbers thousands. Bruce's army is small, excellent raiders, but in pitched battle, very limited. Bruce has bravely but foolishly taken a stand between King Edward's army and Stirling Castle. He will be flanked, encircled, and destroyed."

"Tactics? How are you so well-informed behind convent walls?"

He smiled. "Soldier gossip. Some former Templars have joined Bruce. We talk. I'd almost give my life to be with him even though they are doomed."

He turned away in frustration. After an anxious silence he made a decision.

"Papal bull be damned," he said. "I am a Templar! Brother Brychan, you must make certain the VERITAS coffer does not fall into King Edward's hands!"

"What should I do?"

"Hide it. Until the Jerusalem prophecy happens. Then, the Templars will rise. The new order is 'Watch; pray; be ready.'"

At Brychan's surprised look Mathias added, "Before I became a Franciscan those were my final instructions from the Grand Master if Scotland were lost. Now *you* must carry them out." ✠

Lady Ley Tours was housed in a modest office barely large enough to accommodate Eleanor Harbin and her secretary. The walls were covered with photos of Stonehenge, Glastonbury, and other sites, along with a collage of maps showing a network of ley lines interlocking the entire British Isles.

Ms. Harbin was a solid six feet, plump, and in her fifties with skin that bloomed rosy pink. She bustled about a messy desk talking in a voice pitched for someone a room or two away. "Three statues before a cross?" She peered over her glasses at Thomas and Kate. "Nothing comes to mind. But then, not every site is public. It could be at a family chapel or private estate."

"This would be within twenty miles of Bannockburn," Thomas added.

Eleanor removed her glasses. "What specifically are you looking for? A mausoleum? Gravesite? Is there is some connection with Bannockburn battlefield?"

"It's a Templar grave," Thomas answered.

"Templar?" She brightened. "Oh, they are very rare. Many more of them in France. When we find one here, it's registered. Draws tourists like crazy. The best ones are in churches—crypts with the knight laid out in full body armor carved in stone. Tourists love to make rubbings. It would be impossible for a Templar site to be known and not listed."

She turned to her secretary, a small wispy sparrow with thick glasses. "Imogen," she said, "find that brochure on the Templar tour."

Imogen began searching shelves stacked with pamphlets and tour advertisements.

"Are there any graves from the Bannockburn battle?" Thomas asked.

"Well, certainly no Templars." Eleanor pulled at her lower lip. "Three statues and a cross." She shook her head. "There's nothing like that near Bannockburn."

Imogen held up several pamphlets. "None here either."

"My guess is that your Templar is not in a church or chapel. He's buried outside, probably in a grave not yet discovered near some statues. The site might be—"

Kate interrupted. "But wouldn't a seven-hundred-year-old grave be awfully deep?"

"Not necessarily. Some Saxon graves centuries older have been found as shallow as three feet." She eyed Thomas, testing him. "Are you aware that Templars marked their graves very distinctly?"

"Like with a double-barred cross surrounded by carved figures signifying Solomon's temple—and with the head of the grave always pointing east toward Jerusalem?"

Eleanor smiled; her reserve melted.

"Please Mr. Bardsey," she said. "Do let me know if you find what you are looking for."

They were driving away from Lady Ley Tours when Kate's cell rang. It was Vicky. Kate put it on speaker so Thomas could hear.

"There may be a problem," Vicky said. "Early this morning somebody named Brother Simon called and left a message. He's trying to reach Thomas. Says it's urgent."

"Thanks, we'll call him."

"How is it going in Scotland?"

"We're finally on track."

"Don't take too long. Captain Starger is hard to con. He reads me better than my mama."

Kate hung up and handed Thomas the phone. Thomas, suddenly anxious, called the monastery. Abbot Methodius came on the line.

"How did you know about it?" The Abbot's voice wavered.

"Know what?"

"Simon's death. Isn't that why you called?"

"Oh, no!"

"Barely half an hour ago. A cerebral hemorrhage."

"He died instantly," Thomas heard himself say.

Methodius lowered his voice. "This is astonishing, Brother Thomas. Did you pick it up psychically?"

Thomas was shaken. He had sensed it, but was not fully aware. "I'll call you back."

Kate and Thomas stopped at Caddy's pub before returning to the cottage. Caddy had gone fishing, as usual.

While sitting in a booth they said little until their single malt scotches came. Kate pressed his hand and said, "I'm so sorry, Thomas. Simon was an extraordinary man."

Thomas was stricken numb with grief and rage. "Simon dead? Kate, isn't the timing . . . odd? The day Simon calls me about something urgent, he *dies*?"

Kate held up three fingers, counting. "Two homicides, your abduction, and now Simon is dead. This *stinks* of Fallon!"

A half hour later when Thomas called again, Abbot Methodius was surprised by his request. "An autopsy? Why? Brother Simon had a serious heart condition, was on dialysis, he also was diabetic, and heaven knows what else. I hardly think an autopsy necessary."

Thomas looked at her and said, "He's resisting."

Kate took the phone. "Father Abbot, this is Detective Flynn. I'm ordering an autopsy to see if there is a link between the courier's homicide and Thomas' abduction. Where is Simon's body?"

"At the hospital."

"I'll call the medical examiner to pick him up. Have a good day." She hung up and dialed international for the Santa Barbara medical examiner's office. "This is Detective Sgt. Kate Flynn. I want to speak with pathologist Dr. Moe Cioffi. It's an emergency." She listened for three seconds. "Dammit! Interrupt him!"

Shortly, the ME came on the line. "Kate, if this is about the

Hollander autopsy, like I told you before, I'm only estimating COD by suffocation. Find me her head with enough neck and I'll know more."

"No, Doc, this is a fresh body." She gave a quick background on Brother Simon and his death.

"C'mon, Kate. A monk dies of a stroke in a monastery and you think it's a homicide?"

"It's very tricky, Moe. I've got nothing to go on but coincidence, weird timing, and a bad feeling. Trust me. I don't want anybody but you handling it."

"Got it. When the body arrives, meet me at the morgue."

"I can't. I'm in Scotland. I'm working the case from here."

There was a beat of silence. "Kate, do you make this stuff up?"

"Hell, I just gave you the simple version."

That night, Kate was awakened from the sweet abyss that sometimes followed their making love. Thomas was in his bathrobe; the bedside table light was turned on.

"It's not three statues," he said.

She sat up. "What?"

He showed the brochures Eleanor gave them. "I couldn't sleep. I was still disturbed from my psychic warning about Brother Simon's death. It's like lighting a fire in my brain. At some point I began wondering about the three knight statues, and there was what I call a psychic surge— that I was missing the obvious about Brychan."

"I'm still asleep; be more obvious."

"Brychan knew Celtic lore and legends. One is about huge megaliths standing together. They were believed to be ancient warriors changed through enchantment. It's not three statues of knights. It's three monoliths, warriors turned to stone."

CHAPTER FOURTEEN

BRYCAN WROTE NO more in the diary until he felt it was safe. Should it fall into the Inquisition's hands it would show only events that happened in France and no Templars in Scotland would be compromised. By now, the diary had become as much a part of him as his sword.

In mid-April of 1314, scores of dispatch riders carried a message to all fugitive Templars. They were invited to join King Robert Bruce against the invading army of King Edward of England. Word passed swiftly, true to the saying "Good news makes fast horsemen."

When the Templar Order was destroyed in France, Scotland ignored the papal edict and gave sanctuary to all Templars. Now many were repaying the favor by joining Scotland against the English. As they passed through the countryside, no one suspected their identity, for they dressed as ordinary knights and common soldiers.

Brychan arrived in June at Falkirk, the rally site. They numbered about a hundred and forty knights, sergeants, and troopers, all cavalry. The Templars, as customary, made their camp separate from Bruce's main army. Brychan found the delicious aroma of brewing kahveh in the thick humid air.

"Scotsman! Do ye still fight naked to terrify the enemy with your ugly arse?"

Brychan turned to see the grinning face of Brother James McGill. They embraced with the boisterous laughter that had gotten them in trouble as novitiates. James offered his flagon of steaming kahveh, which they shared as they talked.

No longer a gangling youth, James had fleshed out to a strapping warrior with a few scars of which he might boast. "And what of Ursus, the Great Bear?"

"Fallen."

"Ah! I wot he took a host with him."

"A sherif, two archers, and four foot."

"The Zealote way," James said, and crossed himself.

"What trouble have you been brewing in Scotland?"

"I've taken me a wife—a bonny, bonny Scot's lass. Brychan, I am a wolf tasting blood!" he said with a laugh. "What a price we paid to be monks. No women! Is it any wonder Saracens think us crazy? In battle 'twas not us they feared, but catching our madness!" James playfully tapped him on both shoulders in a mock dubbing. "Now, Sir Knight, how did ye come to answer this call to arms?"

Brychan did not mention Sara. She was biding with a peasant family where a gold besant guaranteed her stay. Instead, he told James of the Inquisition being after him.

Jamie raised his fist in approval. "Good for ye! The Scots army is as good a place to hide as any. As they say, 'hiding among kin is a fortress of many stones.'"

With lively exaggeration James spun a tale of escaping France after King Philip's raid on the Templars. In Scotland he took service with a baron whose chief joy was border-raiding for cattle. James saw the coming war with the English as a blessing from God. He was among the first to answer Robert the Bruce's call.

"Brother Brychan, 'tis me curse to go from bad to worse. I joined Bruce to fight for glory. Yet, for weeks I dig in the ground like a peasant making ditches in a swampy bog, then covering them with sod. I may as well be in a monastery spreading sheep-shit on cabbage."

"Penance for your worldly pride, Jamie."

"Ye've joined a doomed cause, Brychan. The English invade like locusts, with infantry, archers, and a great host of cavalry. Ye could feed all our cavalry horses with three bushels of oats and a dozen sour apples."

"Then why did you join?"

"Why, man! 'Tis the only battle left."

"Are rumors of the English numbers true?"

"Aye! So large they are supplied by sea with ships that follow them along the coast. Though Edward be not the general his daddy ol' Longshanks was, even he cannot lose with this army. Ye recall that back when Longshanks invaded, he brought his own bard to celebrate his victories?"

"The great poet Andrew Baston."

"King Edward has brought the same bard to versify his own victory over the Scots."

"Baston is with Edward's army?"

"That he is." James laughed. "Brother, we shall die in battle but be legends in verse."

ANDREW BASTON, CARMELITE monk, Oxford lecturer, and bard to two kings, sat writing by candlelight in his campaign tent. It was pitched within calling distance of King Edward's tent pavilion. Baston was making notes on events of the day, which he would dictate in verse to Timothy, a novice and his scribe. He was surprised when Timothy entered again, for he had been sent for wine.

"Brother Baston, you have a visitor. A Franciscan."

"Franciscan?"

"He says he knows you."

Baston stood as Brychan entered wearing a brown Franciscan robe. The old monk stared astonished, then both roared with laughter, hugging and pounding each other.

"Brychan! My lad!" He grabbed Brychan's robe. "What is this Franciscan rag? You are Cistercian!" Baston turned to his scribe. "That will be all, Brother Timothy."

The novice, with a curious glance at Brychan, left the tent.

"What madness made you leave Cistercian scholars for Franciscan beggars?"

"I'm neither." Brychan lowered his voice. "I am a Templar."

"Dear heaven, no!"

"And a fugitive. I neither surrendered to King Philip nor joined another order."

"Heavenly host! What a loss," he said. His eyes glowed, remembering. "When you were a child, I predicted your verses would exceed mine."

"Then you are a better poet than prophet."

"Your mother wrote me two years ago. Lady Gwynn only said that you were a monk in France; I should have sensed something dire when she didn't say more."

"She disapproved of my choice. But I think my father, the old warrior, was not displeased."

"I was sorry to hear of his passing." Baston crossed himself, then added, "Do you still write verse?"

"Scribblings. But you! Composing for yet another king! I knew this would be my last chance to see you."

Baston grasped both his arms. "Stay with me! After the battle, we'll go to England. I'll have you writing such verse that your name will sing before every fire."

Brychan was moved. But for a fateful turn of events this great poet might have been his mentor. "My dear friend, I cannot."

"Brychan, you must not fight in this battle! You are a scholar."

"I'm a Scot."

"Jesu! That's no reason! King Edward has more troops than William the Conqueror."

"Yes, yes. So, everyone says."

"You've not heard the half! The English have both cavalry and foot from crown vessels in England and Ireland, and scores of archers from Wales. Infantry from France and Flanders, and Gascogne heavy cavalry! King Edward even has Scots from Cambria and Connaught, whose clans bear old hatreds against Robert Bruce. This army is battle-ready! If old Longshanks had it, he'd have conquered half of Europe."

"Edward is not Longshanks. He's a joke among the Templars." Though Brychan had not heard this, he wanted to rile Baston.

"King Edward is no fool," he argued, "despite his bed favoring men."

"Edward will be at the mercy of his poor commanders," Brychan said.

"Poor? They are among the best! The Earl of Hefford and Earl of Glouster, both seasoned commanders. And Sir John Saint John with his own cavalry."

"Yes, twice our numbers."

"Thrice more! We know your army—peasants armed with long spears, some archers, and a hundred fifty or so cavalry." Baston laughed. "In my verse I will have to give the Scots a few thousand more to appear more evenly matched."

"Would that we had them on the ground."

Baston's tone turned serious. "Hear me, Brychan. Few will survive Bruce's folly. Tomorrow, when an English unit cuts off the south road to Stirling Castle there will be no escape. If you fight, you die."

"I shall die anyway."

"Why do you—ah." The old monk suddenly understood. "The sight—the same as your mother. I never knew a more gifted seer than her ladyship." Arguing against the sight was pointless. "With her vision and your verse, what a bard you would have made!"

Brychan was deeply moved. "I came to beg you to write Lady Gwynn. She will be happy that we talked one last time."

"'Tis is a hard grief she will bear."

"My dear friend." Brychan took his arm in farewell. "Now I must go before I'm discovered by some drunken sentry."

Baston's eyes brimmed. "It is a bitter time when we send poets off to war."

"And have our greatest bard celebrate their slaughter." Brychan hugged him and whispered, "Make us immortal, Brother."

Baston tried to answer, but could only shake his head. After Brychan left, he called angrily to Brother Timothy for wine.

"WHERE IS THIS fool who visits the English?" Prince Edward Bruce bellowed. He was the younger brother of King Robert and appeared late at the Templar camp; the midnight sentries had long been posted. When Brychan returned from seeing Baston, he reported everything to the senior Templar, William Saint Clair. A messenger was immediately dispatched to Edward's pavilion.

Brychan looked Prince Edward over critically, noting his slovenly dress. Under his cloak he wore a filthy night shirt with mud-caked boots. He was attended by two glowering knights.

Sir William introduced him with a ready grin.

"Sire, this is Sir Brychan Houston. A Templar from France, but never fear—a *pure* Scot."

"Houston? Clan Howistean?"

"Yes, Sire." Brychan had heard the many rumors about Edward. King Robert Bruce was thirty, making this Edward two years younger. Where Robert was said to be of moderate temper, this

Prince Edward was a raging hothead. Yet even his severest critics agreed that none exceeded his courage in battle.

"I know of your father Lord Creighton." Edward's tone was taunting. "Is it true that the Houstons always fight on the wrong side?"

"Hopefully not this time, Sire."

"Isn't your family estate nearby?"

"About two hours ride from Stirling Castle."

"Then your knowledge of this terrain could be useful." His tone was accusing. "What were you doing in the English camp, Templar?"

"Visiting their royal bard, Brother Baston, a family friend. He tried to dissuade me from fighting due to their superior numbers."

"Oh, yes! We know their numbers, Sir Knight."

"Good, my Lord. Then you also know that by morning an English detachment moves to cut off the south road leading to Stirling Castle which will outflank the Scots left."

Edward frowned suspiciously. "And did this bard also conveniently reveal to you their commanders and strength?"

"Only that we are greatly outnumbered."

"The south road to Stirling? How far from here?"

Brychan sensed what he was thinking. "If you force march, you could get there before dawn."

Edward looked at his two companions. "Then we could cut the English off at the south road!"

Both knights smiled at the prospect. Edward turned to Brychan.

"If the English do not appear on that south road," he said, "you are a traitor. You'd better pray that your bard is right. If he's wrong, your head will be on my lance leading our next charge."

AFTER A THREE-HOUR night march just before dawn, Brychan found himself in Prince Edward's unit stretched along the south road awaiting the English advance. He was deeply disappointed. The main body of King Robert's army was at Bannockburn in position to engage the main body of the approaching English army. That was where the main battle would be. This small detachment was making a tactical move to prevent the English from outflanking the Scots and marching on Stirling. As he waited, Brychan carefully checked his surroundings; the thick morning fog was heavy as his mood.

From his division, Edward Bruce had selected a modest force of infantry and fifty cavalry to ambush the English. He could risk losing no more. If the English arrived while the fog held, the Scots' force would seem much larger. But if the fog lifted and exposed their inferior numbers, the English ambush would quickly turn into a slaughter of Scots.

As Brychan sat on Dragon waiting, he watched Edward, who yawned in boredom. The prince had first earned his spurs when he and Robert Bruce rode with William Wallace against Longshanks' last invasion. Now as he evaluated their position, Brychan was impressed by Edward's daring tactic: he had placed his infantry well hidden in a narrow line along the road. Their ranks were thin, with surprise their single advantage.

"Templar!" Edward growled. "Where are your English?"

Brychan peered into the misty brume nearly thick as smoke. Where *were* the English?

As if an answer, there was the sound of a horse. Through the swirling haze a knight appeared and saluted Edward. "The north road, Sire."

"Their formation?"

"In column, four wide."

"No outrider scouts riding reconnaissance?"

The knight laughed. "Their left flank is naked as a French whore."

Edward turned to his commanders. "The fog makes their archers useless. Our infantry will assault their infantry front. Our cavalry will charge on the English right."

The infantry commanders saluted and rode away. Edward addressed the cavalry commanders that he would be leading. "Stagger ranks. Ten lengths between. In the fog, we will appear to be coming in waves."

Brychan watched as the men quickly made the alignment. He could see that this was a common maneuver for them.

"Templar!" Edward yelled above the confusion. "The English just saved your head. Let's see if they've left you enough stomach to fight. Stay near me."

Instead of drawing his sword, Brychan selected the mace, curling the strap tightly around his wrist. It had been Ursus'; with its extra-long shank and oversized head it was perfect for chopping down infantry. Settling his weight on Dragon, Brychan firmly pressed his heels down in the stirrups. He felt both a strange calm and a hollow ache; Ursus would not be fighting beside him. It was why he chose Ursus' mace.

Suddenly, without giving a command, Edward spurred his steed and the troop followed. Brychan did not have to urge Dragon, who in a few strides, was at full gallop. The rushing ground ahead was barely visible in the fog.

Breaking through the mist, Brychan was amazed at his first sighting of a Scots schiltrom formation. Each soldier had a twelve-foot spear, their ranks close, with shields touching. When attacking infantry, the long spears kept them well beyond the enemy's reach. If charged by cavalry, they leveled at the horses. If the ranks held, this "hedgehog" was all but impenetrable.

Brychan saw a wall of dead and injured horses impaled before the Scots line—the first to attack. English cavalrymen, having fallen on the ground, were being slaughtered by killing squads that charged out from the schiltrom formation.

The Scots cavalry now hit in waves of ten. Surprised, the English cavalry scattered to regroup in their rear. Instead of pursuing as would be expected, in a perfect show of maneuverability, the entire Scots cavalry wheeled and turned back on the English infantry, now unprotected by cavalry.

In full charge, Brychan raged in a fury of bloodlust, slashing all in reach of his mace. English soldiers scattered or deliberately fell to escape his ferocity. The entire English unit had scattered quickly at the first charge.

With no one left before him, Brychan reined Dragon sharply and looked around to find an English knight for single combat. At the same moment, the two knights saw each other.

The English shield bore three gold lions with the helmet crowned by a coronet, marking a count or baron. His lance broken, the Englishman dropped the truncheon and drew his sword, waving it in challenge to Brychan.

Brychan looped the mace on the saddle pommel, drew his sword, and charged.

The first clash was swords against shields. They passed; both swung quickly around. There was another pass and clash. And another.

With each turn, Brychan was instantly upon the knight. Ursus had trained Dragon so that horse and rider were a ton of single warrior. The Englishman, slightly slower, was vulnerable for an instant after each turn. At the next clash, Brychan landed a solid blow on his opponent's back armor and another on his shield.

As the knight was turning again, Brychan's blade slammed his helmet. The Englishman wavered then fell from the saddle. Brychan spun Dragon around for the kill.

The knight lay on his back, helmet gone, head bloodied. His hand slowly raised in surrender. Brychan lowered his sword.

Prince Edward rode up accompanied by two knights.

"You have a prisoner, Templar," he said. He noted the lions on the crest of the English shield. "Baron of . . . Salisbury, is it not?"

"It is," the man answered and looked up at Brychan. "Who has bested me?"

"Brychan, clan Howistean," Brychan answered with a courteous nod.

"Your blade is fierce, Sir Brychan." The man shakily got to his feet. Now he appeared very old for a warrior, nearly fifty years.

Brychan looked at Edward. "Sire, I do not want a prisoner."

"Very well, Templar." Edward turned to the knight. "Baron, you are now King Robert Bruce's hostage." He turned to his attending knight and said, "Escort him to my pavilion." Edward then ordered that they follow the command in the Book of Proverbs: "*If your enemy is hungry, feed him.*"

In the quickly fading mist, Scots were stripping the English dead of desperately needed weapons. Watching them, Edward said to Brychan, "You fought well, Sir Knight. I would grant you a boon."

"Will the English attack again tomorrow?"

"Providing they do not defeat us today."

"Then, I beg the boon. Some of us wish to fight openly as Templars."

"Glorious!" Edward laughed. "'Tis the perfect insult to the new Pope. The last one excommunicated King Robert."

Brychan saluted, accepting the boon. "Sire, I beg permission to join the Templars with King Robert's division."

"Granted. I have received a messenger from King Robert. The

main body of English are advancing slowly to Bannockburn field on the old Roman road. If you ride fast, you can get there in time."

During the ride to Bruce's division, Brychan's thoughts flooded with gory images of the morning's skirmish. He could not shake a sick feeling of shame: he found combat exhilarating, greater even than making love. God forgive him!

Once again came the realization that he did not know himself. What scholar feeds on bloodlust? What warrior-monk forgets that his duty is to slay the enemies of Christ but to take no joy in the killing? Now he feared for his soul: in this battle lay the prophecy of his own death.

A few hours later, when he arrived at King Robert's camp, he was surprised to discover the King had positioned most of his army hidden in the woods, in the hunting preserve at the top of the hill. From its position they would await the first English units, which were still marching on the Roman road several hours away. Only one troop of Scots schiltroms edged the woods. The arriving English would look uphill into the sun and see only a single Scot's unit. The rest of King Robert's division was hidden in the woods behind.

Brychan dismounted and joined Brother Jamie McGill and ten or so Templar cavalry. Once again, he was disappointed. He was with the reserves, which would only be used as a last measure depending how the battle went. From here he would have a fine view of the battle below; he could only watch and wait. ✞

Eleanor Harbin was awakened by the phone at 6:00 am.

"I must see you," Thomas said.

"Of course, Mr. Bardsey. The office opens at nine."

"This can't wait."

TWIST OF TIME

Thirty minutes later, Eleanor, in pink curlers and wearing a chenille bathrobe of fading violet, answered her front door. She greeted Thomas and Kate cheerily and led them into the kitchen. They were surprised to see tiny Imogen in her blue bathrobe. Obviously, they were a couple. Kate gave Thomas a warning look. For all his sophistication, he was a monk.

"Tea or coffee?" Imogen offered.

"Eleanor," said Thomas, "I've made a stupid mistake. I was working from a medieval verse that referred to three warriors standing before a cross."

"Yes. So you said."

"Last night I came to a different interpretation. Now I believe they're not statues, but three stone monoliths with a cross nearby. Is there anything like that near Bannockburn?"

Eleanor and Imogen exchanged a look.

"Check the brochures, would you, dear?" said Eleanor.

Imogen went into the next room, which from the doorway revealed a wondrous glut of photographs, books, and papers like a paper-hoarder's cache.

Eleanor pursed her lips thoughtfully. "Mr. Bardsey, it is I who must apologize. I should have made the connection—three statues, three stone steles. Imogen, bring the Royal Engineer ordnance map."

With an impatient sweep of her hand, Eleanor cleared the table, sending books and papers flying to the floor.

Imogen spread the map. The scale was one inch to five miles, showing considerable ground detail.

Eleanor put on her glasses and with her thumb followed a ley line on the map. "Here, within your circle. Two standing monoliths."

"Two, not three?"

"A third has fallen, so I think of two standing."

"How did it fall?" Kate asked.

"Bloody vandals," Eleanor sneered. "A stone monument will stand for thousands of years, then some stupid sod will destroy it for fun. I believe these monoliths are sacred, the same as any temple or church. Stele, dolmen, or megalith, their purpose is still unknown—holy site? Sacred burial? If one falls, when it's restored, sometimes it's impossible to get the balance and alignment right. Yet the people who built them didn't have iron or math, just muscle and imagination."

Thomas smiled. "That's quite poetic, Eleanor."

She blushed. "Sometimes, I rave on a bit."

"A bit?" Imogen muttered.

Thomas tapped the map. "How far is this from Bannockburn?"

"Thirty miles—a place called Whitley. In the woods about a hundred or so yards off the road."

"But there is no cross," Imogen reminded him.

Carver had dialed Leo's number repeatedly. There was no answer, not even from Victor. Carver would have to report to Leo that they followed the monk and cop to Paris and lost them. His team was still searching.

When Leo finally phoned, his tone was blunt as a hammer. "Yes, Carver?"

Carver stuttered. "F-for some reason, sir, we can't f-f-find . . ."

"They're in Scotland," Leo interrupted. "Edinburgh or Glasgow. Our sources think Edinburgh. The monk may be checking various tourists' offices." He paused. "I'm very disappointed in you. Shall I try other means?"

Carver felt a rumble in his bowels. Before he could reply Leo hung up.

"My name is Nathanson, Special Agent, Interpol." The man presented his credentials to Eleanor. The second man also flashed his. They had arrived at Eleanor's office as if ready to make an arrest.

She was startled. She had never been questioned by the police, much less Interpol. "Yes? May I help you?"

Carver gave her an official smile. The forged credentials had arrived by Leo's courier just two hours before. He showed Eleanor a grainy surveillance photo of a man. "Do you know him?"

"My goodness. Isn't that Mr. Bardsey?" She looked at Imogen, who nodded wide-eyed.

"Bardsey?" Carver repeated. "That's one of his names. Also, Bentley and Aikens. He's an American; he may be traveling with a woman."

"They were here early this morning," Eleanor said.

"What's he done?" Imogen asked.

"Confidence. Real estate scam. Preys on elderly investors."

Steiner added, his German accent intentionally thicker, "Der scam involves phony treasure, und archeology zites. Who vould belief anyvone could be so easily duped?"

Imogen frowned at Eleanor. "I told you there was something strange about them."

"What did he want to see you about?" Carver asked.

"He was looking for a specific prehistoric site." Eleanor added nervously, "I'm afraid I told him about one."

"That's understandable. He has fooled a lot of people." Carver unfolded a map and held it out to her. "Where did they go?"

CHAPTER FIFTEEN

Thomas and Kate drove on a country road that wound through rolling hills flushed purple with early heather. After about an hour they came to Whitley and its modest string of small businesses stretched along the road. Situated between a grocery and a seed-and-garden store they found Argyll's Tavern, once an ancient coach house.

The barmaid, Frances, was a living Aubrey Beardsley drawing in bold strokes with a raucous laugh to match. The cold lamb sandwiches were rare, the potatoes had a tang of vinegar, and the stout was chilled, a concession to tourists.

When Thomas asked about stone monoliths nearby, Frances gave him a cheery grin. "Just down the road, luv. For ages this was called Three Stones Tavern but after Mickey Argyll bought it, he changed the name. Got tired of people asking if he had three balls." Her bawdy hoot erupted as if telling the story for the first time.

Burns and Sawyer, still tailing Kate and Thomas, were driving separate cars. The Bulldogs stayed cautiously back. It was the first time their subjects left the city search. Obviously, something new was happening.

Kate, following the barmaid's instructions, drove down the road and parked. On one side were a gas station and a few stores, on the opposite, thick woods. There was nothing to indicate a historic site, no sign or marker.

Thomas and Kate entered the dense evergreens of pine and spruce. A little less than a hundred yards they came to a stop. Before them was a sudden clearing—an enchanted battle scene preserved in time. Standing in the mist were two steles twelve feet high. A third lay like a fallen warrior.

"Jesus, Joseph, and Mary," Kate whispered.

"Ab-so-lutely stunning," Thomas added.

They looked up at the proud monuments, their surface pitted as if bites had been hacked into them like a child's soap carving. The top of both steles had been shaped flat by stone working stone, an astonishing feat of craftsmanship. Their sides were stippled with lichen like flaking armor.

Thomas repeated the verse "Before the cross three warriors stand." He looked around the perimeter. "Where was the cross?"

"Why would anybody remove it?" Kate asked.

"Probably a victim in the religious wars. The armies of Henry VII, the Catholics, the Protestants, the Anglicans, and the Puritans were all battling each other. They destroyed churches, convents, and statues. Burned books, then people. Thousands died over religion."

He took Brychan's verse from his wallet and read aloud.

Before the cross three warriors stand
Guarding the last one of our band
Love's face shining shows the way
A warrior's measure ends the lay.

He looked over the ground carefully; there was nothing to suggest a marker. "To find the grave we have to measure from some point. Let's hope it's not the missing cross."

"Measured how? Feet? Meters?"

"Feet or yards, English measures. The French meter came years after this was written."

From habit, Kate surveyed the area counterclockwise, as if examining a crime scene. "See these thick evergreens? That's highly acidic soil. I've known it to reduce a body to a skeleton in as little as six weeks. But the bones survive."

"And hopefully some of Brychan's armor that he was buried in."

Kate tried to imagine his thinking. "He's searching for a place to bury his body and the chest. But what does he measure with?"

"Brychan is on the run, so it's probably something that every knight would have." He repeated the line "A warrior's measure," then asked, "Is it a sword?"

He dialed his mobile phone and Cornelius Higgins answered at the museum. It was an unusual request, borrowing the Houston sword for a day. Just using its measurement was not enough; they wanted the real thing. When Thomas mentioned that he had made Higgins a copy of Brychan's translated letter, arrangements were made to get the sword to them that day.

Kate's gaze searched the ground looking for clues. "How do we figure the number of sword lengths? Are there any numbers in the verse that might apply?"

"Only three warriors. Brychan was weak in math, so there are no tricky number codes. His world was writing."

"Writing what? Describe it."

"Brychan wrote verse in iambic feet, with eight beats per line." He muttered the verse, "No, wait. The first two lines have eight, but the third line has only seven. And the last line has the correct eight again. I noticed it before but thought he was just being artsy. 'Love's face shining shows the way.' If he wanted eight beats, he could easily have said, *my* love's face shining. . . ."

"Why make that line a beat short except to draw attention to it?" Kate asked.

"Then it's either seven sword lengths in that line, or fifteen if you add the two lines together." He slowly looked around. "If I'm Brychan, where would I imagine a place for a cross?"

There was nothing obvious.

Kate's fingers caressed the cool stone of the stele. "How long have they been here?"

"About the same as Stonehenge, three thousand years before Christ." He squeezed his eyes shut. "Before, *before*. Kate, I am an . . . idiot."

"I really wish you'd stop saying that—why this time?"

"I've fallen for Brychan's every word trick. When I think he's being literal, he's being poetic, and vice versa. He says warriors, which can't be live warriors, so I think statues, but no, he means monoliths, warriors turned to stone. Then he says 'before the cross,' so we look for a cross. But seeing it now, I believe he means before the *time* of the cross, *before* Christ, when these stones were first erected. Kate, I don't think there ever was any physical cross here."

"That tricky bastard." She laughed. "I think I love him."

"There is nothing to measure from but the two steles. 'Guarding the last one of our band' must refer to his own grave as one of the last Templars. The next sentence indicates direction—'Love's face shining shows the way.'"

"But where's the face?"

"Maybe carved on one of the stones?"

They carefully searched each stele. There was no face or carving unless it was on the underside of the stone on the ground.

"Could it have eroded?" Kate asked.

"Rock carvings have survived for thousands of years, even in soggy Scotland."

"No cross; no face." She was thinking out loud. "Brychan has to pick a spot for an associate to bury his body and the chest when no one will see him do it. Right?"

"Yes, he could not risk that."

"Then, doesn't burying him at night make more sense?"

"Much more."

She looked around. "At night he can see the two steles. What else could be a marker?"

"There's nothing. Just moon and stars." Thomas looked up. "Love's face shining. Venus, the goddess of love. Kate, he's measuring from a star fix! The chest can *only* be located at night."

WHEN BRYCHAN FIRST arrived at the Templar camp at Bannock, Scots spies watching the English advance knew that it would be at least a day or more before they would arrive for battle. Brychan realized that if the Dominican Pierre was tracking him with soldiers, the Scots army was the best possible refuge. Should he leave its safety he might be captured by the Inquisition. If that happened, at least he would have the opportunity to kill the Dominican. In every prayer since Ursus' death, he reminded himself: Vengeance is mine, sayeth the Lord. Though he prayed desperately, nothing in his heart or mind changed. If he saw Father Pierre, he would kill him.

Yet, for some time, an even greater desire than revenge had been driving him. With the English army a day away, just before dawn he left the camp and rode for an hour to a hunting forest nearby. He was on familiar ground, near the Houston family castle. As the sun rose, he waited and watched.

TWIST OF TIME

. . .

THE BOY WAS tall for his seven years—in this, he resembled his father. He sat the horse easily as he listened to the teaching of old Rothgar. They were on an early morning hunt, a favorite time and tradition in the family.

Once a veteran warrior titled Master of Arms, Rothgar now was hoary-headed, half-deaf, and part lame. But he could still ride well enough to instruct Master Andrew in hawking. A great hooded falcon, Attila, perched on Rothgar's arm, which trembled with the bird's weight.

Andrew's eyes searched the tree line for prey to release Attila. Then he saw the man standing at the edge of the woods—a knight, by his bearing.

"Rothgar, look."

On a rise standing against the murky woods, Brychan had been watching his son and concentrating. Andrew, though absorbed in Rothgar and the falcon, suddenly turned and looked for him. Yes, he too had the gift. And though he was too far away to know for certain, Brychan would have wagered all that his eyes were gray.

Andrew wondered if he might be a ghost. He hesitated, then waved. The figure waved back.

They beheld each other, savoring the long moment, and then the knight turned and slipped into the mist. There was only the fading sound of his horse galloping away.

For the rest of his life Andrew never forgot—it was the day before the battle of Bannockburn. ✠

Ravel, having followed Fallon's two PI's most of the day, spotted another team: two men in a black Audi. They also were tailing

Fallon's Bulldogs—the tails had a tail. Ravel phoned Nora immediately.

Once again, they were parked in Nora's car and breathing a choking mix of her cigarette smoke and a heavy perfume that was eating the oxygen.

She asked, "Are you certain you saw another team?"

"Definitely. Now I will need more help."

"Too late, if they are who I think."

"And who do you think?" The bitch had not told him everything. He fantasized binding her naked to a bed and—maybe later when there was time to make it last, he promised himself.

Nora asked, "What's happening with the monk and the cop?"

"They've found a location in the woods. I couldn't follow them because you insisted on this meeting. Now everybody is tailing them but me."

"Let them." She stubbed out her cigarette.

"And what am I supposed to do?"

"Use the time to find the diary while everyone is concentrating on the monk. He's smart; he won't have it with him in case he's grabbed again. He's hidden it someplace. Find the diary, then we'll look for the chest."

"We've got one helluva problem if the monk finds the chest first."

Her expression was as flat as her tone. "Not if you kill him immediately after he finds it."

At his Lab 5 in Baltimore, Fallon stared at the readouts. Longrieve's physiological readings had improved 12 percent. He was actually getting stronger. There was a blip in projection response data. This rated Longrieve's accuracy in randomly predicting stock quotes, baseball scores, and daily temperature readings. Usually the odds were little better than flipping a coin. Now, there was an overall improvement of 13 percent, a dramatic increase.

The two doctors watched Fallon for a reaction.

"Brief me," he ordered.

"Too early to be certain," Dr. Lizerand answered, "but physiologically GOLEM is taking over some of Herb's stress. He's using less energy because the computer is doing more of the work."

Meyer added, "GOLEM and Herb are connecting on a more efficient level."

"I want to see Herb."

"GOLEM has put him in a deep sleep. He should rest," Meyer said.

"You're right," Fallon agreed. Taking the readouts, he went into his office and closed the door. He tapped a cell number and Burns answered.

"Update," he ordered.

"We're following them now. They apparently found a location in the woods."

"When they find the object, you must *acquire* it in a safe place. Do you copy?"

Burns rolled his eyes. They had been over all this before; no witnesses. "Understood."

As the conversation ended, the Bulldogs watched Kate's car pull in at the hardware store across the parking lot. After twenty minutes they came out carrying a pick and shovel and two shopping bags. Instead of returning to the cottage, they drove into Edinburgh. They went to the Caithness museum where they spent almost an hour.

As they were getting in the car to leave, Kate's cell rang. It was Cioffi, the ME in Santa Barbara.

"Kate. Where are you?"

"Still in Scotland. What about Simon's autopsy? If it's bad news, lie to me."

"It beats anything I ever saw."

"What do you mean?"

"Some kind of computer chip implanted in his head."

"An implant?" She looked at Thomas and touched the speaker button so he could hear.

"Our techie said she never saw anything like the chip. Very advanced."

"Cause of death?"

"Cerebral hemorrhage; probably triggered by the chip. Hurry back, Kate. I can't sit on this very long."

She hung up and looked at Thomas. "An implant?"

"For decades conspiracy freaks have believed that chip implants have been placed in people by aliens and the government. For Simon to have one, there must be a genuine medical reason."

"Could this be Fallon working his animal experiments on Simon?"

"How, Kate? There's no access. Simon's health has kept him confined to the monastery for months."

"Except when he goes to the hospital for dialysis."

"An operation in a hospital without anyone knowing?"

"With Fallon's money he could cover up anything." Then she remembered. "Simon wore a bandage the day I met him. From a fall."

"Yes, when he went in for dialysis."

"That's it!" Kate phoned Vicky and asked her to check Simon's hospital records for an injury or surgery during the month of March.

Thomas was growing impatient. "Wrap it up, Kate. We've got a grave to find."

When the Bulldogs realized that their subjects were headed back to the cottage, they went on ahead. They could not risk being spotted. Once there, they parked half a block away and watched.

Kate drove up, they got out, and Thomas locked the tools and the sword in the trunk. They entered the cottage and turned on the light.

"My god!" Kate gasped.

The room was trashed, books thrown from shelves, pictures torn from the walls, sofa and cushions ripped, drawers dumped. His translation notes were still on the table.

"Move and she dies."

The voice was behind them. Kate felt the press of a gun barrel at the back of her head.

Thomas recognized the voice. "You're the guy from Oxnard."

Kate's look warned him too late; recognizing the man connected him to Hollander's murder.

"That's me, Sherlock," Ravel sneered at his blunder. "Where is it?"

Thomas realized that he might shoot Kate just to make a point.

"The fireplace chimney," he said.

Ravel did a quick pat-down on her, slipped the Beretta from her hip holster and tossed it behind them on the floor. "Get the diary; be *very* careful."

Thomas cautiously stepped through the debris-strewn floor, moving around the cluster of shillelaghs in the rack by the fireplace. At the chimney he removed two loose bricks and took out the plastic-encased diary. He had blackened the loose mortar with soot, making it indistinguishable from the rest.

"Smart," Ravel said as he took it.

Kate was still determined to connect the dots in the Hollander homicide.

"Look, I'm freaking lost," she said. "Do you mind telling me how in hell *you* are connected to the diary?"

He was amused at her unexpected question. "It's what I do."

She felt the press of the gun again.

"You work for that cunt Nora?" Thomas laughed. "You poor pussy!"

When Ravel angrily looked at Thomas, Kate felt the gun move away. She grabbed his wrist, her teeth locked on his flesh; she dropped to the floor pulling him with her. The gun bounced away.

Thomas grabbed a shillelagh from the rack and turned to see Kate crawling after the gun. Ravel desperately hung on to her foot.

Thomas swung, slamming Ravel's arm. He yelped. Kate twisted free to go after the gun.

Ravel rolled aside as Thomas swung again, missing him, and shattering an end table. Ravel scrambled on the floor and from a shin holster pulled an automatic.

Kate fired; its silencer made a hissing pop.

Before Ravel could fire, Thomas swung the shillelagh, sending him rolling.

Kate went to Ravel and felt for a pulse on his neck. She spat the taste of his blood, "He's dead."

The bullet had struck his chest and the shillelagh had shattered his temple.

Thomas pulled Kate to her feet and they stared down at the dead man.

"Who in hell is he?" Kate asked.

In a few seconds she recovered and began searching the body. There was a wallet with mixed currency, and an international driver's license. In an inside coat pocket was a leather holder with four passports: American, Swiss, Spanish, and French, each with different identities but the same ID picture.

"The bastard carries passports like credit cards. A pro hitter," she said, and picked up the phone.

"Who are you calling?"

"The police. It's self-defense, but still homicide."

"Wait."

"For what?"

"Kate, he's dead. And he'll still be dead tomorrow."

"Thomas, don't even think —"

"Tonight, we must do exactly as we planned."

"Do you realize how bad that will look?"

"How much worse can it be? Once we notify the police, we will be tied up for days—weeks? Kate, if this guy found us, we've been followed to the site. That means the others know! We must *not* give them time to search."

"Thomas, I can't delay. I'm a homicide detective, remember?"

"At least give us tonight to find the chest. Then, we can go to the police."

"What about him?"

"Ice him down."

"What?"

"The bathtub. Pack him in ice. He'll keep for days."

Burns and Sawyer were surprised when Thomas came out alone and drove away. They followed him to the next town where he stopped at Duffy's fish market.

They watched from a distance as he loaded bags of ice in the car.

"What is that all about?" Sawyer asked.

"Looks like they're planning one hell of a party," Burns observed. "You can bet your fat ass they found something to celebrate."

UNDER A CLOUDLESS full moon Brychan wandered the evergreens edging the burn. Since he knew the land well, he had been sent to scout a particular section of the terrain in case they made a night assault. The day's ambush against Saint John's force had thrown the English into confusion. Now they were trying to reposition their ranks in the dark, wandering on ground that was half firm and half marsh. In the distance he could hear them noisily trying to regroup.

As he moved through the ground brush, Brychan tried to renew the feeling of his vigil the night he was made a Templar, but memories intruded. Everything in his life had strayed from its intended course. The scholar novice became a warrior monk who was now a knight without a king and a monk without an order. On this twisted path he had shattered every vow, to his deep shame.

Suddenly, there came the same centering he felt yesterday before combat. Perhaps his awen, triggered in dreams, was now working when he was awake. He desperately prayed that he would not fail in this final task, but again his mind wandered and he thought of Sara. Of all that had happened in his life, she was the most unexpected—proof that one with the gift should never read for one's self.

Brother Ursus would say he was bewitched—it was the woman's fault. Dear Ursus. Despite their conflicts, Ursus became closer than a friend or brother. Again, he felt the ache of his death.

He prayed for the guidance scripture promised. "For as heaven is high above the earth, so great is His mercy for those that revere

TWIST OF TIME

Him." And: "As far as East is from the West, so far hath He cast our transgressions from us." All lay in God's mercy. In this final surrender, Brychan felt some peace.

He continued walking until he came to a trickling stream, separating the burn. He drew his sword, laid it down, and knelt in prayer. This was the ground where he would die.

In the distance he heard a cock crowing as a summons. He rose and hurried toward the morning sounds stirring in the Scots' camp. A portion of beans cooked in a pot all night over a sentry's fire, a bite of salted pork and hot kahveh would break his fast. The battle was but hours away. ✟

As Kate drove to the site, they hardly spoke. Both were still numbed by the killing. She alternated speed while continuing to check the mirror. Her instincts had been right about being followed; that bastard was chilling in her bathtub. There must be others, but she did not spot anyone.

Burns and Sawyer were in one car. Knowing the location, they were allowing lead time for the monk to search and find what he was looking for. They parked among the cars in front of the stores and waited.

Kate's car was parked across from the site; they were already in the woods.

Though it was not fully dark, a few stars blinked like early fireflies. Thomas carried pick and shovel, Kate had the sword and a heavy-duty flashlight. The light threw bounding shadows on the great stones, making them loom even larger.

"Okay, professor, how does this work?"

He set down the tools and looked around. "If we're right, Venus should appear over one of the stones. Of course, that depends on longitude, latitude, and the date all being right."

"Gee, and I was afraid this might be complicated."

"The battle was on the twenty-fifth. Today is the twenty-second, so even after seven hundred years, hopefully, the alignment will be close enough."

She had been wanting to ask; now seemed the right moment. "Thomas, do you believe in reincarnation?"

"I'm keeping an open mind. Over two billion people do. Plato said that the soul is immortal and is clothed successively in many bodies. It is a fundamental belief in Buddhism and Hinduism. Even Jesus said that John the Baptist was Elijah reincarnated." He paused. "Are you wondering about the similarities between me and Brychan?"

"Wondering? I am *obsessed*. He was a monk; you both have the psychic thing. He was involved with a Gypsy girl and there's us. We are following the diary and looking for something in Brychan's grave. It just goes on and on."

He started to say something but looked to the sky. Venus was clearly dominant. "Love's face is getting brighter."

"Do we measure seven lengths or add the two lines for fifteen?"

"Let's keep it simple and start with seven. Normally, there would be a second measurement from another position and the two lines intersect over the site. But Brychan had no second marker." He indicated the two monoliths. "They are about eight feet apart and facing different directions. If we pick wrong, we could dig here for months."

"What if the fallen stele is the marker?"

"Then, we're screwed. We don't know the angle it faced when standing. Many monoliths are aligned with celestial positions. Stonehenge has several marking the sun at both the summer and winter solstice. The Maya, who had the most accurate calendar until ours, based it not on the sun, but cycles of Venus. Obviously, these steles also have something to do with Venus. Let's see what she says."

They did not wait long. Venus, growing ever brighter, favored the right stele where it was more centered. The other stone's flat facing was oriented more north-south. The one on their right faced them. Venus had chosen.

Thomas took a position and had Kate walk twenty paces from the stone and aligned herself with the star. Starting at the stele base, he took the sword and measured seven sword lengths as she kept him on the Venus line. He stuck the sword in the ground to mark a spot.

"This feels about right," he said. She spotted the flashlight on the work area.

At the first swing, the pick buried deep. "Soft ground. Thank God."

"Stop when you reach Chinese customs; we don't have visas."

He heaved a shovel of dirt. "I'm not exactly in peak condition. Let's hope it's not too deep."

"Didn't Eleanor Harbin say it could be as shallow as three feet?"

"Brychan probably kept it shallow because he believed the chest would be found very soon."

"Why would he think that?"

"His world had changed little for over a thousand years. Warfare was tactics and having the largest army; the Church controlled literacy; society was locked in feudalism. But the next hundred and fifty years changed everything. The Black Plague wiped out over a third of the population, but the Renaissance followed, which transformed Europe. Luther, the Reformation, and the printing press all broke the monopoly of the Church. Brychan could never imagine it would take seven hundred years for someone to find the chest again." He stopped digging and looked at her. "Also, another piece of the puzzle is beginning to fit."

"Like what?"

"There is a Templar legend that they fought at Bannockburn. Some experts dismiss it, others accept the possibility. At least we know one Templar was there—Brother Brychan."

IT WAS BRYCHAN'S first time to wear the white Templar mantle in combat and also his last. In the ranks he saw a sprinkling of other white cloaks with the red Templar cross. He checked his own white mantle and cross and the blood-red rope around his waist. He felt perfectly dressed for battle. He looked at his brothers.

None were talking. All realized that this was the last Templar battle and, live or die, not a man of them would be elsewhere this day. Their muted silence was a bonding, a profound feeling where words were not necessary.

From the high ground Brychan studied the positions of the Scots' army spread below, trying to read Bruce's strategy. Like many of the nobility, Robert Bruce had spent countless hours studying battles in the British Isles. Most favored were William of Normandy's victorious cavalry at Hastings; and how the barbaric Picts harassed Roman garrisons when Hadrian's Wall failed to contain them; and English Queen Boudicca, an amateur and a woman, outmaneuvering veteran Roman legions.

When Robert Bruce received the unexpected gift of Templar cavalry, his commanders assumed that he would use them as a single unit. Instead, Bruce followed the strategy of Richard Coeur de Lion, who divided the Templars in small groups among his forces to inspire their reluctant comrades.

TWIST OF TIME

At the dawn of June 23 King Robert had three thinly ranked divisions to face the overpowering number of English. He attached some Templar cavalry to each division but held a group of about forty in reserve to attack where needed.

Brychan and James McGill found themselves in this reserve group. Jamie's eyes flashed in excitement; at least he would not die in some paltry cattle raid.

THE TEMPLAR COMMANDER, Sir William Saint Clair, in white mantle, was mounted on a great black charger. At his side rode a cavalry sergeant who bore the white and black Templar battle standard, the Beauseant. It was said of Lord William that none were held in higher esteem in battle. He knew King Robert Bruce well, for it was he who had rallied Templars to his cause.

Their troop stood on a rise of hill behind the Scots' center. On the ground below, Brychan could see all three Scots' divisions. The left was commanded by Lord Randolph, the right by the king's brother Edward, and the center commanded by Bruce himself.

When Robert Bruce appeared from his pavilion, Brychan saw him for the first time. He bore little resemblance to a king. He wore no armor, but a hauberk coat of mail and a basinet helmet circled with a small crown. Instead of a sword, he was armed with a battle axe and he carried no shield. His mount was not the expected cavalry charger but a gray palfrey standing only a hand higher than a cob, which a lady might ride. Chroniclers would later write that Bruce was "ill mounted."

Brychan asked Sir William. "Will the king change horse before the battle?"

"No," William explained. "He will not seek individual combat but rides between his units. A bugler goes with him to signal commands."

Robert Bruce rode down the ranks ordering his men to hold their formation. From the English line he saw a single English knight riding in the field across from him, waving his lance in challenge for single combat. The coat of arms was recognized by many as that of Sir Henry de Brohune, England's second-ranking knight in the joust. He would gain instant glory if he defeated Bruce in front of his army.

Brychan and Jamie exchanged doubtful looks as Bruce rode out, ignoring his own plan to avoid single combat. His gray mount appeared even smaller compared with de Brohune's splendid war stallion. Bruce was armed with only a battle-axe and carried no shield.

At Bruce's approach, the English knight lowered his lance and spurred his charger. The distance between would allow him to speed at full tilt when they met.

Just before connecting, Bruce wrenched his agile horse sideways. De Brohune charged past, his lance barely missing. Robert's axe slammed the side of the knight's helmet, breaking the shaft. De Brohune pitched sideways to the ground, dead with a single blow.

A victorious shout rose from the Scots' ranks! King Robert spun his mount around and with a gesture motioned them to hold ranks. Miraculously, they did not charge; their formation held.

Across the main battlefield, British King Edward was absorbed in watching his army as rank after rank aligned for combat. The King had sworn an oath to annihilate Bruce's army; he would reclaim his father Longshank's title—the hammer of the Scots. Today's victory would finally remove him from his father's heavy shadow.

Edward was attended by two knights, Sir Aymer de Vallance and Sir Giles de Argentine, who agreed that Bruce had wisely placed the Scots with the sun at their backs. The English would be marching into its glare while moving uphill.

As Brychan and James watched the growing spectacle below, James gasped, "Merciful Lord! Has there ever been a more monsterful sight?"

Brychan did not answer. He was thinking that by simply following Templar orders to keep the diary and hide the chest, he somehow ended up on a Scots battlefield! And what irony: the name Bannock was a corruption of the Gaelic phrase *"Gart na Beanacd,"* or field of blessing. There would be scant blessing here this day.

In the Scots' front line Brychan could make out a figure walking. Tall and spare, his ragged robe and cowl marked him a cleric. Brychan had heard that Bruce sent riders to fetch him from the wilderness beyond the Roman ruins of Hadrian's Wall.

The man was Bernard of Iona, a monk of great controversy who spent months alone in the wild. His beard was full; his hair in the old manner of Celtic monks was shaved in front and long at the sides. It caused dismay among his superiors, who demanded all tonsure now conform to the Roman Church style. Because of his reputation as a holy man, none dared rebuke him, not abbot, bishop, or even cardinal.

Bernard strode before the soldiers with arms raised, and in the ringing voice of a prophet, gave a blessing. The Scots, rank by rank, went to their knees to receive it. Even those on horse dismounted and kneeled.

From the distance, King Edward watched, surprised at seeing his enemy fall to their knees.

"Sire, look," Sir Aymer said. "They're kneeling before you. Our numbers alone have convinced them."

"Throne of heaven! They want to surrender." Sir Giles laughed. "Shouldn't you send an emissary to Bruce with terms?"

King Edward looked at his retinue of lords. All were murmuring at the prospect of a bloodless victory. To get the promised spoils of lands and titles without even doing battle would be a wondrous coup and secure King Edward's unique place in history.

"Sir Giles, you will go to Bruce with my terms: the surrender of his army and forfeiture of his crown, which we do not recognize as—"

"Wait, Sire." Sir Aymer pointed.

The Scots were no longer kneeling. Now the ranks were quickly forming into schiltroms, their tall spears a moving, spindly forest.

"They choose to fight!" Edward raged. He turned and shouted for all to hear. "No quarter! Pass on to all ranks. No quarter!"

Brychan watched the English slowly advancing. Each division was composed of infantry center with supporting light cavalry on each wing; the heavy cavalry was formed at the rear. Edging the flanks were small groups of bowmen. Edward, for some reason, was holding the large body of deadly Welsh archers in the rear ranks.

From the English right came a sudden burst of cavalry, several hundred moving to attack the Scots positioned on the low marsh ground. From this mushy bog the Scots had no cavalry to respond, only infantry. Their defeat would be swift.

Brychan read the English strategy: to quickly overwhelm Randolph's infantry with this cavalry assault. Once through the marsh ground, they could easily outflank the Scots and swing around to attack their unprotected rear ensuring certain annihilation.

At the appearance of enemy cavalry, Randolph's ranks tightened their schiltroms, the twelve-foot spears spread outward like hedgehog spines. The English cavalry were thundering in full charge to overwhelm them.

This soggy wooze was where Bruce had laid his trap. Three months of careful preparation were centered on this bog.

As the cavalry hurled into the marsh, horses began tumbling into narrow trenches covered with thin sod. The ranks following tried to hurdle those in front. Horse after horse went down, tramping on thousands of hidden caltrops—iron balls with spikes that were tearing and splitting their hooves. Within minutes, the entire first wave of charging English knights were on the ground.

Killing squads of Scots broke from the schiltrom to attack the fallen English. Axes and war hammers chopped and clubbed the English cavalrymen who were entangled in a mass of crippled, terrified horses. There was no quarter.

The following ranks of English cavalry managed to pull up or veer to the sides. It was impossible to enter the marsh without losing horse. The English could only helplessly watch the slaughter of their comrades. Their commander, unable to relieve or rescue, gave a signal and they retreated to their main line, the cries of the bloody massacre fading behind them.

By well into morning, divisions of both armies were engaged with neither side gaining clear advantage. Brychan was still impatiently waiting with the reserves. Then he saw two riders coming up the hill, Sir Robert Keith and his bugler.

Keith saluted Saint Clair. "King Robert requests your Templars to charge the archers firing on Randolph's division."

Lord William waved agreement and shouted to his cavalry: "Templar charge. On me."

Brychan settled firmly in the saddle and readied his lance. Hated archers—worth the waiting! It was bowmen who had disabled Ursus so that an inferior warrior could slay him.

Since his early days as a novice, Brychan had drilled for countless hours in the Templar charge. It was a disciplined formation moving at half gallop, all riders lining on the Templar banner, which always stayed center. The ranks were in successive lines with each protecting the one in front, should it be overwhelmed by cavalry or infantry. It sacrificed the shock of speed for disciplined control, making the entire troop highly maneuverable. If the formation held tight, all were swept before it in a relentless tide. Even Saracens gave way, preferring retreat to annihilation.

Sir William pointed his sword to the Templar banner and yelled "Beauseant!" The troop echoed the cry and charged down the hill. At the bottom, the ground flattened and the well-disciplined body of cavalry pulled center into tighter formation.

When the black-and-white Beauseant banner veered left with Sir William, the entire troop wheeled on him, bearing the full force of their charge into the archer's exposed flank.

Brychan lowered his lance, singling out a burly English sergeant shouting commands to the bowmen. He was turning around and Brychan felt the impact through his lance, the force of it nearly causing him to lose his grip. The sergeant's scream rang above the battle din as he twisted in the air and hit the ground. Brychan's lance jerked free as he rode past.

He immediately leveled his lance at the next row of men. An archer was facing him with an arrow already strung. As the lance caught him center, he released the arrow high, then he tumbled under Dragon's hooves.

With the cavalry's shockwave, the archers panicked and ran. Those not dropped by lance and sword were trampled under horses "like corn husk dolls," the chroniclers recorded. In the charge of successive cavalry, the body of archers was quickly decimated.

As the Templars reformed, Jamie shouted at Brychan. "Yoicks! They ran lick for leather! Satan on a stallion couldn't catch them!"

Brychan saw the Beauseant banner again turn as William Saint Clair maneuvered to attack the English cavalry at the Bannock burn. To reach the rivulet, they skirted around the edge of the battlefield. In minutes they joined the rest of the Scots as they charged the flanks of the surprised and retreating English.

TWIST OF TIME

Brychan was in the thick of a bloody melee, hacking at infantry on the ground or clashing with cavalry, sword to sword. No lines, no ranks, just slashing blades on every side.

At the peak of frenzy, Brychan suddenly found himself apart and watching to see himself and James McGill disappear in an overwhelming mass of English cavalry.

It was the last any Templar remembered seeing him alive. ✙

Thomas was sitting on the edge of the grave. He told Kate he had to rest, but that was an excuse. It had happened again, a sudden vision. He *saw* Brychan disappear in the confusion of battle. He was not reading the diary, nor in a trance, yet he saw it. It was the same clarity and detail as when Lois died exactly as in his dream. But now he was not dreaming!

"Kate, I just saw Brychan's final minutes in the battle. I wasn't reading, I . . . I actually *saw* it."

Kate thought a moment and nodded.

"Thomas," she said, "I've been wanting to tell you something, and I think this is the time. As you know, I don't understand the psychic, so, let's look at your psychic experiences from a cop's perspective. At first, these events happened when you were dreaming. But now they occur when you're awake. Right?"

"Yes. I don't do anything, it just happens."

"When I'm on a case and the situation changes, I look for anything that contributed to a change in behavior. When you started seeing the event instead of dreaming it, I began watching you as if you were a case."

"Really? What did you see?"

"That *every* time you saw the event, you had just been reading the diary."

"You think what I read suggested the vision I saw?"

Kate shook her head. "Not what you read, what you touched. What do psychics call it when you get information from an object you touch?"

"Psychometry. But that has never been my thing."

"Does a psychic's gift ever change or evolve?"

"Yes, in some people. Edgar Cayce went from healing to being able to see the future and eventually to read the past. This occurred without his doing anything."

"I think something similar is happening to you. You seem to get information from touching the diary that is not connected to what you read."

"Really? Why didn't I recognize this?"

"Maybe you are too close to it."

"But sometimes when it happened, I wasn't handling the diary. Like in Cleveland, when Lois died."

"I went over your whole case. You first dreamed about her death. Later in Cleveland you had been reading her letters. You said you were reading them when you got the phone call. Holding them was the connection with Lois; you saw the car wreck like you dreamed it."

"Lord. I would never have thought of that."

"As I was investigating your case, I began connecting things," Kate continued. "When you were involved in actually looking for the buried chest; measuring the alignment with the stele, poking the ground to find the exact spot, you were holding and using Brychan's sword." She smiled at his surprise. "If my reading you sounds psychic, it's not. I'm just following the evidence."

Thomas slowly shook his head. "Kate, you are incredible."

"Nah. Just a third-generation cop." She shrugged. "So, who won the battle?"

He tried to gather his thoughts. "Ah, the battle." He picked up the shovel and began digging again. "The wily Robert Bruce had a final surprise for the English. From behind the hill where the baggage trains were hidden, thousands of servants—the gillies—came charging and waving flags. The English thought they were hidden reinforcements. They panicked and ran. There was a mass slaughter of several thousand when they were trapped between the two banks trying to cross Bannock stream. Legend says it literally ran red with blood. But I don't know where Brychan was on the battlefield when he. . . "

There was the clunk of metal on metal. He got down on his knees.

"May be something here," he said. "Kate, give me some light."

Kate aimed the flashlight beam in the hole, centering on his hands.

As he worked clearing and brushing dirt, an outline appeared. Emerging from the soil was an iron coffer with a thick green patina—700 years of crusty oxidation.

"Dear . . . God," Kate whispered.

With some effort he heaved the chest to the edge of the pit and looked up at Kate. "Now, let's find Sir Brychan."

He worked the gravesite for another hour. There was not a bone, no scrap of metal, no weapons, nor armor. There was no body. Thomas, sweaty and exhausted, sat on the side of the grave, bewildered.

"Thomas," Kate asked, "who would steal Brychan's body but leave the chest?"

CHAPTER SIXTEEN

✠ LADY GWYNN BORE no love for the Templars. Warriors, fanatics, and drunkards, they had stolen her son away from his true calling of scholar teacher. There was one compensation: as a Cistercian, Thomas was only allowed to write one letter a year, but as a Templar there was no restriction. Brychan wrote to her often, the letters delivered by couriers who were carrying coded messages for the Templar underground.

Word of Sir Brychan's death came the day after the battle of Bannock by courier bearing a pouch signed in English: "James McGill, fellowe Templar knyte eant frynde." Enclosed was a parchment letter in Gaelic from Brychan predicting his death. That he died in Scotland on a battlefield near his home was an additional shock; he was thought to be living in France.

Though there were rumors of an army being raised in Scotland, few knew of the Templars and none of Brychan's presence.

Old Rothgar was dispatched with double-horse cart to bring his body home. At the family's Norman-style stone chapel, it was placed on an oak table in front of the altar. The air was heavy with the waxy aroma from the twenty and nine candles numbering his years. In the stifling heat another odor was growing, for it was the third day. A requiem Mass was set for the morrow.

Watching the laying-out were a haggard Lady Gwynn, brother Duncan pale as a woman in grief, and Vivyan with her son Master Andrew, who stood silently watching. Lady Gwynn with steely grace looked down at the butchered wreckage of her son. Rothgar had warned that he was "fearsome mauled."

HE WAS STILL dressed as he had fallen—battered helmet and chainmail hauberk coat with gloved hands folded across the sword lying on his body. According to Templar tradition, he would be buried clothed in his armor. His Templar cloak was ripped, bloody, and mud-caked. In a final English outrage for being a Templar, his chest was crushed, his heart torn out, and his face destroyed with a war hammer. Lady Gwynn removed his gloves and kissed the fingers that she once taught letters. Vivyan, choking sobs, had to be supported by two servants when her legs gave way.

THAT NIGHT, LADY Gwynn sat lone vigil in the chapel reading her breviary by candlelight.

She had placed sprigs of oak, hawthorn, and holly bobbe along his body, following the Celtic church's tradition.

She looked up from the breviary page.

"I've been waiting," she said.

Brychan stepped from the shadows. "How did you know?"

"When I kissed the fingers there was no ink stain. Yours always were stained, even as a child. That brutish hand never held anything but a weapon. Who was he?"

"An English knight. When Brother James revived me, I could not believe I was alive. It was well into the night. Tens of hundreds of English lay dead. To trick the Inquisition, we searched for a knight my size. We dressed him in my clothes and armor and mauled him in the English manner, especially the face. A Gypsy had given me a bag of medicine for the horses. Brother James covered me with a balm and the expected fever did not come. My heroic demise was nulled by Gypsy medicine for a horse. So much for the glorious prophecy of my death."

"Then it was the right time to prophesy wrong." She spread her hands over the body. "Why have you done this?"

"The Grand Master gave me a charge: to hide a sacred chest."

"After that, will you return to the Church?"

His answer would hurt but there was no way to soften it. "No. Both Pope and Church betrayed us."

"Then the Templars are saints?"

"The Pope sanctioned murder! No guilt proven, yet not one acquittal. One hundred twenty-four burned alive in Paris alone. Even Grand Master de Molay; never a nobler soul."

He moved closer and was startled; her hair beneath the mourning veil had turned white in the seven years since he saw her last. He continued.

"God gives us the sight. Yet, if we use it, we are burned by the Holy Office. I will serve God, not a murdering Pope."

In the candlelight, she now could see that his left arm was in a sling and bound to his body. "And your wound?"

"I am told it will mend, somewhat."

"What do you want here?"

He moved opposite her from across the table. A faint sweetish aroma rose from the body mixed with the canker of death.

"You once ordered me to give you an heir," he said. "I did. Now, I beg a favor. Bury this knight in my grave."

"No English may rot in a Houston grave! How many Houstons have they slaughtered over the years? And my own, the Campbells?" She commanded. "Say the count!"

Since childhood, Brychan knew it by rote, as did all Scots children, even as years added to the toll. "Twelve Houstons, nine Campbells."

"Tomorrow is your requiem Mass. After that you must remove this carrion."

"No, my Lady. In my grave this carrion will keep me alive."

IN A HARD-BLOWING, freezing wind, Father Pierre knocked at the gate of the Sacred Heart Capuchin monastery all but hidden in a desolate valley in the Harz Mountains. The Church's most severe order, the monks spent their days in solitary cells in prayer and meditation, leaving only for two meager meals and the five canon hours.

When Pierre had returned from Scotland to report to the Pope's Cardinal at Avignon, he swore that the Templar Brychan was killed in battle. Pierre had gone to Houston Castle where, invoking Inquisition authority, he ordered the grave opened. He personally viewed the knight's battered remains but failed to recover diary or chest.

Though Pope Clement was dead, the ever-meticulous pontiff had left confidential instructions regarding Pierre's mission. The priest, if successful, would be made a bishop; if not, another course was determined.

Father Pierre arrived at the monastery with orders to bide there "for the good of his soul until receiving further Papal orders."

However, the succeeding pope was not briefed, either through oversight or embarrassment over the mission's existence and failure. Years passed.

The order never came. ✝

Kate was speeding at night on a rough country road, the headlights bouncing with each rolling bump.

"We did it!" she cried.

"Yesss!" he yelled, and they bumped fists.

Kate checked her mirror again. A hundred yards or so behind, car lights appeared then disappeared behind each curve. Each time it was out of sight, it gained on them.

"We've got a tail," she said.

"You sure or just paranoid?"

"Both." She accelerated. "Let's see what he's got."

Burns was driving. Sawyer sat with a .44 Magnum long-barrel in his lap.

"She's spotted us," Burns said.

"Better get them now before we reach another town."

The two cars followed a road that meandered along a ridge edging the hills. Occasional dirt roads cut in from farms and rolling pastures.

Kate watched the mirror and said, "They're closing."

"Can you outrun them?"

"We're about to find out. You can bet your fat glutes they know we've got the chest. Look where we are—no witnesses."

Sawyer was changing the bullets in the Magnum.

"What's that?" Burns asked.

"Armor piercing, my own special load. It can penetrate an engine block."

Kate was trying to remember the road. She had driven it several times during the day but at night there were no familiar landmarks. She passed a sign indicating an intersection ahead. "Grab that handle above your door."

"Why?"

"Just do it."

Fifty yards before the intersection, Kate eased the accelerator, pulled hard on the emergency brake, and cut left. They went into a controlled spin at the crossroad, hung for a nanosecond, and straightened to one-eighty—a bootleg turn. She gunned it straight toward Burns and Sawyer's oncoming car.

"Shit!" Burns yelled.

Kate assumed the driver was an American and used to driving on the right. With luck, he would try to pass on the right.

Burns turned right to get around her. Kate cut hard and clipped his left rear, sending him into a sharp spin.

She hit the brakes, making another complete turnaround as Burns' car stalled dead. She floored it, T-boning him broadside. Then she saw the gun.

"Down!" she shouted, and they ducked below the dashboard as Sawyer's loud shot shattered the windshield.

A second shot slammed into the doorframe. She floored it again.

Kate's car drove Burns sideways to the very edge of the road. Burns jammed the foot brake to lock everything. Too late.

Kate and Thomas peered over the dashboard; there was no car. They heard it tumbling down the hill and saw its lights flashing skyward with each roll.

They jumped out and ran to the edge of the drop. About thirty yards below, the car was upside down, roof crumpled, a giant smashed toy. Both lights glowed at odd angles; one front wheel was still turning and spitting dirt.

"Bastards!" she yelled.

Thomas clicked on a flashlight and started down the hill.

"Thomas, wait," she said.

He looked up at her. "What?"

"We did it!" she cried.

"Yesss!" he yelled, and they bumped fists.

Kate checked her mirror again. A hundred yards or so behind, car lights appeared then disappeared behind each curve. Each time it was out of sight, it gained on them.

"We've got a tail," she said.

"You sure or just paranoid?"

"Both." She accelerated. "Let's see what he's got."

Burns was driving. Sawyer sat with a .44 Magnum long-barrel in his lap.

"She's spotted us," Burns said.

"Better get them now before we reach another town."

The two cars followed a road that meandered along a ridge edging the hills. Occasional dirt roads cut in from farms and rolling pastures.

Kate watched the mirror and said, "They're closing."

"Can you outrun them?"

"We're about to find out. You can bet your fat glutes they know we've got the chest. Look where we are—no witnesses."

Sawyer was changing the bullets in the Magnum.

"What's that?" Burns asked.

"Armor piercing, my own special load. It can penetrate an engine block."

Kate was trying to remember the road. She had driven it several times during the day but at night there were no familiar landmarks. She passed a sign indicating an intersection ahead. "Grab that handle above your door."

"Why?"

TWIST OF TIME

"Just do it."

Fifty yards before the intersection, Kate eased the accelerator, pulled hard on the emergency brake, and cut left. They went into a controlled spin at the crossroad, hung for a nanosecond, and straightened to one-eighty—a bootleg turn. She gunned it straight toward Burns and Sawyer's oncoming car.

"Shit!" Burns yelled.

Kate assumed the driver was an American and used to driving on the right. With luck, he would try to pass on the right.

Burns turned right to get around her. Kate cut hard and clipped his left rear, sending him into a sharp spin.

She hit the brakes, making another complete turnaround as Burns' car stalled dead. She floored it, T-boning him broadside. Then she saw the gun.

"Down!" she shouted, and they ducked below the dashboard as Sawyer's loud shot shattered the windshield.

A second shot slammed into the doorframe. She floored it again.

Kate's car drove Burns sideways to the very edge of the road. Burns jammed the foot brake to lock everything. Too late.

Kate and Thomas peered over the dashboard; there was no car. They heard it tumbling down the hill and saw its lights flashing skyward with each roll.

They jumped out and ran to the edge of the drop. About thirty yards below, the car was upside down, roof crumpled, a giant smashed toy. Both lights glowed at odd angles; one front wheel was still turning and spitting dirt.

"Bastards!" she yelled.

Thomas clicked on a flashlight and started down the hill.

"Thomas, wait," she said.

He looked up at her. "What?"

"They've got high-velocity ammo. These guys are killers. In case something happens. . . ." She hesitated. "I love you. I mean, I am *in love* with you."

It was absurd but there might not be another chance.

"God, Kate—your timing."

Moans were coming from the car. Kate pulled her Beretta. They scrambled down the rolling slope, around jagged rocks and rough boulders. The car's collapsed roof had blown out all the side windows like an explosion.

"Toss out your guns or I'll shoot the gas tank," Kate ordered.

There were muffled noises from inside the car. Two automatics dropped from the window. "That's it," a cramped voice said.

She picked them up, a Magnum and a Ruger, and tossed them downhill.

"Now, your phones," she said.

"Call an ambulance," a different voice croaked.

"Who hired you?" Kate asked.

No answer.

"We're leaving," she warned.

"Wait." From the car window two cell phones dropped to the ground. "Fallon."

She gave Thomas a look. "My favorite perp."

Thomas stooped down to peer into the car, shining the light inside. The two men were hanging upside down by their seat belts. Both faces were bloody. The driver was trembling with shock.

"My leg is b-broken," he said.

"Good," Kate said. "What were Fallon's orders?"

"Shit! I'm bleeding." The man in the passenger seat could now see from the flashlight.

"Fallon told us to get the chest," the driver said.

"Did he also tell you to kill us?"

There was no answer.

While Kate called emergency services at 999, Thomas studied their faces. Incredibly, he had never seen them even though they had been following him for days. Kate asked for an ambulance, gave the location, and hung up.

"Let's get out of here," she said.

Climbing back up on the road they checked the car. The front bumper was twisted at an angle and the intact windshield had etched a crystal labyrinth all the way across with a cabbage-sized hole on the passenger side. The car would still drive.

When they arrived at the cottage, they parked but did not get out of the car. Neither spoke, still trying to absorb what had happened.

Thomas looked at her. "Kate, this, this whole *mess* could ruin you."

"Merely because I lied to my boss, killed the prime suspect in a foreign country, and I haven't an atom of proof to solve Hollander's murder?"

"Think," he said as he took her hand. "If you don't report it. Nobody will know."

"I can't do that."

"You said the hitter was a pro. Do you really believe that whoever sent him will report him missing to the police? He's an assassin. How can they?"

"Thomas, I have no choice. I am a *cop*."

"Bury him."

"What?"

"In Brychan's grave."

"Holy Mary, will that work?"

"It worked for Brychan for seven hundred years."

Once inside the cottage, they set the chest, wrapped in a wool blanket, on the dining room table.

"Coffee coming up," she said, and headed toward the kitchen.

Thomas went to the bathroom to check the tub. He froze—the body was gone.

"Kate!" he called as he rushed back into the room.

Four of the men had guns; a fifth was taking Kate's Beretta from her. She looked at Thomas, her face unreadable.

Another man appeared from the hall, a Black man who by his manner was in charge.

"Who are you?" Thomas asked.

"Leo," he answered and turned to the men. "Carver, you are twenty-three minutes behind schedule. Take the chest to the rendezvous, then dispose of the body."

Steiner and Wojowitz refolded the blanket over the chest, picked it up between them, and went out the front door. Carver and Grigsby waited; Alonzo moved closer to Thomas and looked at him with a half-smile.

"Remember me?" he asked.

Thomas did not recognize him. Alonzo slammed him hard in the stomach. Thomas doubled over, gasping.

"Alonzo!" Leo warned, "Leave."

Carver and Grigsby laughed. Alonzo crossed to the door and the three left together.

Thomas pressed against the wall, fighting for breath.

"Alonzo was the one you gave a concussion to the night you escaped," Leo explained. He waited, listening to the car outside drive away, then looked at Kate. "They've gone."

"Thomas, please, just listen." She paused while he recovered his breath enough to follow what she was saying. "Leo is a cardinal in the Church."

Leo took an amethyst ring from his pocket and slipped it on the third finger of his right hand. "Cardinal in pectore," he said. "It means—"

"A secret cardinal known only to the Pope," Thomas finished for him.

"Yes." Leo nodded, impressed.

Thomas looked angrily at Kate. "So, you're not lapsed."

"Not entirely."

"Kate, please get it," Leo said.

She went to the chimney, removed the clear plastic encased diary from behind the bricks, and handed it to Leo. She glanced at Thomas but said nothing.

He glared at her. "Maybe the Pope will make you a saint for fucking a monk to steal the diary."

"Actually," Leo explained, "the diary was stolen from us."

"Then I presume, your Eminence, those were your goons rescuing me at Oxnard?"

"Yes. To free you and then let you escape."

"Let me escape?"

"How else could you find the chest? After we got you safely away, we planned to let you go and see that you weren't abducted again. Alonzo, whom you clobbered with the briefcase, is my operative in the group. That's why he hit you just now, to maintain his cover."

"Your *operative*?" Thomas suddenly connected. "You are . . . Vatican Intelligence?"

"We've denied it since Napoleon. But after years of speculation, numerous books, and coverage in the media, what's the point?"

"And your thugs—all good Catholics?"

"Oh, no. Only Alonzo. The rest of this particular team are hired help—a mix of rogue intelligence operatives, Cold War flotsam, career criminals. They have no idea who they really work for."

"Your Eminence, isn't your position too exalted to be out grubbing in the field?"

"In special operations like this one, we are hands-on. Obviously, we work well apart from the Vatican. After years in the Vatican Foreign Service, I was secretly named Cardinal in pectore and made Director of Intelligence. Believe me, I didn't want it. But the Holy Father was a difficult man to refuse."

"What was supposed to happen after I found the chest?"

"We'd steal it from you, with Kate's help."

Leo went to the table where there was a tan briefcase. The top edge was loaded with tricked-out hardware. Leo opened it, put the diary inside, and locked the case. He touched a button and there was a crisp hiss of air.

"It's a specially designed case," he said. "Temp controlled, no moisture. Perfect protection for the diary." Leo handed the case to Kate and said, "Get Denise Hollander's killer."

Thomas was surprised. "I thought the diary was critically important to you."

"My mission is to get the chest. The diary was simply the means. We've removed several key pages before turning it over to the police. Kate still has a murderer to catch—the diary is critical evidence, the motive for a tragic homicide of an innocent Catholic woman. Brother Thomas, I presume you have questions."

Thomas' surprise did not soften his anger. "Start with the raid. How did you know where they were hiding me?"

"Surveillance. We were parked outside the monastery keeping a twenty-four-seven watch on you since you were the one most likely to find the diary. When you were abducted, we followed. We made the assault the next night. After you escaped and went back to Kate, she kept us informed of your movements. But I still had to order my men to track you in order to maintain *my* cover. It becomes very tricky when you have to deceive your own people too."

Thomas looked at Kate. "Like you deceived me."

"Please, you must not blame her," Leo said. "The Church can be very persuasive, even to the so-called lapsed."

Several weeks earlier, Kate had received a call from her father. He sounded odd and insisted that she meet him at the beach house. She rushed there, fearing a family crisis.

He was waiting with a stranger, a Black man, well-dressed and with a commanding presence. Behind him, a very large man hovered, his function obvious. She had never seen her father, Captain Grady Flynn, Chief of Homicide, so nervous. He introduced the man as Leo, who then presented Vatican credentials as a Cardinal. Kate was astonished—a Prince of the Church wearing a business suit on a Vatican mission in Santa Barbara?

Leo explained that a woman courier had disappeared carrying a rare book, a diary stolen from the Vatican. She had been murdered. They needed a police officer on the inside when the killer was caught. The diary must be given back to the Church before its contents could be made public. Would she help them?

Kate looked in disbelief at her father, the hard-assed Catholic layman. Even the Cardinal in the Los Angeles archdiocese personally knew him. This dedicated policeman was trying to convince her to steal evidence for the Church! She bit her lip, wanting to ask, "Is it any wonder people like me lapse?" Instead, she listened to the Cardinal while straining her patience to its bearable limits.

Leo's argument was a shrewd mix of candor, logic, and emotional appeal. If she agreed to help, there must be no relationship between them. They had prepared a scenario where Kate would be the lapsed, cynical non-believer with no church connection if she were caught. She must do whatever necessary to be convincing and get the diary.

Kate's thoughts were racing. This was an opportunity to do something unique. Given her maverick streak, it was irresistible. To her own surprise, she agreed.

Leo gave her a recognition password for any communications between them: John 3:16.

"One final item," Leo said. "An Anglican monk named Thomas Bardsey. The diary was being brought to him for translation. Get close to him. He could be invaluable to us."

Leo was explaining the need for secrecy to Thomas. "As you can see, it was absolutely essential that you never know about us."

"What changed your plan?"

"The body in your bathtub. When you went for ice, Kate phoned us. We never leave our people stranded. Never. It is our one unbreakable rule. By killing the assassin, Brother Thomas, you've paid a terrible price. You deserve to know whatever we can tell you."

Kate added, "He was going to bury the body where we found the chest. To protect me."

"Ingenious, but an industrial solvent will be tidier. And untraceable."

"I bow to your expertise, Eminence." Thomas gave an ironic nod. "Who stole the diary from the Church?"

"That took us considerable time to figure out. We discovered that in the 1960s, a radical Belgian priest named Father Meern got himself assigned to the Vatican library. He secretly searched for the diary for several years, found it, and disappeared. He believed it would give him information damaging to the Church."

Thomas frowned; that made no sense. "Why would a priest want that?"

"Father Meern was adamantly opposed to the Vatican II reforms of Blessed Pope John. He was half mad, lost in that terrible limbo between the faithful and the fanatic. He actually thought he could pressure the Vatican to alter its policy."

"What did he do with the diary?"

"It was stolen from him. He spent the rest of his life trying to recover it and failed. When he was dying, he wrote a letter to us confessing his theft. Then the book dealer Lazlo Reiner suddenly appeared with the diary and sold it to Winslow Fallon. Shortly afterward, Reiner was murdered."

"How convenient."

"Oh, not by us. Unlike other Intelligence agencies, we don't kill for Mother Church. But we do maintain the illusion that we have no limits."

"Historically, the Church's willingness to kill is no illusion, your Eminence."

Leo smiled tolerantly. "You and I must argue the Inquisition some other time."

"How did the Church get the diary from Brychan?"

"That I honestly don't know."

AFTER A LIFETIME of service, by late January 1316, Abbot Father Jude the Venerable was frail, shrunken, and worn by a long life of monastic discipline and extraordinary labor. Daily he prayed to retire but his superiors deemed him irreplaceable. For that, God would have to take him.

The Abbot's face was all wrine and wrinkles. One eye, whey-clouded, made reading difficult. He pushed the candle forward, casting more light on his visitor.

She was a Gypsy and though the Abbot would not have agreed to meet a woman in chambers, when she said that this concerned Brychan, he relented.

"How is our beloved Brother Brychan?"

The woman did not answer. He saw that her arm cradled a book bound in dark leather with brass studs. Her other hand rested on her belly, swollen with child.

She set the book in front of him.

He was puzzled. "What is this?"

"A diary. Sir Brychan said that if anything happened to give this to you. It contains codes."

"Codes?"

"For the Church to recover Templar money."

Father Abbot repositioned the candle and opened the book. When he looked up to ask a question, the Gypsy was gone. ✣

Nora, parked half a block from the cottage, sat watching from the darkness of her car. There had been no contact from Ravel. After dialing him repeatedly, she got no answer. While deciding her next move, two men came out of the cottage carrying something wrapped in a blanket and put it in a car parked on the street. It had to be the chest.

Shortly, three more men came out. Nora recognized one of them—Sid Carver, the Broker. In that instant she understood everything. She had lost.

There was only one thing left for her to do. She swallowed three amphetamines and quickly drove away.

Inside the cottage Thomas was firing more questions at Leo. "And your connection with Fallon?"

"A dangerous man—enormous power, zero ethics. Because of his questionable experiments he was on our watch list. Then Lazlo Reiner appeared with the diary. But before we could make an offer, he sold it to Fallon. When the courier Hollander, an innocent woman and lifelong Catholic, was murdered and mutilated, Fallon became our priority to see if he was involved."

"And if he was, would you go after him?"

"No. Just an anonymous call to the police and then mail them any physical evidence through a series of postal letter drops. We always try to work in the background. They never know the source. They would never imagine that some of their anonymous tips come from the Church."

Thomas searched his eyes for a lie. "What is in the chest?"

"My mission is to get it, not speculate. I can only tell you there are powerful forces after it. We try to protect over a billion Catholics worldwide with an organization so small you would not believe me. Surely, that is one argument against the criticism that the Church today lacks relevance."

"How do you manage that?"

"Deception. False flags. Complex scenarios. We recruit specialists—sometimes they know, sometimes not. In this case," he said, and smiled at Kate, "a homicide detective and an obsessed Anglican monk."

Thomas, though irritated by the description, was not to be sidetracked. "Why is the chest and diary so important to everyone?"

"Who benefits the most?" He gave an Italianate shrug. "The Templars had great wealth and a mass of esoteric knowledge, two tempting targets. Winslow Fallon does not need money, so he is after something else. And I seriously doubt that the Church is looking for hidden treasure."

Kate asked, "When you discover what is in the chest, doesn't the public have a right to know?"

"From a biased media? No. For example, I personally have no opinion about the Shroud of Turin. In 1988, the Church let an international scientific team test samples for dating. They reported that the shroud could be no earlier than the medieval period. It made the front pages—the shroud was a fraud." He spread his hands. "Since then, it has been scientifically proven that the test samples were contaminated, which gave a false date. New tests confirm the shroud is at least twice as old, roughly first century—the time of Christ. DNA pollen tests have revealed a variety of plant life particular only to Jerusalem. There is no way that anyone in the past faking the shroud could anticipate the future genetic testing of pollen. Also, a unique stitching pattern on the back of the shroud was found only in first-century Palestine. Forensic and serology tests reveal the shroud of a crucified Jew, type AB blood, and containing nanoparticles, which suggest he was brutally tortured before he died. Whoever he was, the media generally ignored it."

"Then the media is your excuse to stonewall?"

"They simply can't be trusted. Their flavor of the month is a stale re-hash of the old story that Mary Magdalene was Jesus' wife, the Resurrection faked, and she had his baby. It is revived to sell novels and television documentaries—it has no scriptural, factual, or historical merit. But what I am going to tell you does. In 2007, the Vatican announced that they possessed records of the Templar trials that showed that Pope Clement did not believe the Templars were guilty of heresy. Had they believed the Resurrection was false and that Mary Magdalene bore Jesus' child, *that* would be heresy. Pope Clement's statement proves the Templar-Magdalene myth to be completely false." He sighed in exasperation. "There is even a legend that Mary Magdalene hid Christ's mummified body in a cave in the south of France. Brother Thomas, you cannot imagine the crap that comes across my desk."

"What do you think is in the chest?" Kate asked.

"What I think is not important. But several popes knew what it contained. They left instructions stating that it should be protected in every way possible. No matter what anyone believes, in over two thousand years, no historical, Biblical, or archeological discovery has disproved the Crucifixion or the Resurrection. So, whatever is in the chest is not some clichéd conspiracy theory damaging to the Church."

"Then, why the secrecy?"

"Timing. A prophecy to be revealed at the proper time."

"How long did it take you to come up with that?"

"It didn't come from me."

Thomas explained to Kate: "The same occurred with the Church's prophecies from the Blessed Virgin. They were revealed to the public at a chosen time."

The front door opened and a tall, graceful blond walked in. She was startlingly attractive, with a model's face and dressed casually but expensively. Thomas and Kate shared a surprised look.

"The driver wants to know your orders," she said to Leo.

"They've taken the chest to the airport. We'll follow and meet them there," said Leo, and looked at Thomas and Kate. "This is Andrea, my assistant. Actually, Sister Veronica."

She gave them a smile and quickly left. All eyes followed her.

"She's a *nun*?" Kate asked.

"Assigned to Special Security Detail. It was established after the assassination attempt on Pope John Paul." There was a twinkle in his eye as he added, "She's also part of my cover. It costs a small fortune to make her look like that." He looked at Thomas. "Now

I have a question. The Templar's grave contained no remains. What do you think happened?"

"Possibly somebody hid . . ."

"The grave. Of course!" Kate said. "Thomas, I know how it was done!"

"What was?"

"At least one homicide. Your Eminence, may we borrow your jet?"

CHAPTER SEVENTEEN

While driving to the airport Kate explained her theory. For the moment, it was as if nothing was wrong between them; there was a homicide to solve. The diary in its case lay beside them.

Thomas considered her idea. "If you're right," he said, "that's the answer."

"Even if I'm wrong, it still might convict Fallon of Brother Simon's murder." She dialed her cell and looked at her watch. "It's six-twenty in Santa Barbara."

Cioffi answered. Kate laughed and said, "Don't you ever leave, Doc?"

"No. Been expecting your call."

"I'm flying home, Cioffi. I need everything you've got—autopsy, lab reports, and that microchip implant."

"I can't."

"Why not?"

"There are no reports. No implant. Nothing."

"What do you mean?"

"Everything was taken. A crew just showed up. No paperwork. The whole thing never happened."

"That's impossible!"

"There was nothing I could do."

"This is a homicide! The D.A. can—"

"Without all the physical evidence, he refuses to indict."

"Cioffi! We've got to fight this!"

"Kate, I'm eleven months from pension. I'm sorry."

"Sonova-BITCH!"

She hung up and angrily dialed Vicky. "What did you find in Brother Simon's hospital records?" Kate asked.

"Except for his routine dialysis, not a thing," said Vicky. "I've looked everywhere in that damn hospital."

Kate looked at Thomas. "The hospital records have disappeared, too."

"I can see pressuring the coroner, but wouldn't a hospital staff involve too many people?"

"Maybe not. Remember what Fallon said that day at lunch? Something about power is also knowing *who* to bribe?"

At the airport, they sat in the plane while awaiting refueling. Having exhausted the Brother Simon topic, they lapsed into stony silence. Her betrayal was a hard wall between them.

"Kate, were you ordered to seduce me?" Thomas suddenly blurted.

"That not-too-original sin was my own idea. You cannot possibly believe otherwise."

"I don't know what to believe."

"I do. I'm in hell—in love with a monk. You just have an awkward problem at the monastery. Me."

After the past twenty-two grueling hours, both fell into exhausted sleep. They did not wake up until the plane landed in Baltimore on a drizzling Sunday morning.

TWIST OF TIME

* * *

Winslow Fallon was up earlier than usual, anxiously pacing in his apartment at Med-Tek. He seldom slept more than four hours a night with an occasional catnap. Most comfortable in work surroundings, the lab was his womb. This apartment above it, decorated in lavishly bad taste, was an extension of his workplace. Here he could have sex surrounded by walls hung with enlarged photos of erotic sketches by Rembrandt, Dali, and Picasso: no common pornography for him.

Fallon checked the time again—it was a little after nine. On Sunday, the chef arrived at eleven to prepare brunch for Longrieve, who was in the Lab below. There had been no contact with Burns and Sawyer since the previous night. A bad sign.

He sat behind his oversized desk and touched redial on his cell. No response. He looked up, his color drained.

"Gladys?" he said.

Nora waved cheerily. "Hi, Boss."

"You're dead."

"You don't look so good yourself," she said. "Since I'm dead I wasn't removed from the security system. Incredible. The minute I die, everything around here falls apart."

She appeared little changed from the day he lured her away from the NSA. He bitterly remembered how he misjudged her; she should have been the perfect ally. "You faked your death?"

"Hey, that's quick, Boss. Only took you two years."

"Gladys, what do you. . ."

"I prefer Nora," she corrected. "I came to tell you that they got the Templar chest."

"Who?"

"Vatican Intelligence. They were on to it, just like you feared. Looks like the ol' KGB was right—the Vee Eye, Vatican Intelligence, best in the world."

"How do you know it was them?"

"I recognized one of their drones—Carver, the Broker, remember? They've used him before. The imbecile still hasn't a clue who he works for."

"But how did you know they were in Scotland?"

"Jennifer, your secretary. She heard you telling Burns where to go in Edinburgh."

"That fat bitch!"

"Greedy fat bitch. Between bribing Jennifer, hiring my muscle, and creating a new identity, I may file bankruptcy." Her bantering tone changed. "I've got something to show you."

"I don't have time for your . . ." Then he saw the gun: a chrome-plated .32 automatic, small and deadly.

"Let's go down to Toyland and see GOLEM."

They entered his private elevator. She punched the code while holding the gun barrel inches from his groin.

"Little man," she said, "if we run into trouble, you are worse than dead."

He nodded, petrified. He knew she meant it. At the door to Lab 5 he activated the security system and they entered.

Fallon wobbled, almost fainting. The lab was empty of staff. Herbert Longrieve was in his chair in front of GOLEM. A piece of his head was missing. Bits of brain, bone, and blood splattered across GOLEM were still dripping.

"Look." Nora held up a single page. "The printout when I shot him. GOLEM kept him alive for sixteen-point-seven seconds. I thought I was going to have to shoot that damn computer too." Her smile was ice. "That leaves just you."

"You bitch! Do you think that I'm the only one? This movement is unstoppable."

They heard the lab door open. Both turned to see Kate, Thomas, and a security guard with his .45 automatic leveled.

"Drop it," the guard said. He looked eager for somebody to make a mistake. "I mean it!"

Nora stepped behind Fallon. "He dies first!" She jammed the gun barrel against his head and cocked the hammer. His glasses skewed sideways; his eyes bulged in terror.

"Nora." Thomas' tone was gentle. "Killing him won't stop anything."

"Please, *please*," Kate pleaded, "don't do it."

Nora held their position like a tableau for a moment, then visibly sagged. Perhaps, because a woman was asking, or the drugs had burned out, or she was completely exhausted, she muttered, "I am . . . so tired."

Kate gently took the automatic from her. Instead of using handcuffs, she motioned to the guard, and they escorted Nora out.

Thomas was amazed at Kate's reasoning. Brychan's empty grave had triggered the idea: if Dr. Gladys Pullman's death was faked, then Nora fit all the pieces. When she didn't get the chest, her obsessive quest to stop Fallon would force her to kill him. Kate's theory was dead right.

At the Charles Street precinct, Kate met with Homicide Detective Lt. Dan Swartz. They had talked by phone when he sent her Gladys Pullman's file. A veteran of seventeen years, he was lead investigator on Fallon's case because of its high profile and his reputation as a relentless investigator. Second-generation German, Swartz was five-feet-seven of squat fireplug; muscular with a military burr cut and wearing an ugly tie. The room was crowded with homicide detectives who had worked the three cases; all were talking and comparing notes.

Thomas and Kate were interviewed separately, then together. Captain Starger was contacted in Santa Barbara to verify Kate's story. He ordered her to return to Santa Barbara immediately. Severe censure or dismissal from the PD was certain.

When they came back into the squad room, they found Swartz briefing everyone. He announced that Fallon, after signing a statement, had been released. Nora was in jail and charged with the courier Hollander's homicide.

As Swartz was explaining, he was called to the phone in another room. Kate and Thomas moved apart to talk; she was seething. "I get a royal ass-chewing from Captain Starger and Fallon gets off by signing a statement?"

"Well, at least you got Nora."

After some minutes, Swartz returned, shaking his head. "That call was the DA. He is delaying charging Nora or Dr. Pullman, or whoever the hell she is."

"Why?" Kate was incredulous.

"Nora has been rushed to the hospital."

The detectives exploded into cries of "The bitch is faking!" and "Goddamn lawyers!"

Swartz gestured for silence. "I also talked with Dr. Julia Kempt, Nora's physician. She's an oncologist at Johns Hopkins. Nora will be dead in a few months. Lung cancer."

Thomas looked at Kate. "That's why she was in such a hurry," he said.

"And used all her assets." Her tone was touched with admiration.

Early the next morning at her hotel, Kate received a call from Lt. Swartz. "Nora just phoned me and demanded that I come to the hospital and to bring you both with me."

"What for?"

"I don't know. She sounded strange. Meet me there in an hour."

At the Johns Hopkins oncology unit, they found Nora in a private room with a police guard at the door. Lt. Swartz and Kate showed their credentials and explained that Thomas was their forensic advisor. When they entered, Nora was lying in bed, receiving medications from a litter of IV tubes hanging on two racks. Her skin was leaden, her eyes a bit too bright. The handcuffs linking her to the bed reminded Thomas of the similar situation when he was her prisoner cuffed to a metal cot. The irony did not escape her.

"Brother Thomas, I cannot resist the cliché—we must stop meeting like this."

"I am sorry you're sick, Nora."

"Will you pray for your enemy?"

"I have no choice," he said, and smiled. "To love is a commandment, not an option."

"Oh, *pleeez*, I didn't ask you here to preach."

"Why did you ask us?" Kate asked.

"As a scientist facing the inevitable, I don't want loose ends muddling my work. I want full credit, good and bad." Nora glanced at a small pad on which were scribbled notes. "First, the loose ends. Brother Thomas, when you were my prisoner, I told you that I killed someone to get data on Fallon's experiments."

"Yes, you did."

"That was a lie to intimidate you. I was afraid you might refuse my offer to give you the Templar diary for the translation. I was prepared to torture you, even if you died. You escaped the very night we were to begin. That is a strong argument for the existence of guardian angels." She referred to her notes. "The first homicide was the book dealer Lazlo Reiner. My intention was to stop Fallon. If I got the diary, it would greatly impair his GOLEM project. I made a deal with Reiner for the diary. But when he sold it to Fallon for more money, I was furious." She smiled, remembering. "One night I waited outside Reiner's apartment. Two shots in the groin; he squealed like a pig."

She looked at them, waiting for a reaction. When she didn't get one, she shrugged and said, "Well, *I* liked it."

Kate took advantage of the pause. "Since you were already in Fallon's organization, why did you fake your death and leave?"

"My work for Fallon was actually helping the GOLEM project! That had to stop. I suddenly realized that with my knowledge of Fallon's company I could do more harm if he had no idea whom he was fighting. So, I died. He never dreamed it was me. Sometimes the best ideas are so obvious that we miss them." She rubbed her eyes. "I'm afraid the drugs have me a bit addled."

"And the other homicides?" Kate prompted.

"Once I was dead, I was free to move about. Since there was no body, just blood and DNA on my clothes, all I had to do was avoid Fallon seeing me. The second homicide was the courier Hollander. Through my intel contacts I hired a professional assassin, Ravel Marinero. He used a garrote, quick and clean. What he did with head, hands, and feet, I didn't ask. Now that I had the diary I could go after the Templar chest. But when you got the diary in that raid, I had to start all over again." She smiled, relishing the scene. "Finally, I shot Longrieve, who was merely an appendage of GOLEM. Now Fallon will have to find another psychic of Longrieve's caliber, who may not exist. Unfortunately, due to reality issues," she said, gesturing to the medical apparatus, "I failed to kill Fallon."

The three looked at each other amazed. Lt. Swartz asked, "Nora, will you dictate and sign a confession?"

"Certainly. And if you have any other homicides you haven't solved, you can put them on my tab." She gave a ragged sigh. "I'm exhausted. Please leave before I change my mind."

That same day, Kate and Thomas were to meet with Fallon to give him the diary translation. Thomas wanted to get the check for the monastery and leave, but Fallon insisted on a celebration. He arranged for the three of them to meet for dinner at Manna, the most exclusive restaurant in Baltimore. The last time Fallon dined there, a camera crew accompanied him to shoot an episode for the television show *World Class Chefs*. The owner of Manna was an Israeli, the celebrated master chef Saul Raab. In the Bible, manna was the food that God gave the Israelites when they were starving in the wilderness. Its translation from Mosaic Hebrew meant "What is it?" and was an inside joke, as the restaurant provided no menu. The meal depended upon whatever Saul Raab was inspired to create. Manna served only four nights a week, and the waiting list for reservations was over three months unless you were Winslow Fallon. His association with Saul went back decades.

That evening Saul Raab provided a small private dining room for them with their own servers. Fallon's ever-present bodyguards stood watch outside the door. The ten-course meal with rare vintage wines could pay a month's rent of a luxury Baltimore penthouse.

When they finished, Fallon ordered the servers to clear the table, and Fallon turned to Thomas, and said, "Now, the translation."

From his briefcase Thomas took a manila envelope containing loose pages of typed copy.

Kate watched as Fallon began speed-reading; she estimated about ten seconds per page. He occasionally set a page aside, then perused it again.

After several pages he stopped and looked at Kate. "Nine seconds."

"What?"

"My speed per page. Isn't that what you were estimating?"

She didn't answer; the bastard even had that right.

Thomas asked, "How much do you retain?"

"Roughly, ninety-seven percent." He reassembled the pages. "I've seen enough. Excellent work, Brother Thomas." He handed him an envelope. "The check to the monastery plus a little bonus. Please give Father Abbot my compliments." Fallon lit a cigar and said, "Now. Let's talk."

Thomas had been waiting. "No. I ask, you answer. Otherwise tell your Neanderthal goons to take me in the alley behind this ritzy dump and earn their paychecks."

Fallon was surprised. Thomas was not bluffing. His eyes revealed a monk's unyielding determination. Many had been burned at the stake with that look.

"Okay, Thomas. Ask."

"Start with Brother Simon, tell me everything. And make me believe it."

The call had come ten days and twelve hours into monitoring Simon. It took longer than expected; the system was not perfect. As Fallon listened, Simon sounded confused.

"I-I really don't even know why I am making this call," he said, "but this number has been on my mind."

"What is this regarding?" GOLEM's digital voice transformed Fallon's, giving it the inflection, tone, and timbre of a mature, cultured woman. Fallon checked his notes. Various questions had been worked out depending upon what Springer said.

"Is this Simon Springer?" said Fallon.

"Why, yes." Simon was surprised.

"Aren't you associated with Thomas Bardsey?"

"How did you—what is this concerning?"

"Dr. Springer, we have been trying to protect Mr. Bardsey. We believe he is in danger."

"Who are you?"

"A private organization that monitors government intrusion into the lives of citizens. We target DARPA, the Defense Advanced Research Projects Agency, and the DSO, the Defense Sciences Office. They develop advanced technology for the military and intelligence services. This is sometimes used against the very citizens they are supposed to protect."

"Oh, yes. I know all about them. What has that to do with Brother Thomas?"

"He is researching a medieval Templar diary that contains data about a mental discipline with tremendous military potential. If the government found out about us, they would shut us down. It's happened before."

"This is all very confusing. How did I get your number? Why did I feel compelled to call?"

"There's nothing mysterious; I sincerely apologize. We anonymously donated the ambulance that took you to the hospital each time for dialysis. In transit, you were sedated with a DARPA psychopharmaceutical drug used in hypnosis interrogations. You were instructed to think of this number and call us whenever you concentrated on Brother Thomas. Reflex conditioning. It is harmless as Pavlov's dog salivating at the sound of a bell. You are perfectly sane."

"But why didn't you just ask me?"

"To protect ourselves. If you were questioned it would lead to us. They would shut us down and the monk Bardsey would disappear. We had no choice. Again, I apologize."

"What do you want?"

"For you to monitor Thomas Bardsey. He may be tricked into revealing what he discovers in the diary. If so, it is critical that we know. He has been completely deceived."

Simon had often been vetted by both government and industry and knew the game. Given Thomas' naiveté, it all seemed highly plausible.

Fallon toyed with his ashtray as he continued. "Brother Thomas, I knew of your abduction. Detective Flynn told me on the phone. If you and Simon were together again, I still needed him to monitor you."

"Fallon," said Thomas, in near disbelief. "In your way, you are as crazy as Nora."

"Crazy? A diary that cost a fortune was entrusted to you and you ran off with it! Through Simon I was protecting my investment while continuing the GOLEM experiment on him. Frankly, it was brilliant—"

"Wait," Kate interrupted. "Your people performed the chip implant operation *on the brain* in a moving ambulance?"

"Restructured with an interior sterile bubble room I designed. Moving or parked on the street, the surgical procedure only takes about twenty minutes. And there is no record of any surgery, when that's desirable. We perfected it over three years on federal prisoners. As I was saying—"

Kate pressed. "Did they know what was being done to them?"

Fallon paused. Kate was going to stay on the subject until satisfied with his explanation. "Very well, Detective, follow this. It is imperative the subject not know. They might try to resist their own responses. They are conditioned with pharmaceutical drugs. Simon seldom left the monastery, which actually worked in our favor. At the monastery in Santa Barbara the monitoring transmitter for his implant was located in a tree just outside his monk's cell and relayed to a van a block away, then transmitted via satellite to GOLEM here in Baltimore."

"Why did you kill Brother Simon?" Kate asked.

"Kill?" Fallon's eyebrows arched in mock surprise. "I heard he died of a stroke."

Thomas stood, barely controlling his rage. "When I left the country Simon could no longer monitor me. Eventually, a routine head x-ray or CAT scan would reveal his implant and your treachery. He was no further use to you, so you killed him like a lab rat. And considering his multiple health problems, an autopsy was unlikely."

Kate added, "But when I ordered an autopsy, you had to cover it up with your government connections."

"Prove it."

"The evidence is gone but it's still murder."

His eyes went from one to the other. "No evidence, no murder."

When Thomas started to move, Kate stopped him with a look. She changed the subject. "How does Nora fit into all this?"

"NSA. She was their master programmer with her team monitoring global communications. She also worked with DARPA. Her contacts in the intelligence community were phenomenal."

"You put her to work on GOLEM?"

"And my Templar material. She created algorithms to analyze all the collected data, sifting through nine hundred years. That's over three tons of documents. GOLEM found the common factor, precognition. It would have taken a staff decades to find that. The Templars discovered a system, the Al-Din Discipline, developed by the Sufis in Spain under the Moors. It supposedly can enhance the ability of gifted psychics."

"All this just to make a computer psychic?"

"Much more. It is also about singularity—when computers program themselves to the point of having consciousness."

"Artificial intelligence?" Thomas asked.

"Evolution at light speed with no restrictions. The computer and the human being are now inseparable. Very soon, a supercomputer will exceed the functional capacity of the human brain. Each learns from the other. GOLEM's learning programs are patterned after chess algorithms. By playing grand masters, computers learned so well that today no grand master can beat them in a tournament."

"And by interfacing with Longrieve, GOLEM learned from him?"

"It was beautiful! GOLEM will achieve singularity; nothing can prevent it. If we can add a psychic dimension, hyper-evolution will create a human beyond imagining. To that end, we have begun recruiting some of the most brilliant scientific minds."

"To do what?" Kate asked.

"Free science from the control of politics and religion! We want no limits on human experimentation or research."

"The Nazis had that in their concentration camps. It didn't turn out well."

"That was racially motivated. This is *science*! Free of all restrictions we can—"

Thomas interrupted. "Control human behavior?"

"Negative behavior."

"Who determines what is negative?"

"Those in power. Would you prefer political hacks or enlightened thinkers? Scientific minds or religious fanatics?"

"I don't trust any of them."

"You'll have no choice. That is the coming reality." He paused, letting it sink in. "Brother Thomas, I beg you to join us."

"Why? I'm part of the religion you despise."

"You are a monk who committed grand larceny and ran off with a woman. That suggests some flexibility in your religious fervor."

"I'm Episcopalian."

Fallon missed the irony and continued. "Your unique talent would be of inestimable value for what is coming."

"And what is that?" Kate asked.

"The Templar Jerusalem prophecy—Islam and Christianity at war again. With nuclear and bioweapons, they will destroy each other—a very short war, *months*. After that, the Renaissance of Reason. God is not. GOLEM is."

Thomas warily looked at Kate; he had totally underestimated everything.

Fallon smiled, thinking his argument won. "Now will you reconsider?"

Thomas could only shake his head.

"Frankly, I'm disappointed." Fallon made his usual abrupt shift. "However, I have a gift for you from GOLEM."

"What gift?"

"A bit of closure. GOLEM discovered that among Gypsies in England an unusually high number were literate. Legend says that they were taught by a nobleman living among them. Who do you suppose that was?" Fallon abruptly stood. "I confess that I have found you two quite challenging. That doesn't happen to me very often."

With a dismissive nod and a puff of his cigar he turned and walked out.

Kate and Thomas morosely finished the wine, numbed by the reality that Fallon was beyond their reach; sometimes the bad guys win. Now they would have to return to Santa Barbara and separately face whatever was coming.

The morning she arrived at Santa Barbara, Kate reported to Captain Starger. He kept her waiting for nearly an hour, and she was certain this was deliberate. She entered his office and was surprised to find him with a stern-faced woman, Rebecca Layton-Fuller, an attorney from the Office of the Police Commissioner. Kate took a chair opposite the captain's desk. There was an ominous stack of papers in front of him.

"Kate, before we proceed, Ms. Layton-Fuller is here to legally advise both of us when this comes before the Police Review Board. Do you understand?"

"Yes, Captain."

He referred to the documents. "Each of these is a statement of charges explicitly naming you." He held up the first report. "You had an affair, specifically, a sexual relationship with a witness in a homicide case, a monk who goes by the name Brother Thomas Bardsey. Is that an accurate characterization?"

Kate took a breath. "Yes, it is."

He selected another paper. "Also, you withheld evidence from the police when this same witness, Bardsey, was abducted. Comment?"

"That was for his protection. He was a hostage in a similar terrorist scenario that —"

"No terrorist connection was ever established. The question is, did you withhold knowledge of his abduction from your superiors?"

"Yes."

He picked up the next document. "You lied to your superiors, saying you were going to Baltimore when you actually went to Scotland with this same Thomas Bardsey. Any comment?"

"I was following leads to solve the courier Hollander's homicide."

"And to do this, did you lie to your superiors?"

"Yes, Captain."

The next report had a photo attached. "You had in your possession and withheld from the police a document known as the Templar diary that was vital evidence in the Hollander homicide. Comment?"

"I was trying to . . . oh, goddammit! *Yes.*"

Captain Starger looked at Ms. Layton-Fuller, who nodded agreement. Kate had admitted to all the charges.

"Detective Sargent Flynn," said Captain Starger, "I'm putting you on indefinite suspension until the Review Board can sort through all this. Then you will be placed under oath, questioned, and subject to criminal prosecution for obstruction and other charges as they develop. I must ask you to surrender your credentials and your weapon."

Kate laid her badge and police ID card on his desk.

"The weapon is a Beretta," she said, "and personally belongs to me. You gave me special permission to carry it."

"True. However, be advised that now you have no authority to use it." He stood up. "When the Board is ready you will be summoned. Dismissed."

That same day, Thomas returned to the monastery. Abbot Methodius put him on spiritual probation, forbidding all outside communication. Contacting Kate was not possible. A Chapter of Faults with all the monks was set to convene in a few days, with Thomas present as the subject. The outcome would determine his future as a monk. Until then he was assigned to work in the garden, isolated from the others to prevent any interaction. He ate alone in his cell.

While waiting, his intense rage triggered cluster migraines.

Fallon had murdered Brother Simon but was untouchable, protected by wealth, social influence, and dirty politics.

Thomas prayed that his anger be resolved; it did not happen. He remembered Brother Simon quoting the poet Blake: "Prayer without heart and head is better left unsaid."

On the third day, while Thomas was working the monastery garden, Father Abbot Methodius appeared with a man he had never seen. He was James Partain, an attorney looking to speak to Thomas about a matter regarding his Merlin book. Methodius left them alone to talk privately.

Partain then revealed that he was actually a Vatican courier. From his briefcase he removed a mauve envelope marked with a metallic Vatican seal.

"You must swear that after reading, you will burn this," he said. When Thomas agreed, Partain left without another word.

Breaking the seal, Thomas removed a single handwritten page.

Dear Brother Thomas:

While waiting return of the jet we were surprised by an assault to get the VERITAS chest. My team leader, Carver, was killed. I am certain that it was Fallon's men. They failed to get the chest, which, as I write, is in the custody of Swiss Guards on our jet en route to the Vatican. Most importantly, Sister Veronica was killed. It is an unspeakable tragedy. I pray for her soul daily and will until I die. The diary's bloody curse continues.

You should also know we celebrated a special requiem Mass in a Vatican chapel for Brother Simon, who, though not a Roman Catholic, was our mutual Brother in Christ. This is in keeping with the ecumenical views of our Pontiff.

On a more personal note, as one who has spent much of

my life on my knees, I question if you have a monk's vocation. You were meant for other things.

Faithfully,

LEO

"That clever bastard," Thomas said to himself. Leo's thinking was Byzantine: meanings within meanings. Thomas reread it, carefully analyzing every word, phrase, and context.

It began with startling news: Fallon had made another attempt to get the chest. Sister Veronica's tragic death would remind him she was another victim of the diary and her killer roamed free. The Mass said for Brother Simon emphasized that Simon's murderer also was never caught. Finally, a Prince of the Church advised him that he did not have a vocation—he was "meant for other things." In subtext, the document was also a plea to continue his special ties to the Catholic church.

Thomas, as agreed, tore the page into small pieces, burned them, and covered the ashes with dirt.

The following morning at nine he appeared before the Chapter of Faults. Standing in the chill marble corridor outside the common room before the meeting, Thomas waited until all the brother monks filed in. Not a single one would look at him.

In the common room there was a long table with six monks on each side. At one end, and well apart, sat Thomas in a chair. At the opposite end of the table Abbot Methodius presided.

The grueling examination by all the monks covered every event from the first day of the murder investigation to his return from Scotland; it lasted five and a half hours. Thomas mentally noted that it was only half an hour shorter than Christ's crucifixion. Under oath he confessed everything except killing

Ravel. That was clearly self-defense and to reveal it would jeopardize Kate.

Thomas was dismissed so that the brothers could discuss and vote.

Afterward, he met privately with Abbot Methodius, whose face was gray from stress. The chapter of Faults had also been an ordeal for him. It was he who, in the beginning, persuaded them to accept Thomas as a postulate despite his unusual past.

"The brothers were split—six for you to remain, six for your expulsion from the Order. As Abbot, now I must decide." He paused, his distress painful. "For the present you will remain in the Order as a postulant. You will enter into absolute reclusion in your cell to pray and meditate until you determine if you have a vocation. There is no time limit. Only then may you have contact with the outside world."

A week passed. From their last conversation Kate assumed there would be no communication between them until Thomas resolved his situation at the monastery. On Friday she had been unreachable by phone due to a sensitive meeting in the DA's office where cell phones were not permitted. When she came home, she was surprised to find a message on her landline from Thomas. He said he would meet her that evening.

She took special care just for him—an extra touch with her makeup, she wore her favorite dress.

When she opened the door, Thomas was wearing his monk's habit. She had never seen him dressed as a monk. He did not speak, he merely looked at her. After they were seated on the sofa she finally managed to speak.

"I don't know what to say."

"Kate, when I returned to the monastery, because of what happened between us, I was obligated to confess to the Abbot any doubts I had before taking my final vows. I had all but decided to leave." He looked away from her. "This is even harder than I imagined."

"Go on, Thomas."

"There is no rational explanation. Sometime in the middle of the night, I wasn't praying or even meditating, suddenly, there was a moment of *absolute* certainty—I am a monk."

After a painful silence, he said, "Unfortunately, Kate, I was not shown how to tell you. This precious epiphany is matched by . . . the saddest decision of my entire life."

She could only remember that they did not embrace, and he left.

The next days were a numbed void. Kate realized that she must concentrate on something different to get on with her life. She shuddered at the thought that she was "reinventing" herself. Whenever she heard the term, her reaction had always been negative. Now it was the mental game she was forced to play. The future would be very different, and she was resolved to totally focus on the one thing that would demand all her thinking and energy: Fallon.

He had money, power, political influence, and corporate machinery.

She had a determination that was now fanatical.

Kate flew to Baltimore and took a taxi to the Johns Hopkins Hospital. She went to the oncology unit where Nora had been a patient for over two weeks; she was still under arrest for homicide and waiting in a medical-legal limbo. She was in a different room but guarded by the same uniformed officer, whose name was Burt. When Kate entered, she found Nora sitting in a chair. She appeared much stronger than their last meeting. There were no handcuffs or

IV racks. Incredibly, she was absorbed in calculating a maze of mathematics from a board on her lap. She looked up and saw Kate.

"What are you doing here, bitch?"

"I have to see you."

"You are the last person I want to see! I had a gun at Fallon's head, and I let you talk me out of killing him. God *damn* you!"

"I understand how—"

"Not killing Fallon is the regret of my life! If there is a hell, so help me God I will find some way to take you with me. That is one vow I will keep in spite of my status change."

"What change?"

"In these past weeks, the DA insisted on having my psychiatric evaluation and he got it. I am now officially crazy. The legal term is criminally insane. And I am pissed!"

Kate blinked. "Pissed?"

"When I think of all the fun I could have had, all the people I could have gotten even with— scientists who claim my work, idiot politicians who denied me research funding, and especially an uncle who molested me when I was twelve. Being insane, all they could do is put me away someplace nice and cozy, so you bet I'm pissed. Now I dream about how I could have killed Fallon in some deliciously gruesome way."

"Nora," said Kate, "you'll be happy to know I am on suspension for screwing up the Fallon case and most everything else."

"Then there *is* a God. So why are you here?"

"I'm going to nail Fallon for homicide."

"Who did he kill?"

"Brother Simon."

"Who in hell is that?"

"Dr. Simon Springer."

"The cosmologist? Are you crazy? It was all over the media. He died of a stroke."

Kate moved closer. "Yes. And Fallon killed him."

"Jesus, and *I'm* the one on drugs. What are you talking about?"

"Somehow, Fallon used GOLEM as a lethal weapon."

Nora took a few seconds to process. "Kate, the JANUS program only manipulates behavior, it doesn't kill. . . ." She took a breath and started again. "Are you saying Fallon actually killed with GOLEM, and that it wasn't just a reality algorithm?"

"No. It happened."

Nora had the trace of a smile. "Cybercide. Death by computer."

"Maybe the first case; it won't be the last." Kate moved to the window and looked down on the parking lot below. "Nora, I know this is bizarre, but I need your help to prove that Fallon used a computer to commit murder."

"How? You are no longer a cop and I'm . . . here."

Kate turned to her. "Perfect. Fallon won't see us coming."

CHAPTER EIGHTEEN

The following morning, Kate was getting dressed when her phone rang. It was Nora. "I stole a cell phone to make this call. How soon can you come to the hospital?"

"I can leave now. What's wrong?"

"I'll explain when you get here. Bring your gun. And extra ammo."

She hung up.

Forty-five minutes later, at the hospital, Nora was sitting in a chair absorbed in a file folder when the door opened. It was her police guard.

"Miss Nora, you have a visitor. Detective Flynn. You want to see her?"

"Yes, I do. Thanks, Burt."

Kate entered and closed the door. "Looks like you are getting very friendly with your guard."

"Burt can't help himself, it's my lethal charm."

"Why did you ask me to bring a gun?"

"In a few minutes, two of the most powerful men in Washington are coming to see me—a general and a top scientist from DARPA. I'm going to blackmail them. They may go a little crazy."

Kate was wondering if Nora was even remotely rational. "You want me to protect you from a couple of bureaucrats?"

"They are guarded by two SEAL team in plain clothes who will do whatever they are told. I don't know what will happen. Just watch me, play along, and expect anything."

The door opened again; it was Burt. "Miss Nora, two more visitors."

"Show them in."

The two men entered, one in the uniform of an Air Force brigadier general, the other was a stocky civilian in an ill-fitting suit. General Wheeler was African American and described in the media as having the looks of the legendary General Colin Powell and the commanding presence of a pope. As Burt closed the door behind them, Kate caught a glimpse of the SEAL team bodyguards in the hall.

Both men silently glowered at Nora; the tension was instant.

She lit a cigarette that she had managed to sneak into the hospital. "I see that Deputy Secretary Heindorf got my message."

"And here we are," the general said.

"I'll come to the point. Detective Sgt. Flynn is both a witness and my protection." She looked at Kate. "These gentlemen are from DARPA. We go back a long way. General John Jay Wheeler and Dr. Erik Slovac, both from Cyberwar Division."

"Dammit, Nora," Slovac growled, "what is this about?"

Nora took a single page from the folder and held it out to him. "That's a list of items I want from DARPA."

General Wheeler took the list from Slovac and read it. "None of this exists."

"Nevertheless, you will deliver everything to me within twenty-four hours."

"Or what?" Slovac challenged. "You will reveal classified information to the media?" He stepped closer and Kate moved toward him. He stopped. "You faked your death for two years. You confessed to multiple homicides. Now I understand that you have been diagnosed as criminally insane. And you threaten *us*?"

General Wheeler chuckled. "You are one crazy lady. C'mon, Slovac." He moved toward the door to leave.

"ICARUS," Nora said. They both stopped and looked at her. She deliberately took a slow drag from the cigarette, making them wait. "General, at this very moment you have four sub-orbital fighter bombers each separately circling the earth whose two-person crews stay airborne for several weeks without landing. The pilot flies round the clock for six days without sleep, then the second pilot, who has been in self-induced hibernation, takes over. The ICARUS program has been running for over four years and is a direct violation of DARPA's agreement with Congress that *limits* the development of human enhancement programs—so-called Super Warriors. Congress doesn't even know ICARUS exists. If I make one phone call to Senator Reinhardt of the Intelligence Oversight Committee, by the time you two get out of prison, blacksmiths will be pounding swords into plows and war as you know it will be a legend."

"You're bluffing," the general said. "Anyone inside DARPA could have heard of ICARUS. That doesn't mean you actually know anything about it."

"You want details? One of the pilots, Commander Wade Chesterton, is wakened from his sleep state with oxygen containing the aroma of fresh-mown alfalfa—his favorite. He's an Indiana farm boy. He's been conditioned so that this triggers his cardiac system to adjust his pulse from a hibernating 10 to an operational 82 to 88. You see, my NSA team developed the onboard computer's neurological algorithms."

Slovac looked rattled. General Wheeler glared but said nothing.

Nora continued. "I want to spend my remaining time working at home. I can receive medical treatment there. Bert the cop can still guard me. You will use your influence with the Department of Justice to put all that in motion. Immediately. The items on that list are to be delivered to me at my house by noon tomorrow. You know the address." She paused, then said: "Additionally, General, I will also need your help on a matter involving Dr. Winslow Fallon."

The General frowned. "Fallon?"

"Yes, *your* boy Fallon."

Without a word the two men angrily left the room.

Nora took a deep breath. "That was exhausting."

Kate gave her a thumbs up. "Get some rest."

As Kate walked down the hospital corridor, she was astounded by what she had just witnessed. This woman—part genius, part psychopath—who was barely kept alive by drugs, had completely outwitted two government super-players.

Now it was her move.

The next day, Kate arrived shortly before noon at Nora's house. She was surprised to discover Nora lived in a traditional two-story Baltimore rowhouse complete with white marble steps. Burt was standing guard at the front door but in civilian dress. Nora was still technically under arrest. Inside, Kate discovered the first floor had the customary twelve-foot-wide bay with a two-room living space. The entire second floor had been remodeled into a single-room work area. Kate found Nora lying on a sofa waiting for the delivery she'd demanded from General Wheeler and Dr. Slovac.

"Kate, I'm sky high on oxycontin. I'm going to lie here until the goodies arrive."

"I still don't understand exactly what the goodies are."

"Candy from Oz. Chemical compounds developed to create Super Warriors."

"Sounds like a video game of action figures."

"But it's all *too* real, Kate." She closed her eyes. "Poke around all you want, since you will anyway."

Kate relished the opportunity to profile Nora from her environment. She went back down to the first floor living space. The DOI had given her a background file on Nora. She had lived here for over ten years. Kate's surreal impression of the first floor was books, books, books, everywhere. Each wall was lined with shelves of books, and there were multiple stacks on the floor with barely room to walk, as if a library imploded. The few pieces of furniture were spare and utilitarian to the extreme. There were no personal items, not a single picture of friends or family. Only a clutter of ashtrays marked Nora's presence. The bookshelves were jammed with rows of volumes and manuscripts on science and mathematics, titles as meaningless to Kate as if written in Arabic, no novels or light reading.

There was a small kitchenette where Kate found canned tins in the pantry: sardines, mackerel, chili, assorted beans, and potted meats. The refrigerator was empty except for five cans of diet soda. Obviously, Nora did not cook. Nor, apparently, did she drink.

Kate went back upstairs. She noticed against one wall a vintage entertainment center that played cassettes. She checked the artists—mostly Queen, Springsteen, and Elton John, nothing later than the 80s. Nora's music taste was stuck in a time warp.

Kate surveyed the room. The workspace was as orderly as an algebra equation: a worktable, a large desk with two different size computers and printers, two telephones, one red with multiple lines, a super sized Rolodex, and file cabinets. Unlike the first floor with its glut of books, the walls of the second floor were totally free. There was a workboard covered with mathematical numbers and symbols. No television. Little of the outside world intruded. Kate was surprised to find this cozy sanctuary. Nora's workspace was predominantly in her head; she could work in noisy chaos immune to distraction. Kate remembered that at the hospital with all the commotion around her, Nora, unperturbed, was absorbed in working a mathematics problem.

On the sofa Nora had drifted into a twilight sleep. Kate sat in a nearby armchair and began collecting her thoughts for the profile. There were three Noras: the genius mathematical prodigy, the private woman of whom there was little evidence, and the psychopath serial killer. All were driven by one extraordinary mind. From her purse Kate took out a recorder and began dictating.

"As a brilliant scientist Nora fits the description of a chronic loner impossible for an outsider to understand. They communicate best with their own kind. She was a superstar prodigy at NSA even though she was barely twenty when the government recruited her. Exceptional mathematicians bloom early, do their best work in their twenties, and coast on their genius after that. This was true of Einstein, Bohr, and many others. Nora is unusual in that she has continued working at a very high level."

Kate paused, thinking. The next section was more difficult due to lack of information. "Nora, the woman, is difficult to evaluate except that geniuses often have troubled personal relationships. The wives of mathematicians lead the statistics in suicide. Nora does not reveal any association with family, personal, or a love life. It shows in her appearance. She never wears makeup, her hair is blunt-cut short, requiring no grooming, yet many consider her to be attractive. Despite this outsider persona, her intellectual presence dominates any group she is in."

The last section was easier and straight forward. "Nora the

serial killer is different from the typical like Ted Bundy, John Wayne Gacy, and Jeffery Dahmer. They were driven to kill for no apparent reason. For Nora, murder is merely an objective solution to a given problem and not a helpless compulsion. She kills as a solution; there are no moral limitations."

Kate reflected a moment, then added; "I believe that Nora, in her long involvement with Fallon, has realized their similarities—they think and behave very much alike. As Gandhi said, 'You become what you hate.' "

Kate was interrupted by a knock at the door. Burt had opened it, revealing three men, one with a black duffle bag chained to his wrist. The other two stood behind him, obviously his bodyguards. Both men made no effort to hide the assault weapons holstered beneath their open suit coats. One of them produced a key and unlocked the first man's wrist chain; he then gave the duffle bag to Kate. Without a word, the three men walked away. Burt closed the door and took his post outside.

When Kate came back upstairs, she found Nora waiting at the table. "Put the stuff here. This will be our playground."

Kate watched as Nora opened the bag and began laying out its contents. There were various sealed packages and boxes containing packets of paper and plastic containers of assorted pills and capsules in various colors.

"That is Oz Candy?" Kate asked.

"It's just one part of the Super Warrior Enhancement Program, which has been in development for over a decade under various cover names. Super Warriors is the new arms race. What you see here requires the highest security clearance, Crypto 14. Kate, they somehow did a provisional background on you since yesterday. I'm impressed."

"And they simply left it here with you?"

"This building is small and easy to control. There are no hiding places. They've got round-the-clock snipers with spotters targeting every door and window in case anybody comes calling. Their orders are shoot to kill, so don't order a pizza delivery."

"How does this stuff work?"

"I know how it works on a warrior in top physical condition. I haven't a clue as to what it does to a fifty-something woman with cancer and loaded on prescription drugs," said Nora, as she sorted everything on the table into separate groups.

Kate was confused. "You think these drugs can make *you* some kind of Super Warrior?"

"No. But they may help us get Fallon."

"How?"

"Oz Candy works by enhancing the body and mind functions. It must be taken in the right sequence."

"What if you make a mistake?"

"Probable organ damage." Nora paused. "Before we start, Kate, this material is extremely technical—chemical combinations with lots of letters. To make it easier for the candidates, each formula has an easy to remember nickname. So, when you keep track of what I'm taking, just use the nicknames."

"Thank God," Kate said. "The only chemistry I know is explained to me in 'dummy' terms by forensic experts."

Norma held up a container of pills. "This is SS Two—think speed on steroids. Forget sleep. It will keep me awake around the clock for days." She picked up an inch-wide roll of paper with red licorice backing. "We call this Flypaper. Suck on it instead of eating and your metabolism re-fires—more work on less food. It allows Super Warriors to go for weeks on minimal calories and still be highly functional. Instead of bulky food, they carry Flypaper. A warrior who can go without sleep or food has a tremendous advantage over their enemy."

She picked up a red capsule. "When you become tired, this is instant high energy. Z for zombie; it can make a corpse walk. Use too much—cardiac arrest."

Nora indicated a separate group. "Now we get tricky. The brain. It stores data throughout its structure and is divided into left and right hemispheres. This yellow capsule is Tsunami ONE. It floods the brain divider like a dam-busting tide, allowing *simultaneous* access to both hemispheres of the brain at the same time. It was patterned after the brain activity in autistic savants."

"Unbelievable."

"It gets better." Nora picked up two hypodermic syringes. "The Twins. Everything that has ever happened is stored someplace in the brain. These two drugs injected together affect memory. One contains psilocybin, used in drug-enhanced interrogations. Any subject that I know, but have forgotten, I will recall. When I concentrate on Fallon, it's like watching a movie. And that's where you come in. With what I remember, you will be able to build a complete profile on Fallon. We can exploit his weaknesses, like his incredible egomania and his eccentricities. Do you know he can't drive a car? Or that he's obsessed with redheads? I once found a file that I thought was porn. It was all redheaded women, no nudes, just headshots. Classic obsession. We'll focus on his predictable behavior—like the way Fallon is compelled to shock people by saying he married his stepmother."

"Yeah, the day they 'took Daddy off life support.' "

"Kate, want to guess the color of step-mommy's hair?"

"Damn. Really?"

"By knowing how he thinks, we can better predict how he will react in a given situation. It's a mental chess game, Fallon against the two of us."

"But isn't taking these drugs dangerous?"

"I'm dying of cancer. How much damage can it do? It's my one shot to get Fallon. I wouldn't trade that for anything."

"Where do you begin?"

Nora selected a blue tablet. "With this. C Two. It aids concentration by shutting out extraneous stimuli and isolates whatever I'm working on." She popped it in her mouth and swallowed it with water from a plastic bottle.

She stared vacantly for a few seconds then moved to a wall. "I just had a weird thought. If I write on these walls, I can see everything at once without turning pages." She picked up a marker from items on the table. "Poor Kate, you've got the boring part—watching me think."

"Is it okay if I ask questions?"

"My concentration will become very intense; I may not respond."

Kate sat on the sofa with her notebook and the recorder. Nora began aimlessly pacing. After a few minutes she started writing on the wall while talking.

"Mission: prove that Fallon used the GOLEM computer to commit murder," Nora said, then wrote CYBERCIDE in capital letters on the wall, and continued dictating aloud while writing. "Based on the neural algorithms that I worked on, the computer as a weapon has unique features."

As Kate watched, Nora's words began tumbling out. The effect was robotic.

"Jesus," Kate muttered.

Nora had written:

CYBERCIDE
The Computer communicates to an implanted chip that stimulates specific brain circuits. Communication with the computer is via

satellite spanning the planet. The Computer can be operated from separate locations by a computer, laptop, cell phone, or similar device.

Nora continued dictating and writing very fast:
1. *The Killer, the murder Weapon, and the Victim can each be at different locations during the homicide.*
2. *There is no physical evidence: no Blood! no DNA! no Prints!*
3. *The crime scene is the victim's body.*
4. *The victim's death appears to be either heart attack or stroke. A "natural" death.*
5. *An autopsy is the ONLY way to determine if it is homicide.*
6. *Only ten percent of all deaths have an autopsy; it is highly probable that a cyber-homicide will go undetected.*

"My god," Kate said as she stared at the board. "It's a homicide detective's nightmare."

"And think of what's coming." Nora's eyes were bright, her brain was at revving speed. "Computers and implant chips will affect our lives even more in the future. They have already changed medicine, making us dependent on them—think of cardiac pacemakers, artificial hearts, and a whole range of brain devices. Supercomputers are evolving that will make GOLEM look like a toy. One of their abilities will be to non-invasively access anyone's implanted discs and control them. In other words, if you've got a chip, they've got you."

Over the following days, they worked around the clock. They were only interrupted when a nurse practitioner gave Nora her medications intravenously. Kate dictated everything in her diary: which Oz Candy Nora took and its effect, including comments on what Nora wrote on the walls. Nora never ate unless Kate insisted, and then only nibbled a few bites. Kate kept a pot of coffee brewing for herself to keep going. There was only one bed and it was downstairs, so Kate catnapped on the sofa. Nora never slept. She would take a break only long enough to shower.

One night at around two am, Nora took two capsules of S ONE, the savant drug that breaches the separation between the left brain's logic and right brain's creativity. She was writing a sentence on the wall when suddenly she stopped. She moved to the blank wall on her left and began writing a string of mathematic equations with her left hand. Some savants write with their right hand for right-brain function, left hand for left-brain.

"What's that?" Kate asked.

"A mathematical expression of a verbal statement." She re-read the equation. "Gotcha."

"What does it mean?"

"A theory about how Fallon instructs GOLEM to create algorithms for categorizing data."

Nora resumed writing a flurry of equations.

Kate made a fresh pot of coffee. It was going to be another all-nighter.

As the days wore on, exhaustion began taking its toll on Kate. Sometimes, she found herself thinking about Thomas though he was no longer in her life. She also sensed that the more she worked with Nora, her attitude was changing. Ironically, as cop and perp, they were forming a plan that actually might convict their mutual enemy, Fallon.

After several round-the-clock days and nights, they were taking half a day off. Nora was staring into space when she suddenly asked, "Kate, what will you need to arrest Fallon?"

"Hard evidence. Here in Baltimore, Detective Dan Swartz has jurisdiction. He's a good cop; he'll take a lot of convincing. We know Fallon used GOLEM as a weapon, but how? Fallon was in Baltimore when Brother Simon dropped dead of a stroke in Santa Barbara." She pointed to the wall and said, "Just like your example in CYBERCIDE. Fortunately, Fallon is the only person with a motive to kill Brother Simon."

"Kate, when did Brother Simon die?"

"April second at the monastery. Thomas said Simon died after vespers, that's six in the evening, the end of the day; the end of his life."

"On the first week in April, Fallon was here in Baltimore at a hotel leading a seminar convention of techie geeks. He was under constant observation when Simon died. So, that doesn't help us."

"But it does," Kate countered. "It means he went to great lengths to be seen by witnesses at the time he *knew* Simon would die. Establishing an alibi means he needed one. It also tells us exactly when the homicide was committed."

"Ha! I never saw that."

"Fallon is the only one who could have done it. But how did he trigger GOLEM?"

"No problem," Nora answered. "He could have pre-programmed GOLEM to kill Simon at a specific time while he was talking to the group."

"Except that's not Fallon's way."

"What do you mean?"

Kate tapped the desk with her knuckles. "Ego, ego, ego. Given everything we know about him, Fallon needs an audience. Pre-programming GOLEM is too easy. But by performing, his audience is actually watching him commit a murder, but they don't know it."

"While they provide him with an alibi." Nora laughed. "He probably got so excited he had to change his underwear."

Kate was scanning Nora's writing on the other wall. "All murderers have motive, means, and opportunity," she said. "We know Fallon's motive. And he created his opportunity by killing Simon while everyone was watching him do something else. But what does he need as a means to use GOLEM as a weapon?"

Nora, concentrating, was moving her fingers as if working an invisible abacus. "BCI, Brain-Computer Interface," she said. "A computer chip. It's the common factor between GOLEM and all the Super Warriors. "

"Then Fallon must have a chip implanted too!"

They both laughed; it was so obvious, they missed it. Nora added, "And, given Fallon's devout paranoia, he has kept it secret from *everyone*. What happens next?"

"We show Lt. Swartz exactly how Fallon did it. Give him a demonstration."

"How?"

Kate grinned and said, "We find a subject, implant them with a chip like Brother Simon's, and have GOLEM activate it."

"Love it. Who do we kill?"

"A lab rat will do nicely. But it doesn't explain how Fallon triggered GOLEM miles away while he was talking to an audience."

They were silent again. Nora lit a cigarette, slowly savoring the smoke. "Kate, how do detectives get someone to confess to a homicide?"

"The quickest way is if the killer has an accomplice. You put pressure on both until one flips on the other. Unfortunately, Fallon didn't have an accomplice."

"Oh, but he did." Nora pointed to the equations. "A whole lab full, working on JANUS. Most importantly, Dr. Wolf Meyer."

"Who is Meyer?"

"A world-class neurosurgeon. He performed the implants in an ambulance. Fallon couldn't have accomplished JANUS without him. If Fallon has an implant, Meyer had to do it."

Kate had an idea. "How would you describe the good Dr. Meyer?"

"Simple. He's Dr. Mengele to Fallon's Hitler."

"Ambitious?"

"He'd carve up his mother without an anesthetic if it got him the Nobel Prize in Medicine."

"What's his relationship with Fallon?"

"He worships him. Meyer would never turn on Fallon."

"He'll have to. He's our only candidate."

"But how can we persuade him?"

"Look him straight in the eye and lie like hell," Kate answered. "The best con man I ever caught, Joey Rico, said that to trick someone, you don't need the truth, just enough bells and whistles to give the appearance of reality."

"Isn't the brilliant Dr. Meyer too smart for that?"

"So, the smarter the mark, the more bells and whistles we'll need."

An idea was already forming.

CHAPTER NINETEEN

Dr. Wolf Meyer arrived home late, at half past nine, after an exhausting day in the Med-Tek lab. He was hungry, but it was his housekeeper's day off. Rafaela didn't just clean house; she cooked and did everything else but breastfeed him. He decided to skip dinner and went into the den for a drink. He entered, then stopped when he saw Kate.

"Good evening, Dr. Meyer."

"Who are you?"

She showed her credentials. "Detective Sgt. Kate Flynn, Baltimore Homicide."

"Police? In my home?" Meyer snapped. "What do you want?"

"To save your miserable ass," a voice behind him answered.

He turned to see Nora seated in an armchair across the room. "Dr. Pullman?"

"Surprised? I'm supposed to be dying in the hospital. I had to stop dying to be here. Which shows how damn important this is."

He looked at them warily. "What is going on?"

Nora held out a glass of whiskey. "First, you will need this. Jack Daniels, neat, if I remember." She indicated the chair beside her. "And please, sit down."

"Dr. Pullman, I demand to know—"

"Sit!" Kate ordered.

He flinched, then sat. Both women pointedly waited until he took a swallow of whiskey.

Nora's tone was edgy. "Let's skip over our mutual loathing and get to the point. What we are going to tell you is unbelievable and yet, absolutely true. Explain it, Kate."

"I am a homicide detective temporarily assigned to Baltimore Police. You are about to be arrested and indicted on two counts: accessory to first-degree homicide and conspiracy to commit murder."

"What? That's absurd."

She looked at Nora. "Tell him the federal charges."

"You are also charged with conspiracy to reveal top secret information about the Super Warrior program, the GOLEM-JANUS project, to a foreign power. Translation—the FBI wants a piece of your ass."

"Also," Kate added, "there is a federal case of conspiracy with Dr. Winslow Fallon."

"Fallon?"

Nora explained. "Actually, he's really the one we are after. We need some particulars that only you can give us about the homicide."

"Homicide!" He looked at Nora. "Are you insane?"

"Yes. But that's beside the point. The police need your cooperation to make the case airtight."

"I haven't killed anybody!"

"No. But you are involved in everything Fallon does. Your brains are *fused*. It is impossible to separate your work." Nora nodded at Kate to finish the argument.

Kate moved closer, crowding his space. "We are offering you a deal. If you cooperate and tell us what we want to know, you won't be named in the indictment. But if you refuse, you will be accused as an accessory in the murder of Dr. Simon Springer."

At the mention of the name, Meyer looked uncomfortable.

Kate added, "And I find it strange that when I said homicide you didn't ask who was murdered."

He chuckled with a shake of his head. "You are trying to intimidate me. *Me*! Do you know who I am? There is absolutely nothing that connects me with Dr. Springer's death!"

"True," Kate agreed. "But when Fallon goes on trial for murder, we will find a way to include you."

"First, you threaten to arrest me, then you try coercion? That's pathetic." Meyer laughed. "I won't even bother to call my lawyers. Go ahead."

Kate sighed. "I was afraid you might say that." On her cell phone she touched instant dial. When there was an answer Kate said, "I tried. Maybe he will listen to you."

She gave the phone to Meyer. "Hello?"

"Dr. Meyer. This is General Wheeler."

Meyer braced a few inches higher. "General, it's good to talk with—"

"Shut the fuck up and listen. Fallon's arrest for homicide compromises the GOLEM-JANUS project. Do you think the Department of Intelligence, the NSA, DARPA, and God knows who else, will do nothing?" Meyer was slow to respond. "Answer me, goddammit!"

"Uh, no. No sir, I don't know what would hap—"

"The Department of Intelligence must immediately replace Fallon to avoid chaos! And that is you, because nobody can tell whether Fallon or Meyer is doing whatever you freaks do! You have a choice: you can be prosecuted with Fallon as an accessory to murder or you can become head of GOLEM-JANUS—a no-brainer. But either way, you *will* cooperate with Detective Flynn.

Even if it means whoring your fairy ass on Broadway at high noon. Do you understand?"

Meyer was shocked. He had been deep in the closet for over forty years. "I . . . yes, sir."

"Put Detective Flynn on."

Kate took the phone from him. "Yes, General?"

General Wheeler chuckled. "It worked. Kate, about 'outing' him; I made the threat before the Russians will because he is high up and very vulnerable. Better us than them. Do you have the Operation RUNAWAY file?"

"Yes, sir!"

"Time to kick ass, girl." He hung up.

Meyer, stunned, gulped the last of his drink. He shook his head. "This will never, *never* work! Fallon is too smart. Too smart!"

"You may be right," Nora agreed. "But now he has to deal with the combined thinking of one bitchin' homicide cop who never quits, a general who has completely fooled the Department of Intelligence, and a mental freak—me, who is dying to get him. Literally."

Kate laid a file folder on the coffee table in front of Meyer. "Operation RUNAWAY."

"What's that?" he asked.

"Your future. You are about to become a secret celebrity, if there is such a thing. Practically everybody in the intel community will know about you, but nobody outside it," Kate said. She opened the file and held up a page. "This is a letter you will write to Fallon saying that you have resigned your position with him because the Russians have made you a better offer to work on their Super Warrior program."

"Fallon is no fool. He will never buy that!"

"He will when General Wheeler calls him raising hell that it is his fault that you have gone over to the Russians."

"But how can I convince Fallon when *he* questions me?"

"He'll never talk to you. When you have supposedly gone to Russia, you will be in a CIA safe house in Bermuda, where you will stay until Fallon is arrested."

"How are you going to get enough on Fallon to arrest him?" Meyer said.

"Simple. *You* are going to tell us everything you know about how Fallon murdered Dr. Springer."

"But first," Kate asked, "when did you put the chip implant in Fallon?"

"Christ! How did you know that?'

"I'm a cop," Kate answered. The bluff worked.

"Was his chip the same as all the others?" Nora quickly asked.

"No, more advanced. It was developed after you die . . . disappeared."

"How different?"

"Instead of just receiving data from GOLEM, Fallon's implant can mentally send a binary signal back as zero or one. It's triggered by the brain's electric pulses. The same way the brain can be trained to operate a prosthesis limb."

Nora explained to Kate, "Then Fallon and GOLEM can talk to each other in binary code using the chip."

"You mean Fallon could instruct GOLEM to kill Dr. Springer even while he was talking to a group of people?"

"During a few critical pauses, yes," Meyer answered.

As they continued talking Nora opened her purse. From a pill container, she selected a red tablet and swallowed it.

Meyer paused in mid-sentence. "Uh, is that a Z capsule?"

"My second one today," Nora admitted.

"Dr. Pullman, no one over forty should take Z! Don't you realize it could damage your cardiovascular system?"

"Your concern is touching."

"I've got a bigger concern." Meyer looked at Kate. "Why should the Baltimore Police help us?

"They want Fallon for homicide but have never been able to make a case. He's outmaneuvered them every time. We'll convince them that we can *trick* Fallon into confessing that he killed Dr. Springer."

"What? How?"

"By demonstrating exactly how he did it."

The next morning at 8:00 am, Kate planned to confront Fallon at Med-Tek, but Nora did not have the energy. She had fainted twice that week. Kate was anxious about Nora's condition and what would happen if she died from extreme stress while trying to pull this off. Despite trying to keep her emotional distance while working together, Kate's feelings had transformed from enemy to collaborator to get Fallon, to a concern that the strain might kill Nora before they finished. If someone would have told Kate that she would feel this way, she wouldn't have believed it. As a cop, she was working with a serial killer, Nora, to get a mutual enemy, Fallon. "My enemy's enemy is my friend." Nora was a person she had come to care about. The more she knew her, the greater the concern grew.

Kate and Nora spent the rest of the day working on the plan to trick Fallon into confessing to the Springer murder. After they made the necessary phone calls, Kate called Lt. Swartz and explained the strategy with a caution. "I know it sounds crazy, Dan, but it might be our best chance to nail Fallon."

"Kate, I love your whole bat-shit scenario," he said. "We'll set everything up at headquarters, then I'll call Fallon for a meeting tomorrow at Med-Tek. I'll tell him it's about a very serious criminal matter."

"That should get the bastard's attention." Kate laughed.

TWIST OF TIME

* * *

The following day at the Med-Tek lab when Lt. Swartz arrived, Fallon was surprised that Kate was with him. He covered it with his usual aplomb.

"Delighted to see you, Detective Flynn. And where is our monk, Brother Thomas?'

"At the monastery, permanently."

"Then he is a fool to leave you," Fallon said. "Despite our differences, Kate, I would never have chosen God over you, had he existed. I still regret that we never went to Mexico together." With his usual abruptness he turned to Swartz. "What's this about, Lieutenant?"

"We want to question you at headquarters concerning the death of Dr. Simon Springer."

"Why at police headquarters?"

"A demonstration has been assembled there by Dr. Nora Pullman."

"Pullman? I assumed she was dead."

Kate smiled. "Nora is very much alive. It's amazing what these new drugs can do."

Swartz explained, "Dr. Pullman has prepared evidence to show how Dr. Springer was killed by your GOLEM computer. As this will be presented in court, it is only fair that you observe it."

"No matter what it proves about GOLEM, it doesn't involve me with Springer. You should question my associate, Dr. Meyer. He will . . ."

A man burst into the room. "Dr. Fallon!" he said. "Sorry to disturb you —"

"What is it, Dr. Lizerand?" Fallon was annoyed.

Lizerand held out a cell phone. "You have a call from General Wheeler."

Fallon took the phone. "General Wheeler? How are you? I . . . Dr. Meyer? No, I don't know where he . . ." Fallon listened. "Russia?" He turned to Swartz. "Lieutenant, I must take this call privately in my office."

Kate and Swartz exchanged a quick look. General Wheeler had made his call right on time.

"No problem," Swartz agreed. "Let's all meet at Homicide at two this afternoon." His smile disappeared. "Be there."

At Lt. Swartz's precinct, the demonstration was set up in the large briefing room. Swartz had asked them to come early before Fallon arrived. Kate brought Nora who was super-charged with a Z capsule and just enough painkiller to keep going. Kate checked the room layout as she requested. There was a desktop computer and a large flat screen monitor on the wall. Three video cameras would record the demonstration as evidence. Present were Lt. Swartz, Kate, Nora, and two homicide detectives, Lou Fitzroy and Ruth Jonas from Swartz's team. Across the room sat Libby, a lab tech in a white coat. In her lap she held Sheba, a chimpanzee who was looking at everyone curiously.

Swartz asked for everyone's attention. "I want to say something before Fallon gets here. Very honestly, I doubt that we can get enough on Fallon to convict even if you prove motive, means, and opportunity."

"That's usually enough in most cases," Kate argued.

"Fallon is not most cases. He knows that you can't connect him to Dr. Springer despite what he admitted to you and Brother Thomas that night at Manna restaurant. There is no physical evidence."

"Hence, this demonstration," Kate said. "Let's see how Fallon reacts, then decide."

Nora moved to the computer. "The demo is simple. The GOLEM computer is at Med-Tek about twenty miles from here.

Each subject connected with the GOLEM Super Warrior project has a chip implanted with a five-digit binary number, like this." She held up a chip. "The late Dr. Springer's was zero, one, zero, one, one, which has been implanted in Sheba, the chimpanzee."

Everyone looked at Sheba who now had her arms around Libby's neck.

"As you can see, she has a small bandage on her head."

"I thought you were going to use a lab rat in this demonstration," Swartz said.

Kate explained. "We were, Lieutenant. But it was determined we must use a brain as similar to a human's as possible to be accepted as evidence in this case."

Nora continued, "GOLEM has been programmed so that when Springer's number is typed in this computer, and I press the enter key, Sheba will instantly have a fatal cerebral hemorrhage. Which demonstrates how GOLEM killed Doctor Springer."

"We're sorry that Sheba must be sacrificed. But there is no other way," Kate said. "That's how experimental science works in labs all over the world—animals die."

When Fallon arrived, he was accompanied by his two bodyguards. He looked the group over and said, "I'm impressed, Lt. Swartz. Quite a dog and pony show." He saw Nora; they had not seen each other since her arrest. "I'm glad you are looking so well."

"Dude, you ain't seen nothing yet." Nora gave a sly smile.

Fallon looked at Libby holding the chimpanzee. "You have taken Sheba from my lab. I assume she is to be the unfortunate stand-in for Dr. Springer."

Swartz handed him a document. "This is a court order demanding the chimpanzee demonstration as evidence."

Fallon took it, quickly rolled it into a ball, "No matter how many animals you kill, it does not prove that I killed Dr. Springer." He tossed it in a waste can. "Get on with your charade."

Everyone watched Nora as she moved to the computer. She referred to the large monitor on the wall. "The screen will show what I am typing. Springer's number was zero, one, zero, one, one."

She typed: 0 1 0 1.

"Wait," Kate interrupted. "Dr. Fallon, I've been working this damn case from the beginning. I'd like to be a part of the demonstration." She moved beside Nora. "Except, I am going to change the last digit." She typed zero instead of a one. "Okay, Fallon?"

Everyone looked at Fallon. He had turned white.

"Now, I'll press enter."

"No!" Fallon said and leaped toward the keyboard. Kate slammed him in the chest with the heel of both hands, a martial arts move. He fell backward and landed on the floor, hard.

Kate's finger was over the enter key. "Confess, or you're dead."

Fallon looked up at her.

"Then die!"

"Wait! Goddammit . . . I did it."

Lt. Swartz grabbed him and jerked him to his feet. "Winslow Fallon, I am arresting you for the murder of Dr. Simon Springer." He looked at his two detectives, Jonas and Fitzroy. "Cuff this son-of-a-bitch."

Lt. Swartz asked Kate, "What just happened?"

"Fallon has an implant, too. He didn't know that we knew. I entered *his* number. If I pressed enter, he would have died."

"You'll never make this stick." Fallon smirked. "It's clearly entrapment."

The door from the observation room opened and a man entered the room.

Lt. Swartz explained, "This is Dick Abercrombie, the Deputy District Attorney."

Fallon snapped, "I don't care if he's Jesus Christ. It's still entrapment."

Swartz looked at Abercrombie. "Well, Mr. Prosecutor?"

Abercrombie didn't have to think. "Book him. Let the Grand Jury decide."

After detectives Fitzroy and Jonas led Fallon from the room, Abercrombie looked at Swartz. "Damn, Lieutenant. You guys have a lot more fun than we do over at Justice."

Swartz grinned. "Only when Kate is around."

Lt. Swartz turned to Kate. "There's one big question. How in hell did you access GOLEM at Med-Tek to enter Fallon's number for this demo?"

"Dr. Meyer programmed GOLEM for us," Kate answered. "It was the last thing he did before he disappeared."

The week after wrapping up Fallon's indictment in Santa Barbara, Kate still struggled with her battered emotions and bruised psyche. One evening after work she was sitting alone in her car parked outside her apartment building. She found herself sliding into depression; she never knew when it would emerge like a demon crawling out of her subconscious. She had lost Thomas, not to dying love or another woman, but to God. She felt drained, the spirit sucked out of her. It was ten minutes before she mustered the strength to go inside. When she unlocked the door her tomcat Watson was standing there waiting. Kate cleared the doorway, her Beretta covering the room. Watson never met her at the door but always waited on his favorite blanket in the computer chair—always.

When the man saw Kate, he raised his hands.

"Who are you?" she asked.

"James Partain."

"What are you doing in my apartment?"

"I didn't want to be seen loitering outside."

"How'd you get in?"

"I picked the lock. You should have it changed."

"Turn around and face the wall. Put your hands flat, feet apart. Move!" She gave him a hard shove. He hit the wall face first. She pinned him with a stiff arm on his back. "Partain, I recently killed a man who surprised me when I came home. His body disappeared. Want to push your luck?"

"No. I believe you." He grunted in pain.

She did a brisk pat-down; he was clean. She motioned for him to turn around. Height, five-eight to ten; weight, 170 to 180; an unremarkable face, no distinguishing features. A written description of him would be little better than a blank page.

"Okay, what do you want?"

"*John 3:16*," he answered.

Leo's password. Kate was surprised. Entering Leo's world was like walking into a labyrinth in the dark. "What is your position in Vatican Intelligence?"

"Courier."

"Where's the document?"

"There isn't one. I was ordered to speak to you face-to-face. There is to be no record."

"Go ahead."

Partain paused. Every word had to be precise. "Before you commit to the Santa Barbara PD Homicide, please consider becoming a full-time operative for the Vatican. The pay would be commensurate with your current salary. As you have resolved the Fallon case, there are other situations that fit your particular talents. We must have your decision now as it will determine our next move." Partain took a step closer. "What is your answer?"

Kate thought for only seconds. "Tell his Eminence Cardinal Leo that I said . . . yes."

TWIST OF TIME

* * *

It was typical of Thomas' total isolation at the ACO monastery in Santa Barbara that he was not aware of Fallon's trial. The monastery had no access to television, radio, or news media. One day he received a package by courier from Kate. It was the Templar diary, still in its protective case. Included was an article from the *Baltimore Sun*, titled: "Billionaire Winslow Fallon Sentenced to Life in Prison for Homicide."

There also was a note from Kate, "The Templar diary helped convict Fallon. I believe it is your duty to continue writing it as the next monk after Brychan."

Kate was standing on an outcrop of rock pounded by the Atlantic surf fifteen yards below. She carried a ceramic burial urn. As she looked down at the white foam it reminded her of the chalk dust on the blackboard where Nora had written:

Epitaph on the wind:
 "We are made of the same stuff as stars . . ."

Kate took a card from her pocket on which she had made a copy. She removed the top from the urn and tilted it. As the wind caught Nora's ashes Kate read aloud:

"May the atoms of my ashes
Travel the cosmos as far as
Wave and particle of light will
Sprinkle my Stardust."

Kate tossed the empty urn and watched it shatter below on the frothy wet rocks. She touched the crucifix on her neck chain, said a brief prayer, and walked away.

One week later at the City National Bank of Los Angeles, Kate was in a safety deposit box private room. On the table was her deposit box. Whenever she opened it, she felt like she was visiting with her mother and father. She selected a document from among several and read it with a smile. Her parents' marriage certificate declared that Grady Patrick Flynn and Ann Marie McCauley were joined in holy matrimony in 1977 by Monsignor Theodore Doolin at Sacred Heart church. She returned the page beside her mother's rosary. From her inside coat pocket, she opened an envelope, removed a single page, and reread it.

> *Dearest,*
>
> *In my 56 years of a life with many peaks, you gave me the rarest gift: I was your first. It can only be given once.*
>
> *Now I give you all that I have: my ashes to return to the sea.*
>
> *With love,*
>
> *Nora*

Kate closed her eyes, remembering the unexpected surprise and exhilaration of their first kiss, then placed the note among her other memories and returned the deposit box to the safe room.

On Friday the thirteenth of November, Kate arrived in Santa Barbara for a very special occasion, Thomas' ordination as a monk in the Anglican Celtic Order. He was the only monk being ordained and was allowed one guest as a witness. From the moment she received the invitation she struggled with her feelings, though to refuse him would be unthinkable.

In the monastery sanctuary, Kate sat alone in all the empty rows: one initiate, one guest. At exactly midnight a bell tolled twelve and the procession of chanting monks led by Father Abbot Methodius proceeded down the aisle. As the only candidate, Thomas walked behind the abbot. Kate was surprised to see that instead of the usual blue denim, their robes were white with a blood red rope tied at the waist. In the ACO, a monk was ordained the same as a priest in the White Requiem Mass—a requiem for the former man now dead to the world and a Mass celebration for the monk entering a new life.

Kate watched as he approached. She had been apprehensive, but when their eyes met, she felt an instant calm. Whether or not they would ever see each other again, she knew that this was right.

Thomas lay prostrate before the altar as Abbot Methodius continued the ceremony. Kate was unknowingly witnessing the Order's most guarded secret. Their founding in Scotland in 1845 was a well-executed deception. The Order was much older, going back to the seventh century BCE when the Roman Catholic and the Celtic churches were combined. A group of Celtic monks secretly continued the practice of prophecy and precognition, eventually incorporating the Templar New Jerusalem prophecy: "Watch; pray; be ready." This was revealed to Thomas thirty days before his ordination, should he wish to withdraw. He embraced it eagerly.

This ritual fulfils the prophecy that the Templars would be reborn in the third millennium.

The date of ordination is always November 13, when the Templars went underground. The Anglican Celtic Order is the Templars reborn, spiritual warriors hiding in plain sight.

THE BEGINNING

NUGGETS FOR THE CURIOUS

KNIGHTS TEMPLAR

There is probably no subject about which so much has been published and so little actually known as the Templars. Writings about them first appeared in the twelfth century and continue to the present day. Their history, legends, and lore have been reproduced and analyzed in thousands of books and documents. Yet almost all their official records were hidden or destroyed by the Order just before their arrest and persecution by King Philip IV of France.

As a result, there was very little document evidence presented at their Inquisition trials; most of the testimony came from witnesses after being tortured. This, along with the accurate Templar prophecies, has fueled continuous speculation about their mysteries and wealth. Descriptions of their tactics and fierceness in combat have been taken from written eyewitness accounts of both allies and enemy Saracen chroniclers who respected Templar fighting prowess above all Crusaders.

The Zealotes, an exclusive combat group within the Templars, is fictional, though the model follows a long tradition of an elite fighting force developed within many military organizations.

NUGGETS FOR THE CURIOUS

VATICAN INTELLIGENCE

Vatican Intelligence first appeared during the Napoleonic era in the early nineteenth century. Its existence was long denied. However, books and media articles over the years have kept alive confirmation of its existence.

During World War I, its staff numbered about a dozen, with their mission concentrated on codes and ciphers. It is rumored that Vatican codes have never been broken. By World War II, despite the failure of controversial Pope Pius XII to condemn the Nazi regime (an accusation which has since been seriously questioned), a great number of Catholic priests and lay men and women were in the German underground engaged in espionage and sabotage against Hitler's Third Reich.

The Cold War saw Vatican Intelligence greatly expanded and its personnel increased due to the atheist Communist threat worldwide. By this time, it was organized along the same lines as other intelligence services. In the late 1950s, according to U.S. counterintelligence, the Soviet KGB rated Vatican Intelligence number one, Great Britain number two, Israel number three, and the U.S. number four.

Most historical data on Vatican Intelligence comes from published material. Current information is harder to obtain. The description of recruitment and operations are from the author's own sources, two former U.S. counterintelligence agents. One was the handling officer of a Cold War operative working against the Soviets who was recruited away from the U.S. by Vatican Intelligence in 1957. This file is still classified.

The second source, a former counterintelligence agent, was with a surveillance team following two KGB operatives in Vienna when they spotted two men tailing them and their two Soviet subjects. The next day, when writing a report of the incident, he received the daily intelligence summary listing updates from various intel sources. In it was his surveillance of the KGB, reported by Vatican agents using cover names. They had processed and disseminated their data before he could write and file his report.

BATTLE OF BANNOCKBURN

The Battle of Bannockburn in 1314 won Scotland's freedom from England. While there are many versions of the engagement, not all are in agreement. It is generally accepted that the invading English army was twice the size of the Scots; some historians have said even greater. The English were composed of battle-hardened infantry, mounted armored knights, heavy cavalry, and archers. The Scots were well-drilled peasant ground troops relying on the schiltrom "hedgehog" formation armed with twelve-foot-long spears.

The schiltrom was ordinarily used as a defense against infantry and cavalry but was vulnerable to archers. The difference lay in Robert Bruce's preparing the ground he was to defend and his innovative strategy of using the highly mobile schiltrom as an attacking offensive unit. His phenomenal success against overwhelming odds has been studied by military commanders the world over.

The description of the battle tries to conform as much as possible to the several versions using some creative license. Beyond this, any errors are the author's.

In an ironic footnote, Brother Andrew Baston, the famed Oxford poet that English King Edward brought with him to write a poem celebrating his victory over the Scots, was captured by King Robert Bruce. For his ransom, Brother Baston was compelled to write an epic poem celebrating Bruce's victory over the English.

NUGGETS FOR THE CURIOUS

THE SHROUD OF TURIN

The revered and controversial Shroud of Turin, which appears to have been the burial cloth of Jesus, containing his image, has been a religious icon for centuries in the Roman Catholic church. The Church has made no official declaration as to its authenticity. One of the foremost American authorities on the Shroud was an Anglican Episcopal priest, Father Kim Driesbach, who devoted years to studying it while also serving as a parish priest and a Shroud lecturer.

He created an impressive museum with reproductions of photographs and scientific studies, including a remarkable laser-generated three-dimensional model of the Shroud image. Father Driesbach also wrote a definitive history of the Shroud's travels from Jerusalem to Turin, Italy.

It was the author's privilege to know Father Driesbach both as priest and friend, and was given access to his Shroud material before writing this novel.

CELTIC SEER TRADITION

The research on Celtic seers, wizards, prophecy, and precognition comes from a variety of published sources. Most famous are predictions from a fifth-century seer that some historians consider the prototype for the legendary wizard Merlin. His prophecies, written in verse, were believed so accurate that they were studied as predictions of coming events by many royal courts of Europe for several hundred years. The theory that Merlin and Saint Dubricius of the Celtic Church were the same person secretly living two lives has been postulated by some scholars.

GOLEM

Control of human behavior by computers via brain implants has been researched on animals for decades. It has been a popular theme in science fiction. Internet websites monitoring the subject have reported experiments by government contract with major corporations. DARPA (Defense Advanced Research Projects Agency) has been tasked with the mission of developing the neural interface between humans and computers to create Super Warriors. Many of these programs are linked with numerous corporate industries.

Artificial Intelligence—AI—promises to have an impact on computers comparable to what the printing press had on writing.

THE ANGLICAN CELTIC ORDER (ACO)

The Episcopal monastery of Benedictine brothers in Santa Barbara, California that was tragically destroyed by fire was used as a prototype for the fictitious ACO. They are in no way associated with the Templars or the New Jerusalem prophecy; they are a monastic order of the Anglican Episcopal church.

The author also received invaluable information on monastic life when he visited with Trappists at the Roman Catholic Cistercian monastery in Conyers, Georgia.

ABOUT THE AUTHOR

GY WALDRON is an Emmy Award–nominated screenwriter and director who has written chart-topping television sitcoms, dramas, miniseries, and movies. He has created three network series, including *The Dukes of Hazzard.* His writing for theater received an American National Theater and Academy Award.

Whether writing for screen, for the stage, or for readers around the world, Waldron is widely known for his unique blend of action, comedy, and suspense, always leaving audiences highly entertained.

With a background of serving in U.S. counterintelligence in Europe, he has written in both intelligence and real-crime fields. He draws heavily on his experiences when writing fiction.

A native Southerner, he now lives in Malibu, California, in a canyon between the mountains and the ocean where he is writing his next novel, *Fugue.*

Printed in the USA
CPSIA information can be obtained
at www.ICGtesting.com
CBHW031758060924
13930CB00060B/801